CW00362428

THE PRECIOUS GIFT

Also by Tessa Barclay and available from Headline

A Professional Woman
Gleam of Gold
A Hidden Beauty
Her Father's Child
The Millionaire's Woman
The Saturday Girl

The Corvill Weaving series

A Web of Dreams
Broken Threads
The Final Pattern

The Wine Widow Trilogy

The Wine Widow
The Champagne Girls
The Last Heiress

The Craigallan series

A Sower Went Forth
The Stony Places
Harvest of Thorns
The Good Ground

THE PRECIOUS GIFT

Tessa Barclay

HEADLINE

First published in Great Britain in 1997 by
HEADLINE BOOK PUBLISHING

10 9 8 7 6 5 4 3 2 1

All characters in this publication are fictitious and any resemblance to real persons, living or dead, is purely coincidental.

British Library Cataloguing in Publication Data

Barclay, Tessa
The precious gift
I.Title
823.9′14[F]

ISBN 0 7472 1850 1

Typeset by Palimpsest Book Production Limited,
Polmont, Stirlingshire
Printed and bound in Great Britain by
Mackays of Chatham PLC, Chatham, Kent

HEADLINE BOOK PUBLISHING
A division of Hodder Headline PLC
338 Euston Road
London NW1 3BH

THE PRECIOUS GIFT

Chapter One

Catherine had as usual provided the sandwich lunch. Nothing special, but better than the food in the hospital canteen.

'Eat up now,' she coaxed. 'It's your favourite, salmon mayonnaise.'

Dutifully, her sister Laura took a nibble. The truth was, she was too tired to eat. Even here, in the sunshine of the Esplanade Park, with the scent of the wallflowers mingling in the sea breeze, Laura's face hadn't yet lost the grey of fatigue. Overnight duty in Casualty, even in a quiet seaside resort like Hulmesley, was no joke.

Catherine Mertagen worried about her sister. Laura was too vulnerable, too eager to help. She was what people loved to call 'a born nurse'. Ever since she was a child she'd been wanting to 'make it better'. A bird mauled by a cat, a butterfly with a damaged wing, a puppy with a thorn in its paw – Laura Mertagen knew she could heal them all.

So today, of course, when a cry went up from the terrace café, Laura was on her feet at once.

'Sit down, Laura,' Catherine exclaimed, catching at her sleeve. 'You're eating your lunch—'

'But didn't you hear? They're shouting about an ambulance—'

'Well, an ambulance will come—'

'But somebody's hurt, Cath!'

Catherine tried to pull her back, though she knew she was wasting her time. Pulling free, her sister ran along the path to the terrace steps, where a crowd had gathered.

With reluctance Catherine got to her feet. When she reached the group, Laura was on her knees on the shallow steps, loosening the collar and tie of a man who sprawled there.

The crowd, scared but excited, were giving their opinions.

'You oughtn't to touch him—'

'He's having a fit—'

'Probably a heart attack—'

'Mind what you're doing, miss—'

'Please stand back,' Laura said without glancing up from her work. 'He needs air—'

'You ought not to meddle—'

'I'm a nurse from St Leonard's. Now please stand back.'

Everyone at once began to be helpful. 'We sent for the ambulance—'

'I saw him go down, nurse—'

'Hit himself a terrible wallop—'

'Here, take my jacket, he needs something under his head—'

'He's breathing funny, isn't he? Shouldn't you prop him up?'

Catherine moved in among them. 'It's all right,' she soothed. 'She knows her stuff. Now do as she asks, stand back, let her have room to deal with him.'

But the drama of the moment had taken hold of the lunchtime crowd. Something to tell the others in the office when they got back – this fellow plunged down the stone steps at the park café, probably had one too many with his meal, no, it was some sort of attack, he was breathing funny, he came an awful cropper and this pretty girl just stepped in and took over . . .

Catherine, doing her best to get them to move back, caught a glimpse of her sister as she tended the patient. To her astonishment, she saw that Laura was merely making soothing motions with her hands over the man's shirt front. She'd expected to see her taking his pulse or looking for a head injury. Stertorous breathing – hadn't Laura once told her it could be brought on by concussion?

But no, the man wasn't concussed. He opened his eyes and focused on Laura's face. His gaze cleared, the panic that had first stared out of his eyes began to fade.

'Lie still,' Laura murmured as he made as if to raise himself on an elbow. 'You've had a fall. Just lie quiet a minute—'

'But I—'

'Are you hurt? Have you a sharp pain anywhere?'

'No, I—'

'You banged your head – let me feel. Oh my, you're going to have a huge bump there.'

'I feel – I feel—' He stared at her. 'What happened? I had an asthma attack, did I?'

'I know you're bewildered, but just relax. The ambulance is coming.'

'No, that's not necessary—'

'Yes, yes, you must have that head looked at. Now lie back, just stay quiet and everything will be fine.'

She had folded a jacket to cushion his head. Now she rose to her feet, moving back down the steps as she heard the ringing of the ambulance bell. The crowd eddied aside and around her, half wishing to offer her some praise, half lingering to share the excitement of the ambulance's arrival.

A uniformed attendant hurried from the roadway, first aid kit in hand. 'It's all right, Ralph,' Laura said, 'it's not urgent any more. He's got some bruises and a bump on his head, though.'

'Right you are, nurse,' said Ralph, with a nod of recognition. They were old acquaintances from the Casualty Ward. He elbowed his way to his patient. The crowd closed around him again.

Laura joined Catherine at the foot of the shallow steps. 'Everything's okay,' she remarked.

'What happened just then? He was having a terrible time with his breathing and then quite suddenly seemed to calm down—?'

'I don't know.'

'What d'you mean, you don't know? What sort of first aid was that you were doing?'

'It wasn't first aid. I just sort of . . . I just felt impelled to sort of . . . soothe him.'

'Soothe him?'

'Yes, take away his terror, help him to breathe.'

'But how? How did you help him, Laura?'

Laura sank down on the bench where their abandoned lunch had been pecked at by the park sparrows.

'I don't know what I did,' she said in a voice that was almost frightened. 'But it worked . . .'

Catherine put an arm around her sister. She could feel her shivering. 'Don't get upset, dear,' she said gently. This had often been the way in their childhood – Laura would rush to the aid of some wounded or frightened creature, would soothe or cure it, and then this odd reaction would set in. While they were evacuated on the farm during the war, there had been a baby calf Laura had tended just after it was born – and when at last it rose to its feet and staggered gawkily to its mother, Laura had shown this same scared, bewildered exhaustion.

Catherine longed to stay and look after her sister. But the esplanade clock was striking two and it was time for Catherine to get back to the Norfolk Regal Insurance office where she worked.

Her sister Laura was free until she had to report for night duty. She would probably go home to the family flat and would try to get some sleep there, rather than go to her room in the nurses' quarters. From all that Catherine could gather, nurses were very inconsiderate of their colleagues even though they knew how difficult it was to sleep in the daytime.

She looked ruefully at the wreck of their packet of sandwiches. She'd made them before setting out for the office this morning, especially to tempt Laura. She doubted whether her sister would bother to eat now. But she'd try to cook something nice for the evening meal, something suitable for her father's mundane taste and Laura's finicky appetite.

'I've got to dash,' she sighed. 'Go into the café and have some soup or a hot drink, lovey.'

'Yes, all right.'

'Promise?'

'I promise.'

With a quick hug she let her sister go. She would be late back from lunch and Mr Forbush was going to be sarcastic. Well, let him. He knew and she knew that she could walk out of Norfolk Regal Insurance and into another job any day of the week. Jobs were plentiful in 1956 as Britain continued its slow recovery from the war, and Catherine Mertagen was a good shorthand typist. In Hulmesley there were a dozen insurance firms which had moved out while rebuilding went on in London; any one of them would take her on at once, if Mr Forbush got stroppy over her lateness.

Hulmesley had been a quiet little Norfolk seaport until 1938. Then, as war threatened, the Royal Air Force set up airfields on the great flat lands to the south of the town. Once hostilities began, Hulmesley was under constant attack by German bombers. And in one of those air attacks Adele Mertagen, the mother of Catherine and Laura, was killed.

Catherine tried never to think of that night – the drone of the bombers overhead, the thundering of the anti-aircraft guns, the scream of the missiles as they hurtled earthwards, the shuddering of the ground as they hit and exploded in a thousand fragments. The two little girls were safe in the shelter at the foot of the garden. Their mother, who had gone to the doorway to look at the searchlights fingering the sky, was felled by a metal fragment.

Gerald Mertagen, draughtsman and lithographer, had been called up into the aeroplane industry at the outbreak of war. It was one of the great griefs of his life that while he was tucked safely away in a camouflaged building in Cumberland, his wife was killed by the enemy who never once found the secret factory.

On compassionate leave to deal with the crisis, griefstricken, bewildered, he gave his two little girls, aged ten and eleven, into the care of the local authority. A kindly welfare officer sent them to the safety of a farm on the edge of Dartmoor. It was the best Gerald could do. But to the two girls, it was as if he had abandoned them.

Laura, dreamy and quiet, withdrew into herself. Catherine, though the younger, elected herself protector and spokeswoman for the two of them. When Mrs Wendover out of some misguided notion proposed to cut off Laura's long chestnut plaits, Catherine stormed at her until she abandoned the idea. When she – with perfectly good intentions – tried to make them wear her youngest son's cast-off shoes, Catherine dropped them down the well.

In the end the farmer's wife came to understand that the only way to handle the two girls was to consult Catherine first about any issue. Odd though it might seem to have to talk things over with a child of ten, nothing else seemed to work.

By the time peace came, the two girls had grown quite fond of Mrs Wendover, her taciturn husband, and her three sons. But they still longed to go back to the sea coast, to the sedate gaiety of Hulmesley with its esplanade and its Georgian terraces, its bracing sea breeze and its crowded harbour.

Memory and imagination graced the little town with charms that perhaps it had never possessed. The two girls would remind each other of the wonderful big ice-cream cones sold on the sea-front, the trips on the pleasure boats, the bandsmen in their smart gold-braided uniforms on the esplanade. When they returned as almost-young-ladies of eleven and twelve, they found Hulmesley somehow smaller than they'd expected, shabbier of course because the town had suffered in the bombing, but astonishingly full of American Air Force personnel and their families.

Their home – where the air-raid shelter still survived at the far end of the garden – had been taken over as billets. Gerald Mertagen decided to sell it and live in the flat over his shop. He'd formerly been a gallery owner, selling the work of local artists and his own lithographs, but there was no market in 1945 for that kind of thing. People were intent on gathering the bare essentials for home-life – Utility sheets, cutlery made out of far-from-stainless steel, rationed curtain material . . .

So now he re-opened the shop as a picture-framer's and a supplier of souvenirs. The Americans patronised him, he did well enough to provide a livelihood for himself and his two daughters, but the shop was never likely to make a fortune.

When Laura ventured that she would like to train as a nurse, the hope of her earnings adding to the household income vanished.

Nurses were paid the equivalent of pocket-money once the cost of their training, their living quarters and their uniforms had been deducted. Laura, after her first inquiries, came to understand this fact and wanted to relinquish the dream.

'No, no,' cried Gerald, 'we'll manage somehow.' Having been able to keep only intermittent contact with his children during their stay on the farm – for travel from Cumberland to Devon was very difficult in wartime – he was determined to make it up to them now.

The Mertagens did indeed manage somehow. They managed because Catherine gave up art and languages at school; instead she trained in shorthand and typing. The minute she left school she landed a well-paid job. Laura's plans to train as a nurse were at once put into practice.

And that was how things remained: Laura worked for a pittance at the hospital even after her training ended, Gerald's income went up in the tourist season and down in the winter, and so the mainstay of the family was the younger daughter Catherine.

Catherine saw nothing strange in this, although her friends hinted they thought it unfair. Her *particular* friend, Malcolm Sanders, often sighed that her family were holding her back. Malcolm was employed by the Norfolk Regal Insurance Company in civilian life, but at present he was doing his stint of National Service in Cyprus, where there was trouble.

'I see in the company newsletter that there will be vacancies in the new head offices in London when they open,' he would write. 'Why don't you apply? That's where I'm heading once I get out of uniform.'

Once he got out of uniform, it was almost understood between them, they'd become engaged. Malcolm's view was they would both land promotions to the new London office, save a lot of money, and think about marriage when they had enough to put down a deposit on a house.

A good scheme. A lovely scheme. Catherine often looked up from her desk at the Hulmesley office and saw in her mind's eye the house she and Malcolm would buy. Not a suburban semi, but something older and . . . well . . . better. Within Catherine there was an artistic impulse that made her prefer the architecture of other days, just as it caused her to sigh over some of the souvenirs her father had to sell. Too highly-coloured, too carelessly designed . . . If she had only been able to get her GCE in art and go on to art school, she might have taken up design.

Occasionally, when such thoughts came into her head, Catherine would wonder how she'd feel if she were off living in some handsome little house in London, and her sister was still in Hulmesley. They'd been so close for so long. Malcolm was apt to say, when she mentioned this, that it was time Laura learned how to look out for herself. And he was right, Catherine supposed.

But old habits die hard, and Catherine had grown used to worrying about Laura.

That evening she saw to it that her sister ate a decent meal. Then she walked with her back to the nurses' quarters of St Leonard's. Laura still seemed preoccupied, quieter even than usual.

'You're not worrying about something?' Catherine asked as they were about to part.

'No, not a thing.'

'You seem a bit . . . far off.'

'I'm tired, that's all.'

'Night duty is too much for you!' Catherine burst out. 'You've been washed out all day.'

'Night duty has to be done, Cath. We all have to take our turn. In any case, it isn't that . . .'

'What, then?'

'I feel as if . . . I don't know how to express it . . . as if I've used up part of me and I'm waiting for it to be replenished . . .'

Catherine could make nothing of this. 'You're not coming down with a cold or something?'

Her sister gave a little laugh, half-suppressed. 'You're always so practical, Cath.'

'One of us has to be, dear.'

They were at the door of the nurses' home. The porter opened it for them and studied them as they stood talking. Two pretty girls – sisters, yet almost totally different. Laura Mertagen had rounded, gentle features, almost like one of Botticelli's angels. Her hair was a rich brownish-bronze, her eyes a soft, glowing dark amber. She was very like old snapshots of their mother, the same shy curve to the full lips, the same air of living within herself more than the rest of us.

By contrast, Catherine was quite tall and rather too thin. She took after her father in this, and had the same nervous energy in her hazel eyes, the same crackle of electricity in her thick dark hair. Her glance was sharp and direct, her attitude to life was less tolerant than Laura's. But a sense of humour was signalled by the laughter lines at the edges of the wide mouth and, in the firmness of the pointed chin, the ability to control her own energy.

The porter called, 'Come in if you're coming, nurse, that sea breeze is flapping my late-pass lists here!'

Laura kissed Catherine lightly on the cheek. 'See you for lunch on Thursday.'

'Try to get some proper sleep before then.'

'I will, I promise.'

On Thursday it rained so they had lunch in a café close to the harbour. Laura seemed to have more vivacity, and Catherine was content at the improvement. Two weeks went by much as usual. Laura came off night duty and went on days. It always took her a day or two to get accustomed to the change: Catherine wasn't surprised when she seemed a little troubled on an evening visit home.

'Haven't got back your sleep routine?' she inquired, pouring a sherry that she hoped would relax her.

'No, no, it's not that. The most extraordinary thing happened today!'

'At the hospital?' their father inquired, laying aside his newspaper for a moment. 'An accident?'

'No, nothing like that. It was something to do with me – me personally.'

'What?' said father and daughter in unison. They were both alarmed. Although nurses were generally regarded as sacrosanct, almost as untouchable as nuns, from time to time there was trouble. St Leonard's stood on the main road, and nursing staff had been threatened by gangs of youths who descended on the resort to drink and look for trouble.

'No, it wasn't one of the biker gangs, nothing like that,' Laura said, shaking her head at her own clumsiness in startling them. 'No, a man came to see me on the ward this afternoon.'

'What man?' cried Gerald Mertagen, starting up. He was ready to telephone the police if his daughter was being harassed by some importunate male at visiting time.

'You remember that man in the park?' Laura said to Catherine.

'What man?'

'The man who collapsed on the terrace steps?'

'Oh . . . him . . . yes, what about him?' Catherine had an indistinct recollection of a thickish body in a well-tailored tweed jacket and flannel trousers, iron-grey hair . . .

'He came inquiring for me on Buttersford with a huge bunch of hothouse carnations. I couldn't understand it at first, I thought he couldn't find the patient he was visiting—'

'He came to see you on the ward?' Catherine was shocked.

She'd imbibed enough about hospital discipline from her sister to know that this was strictly forbidden.

'Yes, luckily Sister was busy elsewhere at the time! I told him I was on duty, that I wasn't allowed visitors, but he kept on and on so in the end I took him into the kitchenette and told him to be quick. And do you know what? He wanted to thank me for looking after him that day.'

'What?' demanded her father. 'What are you talking about?'

Catherine gave him a brief resumé of the accident in Esplanade Park. 'You never mentioned it?' he queried.

'It didn't seem important,' Laura said with a shrug.

'Well, it was nice of him to want to say thank you,' Catherine suggested.

'That's true. And to bring flowers – shows he meant it.'

'But Dad, he shouldn't have come to the ward! If Sister had caught us I'd have been in trouble.'

'Oh, come on, you can't be blamed if somebody looks you up to say thank you. How did he know where to find you, by the way?'

Laura sipped her sherry, her brow creased in thought. 'It seems I mentioned that I was a nurse from St Leonard's when I wanted the people to let me handle things. And the ambulance attendant knew me, of course. Anyhow, he knew I worked at St Leonard's and apparently he'd been trying to get in touch but of course I've been on night duty so in the daytime I was never around when he came—'

'He's been coming to the hospital looking for you?' Catherine said, a little perturbed.

'Yes.'

'Who is he?' her father asked, once again ready to complain to the authorities. 'Did he introduce himself?'

'Yes, his name's Desmond Colville, he says he lives out Browbourne way.'

'Colville? Big, middle-aged tweedy type, bushy moustache?'

'He has a moustache, yes . . . I'd say he's about fifty . . .'

'You know him, Dad?' Catherine inquired.

'Know him . . . not exactly. I've seen him around, he's on committees and things. Has a big estate out by Browbourne. You remember there was a committee about how to celebrate the Coronation and I went to one or two of the meetings? Colville was on the platform with a bunch of others.'

'So he's a somebody, then,' murmured Catherine.

'Needn't have worried about getting into trouble with Sister,' he pointed out, with a grin. 'He's probably been on the hospital management committee. So, well, you've got someone important giving you flowers, eh?'

Catherine had relaxed as the situation became clearer. A respectable landowner, wishing to show his gratitude, had sought out her sister and given her some flowers. No problem.

Yet Laura still looked distressed.

'What is it?' she asked her.

'It was the things he said. He bothered me.'

'How do you mean?'

'He seemed to make so much of it. He said I'd come to him like an angel, I'd saved him—'

'Oh, that's just complimentary guff,' Catherine said, smiling. 'I mean, it's a bit embarrassing, having to say thank you to somebody who saw you lying like a corpse on a public path.'

'He needn't have done it,' Laura said. 'If he'd felt embarrassed about it he could just have ignored the whole thing. But no – he said he felt he had to come and tell me. He said it was the most important thing that had ever happened to him.'

'What?'

'He said I'd changed his life.'

Chapter Two

Mr Mertagen chuckled and said it took all kinds to make a world. He then switched on the radio to hear the latest cricket scores. Catherine went into the kitchen to take a casserole out of the oven, and drew her sister with her.

'What is it about this man that worried you so much?' she asked as she set the steaming dish on the table. 'I mean, a bit of high-flown compliment to someone who did him a good turn – it doesn't seem all that important to me.'

'You didn't hear him, Cathie. He said that since I looked after him that day he's been much better, his breathing is normal, his asthmatic attacks have stopped.'

'Oh, asthma? Was that what was wrong with him?'

'Yes, that was obvious – short hard breaths, wheezing exhalation, chest hardly expanding, sweat on the face – it couldn't have been anything else that caused him to fall. I expect he was reaching for the balustrade – people having an attack often want to hang on to something – and somehow he lost his footing.'

'Well, he's having a good spell now – I suppose that happens – after an attack there's a bit of a lull?'

'Not necessarily. And anyway that's not what he was telling me. He said he'd been to see his specialist and had X-rays and a series of tests – and he's cured.'

'Well, temporarily, I suppose—'

'No, he says the tests show that his bronchial tubes have become almost normal after being narrowed by asthma for years—'

'That's good. No wonder he's pleased.'

'But you're not listening, Cath. He says *I* did it.'

'Oh, well, if it pleases him to think so, why not?'

Laura sank down on a kitchen chair. 'You don't understand,' she said, almost in a whisper. 'I think he's right.'

'What?'

'What he says – I think it's true. I think I cured him.'

'Now Laura . . .'

'He told me how he felt when I was bending over him. He says he felt a something . . . a force . . . a warmth that spread through his chest.'

'That was just the attack receding—'

'No, because Cath, I felt it too.'

'Felt what?'

'The warmth . . . the sense of something changing . . .'

Catherine's attention was called to the vegetables, which needed to be taken off the stove. She took the saucepan to the sink, strained the potatoes and cauliflower, and tipped them into the serving dishes.

'Supper's ready,' she said.

Laura sighed. 'You don't believe me.'

'Of course I believe you, duckie,' her sister said. As she went by to call their father to the table, she gave her a pat on the shoulder. 'Something happened. You always did have a calming effect on wounded things – trust you to handle a frightened colt or rescue a kitten up a tree. Yes, of course I believe you.' She put her head out of the kitchen door. 'Come on, Dad, supper's ready.'

She was pleased to see that Laura's appetite seemed to have returned. A few more spells of daytime duty would see her back to normal.

Laura didn't resume the topic of Desmond Colville on their walk to the nurses' home except to say, as they were parting, 'What do you think I should do?'

'About what?'

'About what Mr Colville says.'

'I'd forget it if I were you, Laura.'

'But . . . his specialist must be wondering what brought the change about. Oughtn't I to report to him, give him some details from my side of it?'

Catherine sighed. 'Sweetie, you can be sure Mr Colville blurted out all that yarn to his specialist when he went to see him. If the doctor wanted to contact you, he'd have done so.'

'Well . . . that's true. And yet . . .'

'What?'

'What if it happens again?'

'Look here, Laura, you aren't walking up and down the wards curing patients in their beds, now are you?'

'No, of course not. I don't think it's a thing you could do like working on a conveyor belt.'

'So it's just one of those coincidences that happen. You felt concerned about Mr Colville, his attack was getting better anyhow, the pair of you were in some sort of contact for a moment – but the situation isn't going to arise again, is it?'

'No-o.'

'So there you are. Forget it, dear.'

Laura nodded submissively, they kissed each other goodnight, and she went into the building. Catherine turned away into the cool darkness of the sea-coast night, shaking her head at her sister's whimsical notions. Going to see a consultant with the news that she, a newly trained nurse, had cured one of his patients! No surer way of getting your head bitten off, she imagined.

If Laura ever raised the subject again, she would steer her away from it. It would never do if her sister began to acquire a reputation for being odd.

But if the Mertagens were willing to forget it, Desmond Colville was not.

There was no telephone in the upstairs flat, so it was by means of the shop phone that he contacted them. Gerald had taken notes of the conversation. He handed these to Catherine when she came home from the office one evening in early June.

'Good heavens, Dad, why have you written it all down?'

'Because he is who he is, Cathie. I've never had a phone call from a man like that before.'

'Wants to come and see us?' she exclaimed, frowning at the sheet of paper.

'I didn't know what to say, dear. At first I tried to put him off – I mean, even though he's a big noise I thought he might be up to something, for after all Laura's a pretty girl.'

'But it says here he wants to bring his wife.'

'Yes, so of course I had to change my ideas, didn't I? Couldn't be anything underhand if he wants to introduce Mrs Colville.'

'I suppose not.' Catherine was baffled. 'What can he want?'

'Mostly he wants to see Laura and make his wife acquainted, as far as I could gather. I explained that Laura lives in nurses' quarters and only comes home now and again, and he understood all that. In fact, he said he'd already gathered from Laura that it wasn't done to visit her on hospital premises and that's why he'd looked us up in the phone book.'

'What did you tell him in the end?'

'I said I'd pass on his message to Laura and see what she said.'

'Yes, of course.'

'But I wanted to see what you thought before I rang her at the home.'

If Catherine could have dismissed the whole thing, she might have done so. But after all the message had to be passed on to Laura, and for all they knew it could be to her advantage to be on friendly terms with a family as influential as the Colvilles. A little diplomatic inquiry had elicited the information that Desmond Colville owned farms and woodland on quite a grand scale. If he insisted on feeling grateful to Laura for an imaginary blessing, perhaps he oughtn't to be discouraged.

While the evening meal was cooking, Catherine and her father went down to the shop to telephone Laura. The porter told them that Nurse Mertagen was out at the cinema with a group of friends. Since Catherine was meeting her in the hospital canteen on her lunch break next day, she undertook to pass on Desmond Colville's message in person.

'Wants me to meet his wife?' Laura said, pausing with a forkful of salad in mid air. 'What on earth for?'

'Who knows? The whole thing's a bit rum, really. Maybe he's still convinced you brought about a miracle cure and his wife doesn't believe it so he wants you to convince her.'

'Oh no!'

'Come on, Laura, it can't hurt to say a few soothing words to her.'

'But you said I ought to forget the whole thing.'

'Maybe once Colville's brought his wife to meet you, it can be put in cold storage. I'm only guessing, of course, but if our Desmond'd been burbling on about this lovely young angel who came to his aid, it's only natural his wife should be a bit anxious to see you.'

'You think that's what it is?'

'I've no idea, really. Let's agree to having them drop in one evening and see how it goes.'

'Oh, honestly, Cath, I'd rather not!'

'It's up to you, of course.'

'I mean, I don't want to be inspected by a suspicious wife.'

'But if it's causing them to be uneasy with each other? One look at you and Mrs Colville will know she's got nothing to worry about.'

'Oh, thanks very much,' Laura said, laughing. 'You mean I'm so unattractive she'll know I'm no threat?'

'You know I don't mean that. I mean, one look at you and she'll know you don't go round snitching other women's husbands.'

Truth to tell, there was something about Laura that let you know she wasn't interested in men. Something virginal and innocent

. . . For a girl so pretty, she'd had few boyfriends. Most of the girls who'd been in their class when they returned to Hulmesley were by now married and some of them even had babies. One or two were engaged or, like Catherine, semi-engaged. Yet Laura seemed uninterested in romance. And men for the most part were not immediately attracted to her for all her sweet prettiness. Something seemed to fend them off – some invisible barrier.

In the end Laura decided to agree to the suggestion that the Colvilles should drop in. 'What evening shall we say?'

'That's up to you, love.'

'Well, I promised Nancy to help pin up the hem of her new dress tomorrow night, and Thursday there's a lecture in Senior Tutor's Hall about pediatrics – I can't miss that, if I want to get a transfer to the children's ward one day.'

'So that brings us to Friday?'

'I expect they're full up with social engagements,' Laura muttered, looking worried. 'Let's say Friday or either of the weekend evenings.'

'Okay, here's the number—'

'*I'm* not going to ring them!'

'Of course you are – it's you they want to see.'

'Good heavens, Cath, I'd stammer and stutter all over the place! And besides, trying to get to use the telephone in the home is awful – there's always a queue for it and people hang about waiting and can hear every word you say.'

'Ah,' said Catherine.

'So I think you should ring them.'

'All right.'

She used her desk phone at the office. This was strictly against the rules but it was still more or less lunchtime, and the big room was empty.

'May I speak to Mr or Mrs Colville, please?' she asked the maid who answered.

'Who is calling?'

'Miss Mertagen.'

'Hold the line please.'

In a moment the phone was picked up and a rich, vibrant, contralto voice said, 'Miss Mertagen! I'm so pleased to hear from you! My husband's told me so much about you—'

'Mrs Colville? Mrs Colville!' Catherine had to raise her voice to break into the welcoming chorus. 'This is Catherine Mertagen speaking – it's my sister your husband's been talking about.'

'Oh. I'm sorry, I just took it for granted—'

'It's difficult for my sister to get to a phone so she asked me—'

'Desmond's out with our estate manager, but of ourse I can take a message—'

'We thought perhaps you'd like to drop by one evening – Friday, Saturday or Sunday—'

'Oh dear, Friday there's a parish council—'

'Saturday then?'

'Saturday we have friends coming in—'

Catherine began to be a little irritated. Perhaps Mrs Colville didn't see this meeting in the same light as her husband? But no, she was saying with enthusiasm, 'Sunday evening – after evensong – would that be all right with you? It would have to be about seven-thirty – we've got to drive into Hulmesley but if we come straight from St Antony's—'

'Seven-thirty. That would be fine. You know where to find us?'

'The phone book says it's a shop?'

'We live above it. It's about halfway down Mitre Lane, a picture-framer's.'

'I understand. Yes, fine, fine, I've written that down. I'm so pleased, Miss Mertagen. See you on Sunday, then.'

This engagement, when relayed to her father, called forth little delight. 'Parish council on Friday? Coming straight from evensong? They sound awfully churchy.'

The Mertagens were not awfully churchy. The family was of Dutch extraction, sound old-fashioned Presbyterians who had left Holland to teach the business of bulb-growing to the East Anglians at the beginning of the nineteenth century. Gerald had felt it his duty to see that his two girls went through the confirmation ceremony as his wife would have wished. He himself attended morning service perhaps every six weeks, but if Laura and Catherine didn't want to go he never urged them.

Catherine was more concerned about the social side. 'We ought to buy a bottle of decent sherry,' she suggested.

'What's wrong with the bottle we've got?'

'Oh, Dad, it's only a notch or two above Hall's Tonic Wine!'

'What about it? It seems all right to me.'

'Some people would think it too sweet. Perhaps we ought to buy a bottle of something dry.'

'I'll tell you what, they probably prefer gin. Isn't that what the landed gentry drink, pink gin?'

'How do you turn gin pink?'

'Hanged if I know.'

In the end Catherine bought an Amontillado sherry, a bottle of gin, and some tonic water to go with it. All this came out of the housekeeping money, leaving a large hole which Catherine regretted. Yet she was quite looking forward to meeting the Colvilles. It was an event, a dramatic moment in an otherwise humdrum existence.

Laura arrived rather earlier than usual. Hospital routine always seemed more lax over weekends so she had been able to get away promptly. She had changed into an old summer dress of pale blue cotton and had done her long brown hair into a sort of topknot that wasn't particularly becoming.

'What's this for?' Catherine inquired drily when she saw her. 'Are you trying to convince Mrs Colville you're not a *femme fatale*?'

'I see you've gone on the opposite tack,' her sister responded. 'Best dress and new sandals.'

Catherine was wearing what the fashion magazines liked to call 'the little black dress'. It had cost Catherine quite a lot in an end-of-season sale at one of the little dress shops catering for the hunting-shooting-and-fishing set. A straight slim tunic of heavy silk crêpe, it could be 'dressed up', as the magazine writers said, with a bright scarf or a brooch or beads. Catherine had chosen a double strand of imitation pearls this evening. 'This is my hostess outfit,' she said, twirling for Laura's inspection.

'Very smart. Why is it you always look better in your clothes than I do?'

'Oh, nonsense. You can look a dream when you want to. But this evening you don't want to.'

Gerald had already poured himself a drink, of the sweet sherry he preferred. He'd tried the Amontillado and reported it was dry enough to put in a biscuit tin. His attire this evening was much as usual – trousers and shirt and a handknit cardigan. He claimed he was unaffected by the prospect of entertaining two of the richest people in the county. All the same, Catherine noticed that he kept glancing at the clock.

The Colvilles were a little later than arranged. Gerald heard their car draw up in the lane at seven-forty. 'You'd better go down and open the door, Cath.'

'No, let them ring – we don't want to seem eager.'

'Why not?' Laura said, with an urging movement of her hand. So Catherine went quickly down the steep staircase to the door at the side of the shop.

Mitre Lane was a winding row of Georgian terrace houses, the ground floors of which had been turned into shops during the Victorian era. The living accommodation was quite spacious but the stairs were a drawback – and particularly to Mrs Colville who, it seemed, walked with a stick.

She was a buxom, fresh-faced woman in a sensible summer two-piece and with straight brown hair pulled back under a black straw hat. She gave an audible sigh when she saw the staircase. Her husband sprang to her side to offer his arm. There was hardly room for the two of them side by side in the narrow entry, for they were both on the heavy side.

'Miss Mertagen?' Colville said, offering his hand.

'I'm Catherine Mertagen.'

'The one I spoke to,' said Mrs Colville, her rich voice making the narrow hall vibrate. 'Your sister is here?'

'Upstairs, Mrs Colville. Can you manage?'

'Yes, yes, just let me help her – come on, old girl, there's only a dozen steps—'

'More like two dozen.' But with his help she began the ascent.

Laura was hovering at the landing. 'Ah, here's my young rescuer,' cried Desmond Colville. 'Phoebe dear, this is Laura Mertagen.'

'How d'you do, my dear,' panted Phoebe Colville. 'My word, it's like living at the top of Ben Nevis—'

'Nonsense, nonsense – handy little place, right in the town centre – envy you, Mr Colville.' The two men were shaking hands. Mrs Colville was brought into the living-room, where she sank into a chair with a little groan of relief. She hooked her stick over the wooden arm. She put her foot out, straightening her leg in an effort to ease it.

'Now then, everyone, drinks?' Gerald suggested. 'What can I offer you?'

'A whisky would be nice.'

Gerald turned a stricken face to his younger daughter. He'd encouraged her to spend money on gin, the idea of whisky had never entered his head.

'We only have gin or sherry, I'm afraid,' Catherine confessed quickly.

'Oh, then, gin, my dear, gin with a touch of lime juice—'

'Tonic water? We don't have any lime.'

'Come on, Desmond, stop being silly,' commanded his wife. 'You can see these folk haven't got a cellar full of stuff like ours at Browbourne. I'll have a drop of that nice dry sherry, my dear, and my husband will have a gin and tonic.'

Thus called to order, Desmond accepted his drink with thanks and immediately set it down. 'We're not really here to drink your gin,' he said with an embarrassed smile on his bluff features. 'I wanted my wife to meet you, Miss Mertagen—'

'My child, I wanted to thank you in person for what you've done for Desmond,' his wife said, cutting in on his uncertain opening. 'His life has completely changed! You know it's no joke for a farm owner to be out and about in spring and summer, when the flowers and grasses are out and his eyes are running with tears. This year for the first time since I met him, he's been able to get about on the estate without having to call it off by midday.'

'Yes, a world of difference, Miss Mertagen, a world of difference. And I owe it all to you!'

'No, no,' Laura began.

'But yes, yes, my dear! He's a new man! Not but what,' his wife said with fondness, 'I was quite satisfied with the old one. Still, from his point of view it's a vast improvement.'

Desmond launched into a description of his past difficulties. Phoebe addressed herself to getting to know Laura. By and by, it emerged that Desmond was very interested in the making of picture frames and wanted to be taken down to the shop to see the equipment. It seemed to Catherine that a significant glance was exchanged with his wife before he went out with Gerald.

Phoebe Colville finished her sherry and leaned forward in her chair. 'Miss Mertagen,' she said. 'We had more than one reason for coming to see you this evening.'

'Really?'

'I've come to ask for your help.'

'In what way?'

'You noticed, I'm sure, I'm walking with a stick. I've done something stupid to my knee – it's been giving me a terrible time for weeks now, and Dr Glass can't seem to sort it out for me.'

'What is it – an injury? Did you knock it?'

'Not that I'm aware of. It just came on just over three months ago – end of February, I remember, I was kneeling by the pulpit doing the flowers for Quadrigesima Sunday, and when I tried to get up I couldn't, and Maisie Thorpe had to help me up, and then I could scarcely walk, but it went off and I went to bed thinking that was the end of it, but next morning my knee was all swollen, and it's gone on like that ever since, some days worse and some days better, but it never goes away.' She paused for breath. 'So what do you think?'

'It sounds like bursitis,' Laura said.

'Laura,' said Catherine in warning.

Laura seemed to recollect herself at the sound. 'You ought to ask your doctor to send you to St Leonard's,' she said. 'There's probably some fluid there, that needs to be drawn off.'

'I've been to St Leonard's,' grunted Phoebe. 'They drew off some fluid and painted the joint with something and strapped me up in an elastic bandage. But it doesn't seem to get better.'

'These things take time—'

'But that's just what I haven't got,' she interrupted. 'I know you'll think it's silly and vain of me, dear, but I do so want to be able to make my curtsey to the Queen without falling over, and it's only a couple of weeks now—'

'The Queen?'

'She and Prince Philip, you know . . . They're coming to the Agricultural Show in two weeks' time and Desmond and I are supposed to greet them and then I'm supposed to escort her round the horse trials while Desmond talks milk yields and timber quotas with the Duke, but how am I going to manage? I don't want to be hobbling about with a stick on a day like that—'

'No, of course not,' agreed Laura.

'So I wondered . . . you see, it's the Queen's first visit to the Show since her Coronation so it's very special to us and you know . . . since you'd done such wonders for Desmond . . . I wondered whether you'd take a look and see if you could do something for me.'

'No, no,' said Catherine.

'But Cath—'

'No, Laura, you know we talked about this—'

'No we didn't, we just agreed not to think too much about Mr Colville's ideas.'

'Listen, Mrs Colville,' Catherine said, turning to look down with some indignation at their guest, 'Laura's a nurse at St Leonard's. I don't think they'd take a very lenient view if she were to—'

'There could be no harm in taking a look, Cath—'

'There could be no benefit, either. What would be the point?'

'Oh, please don't turn me down,' said Phoebe with a sob in her voice. 'It hurts such a lot, and I try and try to walk without the cane but I just can't manage, and it's going to be so awkward with Her Majesty, and in fact if I can't get something done about it I think I'll have to withdraw and let someone else act as escort. Desmond would be *so* disappointed, he's set his heart on my being the hostess and he's even paid for a Hartnell dress for the occasion and it'll be such a waste if I don't wear it. But what would be the point of putting it on if I was going to sit on a chair in the background all day . . .' The long lament died away, the fine confident voice faltered.

Laura held out her hands to Mrs Colville. 'Come along,' she said, 'we'd better go into my bedroom.'

She didn't even look at Catherine for her approval. But in any case Catherine had no wish to prevent her. It seemed so unkind not even to let her sister take a look at the injury. She was sure Laura could do nothing for Phoebe, and once that was established perhaps a visit to a London specialist might be thought of.

She helped support Phoebe Colville up a second flight of steep stairs and into Laura's room. This was, as usual, impeccably tidy. The bed was made according to hospital principles, with the bedspread cornered and tucked in tight. Laura helped Phoebe sit on the side of the bed, to remove the shoe and stocking on her left leg. The black straw hat and white gloves were given into Catherine's care.

'Now lie back,' Laura commanded. 'Just relax. Close your eyes. Take deep breaths – deep, quiet breaths. How do you feel?'

'I'm all right.'

'Comfortable? Unclasp your hands, Phoebe. Let your arms fall to your sides.'

Phoebe obeyed. Her heavy body pressed into the counterpane, her breathing became slow and steady.

'I'm just going to put a pillow under your damaged knee, Phoebe. It's just for support, it won't hurt you.'

Phoebe's eyes flew open. 'Please don't try to unlock the joint,' she pleaded, 'the physiotherapist tried that and it was agony.'

'I'm not going to do anything like that. Trust me. Just lie still and be calm.'

She went away to bring a chair from the dressing table to the bedside. She sat down by the bed and after sitting for a moment without motion, she leaned towards Phoebe Colville. She laid her two hands very gently on the inflamed, swollen knee joint.

And that was all that happened. She made no attempt to manipulate the joint, she made no movements of massage. She simply sat there, her eyes fixed on some distant point beyond the corner of the ceiling, her hands lying as gently as petals on the knee joint.

Later, when Catherine looked at the clock, she found that almost half an hour had gone by. At the time it seemed a mere instant – or perhaps an eternity. The world seemed to pause, as if in a dream. Even the ticking of the bedside clock seemed hushed.

The first to speak was Phoebe. 'You know, that feels better already, dear.'

'Try to bend it,' Laura suggested.

Gingerly Phoebe drew her knee up a little.

'How is it?'

'So far so good.'

'Try a little more.'

Phoebe drew up the leg so that her knee was fully bent. She put her arms around it and pulled it towards her chest. Her mouth was half-open, as if ready to cry out in pain the moment it began to hurt.

'Is it easier?' Laura asked.

'It's . . . I think it's . . . it's not hurting a bit!'

Laura put her arm about the other woman's shoulders. 'Try getting up and putting your foot on the ground.'

Still with the most intense care, Phoebe allowed herself to be helped to the floor. Her good leg came first. Then she set her left foot on the carpet and lowered her weight on to it.

'Yes!' she cried.

'Two feet on the ground, about twelve inches apart. Right. Now put your full weight on them.'

Phoebe obeyed. There was no yelp of pain. She took hold of her skirt, folded it back against her knees, and looked down. 'Why, it doesn't even look red any more,' she whispered.

And it was true. The left knee looked much the same as the right knee except that there was a silk stocking on the right. Laura knelt to run the cupped fingers of her hand over the kneecap. 'There's a slight inflammation still,' she said. 'If you put a hot compress on it when you get home and renew it two or three times before bedtime, I think that should bring it down completely.'

'It's cured?'

'I don't know if it's permanent,' Laura said. 'It might need another turn or two before it's all sorted out, especially if you walk about a lot or kneel on it. But if you could keep it up for a couple of days . . . I believe it will be all right.'

'It's wonderful,' breathed Mrs Colville. 'I feel wonderful. You marvellous girl, you've cured me!'

Catherine stood by the dressing table, watching Phoebe Colville flexing her knee and glorying in its flexibility.

She had a mental picture of the ugly red swelling that had been there only half an hour ago. It seemed that her sister had banished it, cured it – simply by laying her hands on it.

How could such a thing be happening to an ordinary family like theirs?

Chapter Three

Strange to say, their father wasn't as taken aback by the situation as Catherine expected.

'No, well . . . It *is* a bit of a surprise, but it's in the family, after all.'

'In the family? What on earth do you mean by that, Dad?'

'My grandmother had the power. People in the village used to ask her to help. There wasn't a Health Service in those days, you know, so if you called in a doctor it cost you money, and in hard times folk turned to Granny, so I heard.'

'Where was this? Was this Spondley, where you were born?'

'Yes, although of course Granny and Grandad had this land a mile or two outside the village, where they grew specialist bulbs. People used to walk the two miles to see her, or if they couldn't walk the carrier would take them out there for a penny. Mind you, I don't know anything about it from first hand because she died when I was only about four or five.'

'So really, it could all be just rumour?' Laura asked, disappointment in her brown eyes. Her father's reaction and his first few words had given her a sense of not being some sort of misfit. But now it seemed he knew nothing for certain.

'I remember my father telling me she could soothe nettle rash and charm away warts and cure croup . . . Of course she mended sprains and set broken bones – there was some yarn about the blacksmith dropping his hammer on his own foot and Granny set all the little bones so that he was walking about in a few days . . .'

'Set all the little bones in his foot? But that's impossible, Dad – it would take hours of surgery.'

'Well, it was some tale like that, I can't quite recall. All I know is, he was walking about as good as new a week later, or so the story went.'

'You never mentioned any of this before?'

'No. I'd really almost forgotten about it. Of course, when Laura turned out to have a way with little creatures like kittens and puppies I sort of took it for granted, and' – turning to his elder daughter – 'when you wanted to go in for nursing, dear, it just seemed *right* somehow. Now that I look back, I suppose I just knew you'd inherited something from Granny Mertagen.'

Laura was sitting by the living-room table, the glasses and bottles from the drinks party still standing upon it. She busied herself with putting tops back on bottles.

'She had the power to heal . . .' she mused.

'We don't know that for sure,' Catherine warned. 'It's only what Dad remembers other people saying.'

'Yes, but you know, my father was a stickler for the truth,' Gerald Mertagen said. 'You could rely on his word. If he said his mother had the power to heal, I believe it.'

So perhaps they had had a great-grandmother who was what used to be called a 'wise-woman'. Someone the country people turned to for help, a bone-setter, who knew herbs and home-made remedies, who when she acted as midwife could ensure an easy childbirth.

The two girls looked at each other. Each was thinking, Does that explain it? But neither would put it into words because it seemed so strange.

In the silence that followed, Gerald comforted himself with another glass of sweet sherry. 'I don't think it's anything to *worry* about,' he ventured, after a sip or two.

'Not worry about?' Laura cried, throwing up her hands in consternation. 'If Matron ever heard of this, she'd have me hung up by my thumbs.'

'Good heavens, why? How can it be wrong to help people?'

'It's unscientific, that's what's wrong,' Laura sighed. She let herself lie back against the cushions of the sofa. Truth to tell, the session with Mrs Colville had been tiring, and perhaps more so because of the ebullient gratitude she'd had to endure afterwards.

It had emerged that the Colvilles had come with the express purpose of getting Laura's help. 'He wasn't the least interested in picture-framing,' Gerald reported with some indignation. 'It was just a ploy to get me downstairs out of the way so that his missus could talk to you. And when we got back up here and you'd obviously gone up to the bedroom, he looked as chuffed as anything.'

'I suppose it would have been difficult to plead for Laura's help with us all listening in,' Catherine allowed.

'The minute she hobbled up those stairs, I knew.'

'You did?'

'Oh yes, you could sense the pain she was in, but at first I really didn't want to get involved. It was only . . .'

'What, love?'

'Well, I knew it would be a simple thing to remedy. It seemed – I don't know – churlish to say no.'

'But how did you know it would be simple?' Catherine demanded.

'I don't know, I just knew.'

They sat in silence for a while, trying to come to terms with this new facet to their lives. At length Catherine said, 'I hope the Colvilles will keep their promise and not talk about it.'

'I hope so too.'

A vain hope.

To the inhabitants of Browbourne the fact that the lady of the manor was walking about quite normally and without her stick was important news. The Agricultural Show loomed, the part she was to play in it was well-known – and truth to tell, if Mrs Colville had had to withdraw one or two other ladies were hoping to take her place as escort to Her Majesty. But no, Mrs Colville was back on form and the wonder was, how had she so quickly got the better of her damaged knee? After weeks of treatment by Dr Glass and a useless session at the hospital?

Phoebe really tried not to talk about it. But she was filled with so much innocent delight in her recovery that at last the words came tumbling out.

Catherine got home one evening from the office to meet Laura at the side door seeing some people out. A mother and a boy, about twelve or thirteen years old. Total strangers to Catherine.

Laura blushed a little as Catherine waited to pass into the narrow hall. 'This is Mrs Vanbray and son Eric – my sister Catherine.'

'How do you do?' Mrs Vanbray said in a muted voice. On her face was that look of dazed delight that Catherine had seen on Mrs Colville's. The boy was flexing his right shoulder, levering his arm up and down at about chest level.

'It's great!' he breathed. 'Just great!'

'So we'll say good evening, and thank you again, Miss Mertagen.'

'Good evening.'

The visitors took themselves off to a car parked a little way down the lane. Catherine stepped indoors and studied her sister.

'What's been happening?' she inquired. 'As if I didn't know.'

Laura escaped the question by going rather quickly up the stairs.

In the living-room Gerald was watering the potted fern. He kept his back to Catherine.

'Well?' she demanded.

'They're friends of the Colvilles,' Laura burst out. 'The boy's a junior tennis champion, he'd put his shoulder out somehow—'

'I thought we agreed that we weren't going to let this happen—'

'Oh, come on, Cathie, don't be cross,' her father said, setting down the little watering can. 'Mrs Vanbray rang me this afternoon, practically in tears. The boy had insisted on going to tennis practice this morning and his coach had sent him home with instructions not to use his arm for a month or so – and the play-offs begin next week, so—'

'I didn't know anything about it till I got home,' Laura added. 'So what could I do? I couldn't just *refuse.*'

'I don't see why not.'

'But I couldn't, Cath, I really couldn't.'

There were tears in her voice. At once Catherine was filled with remorse. Her sister only wanted to do good, and here was she, snarling at her about it.

'I'm sorry, Laura, I don't mean to be cross. But I thought you didn't want to because the hospital wouldn't approve?'

'What they don't know won't harm them,' Gerald remarked. 'I mean, who's going to tell them?'

Catherine shook her head but said no more. In the kitchen, Laura joined her to help prepare the evening meal. 'You think I was wrong,' she said.

'I don't know. I just wonder how far this is going to go.'

'I'll only accept people I know I can help, Cath.'

'Are you sure you're always going to know the difference?'

'Yes, I'm sure.'

'Laura, it's all so *weird.*'

'No it isn't, it's perfectly simple, and I've got some sort of gift and I've got to use it.'

'There's no law that says you have to.'

'But I must, Cath. Why else have I got this talent? To hide it under a bushel? You know what it says in the Bible about that. You're meant to put talents to use.'

Catherine had tied on her apron and was rather forcefully scrubbing new potatoes. 'So it doesn't make any difference what I say.'

'I don't want you to be against this, that would make me very unhappy.' Laura came to put an arm around her sister's waist. 'I feel a bit adrift, you see. You've always led the way in the past, this is the first time I've ever gone off on my own.'

A wave of guilt rushed through Catherine. Was this what was wrong? Was she simply resentful because for once her sister had done something without first asking for her approval? Dog in the manger – was that it?

She turned to face her. 'Of course I'm not against you,' she said, wiping wet hands on her apron so as to pat Laura's shoulder. 'It's important for you to feel happy, and if you think you ought to treat people who come to you, then that's the right thing to do. I'm just taken aback, that's all, so don't mind me. I'll get used to it.'

It became part of the family routine that when Laura was off-duty from the hospital she would see people who had been sent to her by former patients. She resisted being paid, but gifts would arrive – boxes of chocolates, bouquets of flowers, bottles of wine, porcelain ornaments, a good leather handbag, tickets for the theatre. Laura persuaded Catherine to come with her to the theatre, and to her embarrassment the giver of the tickets sought them out at the interval.

'I want to introduce my wonderful healer,' cried Miss Stanstead. 'Amy, Freddie – this is Nurse Mertagen, who did such wonders for my bad back.'

She was a businesswoman who supported the local repertory company financially and had brought a party of colleagues to see its production of *Tea and Sympathy*. They stood in a group in the bar, eagerly questioning Laura. Others in the bar listened in with interest. Both sisters were glad to escape back to their place in the stalls when the second act began.

With Catherine's help Laura managed to avoid being taken out to supper after the play. As they walked home, she said, 'That was awful.'

'Can't be helped, love. If you do good to people, they're likely to want to show you off to their friends.'

'If I'd known she was going to be there herself, I'd never have gone.'

'Well, there you are. But as to hiding your light under a bushel, it seems there's no likelihood of that.'

Laura could only agree in silence. She wanted to use her gift, but she must find some way to ensure her privacy. How it was to be done she wasn't sure.

On an afternoon towards the end of September, Laura was off duty until the following day. She had two patients to see, the first a Mr Cyril Patterson, coming at the recommendation of Miss Stanstead. He arrived promptly. She sat with him for a few minutes listening to the tale of his ailment, a stomach disorder that refused to yield to treatment yet which didn't show up in any hospital tests.

Gerald Mertagen was in his workshop at the back of the premises, with his back door open so that he could walk out to the shed in the yard for supplies of beading. He was crossing back to the shop when he heard his daughter scream.

In two strides he had reached the iron staircase at the back of the shop. He ran up, his shoes clattering on the treads. The window on the second floor landing was open to the fine weather. He clambered through, tangling momentarily in the net curtain, falling on the floor.

The door of Laura's bedroom was open. As he scrambled up he caught a glimpse of a struggle. A man had his daughter grasped by the front of her blouse, the blouse dragged up to reveal bare skin and part of her bra. Laura was flailing with her hands at the man's head.

Gerald lashed out with the length of wood in his hand. Like a rod, it hit the assailant on the nape of the neck. With a howl of pain his hands went up to his neck. At that moment Laura was free. She threw herself back out of Patterson's reach.

Her father launched himself at Patterson. The collision brought them down in a tangle, all three. Laura was knocked against the legs of her dressing table. All the brushes and bottles fell off, raining down on her head. She scuttled away into safety behind the bedroom armchair.

Her father was trying to hold Patterson down. Patterson was scrambling to his feet, shielding himself from the blows Gerald was aiming at him. None of the blows had so far reached their mark – Gerald was no scrapper.

'Don't Dad, don't!' Laura cried. 'Don't! You'll hurt him!'

'Hurt him? I'm going to kill him,' panted her father.

But her cry made him falter. Patterson seized the chance to pull himself clear and staggered up.

'How dare you!' he shouted breathlessly.

'What? What? You attack my daughter and you—'

Patterson was buttoning up his shirt, tucking in the tails. He looked about for his jacket. 'You haven't heard the last of this,' he snarled. 'Don't think you can get away with knocking me about—'

'Knocking you about? You're lucky I didn't strangle you—'

'Where's my coat?'

'If you think you're just going to walk out after—'

'Dad, let him go. Here's your jacket.' It was on a hanger on the inside of the door. She grabbed it and thrust it at him, her head averted.

'He's not going until we've settled the account—'

'Oh, money, is it? Blackmail?' He thrust his arms angrily into his coat. 'If you think you're going to get a penny out of me—'

'I don't want your rotten money. I want an apology—'

'For what? For what? *She* started it—'

'I didn't!'

'Your hands were everywhere—'

'That's not true, I was just trying to find out – to see what treatment—'

'Treatment? Treatment? That's a new name for it! And now you think I'm going to pay money to keep it quiet—'

'I don't want to keep it quiet!' shouted Gerald. 'I'm going to call the police! You *attacked* my daugher.'

'Your daughter, is she? Tell me another! How many "daughters" have you got, then? All up to the same trick?'

'It's not a trick,' Laura protested, scarlet with shame. 'You came here for help—'

'That was the story. I was told you were a trained nurse—'

'I *am*, ask anyone, I trained at St Leonard's, you've got it all wrong!'

'It's just a front for funny business, dearie,' Patterson said savagely. 'You haven't heard the last of this, do you hear?'

'Get out,' sobbed Laura. 'Get out, get out, you're absolutely horrible!'

'No, wait, I want him to stay here while I call the police—'

'No, Dad, please! I can't bear it! Let him go!'

Patterson stalked out of the room. Gerald went after him, still in two minds whether to detain him. But he hadn't done too well in the scuffle in the bedroom. He had doubts whether he could keep him by force, and to try and then fail would be too much of a disgrace.

'I ought to charge you with assault,' he said as he thrust open the front door.

'Think twice about that,' said the patient. 'My version could put you in jail.'

'Get out.'

He waited on the doorstep until Patterson had got into his car and driven away. Then he closed the door and hurried back upstairs.

Laura was sitting in the bedroom crying.

'Sweetheart, don't cry,' her father protested, putting an arm around her. 'He's gone, it's all over.'

'He said . . . he said . . .'

'Never mind what he said. He's an oaf. Come on now, stop crying.'

'Honestly, Dad, I didn't do anything, I just sat beside him with my hands on his diaphragm—'

'You don't have to explain yourself to me, love, I know you didn't do anything wrong.'

'I was trying to find out where the problem lay . . .'

'I know, I know.'

'I could sense he was unwell, he was all tensed up. There was a centre of trouble – I was just going to see if I could improve things . . .'

'Laura, I know you were trying to help him. He's got a twisted mind, that's all.' He hugged her. 'Come on now, come down to the kitchen and I'll make you a cup of tea.'

Laura mopped her eyes and got up. He could feel that she was trembling as he led her downstairs. She sank down on a kitchen chair while he filled the kettle and put tea in the pot. When he put a steaming mug of tea before her, she lifted it with shaking hands.

'I'm going to ring the police,' he declared, anger brimming anew at the sight of her distress. 'He's not going to get away with this!'

'No, Dad, don't—'

'But we ought to! I mean, he was *hurting* you—'

'But he'll say it was my fault—'

'Well, nobody's going to believe that—'

'No, we don't know how it might sound. Dad, at least let's ask Cath what she thinks before we do anything.'

That was sound sense. Catherine had a good head on her shoulders. He rang her from the shop.

'There's been a bit of an upset here, Cathie. I think you ought to come home.'

'Upset? What do you mean?'

'Well, Laura's in tears—'

'Is she ill?'

'No, there was a fellow here – he behaved very badly—'

'Oh, lord,' groaned Catherine. 'I'll be there in ten minutes.'

She asked for time off – 'a domestic crisis' – and was allowed to go. She practically ran through the streets. She noticed her father had put the 'Back in ten minutes' sign on the shop door. Before she got her key in the lock he was opening the side door to her.

'What on earth has happened?'

As they hurried upstairs he tried to give her an outline. But her chief concern was to see what had happened to her sister. She found her in the kitchen, eyes red, hair in a mess, hands trembling.

'Oh, Cathie!' Laura wept, and turned to bury her face in her sister's shoulder.

When at last she understood what had occurred, Catherine was stricken. Her poor, trusting sister . . .

'I want to get the police onto him,' Gerald explained, 'but Laura says no.'

Catherine hesitated. 'Who was this man again?'

'Cyril Patterson. He telephoned yesterday, said he'd been recommended by Mrs Stanstead.'

'And why was he coming?'

'He complained of stomach pains but X-rays and tests never show anything. But when I was examining him . . .' Laura burst into fresh tears. 'I don't see *how* he could have thought I was leading him on. Honestly, I was just palpating his diaphragm—'

'I believe you, dearest, of course you didn't do anything. It was just his imagination.' Catherine thought for a moment. 'I'll ring Mrs Stanstead,' she decided, 'see what she says about him.'

Mrs Stanstead could tell her very little. 'He's just a business acquaintance,' she explained. 'He manages a transport firm that we use from time to time.'

'Has he got any kind of a reputation for . . . well . . . picking on women?'

'My dear, I've no idea. He's someone I see from time to time in the office. A bit of a fusspot, is how I'd describe him.'

'Mrs Stanstead, he's behaved very badly. My father is thinking of going to the police.'

'Oh, I wouldn't do that if I were you!' cried her informant. 'Cyril's on the Old Boys' Network – belongs to all the right clubs and business associations. I'm sorry, Miss Mertagen, I really can't be much help except to say . . . well . . . that in a situation where it was your sister's word against Cyril's, the police might listen to Cyril.'

'Thank you. That gives me some idea of what to do. Please keep this confidential, Mrs Stanstead.'

'Of course, of course.'

When Catherine went upstairs again Laura had washed her face and combed her hair. She looked more in control of herself. Her father was pacing up and down, an angry frown on his angular features, his hands clenching and unclenching.

'The situation is,' Catherine reported, 'that Mr Patterson is a mere acquaintance of Mrs Stanstead's—'

'Then she had no right telling him to come to Laura—'

'No, Dad, that's not so,' Laura ventured. 'It's a normal reaction, to tell someone if you know something that might help them.'

'From what she says, Mrs Stanstead views Patterson as an upright businessman. She told me she thought the police would believe him if it came to Laura's word against his.'

'That's more or less what he said to me, too,' Gerald admitted. 'He said, "My version could put you in jail."'

'I don't think we ought to report it.'

'But Cathie, you didn't see it! He had Laura's blouse half-off her—'

'Don't!' Laura protested. 'Don't go on about it. Just let's forget all about it.'

There was a ring at the doorbell of the flat. They all started in surprise. 'Oh, that's my next patient!' Laura cried. 'I'd forgotten all about him.'

'Another man?' Catherine asked.

'It's a boy – the tennis boy – but I can't – I can't—'

'I'll go down and tell him you're not available.'

'But he needs another treatment—'

'*You* need time to recover. I'll send him away.'

She made up a story about her sister having had to return to the hospital on duty. 'She'll be in touch,' she said. Mother and son accepted the lie without demur. The rest of the afternoon and the evening were spent in going over and over the dilemma. But it ended with Gerald Mertagen agreeing to the plea from his daughters to let the matter drop. Laura shrank from having to report the attack, Catherine doubted that Laura would come out of it without harm to her character. Gerald gave in.

Laura had a day's leave next day. Catherine telephoned to ask for a day from her holiday allowance and borrowed the family station wagon to take her sister for a shopping trip to Norwich. Although the shock of the assault was still making Laura uncertain and shaky, they had a good time.

Laura returned to duty the following morning. Catherine went back to the office. The family felt they had put the matter behind them.

That was only until Laura came that evening to share their supper. One look was enough to tell Catherine and her father that something bad had happened.

'What is it, sweetheart?' Gerald asked, sitting her in the armchair by the fire and leaning over her protectively.

'I've been suspended,' she said. 'I'm to go before a disciplinary hearing on Monday. Cyril Patterson reported me to the hospital governors.'

Chapter Four

The news was too staggering to be taken in at first. After a minute or two of stunned silence Catherine recovered. 'I think,' she said with bitterness, 'that a soldier would call it a pre-emptive strike.'

'What does that mean?' Gerald demanded, angry because she seemed to be making a joke.

'Well, Patterson obviously thought you were going to the police. He didn't want that – it might really have gone to court and that's too public. So he got in straight away with a complaint to the hospital. Now if the police contact him he can point out that he's reported it to the proper authorities.'

'But we *didn't* go to the police,' her father groaned. 'We should have!'

'Maybe we should, but it's too late now. It'll look as if we're just doing it to balance out his complaint to the hospital board, if we do it now.'

'It's my fault, Dad wanted to telephone at once but I wouldn't let him—'

'It isn't your fault in any way, it's Patterson's. He's a nasty piece of work.' Catherine couldn't help thinking that in her sister's place she might have sensed the man wasn't to be trusted. That was part of the problem – Laura had always been too trusting. At twenty-three Laura still had a lot of growing up to do.

'What are we going to do now?' her father asked. 'What happens at this hearing?'

'I don't know,' Laura said, white with anxiety. 'I've heard of nurses having to go before a board, but you know . . . it always seemed to be happening a long way off, I was so busy with lectures and studying and ward duty, I never took any notice. Sister told me I should contact our representative, and I did that, and she's coming to see me tomorrow.'

'Representative?'

'From the nursing association, I telephoned her, she's coming from Norwich.'

'And what will she do?' Catherine inquired.

'Well . . . represent me.'

'You mean go with you to the hearing?'

'Yes, you're allowed to have someone to speak for you.'

'God, it sounds like a court martial!' Gerald burst out. 'How can they do this to a young girl?'

'What exactly has Patterson said?'

'Matron read me his letter. He said . . . well . . . you know . . .'

'What, Laura? We need to know what we're up against.'

With trembling lips her sister said, 'He said he let himself be taken in by my . . . my overtures and then when he . . . when he was putting his arms round me a man suddenly burst in claiming to be my father—'

'Claiming?' Gerald echoed, astounded.

'And demanded money or else he'd call the police.'

'But that's—'

'It's a complete distortion of the facts—'

'I know, I know, but the way he's put it, it sounds true, and he claims he's only reporting it because it's dreadful for the hospital's reputation—'

'If I ever get my hands on him again I'll break his neck—'

'Dad, that's no help,' Catherine said. She was dreadfully disturbed at the turn of events. By reporting the affair, and reporting it to the hospital only, Patterson had made himself look like a decent citizen outraged by the immorality of a nurse.

'Who's this staff association person? Is she any good?'

'I've no idea,' Laura said, clasping and unclasping her hands in distress. 'I spoke to her on the telephone from the nurses' home so it wasn't a very thorough discussion. She says she'll pick up a copy of Patterson's letter on her way here tomorrow.'

'Sister told you to get in touch?'

'Yes.'

'Did she speak well of her?'

'She didn't say much. She gave me the telephone number – she had it in a book on her desk – and then she – well – she more or less turned me out of her office. The fact is,' Laura said, 'no one at St Leonard's wants to have much to do with me now.'

Catherine had to work Saturday morning. She would have liked to be present when Miss Walsh, the representative of the staff association, talked to Laura, the more so as their father couldn't be there – he would have to take care of busy Saturday trade in the shop. But she didn't want to ask for any more time off; she was unpopular enough as things stood. On the Friday evening she took Laura through what needed to be said.

'He assaulted you. Dad had to rescue you. There was never any demand for money. He's lying in what he says.'

'Yes, I'm to emphasise that. I understand.'

She got home at one o'clock on Saturday to find Miss Walsh refusing offers of lunch and about to leave. Miss Walsh was about forty-five, tall, leathery, and with a no-nonsense air.

'Just a moment,' Catherine said as the other woman was buttoning up her raincoat ready to go. 'Can I ask what you intend to say at the hearing on Monday?'

'I don't know if I should be discussing—'

'Please tell my sister what you think,' Laura urged.

'Well . . . My view is that with nurses' salaries so low, it's not surprising that anyone should take on a few people for treatment—'

'But didn't Laura tell you? There was no question of money! No one paid her.'

Catherine caught a flicker of scepticism in Miss Walsh's eye.

'It's true! She's treated everyone for free.'

'Be that as it may, it will help if I put it in the context of low earnings. The association wants to hammer away at that point—'

'Look here, Laura's being accused of dreadful things! You can't use her as some sort of weapon against the hospital management—'

'I have to look at the larger picture, Miss Mertagen—'

'No you *don't*! You have to defend my sister against outrageous charges made by a vindictive man—'

'Oh, that's not unusual. A lot of patients make claims of that kind – it's Freudian, you know—'

'Freudian? *Freudian*?'

'The sexual fantasy concerning someone in authority over you – and of course nurses appear to have authority—'

'For heaven's sake!' Catherine burst out. 'Will you talk sense? Laura's charged with getting Patterson into a situation in which he could be blackmailed—'

Miss Walsh drew herself to her full height. She had been a Sister Tutor in her time, well accustomed to dealing with unruly students.

'That kind of attitude will be no help. I advise you to put a bridle on your tongue. I hope to minimise the seriousness of that side of the case by emphasising the economics of nurses' pay—'

'But it's nothing to do with nurses' pay!'

'Everything has to do with nurses' pay, my dear girl. And it will draw their fire—'

'It'll draw their fire by letting them assume that Laura was in it for money, and that's quite untrue!'

'Not many people believe in altruism. It will be far more convincing if we acknowledge that Nurse Mertagen got something out of it—'

'But she didn't! A box of chocolates, that china shepherdess on the mantelpiece—'

'There you are. That shepherdess looks like Chelsea to me – quite valuable.'

'But it was just a way of saying thank you,' Laura said faintly.

'Look, this whole thing is very sticky,' Miss Walsh warned, wagging a bony finger. 'What I'm doing – I'm going to simplify the issue as far as I can—'

'I don't think you even grasp the issue,' Catherine groaned.

'Oh yes I do. Nurse Mertagen is in danger of losing her job. If we do it my way, she might get off with a reprimand.' As far as she was concerned that was the end of the discussion. She nodded at Laura to show her out, leaving Catherine fuming in the living-room.

When Gerald came up from the shop for lunch, he found his two daughters deep in troubled discussion.

'She's *obsessed* with handling it her own way,' Catherine was saying. 'And she's got it all wrong.'

'I know. I wish I'd never called her in.'

'Can you get rid of her, ask for someone else?'

'There isn't anyone else. She's the representative for the area.'

Gerald looked in anxiety from one to the other. 'I take it the lady from the staff association wasn't much help?'

'She's impossible,' Catherine said. 'She seems to want to say that Laura took patients on the side to earn a bit of pin money—'

'But Laura never took any money—'

'We know that, but Miss Walsh doesn't quite believe it.'

All through lunch they went through the problem again and again. None of them ate much. When the table had been cleared and the uneaten food returned to the larder, Catherine went to her father in the living-room.

'What's your view?' she asked.

'I think we ought to hire a proper lawyer.'

'But who? Do we know any lawyers?'

'Lawyers?' Laura echoed as she came in with the coffee tray. 'What's this about lawyers?'

'Dad is saying we ought to hire one.'

'But we couldn't afford it,' Laura protested. 'They cost a lot, don't they?'

Gerald, with memories of how much it cost him to negotiate the lease for the premises, could only nod agreement.

'What we need to do is dispose of this idea that money came into it,' Catherine declared. She look at her father and sister. 'Do you agree?'

'Well, yes, but how could we do that?'

'We could ask the other patients to say so.'

'But the hearing's on Monday—'

'And would they come?' Laura objected.

'We don't need them there in person. We could ring round, ask them to agree to us giving their names to the governors.'

'I don't expect they'd want to be involved—'

'Laura, they must feel indebted to you, surely! It's not much to ask – if they'll agree to the hospital board having their names.'

'It's worth a try,' Gerald urged. 'Can we have your address book, dear?'

Laura kept an exercise book with the names, addresses and complaints of her patients. After some hesitation she brought it from her bedroom, but when urged to go down to the shop to telephone she refused.

'I can't. I wouldn't know how to ask. I simply can't do it, Dad.'

Catherine took the book from her. 'I'll do it,' she said.

The first to try were the Colvilles. But it was Saturday afternoon. The maid told them that the master and mistress were out to lunch with friends. She took a message.

It was a wearisome process. There was no reply at Mrs Stanstead's house, Mrs Vanbray and her son were at some sports gathering. Others were available and agreed at once to have their names mentioned to the hospital board. Some, with obvious embarrassment, refused; it appeared they felt it wasn't quite respectable to have consulted a healer.

By dint of persistence over that evening and part of Sunday, Catherine caught up with everyone and achieved a list of eleven supporters. The Colvilles, who rang back late Sunday afternoon, were extremely concerned. 'I only just found Thompkins' message on the telephone pad,' Phoebe lamented. 'The silly girl never thought to ask if I'd seen it. I hope you haven't been worrying because I didn't ring back. You know you can rely on us.'

'Thank you, Mrs Colville,' Catherine said in relief.

But any sense of comfort was soon done away with on Monday

morning. She had called the insurance office to say, against much disapproval, that she couldn't come in until the afternoon, and went with Laura to meet Miss Walsh at the nurses' home. There, in Laura's room, they held a final council of war before the hearing at eleven.

If Catherine had expected the staff representative to be pleased with what she'd done, she soon found she was wrong.

'I specifically told you I wanted to use shortage of money as a justification for Nurse Mertagen's actions,' she scolded. 'I explained that, now didn't I? It keeps us from having to examine the ethical and moral side—'

'But I don't want to skip the ethical and moral side,' Laura said with unexpected anger. 'I've done nothing for the sake of earning money, I refuse to pretend that I have.'

'If you let them haul you over the coals about these supposed powers of healing—'

'Are you saying I lied to you about that?'

'I think you've been kidding yourself, nurse—'

'You don't understand a thing!' Laura cried. 'I wish I'd never got in touch with you!'

'Well, if you want to know, I feel just the same!' rejoined Miss Walsh with haughty indignation. 'I don't for a minute believe all this highminded nonsense about not taking money and doing it for the good of humanity – and neither will the inquiry.'

Laura went scarlet. 'All right then, let's just part company right here.'

'You're not thinking of appearing before the board on your own?'

'I'll do better by myself than with you spoiling everything!'

'Oh, well, if that's what you feel, we'd better say goodbye right now!'

'All *right*!'

'Laura—' Catherine intervened.

'No, Cath, I mean it. I can't have her in the room with me, misrepresenting everything I've done—'

'If you're dispensing with my services, I need your signature to say so, otherwise HQ will question the outcome.' Miss Walsh fished in her despatch case to produce a form.

'Oh, give it to me, I'll sign it, anything to be able to say what I really feel—'

'Laura, you're getting in a state – think what you're doing—'

'I know what I'm doing, I'm standing up for what I know to be right—'

'Much good may it do you,' Miss Walsh said, heavily ironic. 'When you're standing outside the hospital with your cap and apron in your hand, perhaps you'll remember I warned you.'

Laura's chin went up in defiance. With a gesture she prevented her sister from detaining Miss Walsh when she stalked out. They heard her footsteps descend the wooden staircase then fade away in the outer hall.

'We-ell . . .' sighed Catherine. 'That's that.'

'I don't care,' Laura declared. 'She was horrible.' In her distress she sounded about six years old.

'We didn't see eye to eye with her, that's true. All the same, she has experience of appearing before a board of inquiry. Let me run after her, Laura, she won't have reached her car yet—'

'No!'

'But you've no idea what to expect, dear. You need someone with you.'

'I'll manage.'

'Please let me fetch her back, Laura.'

'No.' Laura got up with sudden energy. 'It's half an hour yet before the inquiry. Just time to make a cup of tea.'

She escaped to the kitchenette where nurses could make hot drinks and light snacks. She put the kettle on the gas ring, fetched a little metal teapot from a cupboard, and spooned tea from a packet. Catherine helped by finding cups and saucers of thick canteen pottery, a bottle of milk in the fridge, and a packet of sugar. All the while she was watching her sister from under her lashes. She said nothing until the tea was poured.

'You've got the list of people who're willing to be contacted as character references?' she prompted.

'In my handbag.' Laura stood at the kitchenette counter with both hands round her cup as if to warm them. She stared past her sister towards the window, where autumn rain clouds were scudding across the sky.

All at once she bowed her head over the counter. 'I can't go in there all by myself,' she confessed in a voice trembling with uncertainty.

'We'll ask them to defer it—'

'What good will that do? We'll only have to go through all this again.'

'It'll give us time to ask the staff association for someone else—'

'*You* come with me, Cath.'

'Me?'

'Why not? You know more about it than anybody.'

'But I'm not qualified—'

'Qualified? What does that mean? Trained to try tricks and twists? All I want is to explain what really happened between me and Mr Patterson, that's all.'

'But am I allowed to be there? Doesn't it have to be someone like a representative or a colleague?'

'I don't know, I never had to do this before. If I just say that I . . . I would like you to be there . . . I mean, what can they object to? You're my sister.'

Catherine was very unwilling. 'You'd be far better to get a deferment and have a qualified—'

'I want it over with. Come with me, Cath, or I'll go alone, just to get it finished.'

There seemed no way round it. 'All right,' she said, but with great misgivings.

They left the untouched tea on the counter top and went to fetch their coats and handbags from Laura's room. Catherine saw that Laura cast a sweeping glance round it as they went out, and it crossed her mind that her sister was perhaps saying goodbye to it.

Laura didn't expect to come well out of the hearing.

They presented themselves to Matron's secretary a few minutes before the appointed hour of eleven o'clock. They were asked to sit on a bench in the corridor. To Catherine it was reminiscent of being summoned to the headmistress's room for some misdeed at school.

Precisely on the hour, the secretary came out of the office to usher them into the boardroom. This was a lofty Victorian room across the corridor from Matron's office, solemn, glistening with furniture polish, and garnished with ornately framed portaits and carved chairs with horsehair seats.

There were five people sitting at one side of a rectangular table. Matron sat at the centre with two men on either side. Laura already knew Miss Apterley from various events and award ceremonies at the hospital. The men were all middle-aged or beyond it, clad in the severe dark suits and sombre ties of the business or professional class.

'Come in, nurse, sit down,' Matron commanded. 'And this is Miss Walsh?'

'This is my sister, Catherine Mertagen.'

'We have met, Matron,' Catherine said with a calmness she was far from feeling.

'I believe we have,' Matron agreed, raising a thin eyebrow. 'And Miss Walsh?'

'I decided to dispense with her services.'

'Is it in order for an outsider to be present?' inquired one of the men.

Matron gave him a crushing glance. 'The respondent is allowed to have a colleague or representative—'

'But can this young lady be categorised as—'

'I'm inclined to allow it, Mr Bowles,' Matron said. 'Unless any member of the board has strong objections?'

The others made negative movements of head or shoulders. Mr Bowles, heavy-jowled and corpulent, huffed and subsided.

'Nurse Mertagen,' Matron said, 'this board of inquiry consists of myself and four members of the hospital management. Mr Bowles is from the Town Council's Health Department, Mr Deemsden is the secretary of the Hulmesley Traders' Association, Mr Pettit is on the management committee of the Combined Charities Fund, and Mr Camara I think you know as a Senior Consultant who joined us last year from London. Have you any objection to these board members, nurse?'

'No, Matron.'

Miss Apterley looked down at a folder lying open before her. 'I received a letter from a Mr Cyril Patterson, a copy of which was made available to the representative from your staff association. She is not present – did she give the letter to you?'

'Yes, Matron.'

'In it he charges you with improper behaviour in a bedroom at your father's premises in Mitre Lane.'

There was a pause.

'What have you to say?' Matron asked.

Another pause.

Catherine looked at her sister. She was as white as a lily petal. Her eyes were bright with unshed tears. Her lips trembled, no words came forth. It was quite clear that, now the moment had come, she was incapable of saying anything in her own defence.

'My sister wants it to be known that Mr Patterson has entirely misrepresented the events,' Catherine said, rather too loudly.

Everyone on the other side of the table turned a startled gaze on her.

'Are you here to conduct a defence of your sister's behaviour?' Mr Bowles inquired in a querulous tone.

'Yes, I am.'

'And what do you know about it, pray?'

'I know more about it than Miss Walsh would have done,' Catherine answered with asperity. 'I know my sister far better than Miss Walsh, and I assure you that what Mr Patterson describes could never have happened.'

'Nurse Mertagen gave me her version of events on Friday. Do you believe her story?'

'Implicitly, Matron.'

'Perhaps you can explain why Mr Patterson should make such an accusation?' demanded Mr Deemsden, tapping the table with a pen to emphasise the question.

'I'm not here to explain Mr Patterson,' Catherine said. 'I'm here to put the case for my sister, who has been greatly shocked by the matter. I myself wasn't in the flat at the time but I heard about it almost at once from my father. He told me he had to rescue my sister from an assault – Mr Patterson was the aggressor and my sister was trying to get away from him.'

'Perhaps,' Mr Camara intervened in a sarcastic tone, 'you would explain what Mr Patterson was doing in your sister's *bedroom*, if he wasn't there by invitation?'

Catherine took the copy of Patterson's letter from her handbag. 'You'll see, if you look at' – she ran her finger down the page – 'line seven, that he says he was there for treatment.'

'Yes, indeed. A very strange phrase. What kind of treatment does a man usually expect in the bedroom of a young woman?'

'He said he had stomach pains,' Laura blurted out, taking the question at face value. 'I was trying to find out what was causing them—'

'You had this man, partially unclothed as he states in his letter, alone in your bedroom—'

'There isn't anywhere else to give treatments,' she explained, her voice rising and breaking on the words.

'Mr Patterson says that he was threatened with a scandal unless he paid money.'

'That's quite untrue, Mr Camara,' Laura said, greatly daring in that she, a mere nurse, was contradicting a consultant. 'My father told him he was going to call the police and Mr Patterson jumped to the conclusion he was being blackmailed.'

'But your father didn't in fact call the police.'

'That was on my advice,' Catherine took it up. 'I rang up Mrs Stanstead, who had recommended Mr Patterson to come to Laura – to my sister – and she said that the police were more likely to believe Mr Patterson. It appears he's a man of some standing in the business community. So we decided to let the matter drop.'

'Mr Patterson is known to me,' said Mr Deemsden. He took out a cigar case and was about to select a cigar until he felt Matron's disapproving eye upon him. 'He . . . er . . . he's a member of the Traders' Association. He runs a very successful business. When he says you attempted to extort money I for one am prepared to take his word.'

'My sister never charges money for her work.' Catherine brought a sheet of paper from her handbag. 'I have here a list of some of her patients who are willing to state, if asked, that they were never asked for money and in fact no money changed hands.'

No one asked to look at the list. All the board members regarded it warily.

Mr Pettit, a gentle-looking white-haired man, spoke for the first time.

'I had a telephone call from Desmond Colville this morning,' he stated, frowning as he consulted a little sheaf of notes. 'I gather his name is on that list, as is that of his wife. He asked me if I was a member of the inquiry board and when I said I was, he was very earnest with me on the point of Nurse Mertagen's bona fides. He told me that Nurse Mertagen has been very helpful to them and has never at any time taken money for her work. He specifically asked me to report this to the board.'

'I wonder if it's ethical to have gone round getting support for Nurse Mertagen in this way?' countered Deemsden, nodding at Catherine's list and looking put out.

Pettit smiled a little. 'I believe we ought to think before we accuse Desmond Colville of doing anything unethical. Before the advent of the National Health Service, Colville was a strong supporter of this hospital. Isn't that so, Matron?'

'That was before my time, Mr Pettit. But I believe that's true.'

'And at present he is very active in several of the local charities, which is how I come to know him. I think if he puts himself forward as a character witness, he should be accepted.'

'Of course, of course,' Deemsden said, backtracking hastily. It was no wish of his to get on the wrong side of one of the most influential men in the district. 'I only meant that . . . I wonder if it's right, to be ringing round asking for good marks like that.'

'My sister is very anxious to clear her name,' Catherine said, sensing that Deemsden was a strong antagonist. 'But if there's any criticism of the list of character references, it was my idea, not Laura's.'

Matron now accepted the list and after glancing over it passed it on to the others. When it reached Mr Camara he waved it at Catherine.

'You made out this list?'

'Yes.'

'And they agreed to bear witness to your sister's good character, and to the fact that she never accepted money.'

'Yes.'

'But my next question must be – *for what* did she not accept money?'

'Eh?' said Deemsden.

'These good people didn't pay Nurse Mertagen – but what did they receive from her?'

'She . . . she gave them treatment for their complaints.'

'What complaints?'

Catherine glanced at Laura. Laura, after a long hesitation, said: 'It would be wrong to go into personal details. But some had joint pains, there was a case of chronic asthma, several had stress headaches and one had eczema.'

'You diagnosed these complaints?'

After another hesitation, Laura said: 'Yes.'

'You are qualified to diagnose medical complaints?'

'I'm qualified to the extent that, in the Casualty Ward, I've had to judge between a simple faint and diabetic coma, or between a broken wrist and a sprain. You know yourself, Mr Camara, that when Casualty is busy, a nurse often begins treatment before a doctor can be free to supervise.'

'So you diagnose. Do you prescribe? And if so, what? Nothing on the official list, I imagine. So it must be aspirin? Herbal remedies?'

After an even longer hesitation Laura said: 'I don't prescribe.'

'You don't? No tonic wine or peppermint tea? No dried seaweed?'

'Nothing.'

He shook his head in disbelief. 'So what are these people so grateful for?'

It was clear Laura was going to say nothing. Catherine drew a deep breath.

'My sister has healing powers,' she said.

'What?' Camara gave a snort of laughter.

'Well, if that doesn't beat everything!' cried Deemsden.

'Faith healing?' Matron burst out, astounded. 'One of my nurses?'

'Excuse me,' Pettit said with obvious unwillingness, 'but Desmond

Colville told me this morning that . . . well . . . he said Nurse Mertagen had cured his asthma merely by touching him.'

'Oh, nonsense!'

'Mr Camara, I'm only passing on what Colville said. I feel it's my duty to do it, although that doesn't mean I believe it. Yet, you know . . . Colville's a sound fellow, a very sound fellow.'

'Faith healing?' Bowles said, blowing out a breath between heavy lips. 'That kind of thing goes with carnival side-shows and crystal balls.'

'I assure you, Colville said . . . and his wife too . . .'

'People do sometimes have results from this sort of thing,' said Mr Camara with scorn in his dark, shrewd eyes. 'Usually the ailment's psychosomatic in the first place—'

'What does that mean, for heaven's sake?'

'Oh, you bring it on yourself – it's a form of hysteria—'

'Do you want me to report back to Desmond Colville that you think his asthma was due to hysteria?' Pettit inquired.

That brought Camara up short. He said crossly, 'Of course not! No doubt his asthma was completely real. But in his case he probably had a spontaneous remission. That does happen, you know. The complaint dies away, and the so-called healer gets the credit.'

'Hold on a minute.' Mr Bowles waved at the others for silence. He was leaning forward in his chair, staring at Laura in disbelief. 'Are you telling me that Cyril Patterson came to you for *faith healing*?'

'Yes. Ask Mrs Stanstead. She recommended him.'

'Well, I don't believe a word of this,' Bowles said. 'I know Patterson. I'd have said he wasn't the type to go in for light relief in a girl's bedroom, but he and his wife are separated, I believe . . . A man might look around for a bit of comfort. But faith healing . . . ? He's too hardheaded for that.'

'When people are in constant pain they seize at any chance,' Laura said. 'Mr Patterson had been in pain for months and his doctor—'

'Yes, his doctor,' Camara interrupted. 'I'd like to hear what his doctor has to say about him. Is there any evidence he really had stomach pains? Why should we believe any of this?'

'It's in his letter,' Catherine said, brandishing her copy. 'He tells you – he went to Laura for treatment—'

'That's just because he doesn't want to admit he was looking for a bit of slap and tickle in a knocking shop—'

'How dare you!' Catherine cried, springing up from her chair.

'How dare you say a thing like that! Who are *you*? You came to this town from somewhere else but my father has lived and worked in Hulmesley all his life except for the war years. He's run an art gallery and now he runs a gift shop. He's paid his rates and his bills and never had a word spoken against him! How dare you imply he's been running a bawdy house—'

'Be quiet, Miss Mertagen,' Matron commanded, terribly perturbed at how things were going. 'I will not have—'

'Don't give me orders!' Catherine stormed, raising her voice to silence Miss Apterley. 'I'm not one of your nurses, you can't tell me what to do—'

'This is my hospital—'

'That doesn't give you the right to order me about, and if you think I'm going to let—'

'Miss Mertagen,' intervened Mr Pettit, standing up and leaning across the table to Catherine, 'I understand your indignation. I share it, in part. I've had a telephone discussion with Mr Colville and his wife which convinces me that Mr Patterson entirely mistook the situation. But we must try to stay calm. Let's all sit down again and try to deal with this.'

'Yes, indeed,' Bowles grunted. 'Mr Camara, I think you ought to withdraw those remarks about Mr Patterson's reasons for visiting Nurse Mertagen. I'm prepared to accept he went there looking for help with a medical problem.'

'Damned idiocy,' muttered Camara. 'These people who go to quacks – they deserve all the trouble they get!'

'Please, Mr Camara, what you said was slanderous to both Mr Patterson and the father of Nurse Mertagen.'

'Oh, all right then . . . I withdraw it.'

'Thank you,' said Pettit the peacemaker. 'Now let's agree that the only reason we're here is to dispose of Mr Patterson's allegations—'

'Excuse me, Mr Pettit, that is not the only reason we are here,' Matron said in her most quelling manner. She was determined to regain control of the meeting. She waited until everyone had resumed their seats and composed themselves before resuming. 'We're here to investigate a complaint which, I will agree, seems to arise out of an error on the part of Mr Patterson. But that doesn't exonerate Nurse Mertagen. She is entirely in the wrong in having laid herself open to mistakes of that kind—'

'Oh, come, Matron, it's hardly Nurse Mertagen's fault if Patterson got the wrong idea—'

'It certainly *is* Nurse Mertagen's fault! She knows that it's against hospital regulations to give private treatment of any kind. Isn't that so, nurse?'

'Yes, Matron, but—'

'There are no buts. When you took up your post here you signed a contract which specifically states—'

'Excuse me, Matron, it forbids giving any treatment for gain—'

'Are you saying you never took any payment of any kind?'

'I refused money. People sent me flowers and things, but—'

'Mr Patterson in his letter says your father talked about money—'

'That's not true, Dad told him he wanted to "settle the account" but he was so angry – it was quite unlike him – he meant he wanted to knock him down—'

'The imagination boggles,' said Mr Camara with a sardonic smile. 'Is this how we want our nurses to be seen? In the middle of a fist-fight?'

'What do you expect?' Catherine demanded. 'The man was assaulting my sister, she was screaming for help—'

'He would never have been there in the first place if Nurse Mertagen hadn't laid herself open in the most unprofessional way to misunderstandings of this kind. Your behaviour has been disgraceful, nurse,' said Miss Apterley.

Laura made no response to this. She looked away. She had always known that she was going outside the bounds of professional ethics in treating those who came to her.

Catherine too was silent. About the ethical side she was uncertain. She'd heard Laura herself say that Matron would disapprove. Her phrase had been that Matron would 'hang her up by her thumbs'.

There was a momentary pause. Then Miss Apterley said, 'Please go outside and wait. The board of inquiry will deliberate.'

The two girls left. They sat on the hard oak bench outside Matron's office and stared at the door of the boardroom.

'That didn't go well,' Laura said wearily.

'What a bunch of stuffed shirts!'

'I think people who get to be governors and committee members are always a bit conventional—'

'Conventional! They're blinkered—'

'No, Cath, it's no use blaming them, what Matron said is true, I was in the wrong.'

'How can you *say* that? How can it be wrong to want to help people?'

Laura shook her head. She didn't have any answers.

Long minutes ticked by. Catherine's watch told her that they'd been in the boardroom for twenty minutes and that another fifteen elapsed before the door was re-opened by Mr Pettit.

'Please come in,' said he. He gave Laura a sympathetic smile as she passed him. Catherine read in it the news that the inquiry had gone against her sister.

'Nurse Mertagen,' said Matron, 'this board has agreed that the accusation brought against you by Mr Cyril Patterson was due to a misunderstanding, aggravated by the fact that your father used physical means to deal with it. We accept that there were no sexual overtures by you and that Mr Patterson was in error.'

'Thank you,' whispered Laura.

'However, you were grossly in the wrong in encouraging patients to come to you for treatment. That is against the regulations of this hospital—'

'But—'

Matron raised a monitory hand to silence her. 'Your behaviour brought the reputation of St Leonard's into grave danger. I cannot have it said that one of my nurses almost caused a public scandal.'

'Without Mr Patterson there would have been no danger of a scandal—' Catherine began.

'Please don't interrupt, Miss Mertagen,' Matron rebuked her. 'I accept that you have been of help in clearing your sister's name with regard to immoral behaviour, but this is now a purely professional matter. Nurse Mertagen knows very well that she has been at fault. Isn't that so, nurse?'

'Yes, Matron,' said Laura, hanging her head.

'In view of your unblemished career so far, the board has decided not to report you to the Royal College of Nursing for behaviour likely to bring the profession into disrepute. But we cannot allow you to continue as a nurse at St Leonard's—'

'Oh, please—'

'We have to contain the damage, Miss Mertagen. We have to reply to Mr Patterson's letter, and anything less than dismissal will certainly not satisfy him. To avoid further outcry from him, and because I now lack faith in your judgement, you are dismissed from your post at St Leonard's.'

'No!'

'You may of course appeal through your staff association, but the board of management will strongly resist any attempt to have you reinstated here. I myself would not welcome you. Is that clear?'

Unable to speak, Laura merely nodded.

Miss Apterley turned to Catherine. 'Miss Mertagen, you don't come within my jurisdiction. But I'd like to point out to you that if you go on championing your sister's cause with too much fervour you may only cause further damage. Discretion is what is needed now.'

'You mean we're to let Patterson get away with this? He *attacked* Laura and now he's lost her her job!'

Matron gave a slight shake of the head and laid her folded hands on the table. As far as she was concerned the matter was closed.

Mr Pettit spoke. 'I'd like to put my view on record. I don't have the same obligation to the nursing profession as Miss Apterley so I don't lay so much blame on Nurse Mertagen. I think she isn't guilty of anything except naivety. But I have to go along with the majority view. For the good of St Leonard's, this is the right decision.'

And the other members of the board nodded agreement.

Chapter Five

For the rest of the week Laura kept almost entirely to herself. To tentative inquiries she replied that she was all right, that her intention was to find a new job, that no one need fret about her.

But fret they did. When she went out, her father kept wondering where she was. When she came home, he worried that she hardly spoke.

'Can't you do anything?' he asked Catherine.

'What? If she doesn't want to talk about it, I can't force her.'

'It's so unlike her to be turned in on herself like this.'

'She's had a big shock, Dad. We just have to wait until she gets over it.'

Catherine was talking good sense, but that didn't mean she was satisfied. She felt she was partly to blame for her sister's dismissal. Perhaps she'd been too vehement in her defence of her. Perhaps she'd put everybody's back up. Miss Walsh might have done better – Catherine should have dragged her back that morning no matter what Laura said. She had no idea what Laura was planning to do now. She longed to have her confide in her.

Seven long, unhappy days went by. On the eighth Catherine came home from work to find Laura in the kitchen making a dessert for the evening meal. Her heart beat a little more lightly at the scene. It was a return to normality.

'Lemon pudding!' she cried. 'My favourite!'

'Yes, it's to make up for being such a gloom-and-misery the last few days.'

'Oh, duckie, you're never a misery,' Catherine said, giving her a hug.

'Careful, you'll get egg white all over you.' Laura held the whisk out of the way.

'So what's brought about this much-needed change?'

'Wait till Dad comes up, I'll tell you both so I won't have to go over it all twice.'

Gerald appeared ten minutes later. Laura had poured a pre-dinner sherry for them all. Her father brightened at the sight. 'Are we celebrating?'

'I've got a new job,' Laura said.

'Marvellous!' He raised his glass to her. 'Congratulations.'

'Nursing?' Catherine asked rather quietly.

Laura's face changed a little but she kept the look of determined brightness. 'In a way,' she agreed. 'I've got a job in a children's day nursery.'

'Oh, you'll like that,' her father declared. 'You always love working with children.'

'Yes, that's why I applied. I . . . I didn't tell the owner anything about the row with St Leonard's, I just said that I wanted to work with children – which is true enough – and that I had my nursing certificate. Mrs Welling didn't go into my training very much, she asked for references and I gave her the Colvilles. They won't mind, will they, Cath?'

'Of course not. We'll ring this evening to let them know.' Catherine sipped her sherry – the remains of the Amontillado bought to impress the Colvilles – and surveyed Laura. Her sister was almost herself again. Not quite the steady, quietly assured girl she used to be, but better than the pale ghost they'd lived with for eight days.

'So, where's this day nursery?'

'It's on the south side of town, near where those expensive new houses were built. The mums there want their children to get accustomed to playing with other children so that when they get to school they'll settle down, at least that's what Mrs Welling says, but I expect some of them have got careers and maybe some of them just like to have a morning or two to themselves . . . Anyhow, it runs from ten till three, and *I* think it's so they can go shopping and have lunch in Norwich!' She said this with a tolerant smile.

'Short hours,' her father commented. 'A lot different from St Leonard's.'

'Yes, and funnily enough, almost the same money! You know, Miss Walsh was right about nurses' pay . . .' She hesitated. 'About Miss Walsh, and all that . . . It turned out she would have been right about not mentioning the healing, Matron was so horror-stricken, I realised then how wrong I'd been. So: I've decided to put all that behind me.'

'You're not going to do the healing?' Gerald said.

'No. I was wrong to let myself be led into that. It was – I don't know – arrogance, self-aggrandisement, to think I knew better than trained doctors—'

'But you did know, Laura.'

'Yes, so far as I'd gone, but Dad, the day might have come when I'd make a wrong diagnosis, or do harm instead of good, and then there was Mr Patterson – I couldn't go through that again.' She shuddered.

'Whatever you want to do, my love, that's fine – isn't that so, Cath?'

'Yes, of course, Dad.'

Through the meal Laura recounted her interview with Mrs Welling and her meeting that morning with some of the children. Clearly she'd loved it. Something like her old radiance returned to her as she talked.

'What d'you think, Cathie?' her father asked when they had a moment alone together.

'Anything's better than that frozen misery of the last few days. But this has changed her, Dad. Have you noticed? She often got in a muddle with what she wanted to say but these days – she talks in a great spate of words – as if she wants to get it all out before you can tell her she's wrong.'

'I don't care how she talks so long as she's happy!'

When Catherine rang the Colvilles, it was Desmond who answered. 'I'm so grieved at the way things went at the inquiry. I've been waiting in hopes that your sister would ask for my help in taking some further steps—'

'No, Mr Colville, thank you for your support but she's accepted the board's decision and—'

'She's not going to appeal?'

'No, she's already found another job, and that's why I'm ringing.' She explained about the day nursery and the need for references.

'Of course, of course – anything I can do. Poor girl! To be rewarded in such an unkind way for all the good she's done—'

'Well, that's over and done with,' Catherine said. 'She's putting it all behind her.'

'That's very brave and sensible,' said Desmond Colville. 'Give her my warmest wishes.'

And thereby was brought about a misunderstanding which was to have important consequences. Colville thought Catherine was saying that her sister had put the distress of the inquiry behind her. Catherine thought Colville understood that it was the healing that was over and done with.

Laura settled into her job. Christmas came, and the New Year, and Laura's birthday. 'Twenty-four!' she said as she opened her cards at breakfast. 'That's a third of my three score years and ten! And what have I done with it?'

'Duckie, you're doing all right,' soothed Catherine.

'But I thought I'd have made it to nurse in charge of a ward by this time.'

'And so you are – in charge of a nursery full of active kiddies,' her father said.

'I'm not in charge. I'm an assistant.' She laughed. 'Oh, it's a heavy nursing job, I put on a bandage if they fall and graze a knee, and give them a cuddle if they bump their heads . . .' She stifled a sigh and rose. 'I've got things to sort out to take to the cleaner,' she said, and went up to her room.

Catherine and Gerald exchanged a glance. 'She misses the hospital more than she lets on,' he said.

'It's only natural. She was *meant* to be a nurse, meant to be a healer in its widest sense.'

'Well, I suppose in time she'll come to terms with it.'

'I suppose so. After all, it's only three months since she was sent away.'

That evening, when she got home, Catherine was waylaid by her father at the shop door. 'Laura's got someone with her,' he said in a stage whisper.

'A friend from the nurses' home, you mean – birthday present?'

'No, I think it's a patient.'

'A *patient*!'

'I know, I was surprised too. But she came home from the day nursery with this woman who seems very distressed, and I think they had tea and a long chat. When I popped up to say I was going out to fetch the evening paper they were gone, and I could hear voices from upstairs. I think they're in Laura's room. Like before,' he added in explanation.

Catherine hesitated. 'Let's go into the shop.'

'I thought perhaps you might go up and – you know – break it up, dear.'

'Break it up? Why should I break it up?'

'Well, didn't that matron say she wasn't to take patients any more?'

They went in among the framed pictures and the paperweights and the pieces of semi-precious stone set as book-ends. Catherine had had time to think.

'You know, Dad, Miss Apterley isn't the Lord Chief Justice, though she may think she is. There's no law that says Laura can't treat people so long as she doesn't set up to be a doctor and write prescriptions for official drugs.'

'There isn't?'

'You must know that, Dad – surely you wouldn't have let Laura do it if you thought it was illegal.'

'No, of course not – no, no, you're right. But didn't Miss Apterley say—'

'Miss Apterley said Laura had broken hospital regulations, and that was true, though heaven knows if a nurse was on the scene of an accident she'd surely treat people. Well, that's not the issue here. Laura has powers that can help people, and because of what Miss Apterley said she decided not to use them. But if people seek her out . . .'

'She's not the type to say no,' her father finished for her. 'So . . . What should we do?'

'Nothing.'

'Really?'

'Dad, Laura is twenty-four years old today. She's entitled to make her own decisions.'

'Yes. Well. Yes, I see that. All right. Okay. I'll just go and get the paper then, shall I?'

'And I'll start the evening meal.'

'Righto.'

Catherine let herself into the flat and went straight to the kitchen after taking off her coat and hat. She was busy with the vegetables when Laura joined her. She turned to study her. Her sister was pale and bright-eyed, a half-smile on her lips that seemed ready to fade if challenged.

'I've just been treating someone who needed my help,' she said, and waited.

'Dad told me you'd brought someone home.'

'Oh, he'd worked it out? Well, he was right, she was a patient, and I felt I just couldn't refuse.'

'I see.'

'I oughtn't to tell you any details, I suppose, because what she said is confidential, but I was so sorry for her, Cath. She's pregnant for the fourth time, lost the other three, she couldn't carry them to term, the doctors don't seem to be able to do anything. This time they've told her she's got to have almost complete bed rest, and she can't *do* that because her husband . . . well . . . he doesn't seem very understanding. And I knew I could help her, I *knew*, Cath.'

'Yes.'

'You aren't going to scold me?'

'Good lord!' Catherine threw down the paring knife and engulfed her sister in a hug. 'Sweetie, whatever you want to do is fine by me! I'm sure you know what's right better than I do.'

'Oh, Cath! That's such a relief! That was the one thing that was bothering me!'

There had been a celebration planned for that evening, because of Laura's birthday. It turned into a bubbling, glowing event. Laura explained how Mrs Jeavons had got the address of the day nursery. 'She's a farmer's wife, a tenant on the Colvilles' estate. Mrs Colville's known her since she got married, knows all about her problems. So she gave Mrs Jeavons the address of the day nursery. I suppose she didn't know I'd decided not to do that any more.'

'But she did – I told her husband.' Catherine paused. 'I *thought* I told him . . .'

'I'm going to see her every week for a bit,' Laura surged on. 'Six or eight weeks, just to make sure everything is all right, and then perhaps just once a month until the baby arrives. I'm going to save that baby! Oh, it's so lovely to be really useful again.'

'"That one talent which 'tis death to hide, Lodged with me useless,"' quoted Catherine.

'What's that?'

'Oh, something dredged up from my schooldays. Milton, I think, lamenting he couldn't write because he'd gone blind.'

'That's just how I felt!' Laura burst out. 'I felt as if I'd cut off some part of me. It was awfully hard to bear.'

'So you're going to go on, then?' Gerald inquired, with a glance of concern towards Catherine.

'Go on? Of course! I should never have stopped! Just because bossy old Apterley smacked my wrist!' Laura was a little *dégagée* because of the wine they'd had with the meal. She would never otherwise have spoken with disrespect of Matron.

'Now wait a minute. Wait a minute,' protested Gerald. 'I can see you've got to do this, but let's be sensible. No male patients.'

'What?'

'Remember what happened. Can't have that again.'

'Don't be silly, Daddy, that wouldn't happen again in a million years—'

'I don't know,' said Gerald. 'You're an awfully pretty girl.'

'But it never happened while I was nursing—'

'No, because you were in a ward with other nurses nearby—'

'That's it,' said Catherine. 'You mustn't be alone with a male patient. That's the answer.'

'If you think I can come traipsing upstairs from the shop to act as guard—'

Laura gave a peal of laughter. 'Oh, yes, I can just see it, Dad. Very reassuring to sick people to have you standing there glowering.'

'I'll do it,' said Catherine. 'I was with you when you examined Mrs Colville that time, because we had to help her up the stairs. I didn't cause any stress, did I?'

'No, that's quite true.'

'I think that's the solution,' Gerald remarked, looking relieved. 'Nobody's going to try anything like that with a witness. Good for you, Cathie, you've solved the problem.'

It turned out to be a bigger commitment than she had foreseen. During the summer of the previous year Laura had seen perhaps twelve or thirteen people. Now that she had resumed her ministrations it seemed as if that trickle had turned into a stream. Four out of the seven evenings in the week were given up to the work.

'It's a bit of a tie but I don't mind it,' Catherine said when writing to her boyfriend Malcolm in Cyprus. 'We all feel it's better not to leave Laura alone with people who after all, at first, are complete strangers. And some have quite the wrong idea. A lady last week wanted Laura to summon up her dead husband and when Laura said she didn't do that, she got quite weepy and we spent an hour calming her down . . .'

Malcolm Sanders, reading this in barracks outside Nicosia, thought the Mertagen family had gone a bit mad. But he didn't take it seriously. Laura had always been a bit fey in his opinion and, compared with his life as a corporal in the Norfolk Infantry Regiment, comforting weeping women and curing chilblains seemed irrelevant.

He looked forward to his return to civilian life. National Service was such a waste of time! He had a life waiting for him back home in Hulmesley – resumption of his career with the Norfolk Regal, special courses to finish his study of statistics and economics, marriage with Cathie, a nice home and children . . .

When he chatted with his mates over a pint of thin Cypriot beer, he gathered that his prospects were superior to some of the others'. They would look at him with a glint of envy in their eyes. Here was a chap who'd planned out his life, who knew what he wanted. Malcolm felt that they were right to envy him. He'd always known he was good with figures, had been Head of School as a boy, had gone into the insurance company because they promised to let him pursue his studies at university. He should have gone into the army at eighteen but it had been put off for two years so that he could get the first certificate in Statistical Studies.

Once back home he'd have demob leave. He'd stay in bed every morning until ten, eat plenty of his mother's magnificent cooking, catch up with his friends at the local. He and Cathie would spend a lot of time together. Go to shows, make a trip to London to hear some of this new pop music, look at houses dreaming of the day when they'd own one: another two years, perhaps, before their savings reached the right level.

Norfolk Regal Insurance would of course have kept his job for him. When he got back to the office there'd be a lot of catching up to do; he'd lost two years out of his upward climb. He intended to be a senior claims executive by the time he was thirty, a branch manager by thirty-three, an investment manager by thirty-five. If he made it to investment manager it meant a desk in the City, control of pension funds, a chance to make his mark in the financial world. The City – that was where adventure lay, where real brains would count.

And all with Cathie by his side, Cathie who had reappeared in Hulmesley as the war ended with all the clear dark shine of seal-brown hair, and hazel eyes, with the colt-like elegance of adolescence. Cathie whom he'd admired from a distance as a teenager because, of course, the girls at Hulmesley High School were more or less unapproachable. She'd appeared in the offices of Norfolk Regal, almost as if fate were telling him to grab his chance. And she was his, and they'd been more or less engaged throughout his National Service, and he'd been almost completely faithful to her despite the temptations of Nicosia.

When he returned with his regiment his father motored into Norwich to collect him off the train, bringing with him his mother, his married brother Tom, and Cathie. There was very little chance for a proper conversation: that evening there was the welcome home party with relations and family friends, which went on until the early hours.

Next day he had a hangover, which he knew served him right: he'd grown accustomed to the light dry wine of Cyprus, he should never have let himself be drawn into all those toasts in port and beer and the lord knew what else. But in any case Cathie had said she wasn't free until the evening. Just as well. It took him most of the day to recover.

When he saw her, it was more or less a repeat of the welcome home party only in the Mertagens' flat and on a smaller scale.

What with the celebrations and the demands of old friends and the need to visit the Norfolk Regal office to discuss his return to work, several days went by before he and Cathie could be alone together. The moment they met, they went into each other's arms. They clung together with an upsurge of the passion that had been long subdued. Two years – they had almost forgotten what the other looked like, and truth to tell each had changed.

'Shall we go to our hideaway?' he murmured, his lips against her hair.

He felt her nod. He gave a little laugh. This was how he had always pictured it, during dreary hours on guard duty or driving across the parched central plains of Cyprus.

Their 'hideaway' was a little harbourside cottage, a little two-up and two-down, a refurbished fisherman's dwelling and one of several properties his father owned for summer letting. On this fine spring afternoon it had no tenant. The tubs of daffodils outside the door were in full bloom, and in one of them the key was hidden. They went in with an arm about each other, and without words climbed the steep wooden staircase to the bedroom.

Their lovemaking, shy and almost tentative at first, soon became fierce and demanding. They relearned old pleasures and discovered new joy and exultation. Cathie found his body had grown more muscular, the skin tanned by hours under the Mediterranean sun. For Malcolm there was the welcome of eager caresses, the perfect happiness of wanting and being wanted.

The evening sun gilded the sloping ceiling when at last they were sated. They tidied up, put the key back among the daffodils, then went in search of a meal. Hulmesley, formerly a fishing town and now a fairly busy harbour, was full of pubs and inns. They chose a quiet place in a lane by the side of the river Hulme, ordered snacks at the bar, then took their glasses to a secluded booth at the back of the room.

They had a lot of catching up to do. So far, at their encounters among friends, the talk had been mainly of his tour in Cyprus and the difficulty of dealing with *Enosis*, the Greek demand for a free Cyprus united with Greece. About Cathie's life there hadn't been time to inquire.

'So tell me, have you made it to office manager yet?' he asked as they sipped. Her position in the offices of Norfolk Regal was something he hadn't thought to raise with the branch manager when he was discussing his own future.

'Well . . . I haven't had time to write and tell you the latest,' she said. 'As a matter of fact, I gave up my job with Norfolk Regal two weeks ago.'

Malcolm was startled. 'What happened? Did you get a better offer?'

'Not exactly. It was the way things worked out. You know Laura's running this sort of clinic now, and when she has a male patient she has to have someone else with her. So I've been doing that in my out-of-office hours but really, it became so difficult to work out a schedule—'

'Just a minute,' he interrupted. 'I think I missed something there. Go back to the beginning. Laura's not at the hospital any more so she's running a clinic from the flat – I got that from your letters. And you've been helping her when you weren't at work – evenings? Weekends?'

'Yes, but I don't actually help, you know. I just – I'm at hand, a presence in the room with her. I told you, she had trouble with this awful man last year—'

'Oh, that . . .' He'd been on a mopping-up patrol in the Kyrenia Mountains at the time, he hadn't paid much attention to the tale of some silly man trying to take advantage of Cathie's sister. 'So okay, I see that, she needs someone handy – but you're not telling me you gave up your job . . . ?'

'Yes I did, Malcolm. It got so there was no alternative. She was seeing patients every day, and we just couldn't keep shovelling the male patients into slots that would fit my free time. So we talked it over and decided it would be best if I gave up my job so as to be on hand all the time.'

He stared at her. 'You must be joking.'

'No, not at all.' Cathie's voice rose a little. 'Why should you say that?'

'I can't believe that anybody with all their marbles would give up a first-class job with Norfolk Regal to be – what? – a sort of dogsbody in a nature-cure clinic! Couldn't Laura have hired somebody?'

'Well . . .' Catherine hesitated. 'The money isn't entirely fore-seeable. We couldn't guarantee a living wage. Besides, I don't think Laura could function with a stranger standing around.'

'The money isn't foreseeable? What sort of charges is she making?'

'She . . . we . . . there isn't an actual charge. Laura doesn't want to ask for money—'

'Good God, why not? If she's putting bandages on cuts and rubbing ointment on stings, she has a perfect right to charge—'

'That's not it, Malcolm. That's not it at all.'

'What, then?' Her tone perplexed him. There was a serious sound to it, almost a rebuke.

'What Laura does can't be assessed in money terms. She heals with her touch.'

He was utterly dumbfounded. He frowned. Dark eyes stared at her out of a thin tanned face.

'I know it sounds strange. I was surprised – almost scared – the first time I saw her do it. I don't know how to describe it. There's a sort of magic in her touch.'

'Don't be silly!'

'It's not silly, Malcolm. Laura is a healer.'

'Oh, for heaven's sake, talk sense—'

'She's always had the power. Even as a little girl, she could handle sick animals, soothe crying babies. But now it's more than that. She can cure sick people.'

'Cathie, you're talking rubbish.'

'No I'm not, it's the truth. Ask anyone. Ask Desmond Colville and his wife. Ask Mrs Jeavons. I could give you a list—'

'Don't bother. Just tell me this – what does Matron at the hospital think of it?'

Catherine drew up her shoulders in an angry shrug. 'Oh, Miss Apterley – anything that happens outside a doctor's surgery must be wrong, as far as she's concerned.'

'Isn't that the usual view? People who run funny clinics are either crooks or cranks—'

'Malcolm, that's my sister you're talking about!'

'Oh, of course, and you can't listen to anything against her, can you? She's always been your first concern. Well, let me tell you, Catherine Mertagen, your sister's a loony and you're encouraging her! You ought to be ashamed of yourself!'

The barmaid approached with the meal. Catherine set down her glass and rose. 'Don't bother to serve mine,' she said to her, 'I'm leaving.'

And with that she walked out.

Chapter Six

It was a serious quarrel, but in two days they made it up. The trouble was, Malcolm believed that with their reconciliation came agreement: that Catherine went along with his view about Laura's activities.

This was at first an unspoken belief on his part. When he put it into words the following evening, he was aghast to find he was mistaken.

'But you can't really want her to go on with this!' he objected. 'She'll get a reputation for being an absolute crackpot—'

'On the contrary, she's gaining a reputation for being a friend and helper—'

'Only among the people deluded enough to—'

'The people who believe in her are the people who've benefited from her talent—'

'Talent! Talent for what – hypnotism? Mumbo-jumbo?'

'Malcolm, you've no idea what you're talking about! Nothing peculiar happens. People come to Laura and she helps them – that's all.'

'By making passes in the air and repeating magic words, I suppose!'

'Why are you so sceptical? People have always had the power to heal. You see it mentioned in history – local healers, counsellors who knew how to calm fears and—'

'But this is a bit more than calming fears, from what you've been saying. Doctors and priests do that sort of thing. You're saying Laura cures disease—'

'It's not unknown. It's even mentioned in the Bible.'

'Oh, next you'll be telling me she's part of the Second Coming—'

Catherine went red with anger. 'That's pretty nearly blasphemous, and you know very well Laura doesn't make any silly claims—'

'I *don't* know that. She cures people by some means other than medical knowledge – so you say. But—'

'Are you saying I'm making it up?'

'Not at all, I think you believe it, but *I* haven't seen it.'

'But I have.'

'All right, let me see a demonstration. Show me how she goes about it. Maybe then I'll believe in it.'

'That's quite impossible—'

'There you are! I knew that's what you'd say!'

'In the first place,' Catherine went on as if he hadn't interrupted, 'I don't think she could do it if someone was standing by sneering at her. And in the second place, I don't think any of the patients would agree to such an intrusion – and why should they, just so you can satisfy your curiosity?'

'It's a bit more than curiosity, for heaven's sake, Cathie. You're asking me to let myself be taken as part of Laura's circle, the people who accept all this. Well, I don't. And I can't imagine what Norfolk Regal would say if they knew someone in my fiancée's family was going in for . . . for . . . well, fake medicine.'

They were out for an evening stroll in the park by the promenade. They had stopped by a tall hedge of Portuguese laurel to shelter from the cool sea breeze. Twilight was well advanced, and in the shadows it was difficult to make out Malcolm's expression.

But his manner was stiff, conveying not only annoyance but embarrassment.

Catherine drew back from him. 'The last thing I'd want is to be a hindrance to you in your career with Norfolk Regal,' she said scathingly.

'You can be disdainful about it if you like. But they've been good to me and I want to make a return for their faith in me. I can't see myself explaining Laura—'

'Who's asking you to explain Laura? She doesn't need you or anyone else to make apologies—'

'But it puts others in a difficult position if she goes on with this nonsense! Couldn't you talk to her, make her see sense?'

'You mean that so as to make things easier for you, my sister should give up her work?'

'Well, she can't really go far with it, can she? From what I can gather, it doesn't bring in much money – what's she going to live on? She can't go on cadging off you and your father—'

'I think we'd better stop talking about it,' Catherine said, busying herself with the fastening of her collar so as to turn away from him.

'What's the use of saying that? We've got to sort it out—'

'As far as I'm concerned, it's sorted. My sister has a very special calling and she's not going to give it up just because it embarrasses you. Either you live with that fact, or—'

'Or what, Cathie?' He took her up sharply. To tell the truth, he was staggered by her attitude. Cathie, who'd always been at one with him on every important point . . . She had been part of his life since he was sixteen years old. Was she saying he had to choose – accept the crackpot sister or end their engagement? Give up the dream that had seen him through the boredom and hardships of National Service, just because Laura was playing the fool?

He tried a new tack. 'I expect you've never stopped to think where this would lead,' he said. 'You've always given first importance to Laura's wishes – that's why you started work for Norfolk Regal, wasn't it, to bring in a steady wage because Laura wanted to be a nurse and that didn't earn much.'

'You're not going to say there was anything wrong with—'

'No, no, I understand you've always had a special feeling – only natural, the way you had to rely on each other while you were evacuated and all that. But it's different now. If she wants to go on with this "healing" thing, she ought to move out, set up somewhere on her own so as not to—'

'Oh, so that's it now, is it? You want to drive her out of her own home—'

'Come on, Cath, I don't mean it like that.' Was she deliberately misinterpreting everything he said? But truth to tell, he'd always felt that Laura was something of a nuisance. He wanted to be fair, but he couldn't help feeling Cathie would get on better without Laura to think about. 'Laura's only able to go on with this because you support her, you and your dad—'

'And we want to do it, because we think it's right! Can you get that through your head? Dad believes in Laura, and so do I, and no sneaky talk about "cadging" is going to change—'

'Sneaky? For God's sake, Cath, I'm only pointing out the plain facts—'

'You're talking as if Laura's up to no good, taking advantage of us, playing some sort of trick on her family and her patients – I won't have it! Goodnight, Malcolm!'

'Hold on, we can't just leave it there. Let's meet tomorrow—'

'Sure you want to be seen with the sister of the confidence trickster?' Catherine called over her shoulder as she stalked away.

But they met, and had another wrangle, and parted on bad terms yet again.

She could see it was going to end in hurting each other deeply. She'd had to bite her tongue more than once to keep from telling Malcolm that in her opinion he was stupid, narrow-minded, self-regarding. Did he really not understand that if Laura were to give up her role as healer, others would be punished? That the sick, the suffering, the anguished would have to struggle along without help?

Moreover, she knew that it would be impossible for Laura to give up now. The power that lived within her was too strong to be subdued. And Catherine would never even dream of asking her to make such a sacrifice – a sacrifice to convention, to Malcolm's view of the world.

Had he always been so conventional? Had he changed – or had she?

Whichever it was, she gradually came to feel that they could never be happy together now. 'Love conquers all', the motto runs – but the love she and Malcolm used to share didn't seem strong enough.

She was very sad. For something like three years now she'd lived with the hope and belief of a life with Malcolm. To give it up was to feel something wither within her, something precious and irreplaceable.

Better to acknowledge that an end had come – and to make the ending quick rather than painful and lingering.

She wrote to him:

Dear Malcolm

I think it would be better if we stopped seeing each other. We seem to argue all the time when we're together, and the argument isn't going to be settled in any way that will satisfy your views. I understand that you've your career to think of and, though I don't agree Laura would damage it, I see that you think so. It would be better, then, to say goodbye now, before we have a quarrel that would turn us into enemies. I'd rather part as friends.

Best wishes,
Catherine.

In some secret recess of her heart, perhaps she hoped he would rush to the telephone, brushing aside their doubts and telling her that he loved her.

But that didn't happen. In a day or two a polite little note arrived.

Dear Catherine

Thank you for your letter. I can't say I was completely surprised by it. Since I got back from Cyprus we don't seem to be in harmony any more. Perhaps it was wrong to take it for granted we could go on from where we left off two years ago. Norfolk Regal are sending me on a 'brush-up' course so perhaps when I get back we might be in touch to see how we feel.

Yours,

Malcolm.

He was gone a month. While he was away she thought she would ring him the minute he got back, but then she would say to herself, 'No, it's better to leave things alone.'

She heard on the local grapevine that he'd returned. He didn't contact her. When her father said to her, 'Aren't you and Malcolm going together any more?' she replied, 'Oh, well, you know . . . both of us changed while he was away.' He tactfully avoided the issue thereafter.

Laura wasn't so easily put off. 'I can't believe you've just let yourselves drift apart, Cath. You were so totally involved with each other.'

'No we weren't.'

'Come on, Cath! You thought the universe revolved around him.'

'Well, even if that's true, that was two years ago. You know the saying, Out of sight, out of mind.'

'But you wrote to him all the time! Don't tell me he was out of your mind!'

'Laura . . . please . . .'

At once, seeing she was hurting her sister, Laura stopped. But at bedtime that night she returned to the topic. She perched on the end of Catherine's bed, hairbrush in hand, and began in a solemn tone. 'Tell me not to blunder about in your private life if you want to,' she said with hesitation, 'but first put me straight about what's happened between you and Malcolm. You didn't write a single letter while he was on that course. Have you actually split up?'

'Yes.'

'For good?'

'It looks like it.'

'What happened?'

Catherine shrugged. 'We changed our minds.'

'But . . . listen, love, you know I wouldn't ever interfere just for the sake of it. But I know how much Malcolm meant to you. After all, I do know you pretty well. I could even tell you the day it got really serious between the two of you for the first time.'

'Don't be silly. How could—'

'It was on that big picnic when we all went to Cromer for the day and you and Malcolm managed to miss the train home.'

'Laura!'

Her sister gave a little laugh and, throwing aside the hairbrush, took her hand. 'It's all right. I never mentioned it to anyone else. But that was when I knew you really loved him, because you would never have gone all the way with anyone else.'

'Oh, Laura,' sighed Catherine, shaking her head and avoiding the smiling, sympathetic gaze.

She'd thought it was their secret, hers and Malcolm's. In the world in which she'd been brought up, 'nice girls' didn't make love until they were married. But on that day three years ago, she and Malcolm had taken the step that – in her opinion – took them over the borderline between friendship and enduring love. It had been a serious commitment.

Often she had marvelled at herself. She hadn't thought physical desire would be so important to her but once they were lovers, she had longed for the stolen moments they could share.

She'd been certain no one ever suspected. How shocked they would all have been, her father, Malcolm's parents . . . The general view was that they were too young to be 'serious'. First National Service, then a year or two for Malcolm to start making his way in the world. *Then*, with everything set fair, marriage with all its conventional trimmings – white gown, orange blossoms, champagne, speeches . . . And a honeymoon in which the young couple would at last taste the joys of physical pleasure.

Conventional, provincial, perhaps puritanical – impossible to let them have even a hint that she and Malcolm had soared over all these barriers already.

Yet all the time, Laura knew.

'It's true, isn't it?' Laura persisted.

Catherine rose so as to occupy herself with hanging up the dress she'd taken off. She was incapable of replying.

'That's why I can't believe you're just letting it all die away,' her sister went on. 'At least, I can see that you *are* letting it happen but I don't understand why.'

'I don't want to talk about it.'

'It can't be that he's found someone else? While he was abroad?'

'No.'

'The company's transferring him? Is that it?'

'No.'

'Cathie, I know you and he were having rows before he went off on that course – I could tell it by how tense you were.'

'It doesn't matter.'

'But you never used to row, you were like two birds in a nest, you agreed about everything. So what—?' She broke off. She picked up her hairbrush from the counterpane, then threw it down again. After a moment she said slowly, 'It's about me, isn't it.' It was a statement, not a question.

Catherine wanted to reject the conclusion. But she always found it difficult to lie to her sister, even for the best of reasons. She stayed silent, and Laura resumed.

'I've felt a difference in his manner to me. In fact, I thought he was avoiding me – but then I thought he was probably just busy, taken up with starting his life all over again, but that's what it is, isn't it – he disapproves of what I do.'

'It's not so much that he disapproves,' Catherine replied, trying to make it less judgemental. 'It's that he just doesn't believe in it.'

'Doesn't believe—? But you told him you'd seen it yourself, surely?'

'He thinks I'm kidding myself. You too. He . . . thinks it's mistaken . . .'

'Mistaken? Although it helps people?'

Catherine couldn't bring herself to relate Malcolm's objections. They would sound self-centred and prim. Instead she said, 'There are folk who can't accept anything that's outside the normal run of things. Those men on the hospital board, for instance . . .'

'But they were all old and set in their ways. Surely Malcolm—'

'Let's forget it, Laura. Talking about it isn't going to change anything.'

'Oh, Cathie, what a lot of trouble I've caused! Dad was so upset about the things Mr Patterson said, and then Matron couldn't get me out of her hospital fast enough, and now Malcolm . . . What did he actually say? He thinks it's all self-delusion, is that it? Or it's some kind of trick?'

'Never mind, love. If people have minds absolutely closed against anything unusual, they're not worth bothering about.'

And with that she pleaded that she was tired and didn't want to pursue the matter any further.

Laura, who would have done anything in the world to put things right for her sister, knew it was no use going to Malcolm herself.

She had no confidence that she could persuade him if Catherine had failed. She had the feeling he'd never cared for her much and had been jealous of the closeness she and Catherine shared. To go to him pleading for understanding would do no good.

Echoing in her head she could hear the kind of thing he'd probably said to Catherine. That she'd thrown up a good job just so as to help Laura, that she was making herself look silly by being involved in this strange endeavour, harming any prospects she might have of a proper career or marriage.

Yet Catherine seemed to come to terms with her loss. In fact, she told Laura she was quite pleased to have left the office of Norfolk Regal, where her job as a shorthand typist hadn't been very enthralling. Now she was keeping the books for her father and filling in his Income Tax forms, thus saving him the cost of an accountant. She took on the same work for one or two of his shopkeeping friends, earning small fees thereby. Others asked for the same help: she earned enough to pay her way.

There was even some book-keeping for Laura because, although she steadfastly refused to ask for money, patients were often insistent on paying. To solve this problem, Catherine placed a Chinese bowl on the little table on the landing with a card saying 'Donations'. Those who had little would put in a shilling or two. But some of Laura's patients put in banknotes of large denomination.

Laura gave ten per cent to charity, a different one each week. Forty per cent went to Gerald for board and lodgings. The rest was Laura's – little enough compared with what she might have demanded, but enough to meet her needs.

As the weeks passed, a certain tranquillity reigned in the Mertagen household. Summer visitors came and went, then the autumn winds arrived and the weekend of Hulmesley's sailing regatta.

Desmond and Phoebe Colville, still strong supporters of Laura's work, tried always to include the two girls in any of their entertaining. For the regatta they had weekend visitors at Browbourne, with a big party the evening after the awarding of the Regatta Cup. Laura and Catherine were invited.

Catherine got out her 'little black dress' again. Laura, dithering between a green taffeta that was five years old and a newish broderie anglaise that was really a day dress, almost decided to give the party a miss.

But she let Catherine persuade her into going. And she was glad that she did. Because at the Colvilles' Laura met Toby Lindham and fell in love.

Chapter Seven

The friends of the Colvilles came mostly from the horse-riding and sailing fraternity. Riding for Catherine and Laura had been restricted to occasional forays on the back of the carthorse on the farm during the war and, though they lived in a coastal town, their sailing experience was limited to a trip around the bay in summer.

Thus they were never entirely at ease with the people they met at the Colvilles'. Aware of this, Phoebe always took care to introduce them here and there among the gathering. To her older friends she would mention that Laura was the young woman who had healed her injured knee; this always aroused an interest which Laura found embarrassing. With younger people Phoebe relied on the good looks of the girls to make their way for them. And in fact Laura's gentle, rounded prettiness and Catherine's gamine appearance usually called out a friendly reaction from the menfolk.

Toby Lindham seemed no exception. 'You live in Hulmesley?' he queried. 'You keep your boat there?'

'We don't have a boat,' Catherine said.

'You don't? Do you crew for someone else, then?'

'No. We're not sailors.'

'What, not at all?'

'Not even a little bit,' said Catherine.

'Oh, then . . .' She thought he was on the verge of asking what on earth they were doing at the party but after a momentary hesitation he said, 'What *do* you do, then? If you're a friend of Phoebe's you either ride, sail, or help to run the parish church.'

'None of those things.'

'Am I allowed three guesses?'

'We're mystery women,' Laura said.

'You intrigue me! Are you into smuggling? No, I've got it – you're property dealers. I hear there's a lot of interest in Norfolk as a place to have a weekend cottage. That's it, isn't it?'

'More to the point, what do *you* do?' Laura countered. 'I know you're a sailor, of course.'

'How do you know that? Phoebe told you, I suppose.'

'No, I know because the first question you asked was about sailing.'

'Well now, that's rather clever!'

'And I further deduce that you didn't win any of the prizes in the regatta,' Laura went on.

'You guessed because of my air of gloom and despondency?'

'No, before we were introduced I noticed you weren't with the group exchanging photographs of themselves holding the cups.'

'Oh, so you were taking notice of me, were you?'

'Just a polite interest,' Laura said, and smiled.

Why, she's *flirting* with him, Catherine said to herself in astonishment. It was so long since her sister had shown any interest in romance that Catherine had almost forgotten when it happened. All during her long period of training to be a nurse there had been almost no time for any kind of distraction, and now that she had healing sessions almost every day, there seemed no chance of meeting men in ordinary circumstances.

But now here they were at Browbourne House and Laura was making a decided effort to attract Toby Lindham. And there was no denying that he was a man worth attracting.

Catherine put his age at about twenty-seven or twenty-eight. He was above middle height, sparely built but broad-shouldered. His fair hair showed the effects of salt water and sun by its rather rough texture. His skin was tanned, he had fine, even, white teeth in a wide mouth and greyish eyes set wide apart. His sports jacket and slacks had been bought from a good tailor but showed signs of wear, which probably meant that he wasn't among the richest of the Colvilles' friends. And his badly ironed open-necked shirt meant that he had no wife looking after him.

All this was quite satisfactory to Catherine. If her sister wanted to pair up for the evening with a young man, all the better if he were goodlooking and unmarried.

She left the conversation to develop between them and at an opportune moment slipped away. When the carpet was rolled back in the drawing-room for dancing, she was pleased to see that Toby Lindham had his arm around Laura for the sprightly opening bars of 'The Yellow Rose of Texas'.

Later, when Desmond Colville had changed the record, he claimed Catherine for the next dance. 'I always try to put on a waltz when Phoebe tells me to change the record. I can do the waltz.' This he proved by sweeping her round in a masterful circle. 'How are things going for Laura?'

'Pretty well. She has as much as she can handle – all personal recommendations, you know.'

'I gather you've given up your own job to work with her?'

'Oh, hardly that. I do the donkey work – keep the appointment book, act as chaperone.'

'It's very good of you. Phoebe was only saying to me the other day, not many girls would do so much for a sister. Quite a sacrifice.'

'No, no . . .'

'You used to work for Norfolk Regal Insurance, didn't you?'

'In the office, yes.'

'One of their regional directors is here tonight. Edward Dudley, d'you know him?'

'Oh, I wasn't on the directorial level, Mr Colville,' she laughed.

When the dance ended and he had to attend to the gramophone, he took her to Mr Dudley. 'This is Catherine Mertagen who used to work in your Hulmesley office,' he said. 'Look after her while I put something else on the turntable.'

'Hulmesley office, eh?' Mr Dudley said, taking his pipe out of his mouth and shaking hands. 'What were you, sales side? Claims?'

'Neither, I was just a shorthand typist—'

'And you left to better yourself, I imagine. Good for you. Though mind you, if you'd had a word with me before you went, I might have been able to do something. Any friend of Desmond's, you know . . .'

'Thank you, you're very kind, but I left to work from home with my sister.'

'Self-employed, is that it? Well, that suits some people. I've nothing against it. But mind you, with the career structure we're offering now at the old Norfolk Regal, I'd hate to lose a promising candidate. You can go a long way these days in the insurance business. Pension funds are going to be big.'

Catherine made complimentary noises, looking round for a way of escape, when her attention was recalled by the mention of Malcolm Sanders' name. 'I beg your pardon?' she said, leaning towards him to be sure to hear above the music.

'D'you know him, by any chance?'

'Yes, he was at the office when I first started there.'

'Bright lad. We picked him out as a star player quite a while ago, almost as soon as he joined us. This blasted National Service, of course – puts a damper on things for a couple of years but he's all ready to go forging ahead now. We'll be giving him a branch office pretty soon in one of the big towns – a big step up for him.'

'That sounds wonderful,' said Catherine, sighing inwardly at the unimportance of news that once would have meant so much to her.

'It's a bit early, perhaps, but you know, young men who've coped with service life and been abroad and seen a bit of the world . . . they shouldn't be held back, that's my view. And then, of course, with marriage on the horizon—'

'Malcolm is getting married?'

'Romantic, my dear!' Mr Dudley made a sweeping gesture with the hand not holding the pipe. 'A gorgeous girl he met in Cyprus – I didn't see her photograph myself but he was showing it around and they say she's a real beauty. From some family regarded as very high-up in the Greek Cypriot world – landowners, wine-growers, something like that.'

'That does sound romantic,' Catherine agreed, thinking that she would never have believed it. She nerved herself to hear the rest, which Dudley was dying to tell her.

'Oh, there's more! Her folk weren't keen to let her marry a foreigner in the first place, and then they're the kind that would want someone like a lawyer or a diplomat, someone with good prospects, you know. So his promotion came along at just the right time. That's what's called giving Cupid a hand.' Mr Dudley put his pipe between his lips, puffed happily, and looked pleased with himself.

'That's wonderful,' murmured Catherine, and was glad music was pouring from the gramophone to conceal the unsteadiness of her voice.

Marrying . . . And so soon after they had broken up . . .

But she banished the strange feeling of loss. She and Malcolm meant nothing to each other these days except that, for her, he would always be her first love. She'd read somewhere that women cherish the memory but that men soon forget. So Malcolm had soon forgotten.

Yet, in a way, she was surprised by his choice. A Greek Cypriot girl hardly seemed to fit in with the plans they'd so often discussed, for a typically English house and garden. But then . . . plans can change as hearts change.

Mr Dudley began to chat about the regatta, some of the prizes having been donated by Norfolk Regal. Soon after, she was invited to dance. By and by midnight came, time to go. She went in search of her sister and found her in a nook of the verandah, deep in conversation with Toby Lindham.

'Come on, Laura, we promised Dad we'd be home before one.'
'What? Oh, what time is it?'
'Ten past twelve.'
'Really? Good heavens.' With obvious reluctance Laura rose from the basket settee she'd been sharing.
'Don't go.'
'I must, Toby. It's a bit of a drive to Hulmesley—'
'But it's early – the party won't break up for another hour yet—'
'I'm sorry,' Catherine said. 'But Dad doesn't like me out on country roads in the middle of the night. He doesn't have a high opinion of my driving.'
'A bit of a tyrant, is he?'
Laura laughed at this inaccurate description of Gerald. 'No, no, he's a bit of a fusspot, that's all. But Cath's right, we do have to go—'
'If it's Cath's driving he distrusts, perhaps she'd better get home and set his mind at rest. But there's no reason why you should go.'
'But Cathie's got the car—'
'I can drive you back—'
'But it would be miles out of your way—'
'What about it? There used to be a song, didn't there? "Let's take the long way home" . . .'
'Are you coming, Laura?' Catherine demanded, rather more sharply than she intended.
'No, stay,' urged Toby. 'The night's still young.'
'Well . . . if you don't mind going on your own, Cath?'
'But—'
'Tell Dad I'll be along later.'
Catherine looked at Laura's flushed face and glowing eyes. Useless to say that they had a busy day ahead, that a few hours' sleep was poor preparation for it.
'All right, see you later.'
'Don't wait up, Cath,' Laura rejoined in a faintly reproving tone and with something of a frown.
'No, of course not,' she agreed. 'Goodnight, Toby, nice to have met you.'
'Goodnight, Cath.'
Cath . . . She'd hardly exchanged ten words with him and already he was calling her Cath. Quick on the uptake, this young man who had so enthralled her sister.

She drove home in the old estate car, trying to persuade herself she wasn't in the least hurt at being sent off on her own. After all, when she and Malcolm had been a pair, Laura had often been left to her own devices.

But that was different, argued an inner voice. Laura had been living in nurses' quarters, busy with her training, never at a loss for companionship. Whereas I . . .

And it dawned on Catherine that for the last few years her attention had been concentrated on two people – on Laura and on Malcolm.

Malcolm was gone. And now, for the first time, it came to her that Laura too might go – probably would go, to a man with whom she would want to spend the rest of her life. It would be only natural, and right, and she must foresee that time, and accept it.

I've been a fool, she said to herself. Where are all the friends I should have had, the hobbies and pastimes I should have cultivated, the life of my own I should have been building?

The countryside around her was a dark void, with only an occasional pinprick of light from some farm window. The car headlights drew her along the highway towards – what? What was her future? The thought occupied her mind until she reached home.

She put the car in the alley at the back of the shop. As quietly as she could, she went indoors. As she crept past her father's room he murmured, 'That you, kiddies?'

'Yes, Dad.'

'Had a nice time?'

'Lovely.'

'G'night.'

''Night.'

She lay awake a long time. She wasn't waiting for Laura to come home, her mind was elsewhere. She was asking herself how it came about that, at twenty-three years old, she felt as if she had nothing of her own to look forward to.

An absurd thought. There was still time to find new friends. She would go out more. She needn't stay in the flat if Laura had only female patients, and she needn't spend so much time working on account books . . .

Despite the late night she was up and about at her usual hour. In a way, today was an important day, domestically. Her father had decided to have central heating put in the old building, and the heating consultant was due at ten. Over breakfast Gerald began once again on his plans. 'You know that idea of mine for a consulting room for Laura . . .'

'The problem is, where?'
'It ought to be on the first floor.'
'But Dad, that means giving up the living-room—'
'Well, we can make the dining-room into a dining-cum-living-room – we'll have to get rid of some of the furniture, but—'
'I quite see it would be better if patients didn't have to clamber up two flights of stairs to Laura's bedroom—'
'There you are then—'
'But honestly, it would mean buying things – there'd have to be a couch – not the one we've got, that's a settee, what we'd need would be more of a chaise longue—'
'Well, we can do that—'
'Look, Dad, I'd better get Laura up or this central heating man will arrive while she's still in her dressing-gown.'
Her sister was in the bath. She knocked and called, 'This heating consultant will be here in half an hour.'
'Who?'
'About the radiators.'
'Oh yes.' In a moment Laura, in a bathrobe and smiling a lazy smile, opened the door. 'I'm only half-awake. I'll hurry up, Cath.'
She'd only just made it to the kitchen for toast and coffee when the central heating engineer arrived. Gerald had put the 'Back in ten minutes' sign on the shop door. 'I can't really stay,' he explained. 'I've got a customer collecting a set of prints any minute now. We already talked about this on the phone, you understand what's wanted. My daughters will show you the problem places.'
With that he hurried off, leaving Catherine in charge while Laura hastily swallowed the last of her toast.
She joined Catherine and the heating engineer in the living-room. Catherine was moving a table with a chess problem on it so that the man could examine the wall.
'This plaster's not good,' he remarked. 'If I site a radiator against it, I think you'll get not only cracks but crumbling.'
'What does that mean, then?'
'Well, the wall would have to be re-plastered first.'
'That might be quite a good idea. We're thinking of making changes anyway – taking out a lot of the furniture, having the room redecorated.'
'Since when?' Laura inquired, looking with raised eyebrows at Catherine.
'It's an idea of Dad's – I'll tell you about it.'

The consultant spent more than an hour going from room to room. It ended with the opinion that several of the walls would need new plaster and so they might think about redecoration to go with the installation of the heating.

'It looks like costing a lot more than we expected,' Catherine said as she saw him out. 'We'll let you know.'

Laura was in the kitchen when she got upstairs, making a new pot of coffee. 'What was that about altering the living-room?' she called.

'Dad's thinking of making it a consulting room for you.'

'Good heavens, what brought that on?'

'Well, we've been going on in a sort of improvised way for over a year now, Laura. It's time to think about how to handle it as a permanent thing.'

Laura looked up from measuring spoonfuls of coffee into the jug. 'Well, what an extraordinary coincidence!'

'What is?'

'That's just what Toby and I were talking about last night!'

'Oh, that's what you were doing?' Catherine said with an ironic smile. 'Discussing professional matters?'

Laura blushed. 'Not all the time,' she admitted. 'Toby and I . . . Catherine, don't you think he's great?'

'He seemed very nice,' Catherine said.

'He's got a business of his own, you know – well, at least, not entirely his own because the Colvilles have got money invested in it, or at least are thinking of investing. Yacht-building, converting ex-landing-craft into houseboats, that kind of thing. He's got a good business head. That's what we'd been talking about when you came to tell me it was going-home time.'

'Fascinating. What time did you get home, eventually?'

'I think it was about four,' she confessed.

'And all that time you were discussing boat-building?'

Laura giggled with embarrassment. 'No, of course not. Later we . . . well . . . Laura, he's so marvellous! He said the minute he saw me, he knew I was the girl he'd been looking for all his life! I never thought I'd ever be so lucky as to find someone like him. Isn't it great that we should find each other?'

'Laura, don't you think it's a bit soon—'

'And he's so interested in everything I do! It was really strange – we'd been dancing and we were just going to separate – and I can tell you, I didn't want to, not at all! But then Mrs Colville came along with one of her friends and started talking about my work. And Toby stood by, listening with all ears – he was *fascinated*.'

'Well, that was good—'

'Yes, wasn't it, because you know how it is . . . I must admit, I dreaded what he might say because you know, some people . . . But no, he understood, he took it all in, accepting, you know, not being sceptical and difficult. Of course Mrs Colville – you know what she's like, she talks as if I'm Florence Nightingale and Sister Kenny rolled into one – she went on and on, I thought she'd bore him to death. But when at last she took her friend off he made me explain it all to him from beginning to end – well, of course, I couldn't really *explain*, but I told him what's been happening. And he asked sensible questions, rather practical, and yet . . . I felt so . . . so *in tune* with him . . .'

Laura's happy chatter faded. She stood staring with a half-smile into some unseen future. The kettle boiled but she didn't notice. Catherine picked it up and poured hot water into the coffee jug.

'What was that you were saying about discussing the future with Toby?'

'What?'

'You said it was a coincidence that Dad was talking about making a proper consulting room—'

'Oh yes. Yes! That's amazing! When Toby heard all about it from Mrs Colville he said that from the sound of it what I needed was a proper consulting room. Mrs Colville had been telling him how we live above the shop and he was shaking his head and saying, "That's not very suitable," and she of course had to agree, because you remember how she had to clamber up those dreadful stairs. In fact she laughed and said she almost gave up there and then. But she thanks heaven she didn't and really . . . Now I come to look back on it . . . Well, things might have been absolutely different if she'd changed her mind and backed off, so you see, Cath, perhaps it isn't suitable. Using my bedroom, up two flights, I mean. Toby says it isn't.'

There was no doubt he was right. Yet, to her own dismay, it irked Catherine to hear him get all the credit when their own father had already come up with the idea.

Come, come, she told herself, you mustn't get into the habit of blaming him if Laura puts him first. It seemed it was something she was going to have to get used to. Laura had fallen in love as if she had toppled into a chasm. From now on, everything was going to be different.

That's to say, things were going to be different if Laura's view of the romance was correct – if Toby Lindham was as interested in Laura as she was in him.

Why she should doubt this, she couldn't quite explain, even to herself. Laura was a pretty girl, intelligent, sweet-natured. It was just that Catherine had read Toby differently, read him as the kind of man who would want someone smarter, more sophisticated.

But she soon saw she was wrong. Toby called for Laura that evening, was introduced to their father, and after a drink and a few minutes' conversation was taken on a tour of the premises to give his opinion of the consulting room plan.

'Good God!' he exclaimed as he finished toiling up the steep flights of stairs. 'You can't really ask sick people to climb Everest to get to you. It doesn't make sense, darling.'

'No, Dad quite agrees with you, and we're going to turn the living-room into a consulting room—'

'But that still means the first flight from the ground floor – how many steps are there? Sixteen?'

'Seventeen,' amended Catherine, who had counted them mentally many a time as she staggered up with shopping in her arms.

'There you are! It's not fair on anybody who's a bit under the weather to ask them to make an ascent like that! And the side door of a shop! Don't you see, Laura, that if a person is unwell, and a bit uncertain about whether to consult a non-medical practitioner, they might very well give up at the threshold.' He turned to Gerald. 'You're a businessman, Mr Mertagen. Don't you agree the set-up needs improving?'

'Well, that's what I'm actually planning to—'

'Yes, I see what you have in mind, and in fact, that's a very nice room, your living-room.' They went downstairs again in a body, to stand in the doorway of the living-room, surveying it as if it were terra incognita. 'Nice high ceilings, tall windows – yes, these old Georgian buildings have a lot of good points.'

'Well, we like it,' Gerald acknowledged. 'Shame in a way to have to change it – west-facing windows, you know, nice for us to sit in in the evening. But there you are, we can't very well give up the dining-room for a consulting room because the kitchen's right next door.'

'Right, very unprofessional, the smell of apple pie being baked.' Toby laughed, and they all laughed with him. By this time it seemed perfectly natural that he, a man whom Gerald had only just met, whom Laura herself had only known for twenty-four hours, should be playing such a large part in their discussions.

Gerald poured more sherry for himself and some of the long-stored gin for Toby. They chatted for a while. Then Laura and Toby took themselves off.

Gerald collected up the glasses on a tray. 'Serious, is it?' he inquired of his younger daughter.

She suppressed a sigh. What was there to sigh about? 'I think so.'

'Seems a nice lad?'

'As you gathered, he's a friend of the Colvilles.'

'Must be all right then.'

She nodded agreement.

'Seems funny, Laura with a boyfriend,' he went on. 'I've always thought of her as a dedicated nurse. Still, even nurses fall in love and get married, eh?'

'Right,' she said.

A neighbour was coming in to continue the chess match set up on the coffee table. Catherine took herself off to the cinema. The film scarcely held her attention. She found herself thinking about Toby Lindham.

And what she was thinking was this: why was he bothering himself over Laura?

This harsh thought astounded her when she paused to examine it. She thrust it away, forced her mind back to Bette Davis as the Virgin Queen, but it was no use.

Since it seemed she must think about it, she set herself to think about it logically.

Of course her sister had had boyfriends. There had been teenage romances. Yet Catherine knew by some instinct that Laura wasn't the type to attract the likes of Toby.

The first encounter had been led by Laura. She it was who made the running. Toby had responded – and why not?

But Laura herself had reported that they were about to part after their first dance at the party. It was the arrival of Mrs Colville with her paeans of praise about Laura's healing talents that had made him stay.

Was Toby Lindham really the kind to accept and be interested in that kind of thing? Instinct once again said no. Yet he had listened to her account of her work, and hadn't laughed or sneered . . . Quite the contrary. He had monopolised her all night after that.

Then an explanation came to Catherine. He hadn't laughed because the Colvilles wouldn't have liked that. And Toby *needed* the Colvilles. Hadn't Laura said they were investing money in his yacht-building business?

There it was, an explanation that made sense.

She thrust it away. How could she be so unkind? Was she really saying that Laura's belief in Toby was mistaken, that he was only out for the main chance?

Don't be silly, don't be grudging, she said to herself. She's in love, don't spoil it by thinking things like that.

Yet how better to get the goodwill of the Colvilles than by making friends with Laura? They thought the world of her. The girl who had cured Desmond's asthma and made Phoebe well enough to greet the Queen – here was someone whose influence with them could be useful.

No. Silly, cruel and wrong. Laura had met a man she liked and he in return liked her. That was the real story. All the rest, she berated herself, was envy, the fear of being shut out, of rejection, of loneliness.

So she walked home from the cinema, determined to take a sisterly interest in Laura's romance and not to look for faults. Laura thought him wonderful. Very well, he was to be accepted as wonderful.

In the ensuing days she kept to this resolution. Laura was so happy that almost all her conversation was about Toby: how clever he was, how much business sense he had, how sensibly he thought things through, how quick he was to take her meaning when they talked, how seriously he listened to her musings on her work.

'We're so in tune, Cath, it's amazing! He was saying to Desmond the other evening that he sometimes pauses in his work and can sense what I'm doing. Isn't that wonderful?'

'It certainly is.' She hesitated. 'Does Mr Colville – Desmond – intend to put money into the boatyard?'

If he did, she had an awful fear that Toby would cease to find Laura so wonderful.

'Well . . . no . . . that's a bit disappointing, in fact. Toby thought he was going to get a contract to convert three ex-landing-craft into houseboats for a site up the coast, the local council was going to allow them to be registered as dwellings or holiday homes. Anyhow, that's fallen through, and though Desmond thinks business may pick up in a year or two, he was recommending Toby to take on repair work.'

'And is Toby going to do that?' Catherine asked, feeling certain that repair work was too unglamorous.

'Well, his partner is quite in favour – Ken, his name is, been in the business all his life, says he's always made a living. But Toby says he could have stayed on in the Navy and made better money than if he goes in with Ken just doing repairs – and I do see his point, don't you?'

'So he isn't going to?'

Laura gave a happy little shrug, which said that whatever Toby did was bound to be right. Catherine thought to herself, He'll drop her now, she's no longer any use to him.

But no, she was quite mistaken. If anything Laura and Toby seemed to spend more time together. To Catherine it became quite clear that they were lovers. There was a flush to Laura's warm colouring, a glow to her smile, that told the tale. As for Toby, he was all that a woman could ask for – courteous, considerate, devoted. To see them together was to say, There goes an ideal couple.

Toby went home to Lancashire for Christmas. Laura moped about, trying not to show how much she missed him. He returned in good time to escort her to a New Year lunch at the Colvilles'. They came back from it all alight with plans and hopes.

It almost looked as if they were about to announce their engagement.

Not quite that. Toby produced a bottle of champagne and said, 'We've something to tell you, and it deserves a toast. What do you think has happened?'

'What?' chorused Catherine and her father.

'Desmond Colville and I are going into business together! He's offered the money to set Laura up in practice in proper premises – I've got one or two places in mind, one of them just off Higham Square—'

'But I don't understand,' Gerald interrupted, half laughing. 'You said you and Colville – but it's Laura – where do you come in?'

'It's going to be so wonderful,' Laura cried. 'There's to be a proper reception area and a consulting room, all in a prestige building, and Toby's going to manage it for me!'

Chapter Eight

Gerald was laughing and hugging Laura. Toby was busy peeling the foil from the champagne bottle. An air of celebration hovered as Catherine went to fetch glasses for the toast.

Better premises. A proper consulting room. Opportunities to extend the work. All that. Yes, it was something to celebrate.

Why then did she experience this faint sense of misgiving?

The explanation emerged a few days later. They had all gone on a Sunday to view the rooms Toby had leased, in Saltcut Crescent, one of the old rows of 'gentlemen's residences' off Higham Square. The entrance hall which served all the office suites was vast and echoing, with a stone floor. Catherine felt sorry for the servants who once had to clean a mansion like this.

The rooms were on the ground floor, towards the back of the building. There was a light and spacious vestibule with a desk, some comfortable seats upholstered in royal blue, and the obligatory Swiss-cheese plant in a big white pot.

Beyond that was the consulting room, looking out through tall windows on a back garden of lawn and laurel bushes. The original Georgian panelling had been restored, painted white with a thin gold trim. Here there was no desk, but instead a low table with a group of easy chairs as if for relaxed conversation. There was an examination table in one corner behind a screen, and a more comfortable couch under one of the windows, spread with a washable cover of royal blue cotton.

There were floral pictures on the walls, reproductions of Dutch masters. Everything looked friendly, not the least intimidating, while at the same time having a very professional air.

'Splendid,' remarked Gerald, looking round with something like ownership – for this was to be his daughter's domain. 'Plenty of elbow room. Much better than having to manage in your bedroom, dear.'

'Yes, it's a great improvement,' Laura agreed. 'And no stairs!'

'Treatments will be by appointment only,' Toby said. 'Mrs Thorpe will keep the appointment book and—'

'Who's Mrs Thorpe?' Gerald inquired, puzzled.

'The receptionist. She's worked for the last four or five years at one of those residential clinics—'

'Receptionist?' Catherine repeated.

'Yes, Desmond and I thought it would be best to have someone—'

'But *I'm* Laura's receptionist.' Despite herself, the words came out as a complaint.

'Well . . .' There was an awkward pause. Then Toby hurried on, 'Don't you think it's time for a change, Cath? Desmond and I talked it over, and we felt . . . it has an amateurish air about it, if you know what I mean. Of course at the outset you pitched in because in a way there was nobody else to do things for Laura, but now we're setting it up on a proper basis—'

'Is this what you want, Laura?' Catherine broke in, turning to look at her sister.

Laura flushed. She too hesitated, and for longer than Toby. 'At first I . . . You know I don't like change at the best of times, I like things to stay the way they are. But what Desmond says is right . . .'

'An older woman,' Toby explained soothingly. 'I mean, let's face it, Laura looks almost like a schoolgirl, and you're a year younger, so to be faced with a couple of kids when you yourself are maybe fiftyish and suffering from rheumatism . . . it's just another barrier for the patient. Desmond and I felt that Mrs Thorpe would be a soothing presence, and of course she can act as chaperone when necessary, and being older – she's forty-one – well, all in all we thought it would have a steadying effect.'

'I see.'

'After all,' Toby went on, smiling in placation at Catherine, 'you couldn't have envisaged spending the rest of your life acting as general factotum to Laura?'

'It really wasn't right,' Laura took it up. 'I didn't realise how selfish I was being until Toby pointed it out.'

'There was nothing selfish in it,' Catherine returned. 'We did what we thought was right at the time.' She paused. 'But now . . .'

'Now you see it's better to change things?'

Catherine was slowly nodding. 'Yes, Laura, perhaps it was time for a change.'

The first explanation from Toby had been like a douche of cold water. But now the shock was past. Now she could begin to look at it dispassionately.

Hadn't she just been saying to herself a few weeks ago that she'd allowed her life to be monopolised by two people, by Malcolm and Laura? Now Malcolm was gone, and Laura was opening the door of the cage. She'd never before thought of herself as in a cage but now – freedom beckoned.

She could start all over again. She could find a job, a proper job, something that might lead on to a career. She could make new friends, take up new pastimes. Art lessons . . . she'd sometimes thought she'd like to study painting or drawing.

'It'll be great,' Toby was enthusing. 'Desmond has promised his support for at least a year, but I'm certain we'll be well established in six months. We're going to call it The Mertagen Clinic – sounds good, doesn't it? We had to decide on a name to put in the phone book, you see.'

'It sounds excellent.'

'Desmond wanted to call it The Laura Mertagen Clinic but I thought that was too much,' Laura confessed, blushing.

Catherine and her father left Toby and Laura discussing letter-heads and a brass name plate for the outer door. As they walked back to Mitre Lane Gerald said with faint envy, 'He's a go-getter, isn't he, that Toby!'

'He certainly is. You and I would still be fiddling about trying to make a consulting room out of the living-room.'

'Well, the two of us wouldn't ever have thought of approaching Desmond Colville for backing.'

'No.' Catherine thought it over. 'I wonder how much of this is really Toby's idea?'

'How d'you mean?'

'If Mr Colville had wanted to back Laura financially, he could have made the offer any time in the last couple of years.'

'That's true. So you feel Toby thought of it, really?'

'I'd say so.'

'But then, you know, if Mr Colville had approached Laura off his own bat with a scheme like this, she'd have been too scared to take it on. It needed someone like Toby to give her the confidence.'

'That's true, too, Dad.'

'And you don't feel too bad about this Mrs Thorpe?'

'Goodness, we all want what's best for Laura—'

'Yes, but I could see by your face you'd had a blow, my lamb. You got over it quickly, but all the same—'

'It'll be all right. I'd been thinking just recently that I'd got into a bit of a rut, so perhaps this has come just at the right time.'

'What'll you do, then, Cathie?'

'Oh, find a job – office work – *you* know—'

'If that's what you want. I've often thought . . . You went right into shorthand and typing but perhaps there was something you'd rather have done, eh? Something more exciting?'

She laughed. 'Rock climbing? Ski-jumping?'

With that they let the matter drop. In truth, Catherine had as yet no idea what she might do.

Laura came home at mid-evening, to Catherine's surprise. Their father had gone to a chess game at the neighbour's house, where he would be given supper. Catherine was in her bedroom reviewing her wardrobe when she heard Laura's step on the stairs.

'Hello, I thought you and Toby were going out for a meal?' she remarked, turning from the spring dresses she'd been studying.

'We decided not to.'

'Oh, why?'

'We . . . we . . . We had a quarrel.'

'*What?*' Catherine sat down on her bed in surprise. Laura seldom quarrelled with anyone and to quarrel with Toby was the least likely thing in the world.

'Oh, Cath, it's so awful! He wants me to charge people for treatment!'

Catherine was truly shocked. She stared at her sister.

'He said it was the professional thing to do. But you know it's always been a principle with me—'

'Of course, of course – how can he think you should charge fees – he must know how you feel. Laura, I don't understand!'

'Neither do I! I'd no idea he had such a thing in mind—'

'He'd never mentioned it?'

'No, although he did say he wanted to put the clinic on a proper financial footing—'

'What does that mean? Does he mean he thinks it ought to make a profit? Because of course we never have—'

Laura, still in her outdoor coat, sank down on the bed beside her sister. Huddled into the brown tweed, she looked like a thrush that had been battered by a gale.

'He says we have to cover the cost of leasing the premises, he says Desmond Colville expects the money he's advancing to be repaid out of the fees, I'd no idea . . . I thought Mr Colville was making a gift of the money . . . I should have asked, I suppose, but it's so embarrassing to talk about things like that . . .'

Catherine was silent. Her hands were occupied folding the

dresses to put them away but her mind was busy with what Laura had said.

'Mr Colville has advanced the money to pay for the lease?' she asked.

'Yes, and a bit more, to buy the equipment and pay the bills for the first few months – things like electricity and the phone.'

'I'd imagine it's quite a lot.' She thought about the houses in Saltcut Crescent, elegant and substantial, offices for lawyers and estate agents and accountants. Even a six months' lease on a suite in an area like that must cost a fair bit. 'So what's the plan – there are to be set fees?'

'By the hour.'

'Just to cover the cost of the rent and heating and lighting and so on.'

'Yes.'

She considered it.

'What do you think?' Laura asked, looking seriously into her face.

'Well . . . you have to admit . . . it does sound reasonable.'

'Do you think so?'

'I suppose I do,' she said, rather unwillingly. Logic seemed to urge her to that conclusion, although it went against all the ideals of the past two years. 'You see,' she explained, 'when we were using our own home, there was no question of Dad asking for anything except your board and lodgings. But after all there was the use of the shop telephone and wear and tear of people coming in and out and I suppose heating all day in your bedroom . . . Dad wouldn't have dreamed of asking you anything like a business rent—'

'To tell the truth,' Laura broke in, her mouth trembling with emotion, 'I never even thought of offering it! What a selfish beast I am! It never even crossed my mind!'

'No, no,' said Catherine, putting a comforting arm about her, 'you're not selfish, not at all. And if it's any comfort to you, I never thought of it either, not until this minute.'

'Just think what a *nuisance* I must have been to him,' Laura raced on, scarcely heeding what her sister was saying. 'People coming and going in his home at all hours of the day and evening – and having to take messages for me on the shop phone – and if you even think about the wear and tear on the stair carpet—'

'Oh, I don't think we need weep too many tears over the stair carpet,' Catherine interrupted, half-laughing. 'Really, Laura, I think we can accept that Dad was pleased to do anything he could to help you and wouldn't have done otherwise. Yet all the same . . . There's truth in what Toby says. If you're going to have a proper clinic, it has to be paid for. And in a way, I suppose making a set charge is just another version of accepting donations in a bowl on the landing table.'

'What?'

'That bowl on the landing . . . It says "Donations" and I expect most people put something in. But perhaps they've stood there dithering, wondering how much they should donate. Is one pound enough? Is it too little? Is five pounds showing off, being ostentatious? Is ten shillings an insult?'

'You think they'd rather know how much they're going to pay?' Laura wondered.

Catherine shrugged. 'They might. But the point is, how would *you* feel about it?'

'We-ell . . . I don't like taking money for something that came to me as a gift.'

'I understand. But you won't have to take the money. Mrs Thorpe will do all that.'

'I suppose she will.' Laura brightened. 'That's something, isn't it? I needn't ever have to accept it, or watch someone writing out a cheque, or anything like that.'

'You can work out how much to charge by estimating how much you have to repay to Mr Colville and dividing it up into so much per month.'

'Yes, that ought to work. Or at least, Toby will do all that, because he's the business manager.'

Catherine observed that Laura's quarrel with Toby had already receded into the mists of the past. Everything was as it had been. And when about an hour later Toby himself arrived at the door with a bunch of crimson carnations and a humble apology, she saw Laura off for a walk in the winter dark and a scene of happy reconciliation.

Next morning Laura confided that everything was sorted out. 'I told Toby you and I had discussed the thing about charging fees and he agreed with the points you made and so . . . well . . . that's the way it'll be.'

'You're not unhappy about it?'

'Goodness, I'd be a goose to be unhappy when I've got someone as wonderful as Toby to look after things for me!'

It crossed Catherine's mind to inquire how much the business manager was to be paid out of the earnings of the clinic. But she thought better of it. Toby would surely be taking only expenses out of the fees. He had his boat-building firm as his main source of income: what he was doing for the clinic would be a part-time occupation.

Yet as winter melted into spring, he seemed more and more concerned in the running of the clinic. Laura was busy, with little time to relate the day's happenings to her sister. When she was at liberty, she was usually out with Toby. From being an important part of her sister's work, Catherine began to feel absolutely unwanted.

She had gone on with the book-keeping for her father and his business acquaintances. She took a part-time job in the harbourmaster's office. But it was unsatisfying.

One day in early summer she ate a sandwich lunch in a café by the harbour. As she often did, she was glancing through the job vacancies in the newspaper. Office work . . . Did she want to go back into full-time office work?

She said to herself, Either I've got to get qualified as an accountant and take the book-keeping business seriously, or I've got to take a proper job with a proper salary and prospects.

But there were no alluring posts in the regional newspaper. She folded it and put it in her handbag.

If she was serious about changing her life, she'd have to do something more constructive than look dismissively at the local job columns and drink bad coffee from a thick white cup in a harbour café.

She made a resolution. From tomorrow on she would buy one of the Fleet Street papers every morning and take immediate action if she saw something she liked. If there was nothing in Hulmesley that tempted her, she would up sticks and move to London.

Chapter Nine

When Thelma Axford offered Catherine the job, it was because she wanted more than just a secretary. She wanted an assistant, a sounding board, a talent scout: someone of an artistic bent, with an instinct for good design, a girl to whom she might one day delegate some of the ever-increasing responsibilities of her job.

'But I've had no training,' Catherine told her.

'You say your father used to run a gallery – had had training in graphics?'

'Yes, but there's no sign I've inherited that kind of thing—'

'When I showed you the advance pattern book, you picked out the very designs I've chosen for special promotion.'

'Maybe that was just luck.'

Mrs Axford laughed. 'Don't you want this job?' she inquired.

'Yes, I do!'

'Then stop putting obstacles in the way.' She paused to lean back in her swivel chair and think things over. She decided on frankness. 'I've seen four other girls and one young man. They all had business training but none of them seemed to be on my wavelength. I need someone I can rely on and, for some reason, I think I could rely on you. What do you say? Think you could be secretarial assistant to the Fashion Fabric Buyer at Velton's?'

'Yes, I'm sure I could,' Catherine said, though she was far from sure.

It was a bigger job than she'd expected. The advertisement had sought a 'keen young person as secretary to a senior buyer' and had given a box number. Only after she'd applied did she discover the firm was one of the biggest department stores in London. Only at the actual interview had any mention of artistic ability come into it.

She very much wanted the job. Making her way to the staff entrance of the store had been exciting enough, but the behind-the-scenes view as she was shown up to Mrs Axworth's office had thrilled her. This was *Velton's*, famous throughout the world for its fashions, its fabrics, its summer and holiday clothes, its swimwear, its gloves and scarves and costume jewellery.

She and her guide had to make way for a porter pushing a rack of rainbow-coloured, floating silk dresses. A window-dresser with her arms full of pastel suede coats came into the lift with them. As they passed the evening-wear department Catherine glimpsed an alteration hand with a tape measure round her neck hurrying to a fitting room. On every floor, in the waiting area by the lift doors, a beautiful flower arrangement lent elegance and freshness to the scene. The whole store was arranged so that it had the feel of a country house.

To work here would be more than just a living. It would be an education.

Thelma Axford was a fortyish woman of ample proportions, with strong features and sharp black eyes. Her dark hair had reddish tints supplied by her hairdresser. Her manner was forthright with an undercurrent of cynicism. She conducted the interview at high speed, barking questions and scribbling notes at Catherine's replies.

Nevertheless, Catherine took to her. There was something very attractive about the energy, the unforced efficiency of the woman. What was even more important, she sensed that Thelma Axford had taken to her.

When she reported to her family that she'd got the job, the news was greeted with cheers and congratulations. If her father looked a little wistful, if Laura seemed to be struggling against tears, the general atmosphere was approving.

After all, things had changed so much in the Mertagen family lately that one more change was soon accepted. It was only right: Catherine should have her chance at making a career even if it meant going away from home.

On Toby Lindham, Catherine noticed, the news had an odd effect. For the first time he looked at her with something like respect. Until then she'd always been just 'Laura's sister Cath', the one who remembered to pay the milkman and order the weekend joint. Now all of a sudden she was Miss Mertagen, secretary to a very influential fashion buyer, off to live in a studio flat on the banks of the Thames.

The banks of the Thames. From the depression that settled on Laura, you'd have thought it was the banks of the Niger.

'I'm not going to the ends of the earth,' Catherine soothed. 'It's only the other end of a train journey. I'll be home for weekends, and you'll come to London for a show or some shopping.'

'But we've never b-been apart,' Laura faltered.

'I know, duckie, and it will seem strange to me too.' She didn't add that for her it would seem strange indeed, for she would be alone in London, with no adoring Toby to look after her. Instead she said, 'It will be a big change for Dad. He's been used to having one of us around most of the time.'

'I promise to be at home more. Toby understands, he's quite looking forward to coming to the flat for a meal or two. I promise not to let Dad be lonely, Cath.'

'I'm sure it'll work out fine. The new cleaning lady seems a decent soul, and then there's his chess games with Ernest Goode. Ernest's wife is always eager to have him stay for a meal. And Dad's got other friends, he won't let himself wither away.'

'No, I'll see he doesn't.'

Gerald arrived upstairs at that moment to take Catherine's luggage out to the old station wagon. On a fine Saturday in early May, Catherine was driven to the station for the London train.

The studio flat was in Hammersmith, in a corner of an Edwardian house which did in fact overlook the Thames. Catherine hurried out to the market near the station to stock up with milk and tea and bread. Cooking facilities were minimal but she could make toast and had a jar of home-made marmalade for breakfasts.

Sunday she spent exploring the area. Hammersmith had suffered in the bombing of the war, and was still shabby. Yet there were some beautiful areas, old houses and warehouses from the days when goods were extensively moved by river barge; gardens and parks with stately plane trees, neat flowerbeds, and a fine show of tulips; and always the river itself, silvery when the flow was from the source, dark pewter when the tide-water from the estuary surged upstream.

She discovered the public library not far off, and a few good shops handy on the way home from the Tube station. Altogether a satisfactory place to live, she felt.

For the first couple of weeks of work, she was too exhausted to explore further. She fell into a routine: she would arrive at Velton's at eight-thirty, to open the post and plug in the coffee percolator. Thelma would appear at nine on the dot, crying out for coffee and the important letters. She would already have read the morning papers, would drop them on Catherine's desk with columns marked for attention. Women celebrities visiting London were to be telephoned with an invitation to see Velton's latest imported silks and brocades over afternoon tea. Any item about textiles was to be clipped and filed. Fashion shows in other stores – which Thelma always called 'the Opposition' – were to be snooped upon.

The possibility of eating lunch depended on Thelma's diary. If she herself had a luncheon engagement then Catherine had time to go to the canteen for a proper meal. If not, they might work straight through, grabbing a sandwich and yet another cup of the ever-freshly-made coffee.

The day ended when Thelma said it did. Catherine might be given permission to leave at four, ordered to type up six letters at five, take dictation at six, search the files for necessary background material at seven, and wait for a phone call from some distant part of the world at eight.

She would leave the building, eat a snack in one of the nearby Lyons tea-shops, take the Tube home, and fall into bed.

Perhaps it was as well that she was in this half-dazed condition when she was given the news about Malcolm Sanders.

Her father passed it on in one of his weekend phone calls. 'Quite a do, it was, as far as I can gather,' Gerald told her. 'A big church ceremony in Nicosia – Greek Orthodox, is it? – and then a party that went on all weekend with her relatives from all over Cyprus. Of course Malcolm's mother and father were there. To hear them tell it, it was like a three-ring circus! They were there a month and came back with the newly-weds a while ago. There was a bit in the *Hulmesley Herald* about it. Shall I send you the cutting?'

She shied away from the idea. She was more interested in knowing the personal side of things. 'What did Mrs Sanders say about it?'

'To tell the truth, lovey, I think she found it all a bit overwhelming! And from something she said . . . I don't quite recall what . . . I got the impression the family weren't too keen on the girl marrying a foreigner. The negotiations seem to have gone on for months before the engagement was announced.'

'And the bride – the new Mrs Sanders – what's she like?' she asked, with an effort at sounding casual.

'Mari – her name's Mari, it's short for Mariana or something. Well, she's a real beauty – lovely olive skin, black hair, flashing eyes – I tell you, you only have to see her once to know she was never born and brought up in Hulmesley!'

She managed a laugh. 'And do you think she'll settle down in Hulmesley?'

'Oh, I gather Malcolm's been given a branch office in Manchester,' her father reported. 'They went off almost as soon as she got here – just a short stay to get to know her in-laws, you know, and now she'll be setting up home in the big city. Poor little thing,' he added, 'I wonder if she knows what she's taking on? She's never seen the likes of Manchester in the rain, I bet! Sunshine and blue skies, that's what she's used to.'

Catherine felt that Mari Sanders didn't need her sympathy. Any girl lucky enough to marry Malcolm could put up with a little rain and city grime. And any girl silly enough to have lost him would just have to find consolation where she could.

Though she said this to herself, she thought at first she'd never survive the shock of the news on top of the loneliness of her London life. But as the days went by, her mind came to terms with it. She'd known since the regatta party that Malcolm was marrying a Cypriot girl. Now it had happened: it was an accomplished fact. A bitter fact, but real and unchanging.

Then gradually her body seemed to adapt to the stresses and rhythms of this new life. She learned to relax at weekends, to take advantage of all the entertainments that London had to offer, and to throw herself into her work with enthusiasm. By the time summer came, she was revelling in it. Looking back at her days in Hulmesley, she felt she'd only been half-awake there.

Her family – which these days seemed to include Toby – came for a weekend at a Bayswater hotel in July. It was a package deal to do with a trade show which meant they had to attend a formal dinner on the Friday. On Saturday, after touring the exhibition of office equipment, they all came to view her new home and find out how she was faring.

Her description of her home as a 'one-room flat' had led them to expect a version of student digs. They found a big, airy room, with its kitchen corner deftly screened by a plant-decked room divider, and with great windows looking out over a walkway to the river.

'Not bad,' Toby allowed, raising his eyebrows. 'In fact, I think it's what the estate agents would call "desirable".'

'I'd never have got it if Thelma hadn't put in a word.'

'Thelma?'

'Mrs Axford. She's got a lot of contacts, and not just in the textile world.'

'You call her Thelma?'

'Oh yes, she insists on that. She said from the outset she wanted me to think of us as colleagues, not employer and employee.'

'Sounds like a nice woman,' her father mused. 'Bit of luck, landing a job with someone like her.'

'And I hope you'll use the luck,' Toby added. 'What I always say is, if something's handed to you on a platter, you ought to have a good meal.'

'In other words, seize your chance with both hands?'

'Well, one hand might not be strong enough,' he laughed.

But she saw him suppress a little shrug at the edge of criticism he'd detected in her voice. She suspected that from Toby's point of view, contacts were meant to be used. Foolish, to have someone important as your acquaintance or friend, if you didn't take advantage of the fact.

Catherine had certainly come to London with the intention of making a career. But she had never intended to use her jobs as a series of taking-off points, as rungs on a ladder to success. On the contrary, she'd thought of them as opportunities to learn. In any case, the idea of 'using' Thelma Axford was laughable. In time, Thelma might offer help. But nothing Catherine could do would hurry her into making that offer.

And besides, Catherine didn't want to hurry her. She was enjoying her job too much. Every day she learned more about fabrics, about their design and manufacture and marketing.

When she first began at Velton's, fabrics were interesting because that was what Thelma Axford bought for the firm. But before long they began to have an appeal, a magic, all of their own. To handle a newly woven silk, to spread out an expanse of gaudy tropical cotton, to walk through a showroom of bright ginghams and paisleys, watch a cutter turn a length of dogstooth check into the beginnings of a riding jacket . . . She found it more and more enthralling. She began to feel that, by accident, she had wandered into the very path that she would have chosen before any other.

She had to acknowledge to herself that she had no skill as an artist. She started evening classes in sketching and drawing in the autumn, but although her work was adequate she knew it had no real spark. The interesting thing was, she could spot talent in others. At tea-break, when she strolled between the easels to make for the cafeteria, she would pick out work that was good, and linger by a sketch that she felt was more than good.

And the teacher's assessment almost always coincided with her view.

This was a comfort and support to her as, through the autumn, Thelma delegated some of her tasks to Catherine.

'You've got more than six months' experience behind you now, kiddo; if you haven't got the hang of what's right for Velton's by this time, you never will. I want you to go to

Hewitt's in Manchester and choose six designs for next summer's dirndls.'

'What on earth's a dirndl?'

'It's a gathered skirt made of figured cotton and all of a sudden it's going to be big next summer. It's one of those come-and-go fashions so we don't want to waste too much time on it, but we've got to have it. Go to the library and get some books about Austrian peasant costume. They'll have pictures or drawings of dirdnls – no, drat it, it's dirndls. Well, however you pronounce it, I suddenly need to have the fabrics sent to the makers-up, so hop to it.'

'But how shall I know—'

'The books will show you.'

'But suppose Hewitt's aren't making any cottons that will do?'

'Hewitt's make everything that can be made in a cotton mill – you should know that by now. Choose what you think will make up well and be a credit to Velton's.'

'I'll do my best.'

She was scared all through the next four days. But when Thelma saw the samples she'd chosen, she smiled.

'Clever little kitten! Rustic without being dull, peasant-like without being heavy. Tell the maker-up that the order's gone in.'

'Would you have chosen those?' Catherine asked with anxiety.

'Perhaps not, but that's why I gave the job to you – I know I always go for what's striking, and that's not always appropriate. It's a struggle not to stamp my own character on the choices for Velton's. Time to have another eye making some of the decisions.'

Catherine was very flattered.

As it happened, Toby Lindham telephoned during that morning to invite her out to lunch. 'I'm in London on business, thought it would be nice if we could meet.'

'What a surprise! I'd love to, but I don't know whether . . .'

She tapped on Thelma's door, put her head round, and asked if she would be needed from one to two.

'Well,' barked Thelma, 'what's this? Taking advantage of my good opinion of you?' But her grin and her nod of the head told Catherine she was free to take a normal lunch hour.

She poured out her success story to Toby – she knew she was boasting but it was so good to feel she had done well, and to have someone to tell it to.

'Good for you,' Toby commented. 'I'd imagine your boss isn't the kind to throw compliments around?'

'No, quite the contrary, she's rather tough. So I'm really pleased.'

They were in a busy restaurant in a turning off Oxford Street. Christmas shoppers and their parcels crowded them on all sides. Catherine asked for the news from home and was rewarded with a brief report: Laura busy and happy, her father delighted with a win over a postal opponent at chess, the central heating was still not installed in the flat in Mitre Lane, Desmond Colville had been newly appointed local magistrate . . . All the dear trivia of home town gossip.

And yet it had the faint aspect of something seen through binoculars. Far-off, important yet not immediate.

'Doesn't seem to matter much, now that you're a big-town girl?' Toby suggested with surprising acumen.

'Of course it matters.' A quick denial. Yet there was faint apology in her tone and she knew Toby caught it.

He was open in his admiration of her success. She was doing well at her job, and she looked good – she'd always dressed well for a provincial, but now that she was working for a fashion store, she had something more, so that her hair style, her shoes, even her lipstick were a statement of good taste. Cath certainly outshone every girl in the country-lady set back in Hulmesley.

Moreover, it was easy to tell that her boss, the formidable Mrs Axworth, took a big interest in her. Toby very much wanted to get to know Mrs Axworth. She was friendly with important people, from the names that Cath mentioned so casually in passing.

Toby had learned from his encounters with the Colvilles and the rest of the county set that it wasn't *what* you knew but *who* you knew that mattered. A woman like this Mrs Axworth, who hobnobbed with visiting film stars and had met the Queen Mother . . . well, obviously, she was worth getting to know. Any VIP he could get hold of might help with publicity for the clinic.

So he insisted on seeing her back to the store after lunch. 'I'd love to see where you work,' he remarked as they reached the entrance.

'Oh, sorry, I'm afraid that's impossible. No one is allowed inside the office area without invitation.'

'Well, invite me!'

'That wouldn't work,' she laughed. 'The porter has a list of people who've been invited and you certainly aren't on it.'

'Oh, come on – you could vouch for me.'

'No, no, Gittings wouldn't stand for that. He has to have either a name on a list or he telephones to the specific office and checks that the visitor's expected—'

'Well, go on up and be ready to vouch for me when he telephones—'

'But I really can't, Toby. I've got to get straight back to work when—'

He put an arm round her shoulders to urge compliance. At that moment there was a heavy footfall behind them and a voice said, 'Now, now, what's this? Jitterbugging in the entrance?'

'Oh – Thelma – we were just—' Catherine was unreasonably flustered. She removed herself from Toby's embrace. 'This is Toby Lindham, he was just seeing me back to the office.'

Toby gave a polite little bow of acknowledgement.

'Er – this is my boss, Mrs Axworth,' Catherine said, wishing him a thousand miles away. What would Thelma think, seeing her swaying about in the circle of a man's arm?

'How d'you do?' said Thelma. 'Have a nice lunch?'

'Yes, thank you. I'm very honoured to meet you, Mrs Axworth.'

'Oh? Why's that?'

'Cath's told me so much about you.'

'She has? Then she's told you I've got a lot of work to do, and I've got to get back to it. See you in a minute, Catherine.'

With that she walked through the entrance and they could hear Gittings' respectful greeting. Toby gave a grimace. 'That was what they call the brush-off,' he observed.

'Well, now you understand why I wasn't going to take you up to the office just because you felt inquisitive.'

'I take your point. And as the Dragon Lady is waiting for you up there, I'll say bye-bye for now.' He gave her a quick kiss on the cheek and was gone.

When Catherine reached her desk, Thelma came out of her office. 'Did I scare off your boyfriend?'

'No – well, yes, he left rather quickly. But he's not my boyfriend.'

'Really? You could have fooled me.'

'He's engaged to my sister.' Was he engaged to Laura? As she said it, Catherine wondered yet again when, if ever, those two were going to get married.

'Oh,' Thelma said on a note of heavy warning.

'Oh what?'

'He struck me as being . . .' She hesitated. 'Well, better not read too much into one glimpse of him.'

'Tell me what you read in him.'

'Ready to strike while the iron's hot. "Honoured to meet me" – what a line!'

'You didn't take to him.'

Thelma studied her. 'Does it matter whether I take to him?'

'Well, he and my sister . . .'

'Ah yes.' Thelma had heard Catherine speak of Laura – not much, because theirs was a business relationship, but enough to understand a little about the family. 'It's hard to tell, Catherine. Sometimes a man who's all out for himself will surprise you by falling for someone who brings out something you didn't know was there. With her, it's quite possible he's – you know – generous, caring. But if I were talking business with your Toby, I'd mind my step.'

'He's not my Toby,' Catherine assured her.

'So much the better. And now get Salomini Silks on the line, I want to know why they sent samples labelled suitable for next summer's Presentation Gowns when I've already told them the very last debutantes were presented in July!'

Back to work. Catherine obeyed at once, but throughout the afternoon one part of her mind was busy with Thelma's opinion of Toby. What bothered her was that it so much coincided with her own. From the very first she'd had this feeling that Toby was on the make. She'd chided herself for being unkind and ungenerous, because after all, what advantage could Toby gain from an involvement with Laura?

And the answer to that had always been, approval from the Colvilles. Their approval was important in a small place like Hulmesley.

Now, perhaps, he was growing a little bored with the whole thing. By now he'd hoped to have moved on, to have got some financial investment in his own boat-building firm – but from all that Catherine had heard, nothing of the kind had happened.

So perhaps he was looking around, casting his net . . . Perhaps he was trying through Catherine to meet the influential Thelma Axford, and through Mrs Axford, others who might be useful to him.

At Christmas Catherine went home for a few days. Her sister seemed happy, still starry-eyed in the first joy of being in love. Toby seemed as devoted as ever. Catherine was ashamed of having been too influenced by Thelma's views.

Yet when she happened on old acquaintances, she heard little remarks that troubled her. 'I marvel your sister can hold on to him,' Joan Luvett said. 'He's got such a roving eye . . .'

‘That’s not true, Joan. He and Laura are absolutely bound up in each other.’

‘If you say so. But I heard there was almost a divorce in Gollesfield over Toby Lindham.’

‘Who? Who’s he supposed to have been seeing in Gollesfield?’

But the answer was a shrug and a denial of any further knowledge. And most people were the same – they’d heard such-and-such, or someone else had hinted that so-and-so had been seen with Toby. Actual facts weren’t forthcoming, and so Catherine decided to put it all out of her mind.

During the early months of 1959 Toby still came to London from time to time on business. He was still seeking investment for the boat-building firm, had a Dutch company interested. Catherine heard about the ups and downs of negotiation, offered advice and sympathy – and was aware that she was letting herself become too involved.

Truth to tell she was at rather a low ebb herself. Because she was so busy, she’d made few friends in London except at the art class. Although she loved her job, there were times when the winter evenings seemed long and lonely.

So it was that Catherine allowed herself to drift into something like a dependency on Toby Lindham. She almost looked forward to his visits to London. She even stopped reminding herself to think of Laura. Where it was likely to end, she didn’t allow herself to think. But the time came when she had to think – and make a choice.

She went home at Easter, arriving at Hulmesley Station on Good Friday on a train that was supposed to have been in time for lunch. Toby was outside the station in his car.

‘You’re half an hour late,’ he complained as he put her case in the boot. ‘I almost gave up and went away.’

‘Glad you didn’t,’ she said, ducking into her seat out of the cold March rain.

‘Well, I had special plans, you see.’

‘Really?’ She settled herself in and they drove off, in a dashing U-turn that caused angry hooting from the taxis collecting other travellers.

Hulmesley Station, like many another of the Victorian era, had been built some way out of the town – on the grounds that sparks from the fireboxes of steam engines might set fire to town houses. So it was a few minutes before she realised they weren’t taking the road to the town centre.

‘Where are we off to?’ she inquired.

‘I thought we’d take a run out to Flagghead Quay – one of my recent conversions, you know, from landing barge to houseboat – she's moored there.'

Catherine frowned at the swishing windscreen-wipers. This was hardly the weather to make a side-trip to view a houseboat.

'I'd rather go home, thanks, Toby. Dad will be expecting me.'

'Oh, he's busy making picture frames, isn't he? And Laura's tied up with a patient. So this seemed the ideal opportunity.'

'Opportunity to look at a houseboat?' she countered, completely baffled.

'Oh, we're not just going to look at it. We're going aboard. It's a comfortable little craft, though I do say it myself as designed it. You'll like it.'

'Toby, I'm sure it's lovely, but it's cold and wet—'

'But we'll find a way to be snug and warm,' he broke in, turning to smile at her. 'Come on, Cath. Your conscience has kept you from inviting me into your flat the last two or three times we met in London, but now we're on my home ground and so I'm taking the initiative.'

'The initiative!'

'Nobody's going to miss us if we snatch an hour or so—'

'But you must know I—'

'I know you want to, Cath. I've seen it in your eyes more than once. You need someone to love you and now's the day for it.'

'You're mad,' she gasped. 'You can't really imagine—'

'I don't have to imagine. From what I've heard about you and that former boyfriend of yours, there was some really hot stuff going on. Don't tell me you don't miss it, sweetheart. It leaves a great big glaring gap when it's gone – and why should you have to live with that, eh? Especially when I'm here?'

'Stop the car,' Catherine said.

'What?'

'Stop the car. I'm getting out.'

'Don't be absurd. It's pouring wet out there!'

'That's preferable to what's on offer inside! *Stop the car!*'

Toby slowed enough to be able to study her without endangering his driving. 'Why are you putting on this silly act?' he demanded. 'You want it and I want it – why the fuss?'

'You've got it all wrong, Toby. Will you pull up or am I going to have to jump out while you're still going?'

He muttered something under his breath, but guided the car into the side of the road and put on the brake. He turned so as to reach over and prevent her from opening the passenger door. Leaning into her, he brought his mouth against hers.

It was an angry, insolent kiss. She squirmed away from it. He forced her back into the passenger seat more harshly and tried once again to kiss her, but she had her head turned away. She hunched up her shoulders to protect her face. At last he drew back.

'Is this just playing hard to get?'

'Hard to get? Good God, why should you even want me? You're Laura's man—'

'Oh, that! Oh, of course, that conscience of yours—'

'Laura *loves* you! Why are you running after someone else?'

'You know what they say, dear. Variety is the spice of life.'

She unlocked the car door.

'You're not really getting out? It's pouring!'

She stepped out into the downpour. She slammed the car door. 'Goodbye,' she said.

He leaned over to reply. 'But your case is in the boot—'

'Deliver it to Mitre Lane.'

'Get back in. This is irrational!'

She turned and began to walk back in the direction of Hulmesley. Toby didn't start the car. She knew he was watching her in the rear mirror. After a moment she heard the car door open and footsteps behind her.

'Don't be silly, Cath! It's a mile or more into Hulmesley.'

'There's a bus.'

'For heaven's sake, stand still!' She paid no heed but he caught up with her and grabbed her arm. 'What happens when you get to Mitre Lane soaking wet? How're you going to explain it?'

'Worried, are you? Afraid I'll give you away?'

'Look here, Cath, don't you go making trouble between Laura and me! You'll be sorry if you do!'

'You don't think my sister deserves to be told she's throwing herself away on you?'

'She wouldn't believe you. Laura'd be lost without me.'

'She managed all right before you came along—'

'So that's it! You want to go back to being the big influence in her life—'

'Toby, I've got a job I adore and a life of my own. That's not what this is about. It's about the contempt you show when you think you can drag me into bed just by crooking your finger—'

'You mean you wanted it wrapped up in violins and red roses? Good lord, we're grown-ups, we don't have to kid ourselves with romantic trimmings. You want me and I want you—'

'You're wrong. You're so wrong. Nothing would induce me to—'

'That's not the message I was getting when we'd part on your doorstep in London. We both knew then that I only had to put my arms round you and go up with you and we'd—'

'Is that really what you've been telling yourself? That I've been longing for you, and only held back because of Laura?'

'Well, it's true, isn't it?'

'No, it isn't. And even if it were, *that's a good enough reason to say no.* You and my sister belong together—'

'Only if I say so.'

'And you and I become lovers only if I say so and I say no.'

Other cars were going by, their drivers casting curious glances at the pair by the roadside in the streaming rain. Toby pulled the collar of his raincoat closer to his neck before turning away. 'Suit yourself,' he said. 'But mind what I say – don't cause trouble, because it's Laura who'll suffer.'

'She's got to find out some day, Toby.'

'What she doesn't know won't hurt her. But of course if you think it would be fun to see her crying—'

'Why do you bother with her?' she burst out. 'Surely the Colvilles aren't so important to you now you've got this Dutch investor?'

She saw that she'd startled him by her insight. He paused and turned back. He was frowning. 'You really are the clever one of the family,' he muttered. 'Quick on the uptake, aren't you?'

'I've always felt you only got involved with Laura because it was a way of being close to the Colvilles.'

'Well.' He hesitated. 'Say you're right. Say their goodwill is still important to me. How's it going to help Laura to tell her anything like that?'

'But you treat her like a pawn in a chess game—'

'No I don't. Ask her. I make her happy. Can you do that, clever clogs? No, I don't think you can. So don't do anything silly, or the whole Mertagen family will be weeping and wailing for the next six months.' He gestured back towards the car. 'Come on, get in, and I'll run you home.'

She shook her head.

'Come on. I promise – no funny business. But for heaven's sake get in before we drown.'

Sighing at having to accept, she returned to the car. He made a flashy three-point turn and drove back to Hulmesley without a word being exchanged between them. Once in Mitre Lane, he got her suitcase out of the boot, handed it to her, and backed off.

He could glimpse Gerald coming to the shop door to greet his daughter.

'Remember,' he warned, 'don't cause trouble.' And with that he was gone.

Gerald came out of the shop as she was putting her key in the side door. 'My word, you're drenched,' he said. 'What happened?'

'Oh, Toby turned up to offer me a lift home but then something went wrong with the car and we had to get out. I'll just run up and change.'

'Righto, Cathie. Have a nice hot drink. See you later.'

She changed into dry clothes. She moved to the door of her bedroom to obey instructions and make herself a hot drink. Then she drew back, to sink down on the dressing stool. She leaned her head down on the dressing table and began to cry.

How could she ever have let such a thing happen? For it was her fault – she knew that. She'd been giving the wrong signals to Toby when he came to London, wanting to see him not just for his company but perhaps for something more, for the admiration, for the excitement of his sexual attraction.

She'd thought about letting Toby kiss her with passion. She'd half daydreamed the drawing back, the quietly firm shake of the head. 'No, Toby, we mustn't, because of Laura.' That was how it was supposed to go.

To be propositioned so blatantly . . . Never mind proper feelings, never mind common decency, let's just hop into bed together. It was insulting, and though she knew she'd brought it on herself, that didn't excuse Toby. It showed him as unfaithful – well, she'd half suspected that. But as unfeeling, insensitive, grasping . . .

To think that her sister was in love with a man like that . . .

Chapter Ten

Halfway through Wednesday morning Thelma Axworth called Catherine into her office to take dictation. That done, she spread out some fabric samples for discussion. Catherine took notes of their decisions.

'Something wrong?' Thelma asked as her assistant tidied away the samples.

'No, nothing. Why?'

'I expected a lot more vehemence from you over those new American prints. They're just the kind of jazzy thing you hate.'

'I suppose they are,' Catherine agreed.

'Well?'

'Well, as you said, we mustn't stamp our own taste too much on the range we choose for Velton's. I'm quite prepared to accept that some women would go for those colours.'

'So what happened over Easter to upset you?'

Catherine gave a startled laugh. 'How do you get from jazzy print to being upset?'

'Something's on your mind or you'd have stood out against that design. And from the way you seem to have lost your smile, what's bothering you isn't pleasant.'

'I'm quite all right. Really. Sorry if I haven't been pulling my weight.'

'Cathie, I wasn't complaining about not pulling your weight. I want to know what's on your mind.'

'It's nothing. Just a family thing.'

'Somebody ill?'

'Oh no. No, just a disagreement.'

'Thought your family didn't go in for disagreements?'

'No, we don't. We never had a cross word between us until . . .' Her words tailed off.

'Until what?'

'Nothing.'

'You had a row with your sister?'

'Not a row. Not exactly.'

'But you squabbled.'

'I suppose you could say that.'

'Then it was about that young man.'

'What? How did you—' She broke off, going red.

'So it was him, was it? Mr Quick-off-the-mark – Toby, wasn't that his name?'

'Yes, Toby.'

'You quarrelled with your sister over Toby?'

Catherine said nothing. But silence means consent.

'Thought you had more sense than to fall for a man like that.'

'I haven't fallen for him,' Catherine protested. 'That's partly the trouble.'

'I don't follow that, dearie.'

'Oh, it's too complicated to go into. But I tried to tell Laura . . . warn her . . . and it went wrong.'

It had proved quite difficult to get a moment alone with her sister over Easter. In days gone by, they'd almost always spend time together before going to bed, pottering about in each other's rooms, comparing notes, looking ahead to the tasks for next day, making plans, sharing hopes. But now it was different. It was with Toby that Laura shared her life.

But on the evening of Easter Monday, as Catherine was preparing to leave for the train, Laura came into her room with a silk scarf she'd found behind a cushion. 'Don't forget this.'

'Oh, thanks. I wondered where it had got to.'

'Can I do anything to help?'

'No, there's really nothing much to pack.' Laura was about to go when Catherine called her back. 'Sit down, Laura, we never seem to have time to catch up these days.'

Laura smiled in happiness. 'No, we're a lucky pair, aren't we! Both of us busy with work we love doing. The hours just seem to fly past. I often mean to ring you and have a long chat, but somehow . . . you know . . . there never seems to be time.'

'So you're still enjoying the work at the clinic?'

'Oh, of course! It's more tiring than it used to be, I admit, more patients, you see – they come from all over, it's amazing, but the schedule runs like clockwork, thanks to Toby, I can't imagine how I'd manage without him.'

'Laura, about Toby . . .'

'Yes?'

'I wonder if you're not . . . counting on him too much?'

'But he likes me to count on him. "Leave the donkey-work to

me, darling," he keeps saying, and he's so marvellous, he's got it so beautifully organised—'

'I didn't mean so much about the clinic, Laura. I was thinking . . . I wonder if you're not too wrapped up in him?'

'That's a silly thing to say, Cath. I love him.'

'Yes, I know, I understand—'

'I wonder if you do? Just because you broke up with Malcolm, that doesn't mean other people can't make a go of it—'

'It's nothing to do with Malcolm, Laura. All I'm trying to say is that Toby's human, after all—'

'Well, of course he is – and if you're going to say he's got faults, don't bother, because I don't mind if he's ambitious and wants to get on, that's only natural in someone with so much energy—'

'I'm not arguing about his business ability, lamb. I'm just saying that you oughtn't to let him take you over completely—'

'But why not?'

'Well, suppose . . .'

'Suppose what?'

'Suppose things changed. Suppose that your feelings changed.'

'Don't be silly.'

'Or that Toby's feelings changed.'

'Ah!' Laura held up a finger like someone calling attention. 'I know what this is about. It's that silly bit of gossip about Celia Kingsley—'

'Celia Kingsley? I never heard of—'

'Her husband was supposed to be going to divorce her. Is that what this is about?'

'I . . . did hear something about a divorce . . .'

'The whole thing is utter invention! I asked Toby about it and he explained. It's true he knows the Kingsleys – Lonnie Kingsley was thinking of buying a boat from Toby. But he couldn't put up enough money for the deposit and it fell through, and Lonnie Kingsley was a bit put out and got cross over that, and somehow people think it had something to do with his wife Celia but it hadn't, and there *wasn't* a divorce or even the start of one, so what are people going on about? I do think it's unkind to pass on that sort of gossip, even at the hairdresser's where of course women do tend to talk about everybody, but I told Ethel – that's my hairdresser, she's awfully good – I said she shouldn't tell stories like that because it could be really upsetting and she said she was sorry. So you see there was nothing in it, it's just one of those fairy tales.'

'You actually asked Toby?'

'Well, I was really shocked when I heard it, because Ethel said she knew for a fact that Lonnie was going to cite Toby in the divorce proceedings, and Toby asked me why I was crying and I sort of couldn't prevent myself from asking, although I *knew* it couldn't be true, and he sorted it all out and that's the truth of it. So don't talk to me about Gollesfield and Celia Kingsley,' Laura ended with indignation, 'because I know Toby is true to me and would never so much as look at another woman and people who try to say otherwise are just jealous of how much we love and trust each other.'

'But I heard . . . someone told me . . . that Celia Kingsley wasn't the only one—'

'Oh, Cath, how can you! You ought to know better than to listen to things like that! I'm sorry to have to say it, but you sometimes do seem to be a bit down on Toby, and if you're going to bring tales like that to me about him, I shall have to accept the fact that you're not his friend.'

'I'm only trying to—'

'I don't want to hear another word! You ought to know better! I never thought my own sister would be mean or envious—'

'Laura, don't get angry about it. Of course I worry about you and Toby—'

'Well, there's absolutely no need, thank you very much! I'll thank you to keep worries like that to yourself, where they started, because *I'm* not worried – I know I'm the luckiest woman alive and so I try to be tolerant when somebody tries to spoil things but I must say, Cath – I didn't expect smallmindedness from *you*.'

Clearly it was useless to go on with the conversation. Her sister simply didn't want to hear criticism of Toby. She couldn't bring herself to break in on Laura's defences with the stark facts of Friday's encounter. 'He tried to get me into bed with him' – it was an impossible thing to say. Too wounding, too callous. After a lifetime of trying to look after Laura, she couldn't bring herself to say or do anything to hurt her.

She wouldn't have dreamed of confiding any of this to Thelma Axworth. But under pressure she did admit that there had been trouble not only between herself and Laura, but with Toby as well.

Thelma's black eyes flashed with irritation. 'I knew he was a snake the minute I laid eyes on him,' she said. 'You don't have to tell me the kind of trouble you had with him, I can guess.'

'Honestly, Thelma, it was just one of those stupid things . . .'

She sighed. 'I suppose it happens in every family – ups and downs that somehow you live through.'

'That's a good philosophy. Why doesn't it cheer you up, then?'

'I don't know . . .' But she did. All her life until a few months ago, she had regarded her sister Laura as her other self. They'd had no secrets from each other, each knew that the other could be depended on at all times. Now Catherine felt as if something had been cut off, almost as if she had lost a limb.

She'd known, at their parting on Easter Monday, that things could never be the same again. She'd always accepted that one day there would be a change, that either or both would fall in love and get married, yet she'd never thought they would be parted on the emotional level.

Now she knew better. Laura had warned her off.

What made it worse was that as Toby shook hands on leave-taking, he'd remarked, 'See you again soon.'

'What?' She was taken aback.

'I'll be in London a couple of times in the near future. See you then.'

'Oh – I'll be busy – we're putting the spring fashions into the departments—'

Laura gave her a reproachful glance. 'Surely you'll be able to find time, Cath?' Her tone implied, I knew you weren't his friend.

'That's right, Cath, I'm sure you'll find time,' Toby echoed, and smiled as if to say she wouldn't elude him so easily.

She looked up to find Thelma Axworth regarding her with something akin to pity.

'Tell me,' she urged.

'It's nothing.'

'You're afraid your sister's going to get hurt?'

'Well, you see, he comes to London every so often . . . on business. I want to stay out of his way but it's going to seem so odd.'

'Mm . . .' Thelma caught all the nuances of that reply. She sat looking thoughtful.

'I'll just tell him I can't get away, I have to work late.'

'Hold on. I believe I can do better than that.'

'How do you mean?'

'I can spirit you away for a couple of weeks.'

'You want me to go to the Midlands again? To the mills?'

'Duckie,' said Thelma, making up her mind, 'I'm going to take you to Italy.'

'Italy?'

'Never do things by halves, is what I always say. I want to look at Milanese silks and voiles for a special "Dressmaking for Parties" event next winter. How about it? Think you'd like it?'

Catherine could hardly believe her ears. She stared speechless at her employer.

'Righto, that's settled. We'll fly Saturday the eleventh and be away till the twenty-second, that's the Wednesday.' She was flicking over her desk diary pages as she spoke. 'I may leave you there a couple of days longer – I have to be back for the Thursday because I'm meeting the dress-pattern publishers that afternoon. But it might be handy to have you stay on and accept the samples and swatches in person rather than have them sent on after us. There's always a delay if you leave them to be mailed on later.'

'But I can't speak any Italian!' Catherine cried, scared at the idea of being left alone in Milan with business to conduct.

'Neither can I, child! *"Spaghetti bolognese, o sole mio,"* that's my lot. But you're the customer, child – they'll run round after you if they think you're going to spend money with them.'

It proved that Thelma spoke more Italian than she'd claimed, but as she'd predicted, their business confrères were so attentive that the buyer from the important London store and her charming young assistant scarcely needed to raise a finger. They were chauffeured from factory to showroom to warehouse to managerial offices. Handsome young men danced attendance on them. They were escorted to the opera at La Scala, wined and dined at the finest restaurants in Milan, presented with flowers and trinkets and boxes of Italian sweetmeats.

'Enjoying yourself?' Thelma inquired as they trundled upwards in the ancient lift of their hotel. They had just come back from an open air concert in the park at Sforza Castle. The hour was late, the air had been heavy all day, Catherine was dead on her feet.

But yes – she was enjoying herself!

After Thelma left for London, the attentions of the handsome young men redoubled. Of course, they would be attentive to any prospective buyer – but all the more so if the buyer proved to be young, attractive, chic and intelligent. Catherine found it almost embarrassing to be so much in demand. Thelma had warned her to be careful: 'Don't fall in love with any Latin charmer, dear, they're all either safely married or have been betrothed since their cradles.' Then she'd added, 'But have fun!'

So Catherine had fun, and returned home with a different view of life. Toby Lindham no longer seemed hard to handle. When it came to making conquests, he had a lot to learn from his Latin cousins, she felt. And as to Laura's devotion to him . . . well, it made her happy, so Catherine would do nothing to mar her view of him.

That one last gift Catherine could offer to the sister who had turned away from her. She could leave her the dream in which she was living.

The trip to Milan marked a turning point in Catherine's career. Thelma Axworth was more than pleased with the silks they'd found and the part Catherine had played. She delegated more tasks, and let it be known she was grooming her for promotion.

Promotion came in the early months of 1960. Velton's had decided to set up a new department, for 'Leisure Wear'. This was a new category of clothes, made possible by the financial climate encapsulated in Harold Macmillan's phrase, 'You've never had it so good.' Paid holidays were now universal and many more people were able to head for the sun. The demand for poolside clothes and sundresses was growing every year.

Velton's would, as usual, be offering many garments specially made for them in the fabrics for which they were famous. Thelma Axworth was instructed to confer with the fashion buyer over themes for the fabrics – should they go for the 'tropical' look, with hot colours and bold designs, or for a more soignée Mediterranean style?

'I've really got enough on my plate already,' she protested. 'Although of course I know Miss Aymes has picked the main outlines for the swimwear and dresses, I think we should create a new post of assistant buyer to get the fabrics.'

No no, too costly, besides, there was no time to look for new staff, the planning meeting rejoined.

'I've got just the girl,' Thelma announced.

'Me?' gasped Catherine when the news was passed on to her.

'Why not you?'

'But I've never handled a department.'

'Now's you chance.'

'But . . . but . . .'

'Feel you're too stupid to do it?'

'No, of course not!'

'Then stop dithering and say thank you.'

'Oh, Thelma, I do say thank you – I know I'd never have been given this chance if you hadn't wangled it.'

'Not so much of the "wangle", if you don't mind. It's all honest and above board. I think you've got the eye for good fabric design, and it's a sure thing that you know more about sleeveless dresses than I do with *my* figure.'

Catherine laughed. Although held in by the very best corsetry that Velton's could supply, Thelma was never going to look good in a sundress.

'Bring us some ideas,' Thelma said, waving the laughter aside with a plump hand. 'Don't hang about, either – Janet Aymes and I want this department up and running by Easter, and that only gives us until the middle of April.'

Catherine had been looking at fabric design for nearly two years now. She'd kept notes and samples from studios that particularly appealed to her. She came back to Thelma on Monday morning with a portfolio under her arm.

She offered the portfolio. 'You'll find in there brief studies of the work of nine fabric designers working here in Britain. I thought it might be a good selling point to use only British designers. Some I've met, some it just so happens I've seen their work. You'll note they all have a particular talent for floral and "natural" themes – look at this man, he uses shells and strands of grass and fern . . .'

'Yes . . .'

'Here.' She unfolded a cardboard wallet to show bright designs using poppies – red poppies on a grass-green background, yellow poppies on a beige background, blue poppies on a cream background. 'These could be woven in almost any colourways you like to ask for. They're on linen but they could be screen-printed on silk for resort evening-wear.'

'Well now, those are *good* . . .'

'Here's this girl who does nautical designs – no, not anchors and cables, look.' She spread a piece of cotton print over her arm. It showed a ship, prow on, with the waves dividing around the sides and dissolving into a grey-blue plume.

'I like that, it's unusual.'

'I thought we'd try for an all-British collection for the launch. Do you think Janet Aymes will go for it?'

'Let's go and ask her.'

They spent two days discussing, arguing and choosing. The upshot was that Catherine was charged with buying the designs and commissioning the immediate manufacture of enough fabrics for the first run of Velton's leisure-wear collection.

The makers-up were aghast. 'What, ready by April and the cloth hasn't even left the mills yet?'

'You'll manage,' soothed Catherine.

'We'll have to go on overtime.'

'I'm empowered to allow that so long as you don't lay it on too thick,' she said, although she'd been given no such permission.

'Ah well then . . . we'll see what we can do.'

The only difficulty arose with the artist who had produced the poppy design. 'I'm not going to let you mess it about putting it into twenty different colours!' he protested.

'We're not putting it into twenty colours, Mr Chelburne. You've painted it in three contrasts, we'd like to extend it to seven and call it "Fieldflower"—'

'No, no, no! I only saw it in those three tints—'

'Don't you think it would look good with terracotta blossoms against grey? Or crimson against black?'

'No, I don't! At least . . . Well, crimson and black might not be bad . . .' Fenner Chelburne's annoyance died a little as he thought about it. 'What was your name again?'

'Catherine Mertagen.'

'I thought the fashion fabrics for Velton's were bought by Mrs Axworth?'

'Usually, yes, but these are for a special leisure-wear collection—'

'Leisure-wear? I'm not letting my fabrics be turned into shorts—'

'Mr Chelburne, if you sell us the designs we'll have the right to use the fabric for anything we choose—'

'In that case I refuse to sign.'

'But I might make a personal promise not to use "Fieldflower" for shorts.' This was a rapid invention on her part in response to the grouchy, resentful manner. To no one else had she offered special terms. Freelance designers didn't expect them. But in any case, the poppy design wouldn't look good on shorts, she thought to herself. If it would soothe this prickly man to be told she was making special terms for him, so much the better.

Fenner Chelburne lived in a cottage in Somerset. But there was nothing charmingly rural about it. It stood at the end of a row of cottages in a village that had once been a carpet-weaving centre, so that the appearance of the place was workmanlike, especially on a cold February afternoon. The interior of his cottage was just as workaday. He had had the upstairs windows enlarged for a good northern light under which stood easel, draughtsman's table, neat boxes of pencils, crayons, pastels and watercolours, and the other tools of the artist. A few canvases leaned against one wall with their backs facing outwards: the cases of oil paints were stacked nearby.

Chelburne himself was a big man with the long bones and fair skin of the Saxons. There was nothing about him of the artist in appearance: rather he looked like a farmer or a gamekeeper. He was clad in grey corduroys, a black sweater, and an ex-army body-warmer made very necessary by an entire lack of heating in the cottage. At the moment the fair skin was flushed with annoyance and the light blue eyes glowed with the warmth of battle.

He was different from other freelance designers Catherine had dealt with. Most of them were only too eager to sign a contract for their work, and all the more so if the contract was with Velton's. To have your designs accepted and used by Velton's was the entry to the Hall of Fame. Where Velton's had led, other firms would follow. Catherine had never yet met with an artist who wanted to alter the standard conditions of the contract.

Commonsense told her to shrug and walk away. If Fenner Chelburne didn't want to sell his work to her, plenty of others would rush forward to take his place.

Yet she wanted the poppies. Before she met Chelburne, she'd already seen in her mind's eye cotton sundresses, casual jackets of linen, swirling skirts to wear with plain tops of the background shade, and simple silk sheaths for evening, all in some version of the poppies design.

Moreover, the designer himself intrigued her. In the first place he had a high opinion of himself. In the second, he didn't make any attempt to persuade her to take his work or show any other offerings: no flattery, no eagerness, no anxiety for her good opinion.

After weeks of contact with designers, mill owners and factory managers desperate to sell to her, Fenner Chelburne came as a pleasant surprise.

He was grumbling on about the commercial side of design. 'You say this was for a new line of leisure-wear. I don't want my work trotting around Cannes and Jesolo on the haunches of rich fatties—'

'Mr Chelburne,' she intervened, rousing herself to do battle, 'if you have these reservations about how your work is used, what are you doing in fabric design?'

'I'm trying to earn a living until I can get my serious work looked at, that's what!' His glance flicked towards the canvases stacked against the wall, but he didn't offer to show them. 'There's money in fabric design, it's what pays the rent and puts bread on the table.'

From the lack of a fire in the living-room and the sparseness of the furnishing she'd passed as he led her up to the studio, Catherine deduced that Chelburne had been trying to manage on sales of 'serious' work. But, like many another, he had had to turn to commercialism to survive.

'Be sensible,' she urged, her tone kindly. 'Sell me the poppy design and then don't think about how it will be used. Close it off in your mind—'

'That's not so easy. I sold a real beauty to a manufacturer of furnishing fabric last year – Tudor Tree, it was called – and where did I see it but on dreadful three-piece suites in furniture chain stores all over the country. It should have gone into stately homes and manor houses, not into semi-detacheds!'

She couldn't help but laugh. 'Delusions of grandeur,' she said. 'You've either got to put up with ordinary people using your designs or go into something else to earn an honest penny.'

'What else?' he said gloomily. 'Some chaps take up pottery but I'm no good at that, and as to murals for town halls and business premises, commissions are few and far between. Portraits of politicians . . .' His shrug told her what he thought of politicians. 'Besides,' he added, with a slight lessening of resentment, 'I rather like fabric design.'

'That's right. What was good enough for William Morris should be good enough for you.'

'Don't start telling me to follow in the footsteps of Morris. He had rich friends, he didn't have to sell his designs to grasping mill owners.'

'Well, neither will you if you sign the contract with Velton's. Come on, grab the chance. We'll have the design woven by the mills who've worked for us for years, which means to a very high standard of colour accuracy and detail. If we go for screen-printing, you know Velton's has its own factory so it will be beautifully done. The clothes made from the fabrics will be a special feature, your name will get known, and you'll be able to afford an electric fire for your living-room.'

'Never mind the living-room, it's the studio where it matters,' he replied with the beginnings of a smile. 'Ever tried to do shading with a camel-hair brush when your fingers are too cold to feel the contact with the paper?'

'There you are. Let Velton's have your poppies and you can work in comfort.'

'Humph.' He surveyed Catherine, and seemed for the first time to notice she was still wrapped in her outdoor coat. 'I suppose I ought to offer you a hot cup of tea.'

'Better still,' she amended, 'come back with me to Bridgwater and we'll have a drink and a meal.' She thought longingly of the comfortable old coaching inn and its glowing log fire.

'Bridgwater? You're staying there?'

'Just overnight, at the Angel. I heard it was quite good.'

'Oh yes, very posh – at least by country town standards.' He moved indecisively about the studio, picking up a pencil and a ruler to tidy them away in a drawer.

Outside the sky had darkened. The big uncurtained windows dominating the studio were squares of slate grey, as if the night were pressing against the glass. He switched on a lamp. Clearly whatever he earned went into good equipment for, though he might lack an electric fire, he had the very best Swedish cantilever light.

'All right then,' he agreed, 'you can pay for a hearty meal at the Angel. But that doesn't mean I'm going to sell you my poppies.'

'I'll ply you with strong drink. When your head is reeling, I'll get you to sign.'

'Ho ho. You don't know how hard my head is.'

Catherine drove him to Bridgwater, along winding roads where a cold mist had formed. She asked him where he had trained and how long he'd been painting, and received some shreds of personal information. She was able to gather that there had been a wife at some point, who'd walked out – presumably because she didn't like living in a cottage miles from a town and with no heating.

The dining-room at the Angel didn't open till seven. Catherine took her guest into the lounge and ordered drinks. 'Can you amuse yourself with the newspaper while I go up to my room and leave my coat?'

'Why not? I'll catch up with what's going on in the big world – normally I never look at newspapers.' He didn't say, though she guessed, that he didn't want to spare the money for them.

She left him with that morning's *Times* and a malt whisky. She took the time to brush her hair and freshen her make-up, though exactly why was difficult to explain. What did it matter how she looked – this was just a business occasion in a country town. All the same, she was glad she was wearing a good plain tweed skirt and a bronze-coloured silk shirt that set off her dark colouring.

When she got back to the lounge it was to find that her guest had finished his drink and ordered a second.

'You don't mind,' he told her. 'Velton's have got pots of money.'

'Quite right. And I did say I was going to ply you with strong drink.'

'Ply away. We'll see who slides under the table first.'

Catherine made no attempt to keep up with his consumption. He seemed to have a head made of oak, for even a third whisky had no effect on it. The only result was a slight lowering of his guard.

'Have you seen this?' he demanded, brandishing *The Times*. 'Harold Macmillan's out in Cape Town telling them that the "wind of change" is blowing. Politicians . . . ! Any excuse to go off somewhere in the wintertime where it's warm and sunny.'

'I can't say I blame him,' Catherine said, holding out her hands towards the logs in the firebasket of the lounge fireplace.

'Well, no . . . I suppose I'd do the same myself. Greece – if I were a politician I'd invent excuses to go to Greece.'

'Greece is going to be a big tourist attraction now that air fares are coming down. Velton's sell a lot of yachting clothes already to people who sail among the islands.'

'Is Velton's your only point of contact with the rest of humanity?' he demanded, but with a grin and a shrug that robbed the words of unkindness.

'I like working for them,' she said simply. 'I like finding fabrics for them, and finding the designers who'll produce good fabrics.'

It seemed there was a diminution in his antagonism towards commercial art as represented by Velton's. He allowed himself to be led into a conversation about it.

'Why're you so keen on my design?' he inquired, stretching out long legs towards the log fire. 'There must be hundreds of others you could use.'

She nodded agreement. 'I've looked at hundreds of designs for this project. If you insist on being difficult I can fill the gap by going to one of a dozen others on my list. But I get paid for choosing *good* design. And your poppies have something that seems just . . . special. Strong, energetic, rich . . . I mean rich in life, in the flower's will to survive . . .'

He frowned. 'That's laying on the flattery a bit thick.'

'It's not flattery. That's what I see in the design.'

'Well . . .'

'What?'

'You're not the usual run-of-the-mill buyer.'

'Now you're laying on the flattery,' she countered, smiling.

'Me? The day you hear me flattering a woman, you can have me toasted and served on brown bread.' He sipped the last of his whisky. 'Catherine, your name is? What do they call you? Kitty?'

'The day anyone calls me Kitty you can lay me out with lilies on my chest.'

'What then?' He studied her. 'I'll call you Cathie.'

'And what do I call you?'

'My friends call me Fenn.'

She didn't ask, Am I your friend? Because she already knew that they had formed a bond that would last, and that it had only partly to do with business.

Chapter Eleven

Thelma Axworth was pleased with the results of Catherine's efforts until she came to the contract with Fenner Chelburne. 'What's this? Limited use? Only seven colourways? What on earth possessed you to make an agreement like this?'

Catherine was expecting the complaint. 'We weren't going to get his design unless we made some concessions about colours,' she replied. 'He had decided views about colour and he's a very touchy character.'

'Oh is he, indeed! Freelance designers can't afford to be touchy.'

'Quite true as a rule. This one is living hand to mouth but he's quite prepared to starve rather than let us play about with his work.'

'Play about? Play about? Since when has Velton's ever played about with textile design?' Thelma was quite vexed. 'I hope you told him in no uncertain terms that we—'

'No, I didn't, Thelma. I had to be tactful with him, otherwise we'd have lost him.'

'Huh! Plenty more where he came from.'

'Not as good as Fenn.'

Thelma threw down the contract to focus the gaze of her shrewd black eyes upon Catherine. 'Fenn, is it? Do I take it he's tall, dark, and handsome?'

'He's tall, fairish, and . . . well, not badlooking.'

'Tell me more.'

'There isn't more to tell.'

'Yet. Do I hear a "yet" in your voice?'

Catherine laughed. 'Now, now, don't read more into it than is really there. I admire his work, I liked him for sticking up for his rights—'

'His rights? A few more like him and we'd have to ask the legal department to take a microscope to every contract! Don't do it again, Cathie. I'll forgive you this once since he's tall, fairish, and not badlooking, but don't make a habit of allowing limitations on Velton's "right-to-use".'

'I'm sorry. I thought it was worth it in this case.'

'I'm not saying you're wrong. Just don't do it again.'

But Thelma wasn't as cross as she sounded. It pleased her to hear a certain note in her assistant's voice; it was time she found herself a proper boyfriend, someone better than that Clever-Dick who'd been hanging around. Thelma would take the first opportunity of inspecting Fenner Chelburne to see if he was good enough for Catherine.

Together they went down to Somerset about a week later. The mills had produced two samples of the poppy design on cotton. There was no clause in the contract that said they had to show the cloth to the designer for his approval but Catherine had promised Fenn she'd let him have a look. And Thelma for her part wanted to have a look at Fenn.

The spartan living conditions startled her. He must be very serious about his work if he was prepared to make conditions over manufacture, for clearly he was in desperate need of the money.

He refused to be over-impressed by the samples. 'Not bad,' he grunted. 'They've got the shading tones quite well.'

'My dear man, it's a beautiful piece of weaving,' Thelma lectured. 'Feel it, it handles like silk – and when you imagine the fabric pleated or gathered, the collecting of the colours will be lovely.'

'I'm not concerned with the dressmaking side—'

'You'll have to learn to be if you want to make money in designing for fashion fabrics—'

'Who said I do?'

Thelma hesitated. Her glance took in the uncurtained windows of the living-room, the shabby paintwork. 'Come on now,' she coaxed. 'You need to make a living and Velton's needs good fabric design. We can be partners if you'll unbend a little.'

'I'll unbend to the extent of doing work I think you might like. But I won't be ordered about or chivvied.'

'Chivvied? I've never chivvied anybody – have I, Cathie?'

'No, never,' Catherine said with a broad smile that belied the words.

Fenn gave a faint shrug. 'I'll give it a try,' he remarked. 'I admit I need the money. But that's not my first priority – do you understand that?'

Thelma at once gave Fenn assurances of due respect.

The mannequin show at Easter attracted a full take-up of tickets at every performance, then almost immediately afterwards the customers began to turn up inspecting the garment racks on the second floor.

The idea of an all-British collection, both fabrics and styles, had aroused press comment. Television, now firmly established as a national pastime, took an interest: Velton's resort collection was featured in a news-magazine programme one evening. Next afternoon women from as far off as the Midlands were in the store, asking to see the clothes.

There was no doubt the British fabrics were popular. And the biggest hit of all was the design 'Fieldflower', or in other words Fenn's poppies. And the most popular of the colourways was one that Fenn had had to be argued into – much to Catherine's delight.

'Stop walking around with that "I told you so" look on your face,' he scolded. But he was grinning. No matter what he might imply about despising commercialism, he had a natural pleasure in having produced something not only good from the artistic viewpoint but popular with the public.

At Catherine's coaxing, he had accepted an exclusive two-year design contract with Velton's. 'This won't affect my serious work,' he mused as he sat with the pen in his hand. 'The store can't prevent me if I want to do some landscapes – or take on a commission for a portrait.'

'Of course not, read the terms – "designs for fabrics to be used in the manufacture of clothing" – nothing else, Fenn. And you remember that fern you were sketching in black and white a few weeks ago – that would be ideal for autumn styles, so get started on something like that in colour.'

'Slave-driver,' he groaned, but he was pleased.

As spring slipped into summer, Thelma Axworth saw him from time to time to assess further examples of his work and came to like him. Yet she had reservations. She'd been dealing with people all her working life and experience told her that Fenn wasn't falling in love nearly so deeply as Catherine.

Catherine had no such uncertainty. She felt that the empty place in her life had been filled at last. Because she had kept busy, she'd pushed away the awareness of how lonely she felt. Only at night, when the rest of the world was asleep, she would remember there was no one who longed for her, no one whose arms would be a haven against the dark and the chill.

A long time had gone by since she had been swept away by physical longing. To join with Fenn in the transcendental moment of passion, the forgetfulness of self and the world, was a reward she'd felt was gone for ever. Like finding shelter after a snowstorm, like cool water in a parched desert, love made her live again.

She wouldn't let herself compare this relationship with the feelings she'd had for Malcolm. That had been her first love, but she had put it away in some attic of the memory, like an album of faded photographs. If some treacherous voice whispered that she and Fenn were not equal partners, she hushed it: he gave her something that had been missing for years now, the feeling of being wanted. But the relationship was less direct than the one she'd shared with Malcolm. Fenn was less simple, needed more tact and care – for he proved to be as touchy in private life as he was in matters of art.

For instance, he resisted when she tried to import some comfort into his cottage.

'Easy chairs? Who needs easy chairs? That's just a waste of money—'

'Darling, when I get here after a draughty train journey and a taxi ride, I'm tired, I want somewhere comfortable to flop down—'

'There's always the divan—'

'And that's another thing – I want us to buy a new one, that one's about to fall to pieces.'

'Nonsense, I've had it for years, it's as strong as an oak tree—'

'And about as comfortable! Come on, sweetheart, let me make the place a bit more liveable. I promise not to go in for wall-to-wall carpet, but a few rugs in the kitchen and a decent stove—'

'What's wrong with the old range?'

'It takes twenty minutes to boil a kettle, and over an hour to clean, that's what's wrong with it.'

'Oh, *women*!' growled Fenn, and stamped out of the house.

He was gone for nearly two hours, in a gale of wind and without a coat. When he returned at dusk, she was on the verge of going out with a torch to look for him, afraid he'd missed his footing in the marshy ground beyond the alders. She'd pictured him lying injured out there in the cold and dark.

She threw her arms around him. 'Where have you been? You went out without a jacket! My God, you're absolutely frozen, Fenn! Now come on, put on this sweater, sit close to the fire—'

'Stop fussing or I'll turn round and go right out again!'

But his hands were stiff with cold, his face was pinched and pale so that his Saxon-blue eyes gleamed like a winter sea above angular cheekbones. His commonsense returned – no use giving himself pneumonia over a triviality. He put on the sweater, accepted hot soup and fresh toast, and at last managed a smile. 'Might not be bad to have a cosy chair to draw up to the fire,' he acknowledged.

So the quarrel was made up, not for the first or last time, by kisses and embraces and the sweet compensations of love. In those moments, Catherine felt that she had nothing in the world to ask for – simply to be in his arms was the ultimate reward.

Now that she spent most weekends in Somerset, she went home to Hulmesley infrequently. She kept in touch by telephone. In general it was her father who answered when she rang. Laura was still living at home but was seldom there in the evenings.

'She's at the Colvilles',' Gerald would report, rather proudly. Or, 'Toby's taken her to Lincoln to meet up with some bigwigs.'

The result of these meetings startled her when at last she learned of it.

'What d'you think?' her father demanded one evening almost as soon as they'd said hello. 'Laura's going to have her name in print! Toby's getting out a series of little books about how to lead a healthy life and all that sort of thing. There's a printer in Lincoln who has been doing lay-outs and so forth, and they're starting off with two, with two more to come in the autumn.'

'Books about a healthy life?' Catherine repeated, at a loss.

'Only short, you know. Paperback. Toby's put it together for her. The first one looks very nice – the cover's going to be white printing on blue – *The Mertagen Message*—'

'But Dad, Laura isn't in the business of giving advice, surely?' she interrupted. 'I mean, of course I remember she used to, to people she'd treated – specific recommendations about how to avoid further trouble if she thought it necessary. But general advice?'

She could almost see Gerald frown. 'What's wrong with it?' he asked, quick to take offence on Laura's behalf. 'People *do* need advice, and a lot of them ask Laura – they'll talk about their relatives, ask what she thinks – so Toby thought she might as well put it into a little book.'

'She used to say, if a patient asked for help with someone else's problems, that she'd have to see them herself before she could make any suggestions—'

'But she's got so much on her plate already, Cathie, I don't think you've any idea how much she has to do these days! She couldn't really take on much more. Toby says the books are a good way of dealing with that.'

'Have you read one? What does it actually say?'

'Well, the first one's about how you live and how to improve things – eight hours' sleep, how to relax when you're tense, getting enough exercise and what kind for your time of life – that sort of thing.'

'I see.'

'I never thought I'd have a daughter who got her name on a book! Isn't it wonderful?'

'Yes, wonderful,' agreed Catherine with a sinking heart.

'You don't sound very enthusiastic?'

'I'm just surprised, that's all.'

'I suppose you thought she wasn't clever enough with words to be an author. I have to confess, I was the same – I always thought you were the brains of the family. But you see? Laura's got talent and with Toby to help her, there's no knowing what she'll do.'

She went along with the approbation in Gerald's tone but was glad when they said goodnight. Because, in her heart of hearts, she thought it was cheapening for Laura to put her name to generalised chit-chat about health. Laura had a gift, a touch of magic – something she gave to just one person at a time in a close encounter, infinitely superior to mundane advice about fresh air and exercise.

She'd seen Toby in London, but she'd talked about Fenn on these occasions and Toby had soon got the message – he'd be wasting his time on courtship. So instead his part of the conversation had been about the world of Hulmesley that now seemed so far away. Not once had he mentioned anything about books. She couldn't help thinking the concealment had been deliberate, because he knew she'd try to talk Laura out of it. But it was too late now.

And besides, what right had she to try to influence her sister these days? Each had chosen her own path, and it seemed those paths seldom converged.

Yet she found that it grieved her to think of Laura's name being used to sell empty phrases in a prettied-up cover.

When she tried to express some of these doubts to Fenn, she found to her surprise that he was rather on Toby's side.

'If the public want to buy things like that, why not supply them?' he remarked.

'Don't you think it's a bit . . . opportunistic?'

'What's that mean?' He was sketching with charcoal, a skeletal fern on matt white.

'You know what it means – grabbing at the chance to make money.'

'Right. That's what commerce is about, isn't it? What Velton's does – buys things and exploits them. It's what I do when I fiddle about with things like this fern, to sell it as a fabric design. Why shouldn't Toby make money from the clinic? I gather it was his idea to set it up in the first place, so he's entitled to exploit it.'

Catherine was often unsure if Fenn was in earnest or making fun of her. She decided to take this argument at face value. 'But the clinic only exists because my sister has this power to heal—'

'So you say, puss, and I'll take your word for it. But who can tell how long a thing like that will last? I'd say Toby was showing sense, laying in a bit of money while they have the chance.'

She shook her head. She couldn't quite put it into convincing words, but she somehow couldn't resign herself to the idea of money-making schemes connected with Laura. To Catherine, the purity, the wholesomeness were being damaged.

After her next weekend in the country Fenn came up to London with her to show a folio of designs to Thelma. On such occasions he would stay with Catherine in her Hammersmith flat. Toby rang to say he would be in town on business. It seemed a good opportunity to introduce him to Fenn, to include Fenn in her family circle, to talk about the publication of the booklets over a drink, to take the chance to voice her reservations. With this multi-layered aim in view, she arranged to meet in the quiet, secluded bar of the Bellamy Hotel.

Toby was there first. He gave a hard stare at Fenn as he and Catherine walked in together. Catherine wondered if he was looking at Fenn as a rival – but that was foolish of him because there never could have been any justification for it. Yet she sensed that he had decided to regard him as unimportant. An artist, after all – a dabbler in paints and colours, with no business sense from all he'd heard. He could hardly wait for introductions to be over so he could tell them about his success.

'The book's selling already!' he announced. 'We only put the advertisement in ten days ago and we've made nearly two hundred sales—'

'But how did you get it into the bookshops so quickly?'

'Bookshops? We're not bothering with shops. We're selling mail order. That way we get names and addresses, so we can send them an order form when the next book is ready.'

'Very astute,' said Fenn. He gave a sidelong grin at Catherine. She couldn't be sure whether he was inviting her to admire Toby or laugh at him.

'I brought you a copy of the first title, and a proof of the second,' Toby went on, producing them from his pigskin briefcase. 'Good to look at, aren't they? Dignified.'

'Neat not gaudy,' Fenn supplied.

Catherine was thankful to see that in fact the paperbacks had a good appearance. She'd been afraid of some blatant publicity concerning Laura's healing powers. Not so. Laura's name was on the cover but no claims were made, except at the end of the text. There a footnote informed the reader that the author treated patients at the famous Mertagen Clinic. Further information could be obtained by writing to the address in Hulmesley, Norfolk, or telephoning the number supplied.

'I'm ordering a reprint,' said Toby with evident satisfaction. 'And I've increased the print run on Book Two. What we want now is a mention or two in the newspapers and magazines—'

'That's not very likely,' Catherine put in. She knew from experience how difficult it was to interest journalists in anything except show business or politics. Velton's had a publicity staff who worked on the problem every day of the week with very little success.

'Well, we can but try, Cath. I've hired a firm that's got some good contacts – costs a bit but it'll pay off.' He chatted on for a while about the difference between ordinary local advertising and national publicity of the kind he was now seeking. Catherine could feel Fenn at her side, fidgeting with boredom. He had absolutely no interest in publicity.

'You've gone into it pretty thoroughly,' she murmured, hoping to break the flow.

'Of course. I want to get the clinic appreciated.'

'In what way?' asked Fenn. 'I mean, what do you want to achieve?'

'More book sales, in the first place. And then I've got other ideas . . . Well, we'll see.' He checked himself with some difficulty. Clearly he had great plans – but not for immediate dissemination.

He finished his gin and tonic and glanced at his watch. 'Must dash,' he said, getting up. 'I'm meeting one of the publicity people for dinner. Nice to meet you, Fenn. Everyone at home sends their love, Cath. Bye!' He hurried out so quickly that Catherine's messages to her father and Laura were lost in his wake.

She turned to Fenn. Without putting it into words she was asking for his opinion of Toby.

'He's a real go-getter, isn't he?' he responded. 'Savile Row suit, Rolex watch, handsewn shoes – all the hallmarks of success. I bet he tips the doorman to get him a taxi – too important to stand on the kerb looking for one.' He rose with his drink in his hand, sauntering to the window of the bar to survey Toby coming out of the hotel entrance. Catherine saw him stare, then draw back a little. 'Well, well,' he said.

'What?'

'Doesn't need a taxi, there's a smart little MG picking him up.'

Wondering for the moment what an MG might be, Catherine joined him at the window. 'Oh, a sports car.'

Their presence was to some extent masked from the outside by the plants in the window boxes. She was going to say jokingly, 'Are we spying on him?' but the words died on her lips.

A dark-haired girl in a blue silk Hardy Amies suit had jumped out of the MG and was kissing Toby with a great deal of fervour. And he was returning the kiss, arms around her so that both hands clasped his briefcase which in its turn pressed her body close against his.

'So that's the publicity person, is it,' Fenn remarked. 'Very nice.'

Catherine, sighing, turned away.

'You're not surprised?' Fenn asked, rejoining her at their table.

'Not a bit.'

'Does your sister know about it, do you suppose?'

'Of course not! Laura sees him as the love of her life, as devoted to her as she is to him.'

'Oh dear.'

'Fenn, I'm going to have to tell her—'

But he was shaking his head at her. 'Don't interfere, puss. She won't thank you. If she's happy with what she's got, why spoil things?'

'But it's all based on a lie—'

'So are most things, Cathie. We all put up a front and kid the rest of the world when we can. Toby's just doing what's natural—'

'He's using my sister as a way of making money—'

'Oh, come on, he's hardly going to make a fortune out of selling paperback health books through the mail.'

'You sound as if you don't see anything wrong in it!'

'No, I don't see much wrong in it, if you want to know. As far as I can gather, your sister went along with the idea. Your objection seems to be based on some idealistic view of her . . .'

Was she being unrealistic? Over-sensitive on Laura's behalf? She had to remind herself that she didn't know her sister as well as she used to. If Laura accepted Toby's business outlook, why should she try to interfere? And as to the girl in the Hardy Amies suit . . . What good would it do to take the story to Laura? Toby would explain it all away as he had before, would claim that she'd misjudged the situation. A friendly kiss between business associates . . .

'I don't know,' she sighed. 'It would break my sister's heart if she'd seen what we saw.'

'Then for the sake of keeping her heart in good shape, forget it.'

She accepted the advice. Luckily her attention was called elsewhere by the huge success of Velton's new leisure-wear department. Thelma Axworth had given her the chance to show what she was capable of: she was determined not to let her down. As for Fenn, he was enjoying himself although he would never have admitted it.

He worked hard through the summer. Catherine unobtrusively made improvements at the cottage. Life flowed on like an untroubled stream.

Then one evening at about the usual time, Catherine received a telephone call from her father. He sounded perturbed even as they were greeting each other.

'Is something wrong?' she asked.

'I suppose not. I mean, it's not really for me to say. It's just that it seems so unlike what I ever expected for Laura. She's always been so reticent, almost shy – hasn't she, Cathie?'

'Yes, she has. What is it, Dad?' By now her imagination had conjured up all sorts of disasters.

'Toby's suggesting that Laura should make public appearances.'

'What? I don't understand.'

'He says it's done all the time, especially in the States—'

'You mean he wants to put Laura on the lecture circuit? Women's Institutes, Rotary Clubs?'

'No. No, not from what I gather. No, Toby says the thing is to hire a hotel ballroom, or something like that—'

'In Hulmesley?'

'Not only Hulmesley. Toby's saying he thinks she should take her message to all the big cities, right up and down the country—'

'Her message!'

'Yes, you know, that's what the series of books is called – *The Mertagen Message*. So he's planning to make a sort of tour, and Laura will speak and demonstrate her powers of healing—'

'*Demonstrate*?'

'Yes, and Laura's being talked into it but . . . but . . . To tell the truth, I think the idea terrifies her!' Gerald made a sound halfway between a sigh and a sob. 'I don't know what to do, Cathie, if I speak against Toby she gets very upset.'

Catherine said nothing. She herself had tried to criticise Toby, with the result that she and her sister had had their first real quarrel.

'Cathie? What should I do?'

'Don't do anything,' she said. 'I'll drive up first thing in the morning.'

Chapter Twelve

Not since the accusation of misconduct against Laura had there been such an air of crisis. The living-room above the shop crackled with tension. Gerald Mertagen had his anxiety under control but only just. As for Laura, she was pale, weary, and much too quiet.

Catherine had arrived home at mid-morning but it had been impossible to talk to Laura at that time. She was tied up at the clinic for the rest of the day – even lunchtime, because patients came to her in their lunch hour. Catherine had spoken to her on the phone, briefly, to say that she wanted to have a serious talk.

'Today,' she insisted. 'As soon as you're free.'

'That won't be until about four o'clock—'

'All right, see you at home at about four—'

'But Toby's taking me to Norwich—'

'What for?'

'To look at cars – he feels we ought to have a bigger car—'

'Put it off.'

'No, the dealer's got one specially for us to see—'

'Put it off, Cath. The car will still be there tomorrow.'

'But tomorrow's schedule is—'

'Cath, we've really got to talk. Dad's worried about you.'

A long hesitation. Then her sister said, perhaps with a hint of relief, 'All right, see you soon after four.'

To Catherine it was clear that her sister knew what they wanted to discuss. And that she half-hoped they would suggest some way to change the path laid out before her. It seemed Laura didn't feel happy about the proposed lecture tour, had been argued into it by her dependence on Toby's judgement. If her family could put up some good arguments against it, perhaps Toby could be persuaded to call the whole thing off.

Catherine made lunch for herself and her father, then spent the afternoon at his suggestion going through the file concerning the proposed tour.

There were in fact two of them, one to take place over two

weeks in November and one to take place in the latter part of January. They were alarming enough at first glance: Laura was to speak in Norwich one evening, accept patients next day but make no evening appearance, speak in Lincoln next evening, accept patients next day in that city, have a free day on Friday, and on Saturday speak in Nottingham.

So on across England, the two-week tour ending in Leeds. The two weeks for the end of January took her from one industrial city to another – Coventry, Birmingham, Wolverhampton, Stoke-on-Trent, and so on until the last evening in Manchester.

For an experienced speaker – for a politician or a campaigner for some cause, for a teacher or a lecturer – it might not have seemed daunting: six evening talks over two weeks, with rests in between. But as Catherine read through the programme she could tell that for Laura, unused to public appearances, reticent, not quick-witted or ready with a response, it could be torture.

She fumed over the papers and lists and schedules. When her father, having closed the shop early, came upstairs, she was about ready to throw the whole file into the dustbin.

'She'll never survive this!' she exclaimed as Gerald came in. 'That man is going to drive her to a nervous breakdown.'

'Try telling him that. He says she'll be all right, she's just got to be herself and everybody will love her. It doesn't seem to occur to him that she *can't* be herself if she's put on display like a showgirl.'

It was unusual for her father to disagree with anything that Toby proposed. He had always had a high opinion of him, firstly because the Colvilles approved of him, secondly because his daughter adored him, and thirdly because there was no doubt that Toby's management of the clinic had brought in a lot of money. Gerald was in business himself; he had a high respect for a moneymaker.

'I can't think why she's agreed to it,' Catherine mourned, shuffling the papers into the file.

'It's because Toby thinks it's a good idea. Anything Toby thinks must be right.' Was there a hint of jealousy in his tone? Perhaps every father feels something of the kind for the man his daughter loves. Whatever the cause, Gerald was not feeling kindly disposed towards Toby.

'Toby's advice is important to her, Dad. But she shouldn't follow it if she doesn't feel up to it. He mustn't force her into it against her will.'

'Don't be angry with *me*, Cathie. I've tried to argue against it.

But you know her whole life revolves around him. What Toby says goes. And you know,' he added, his sense of fairness prompting him, 'he's been proved right in the past. It was his idea to open the clinic, and look what a success that's been.'

'Has it? Selling packets of herb tea and paperback books about living a healthy life? Is that what Laura's talent is about?'

'Oh . . . well . . .' Gerald retreated into the kitchen to put on the kettle for tea. Challenged to identify what made his elder daughter special, he had no words to express it.

Catherine followed him, busying herself with the small tasks of getting out cups and saucers, setting a tray.

'I suppose you could say that Toby has commercialised the clinic,' he went on with some reluctance. 'And I must admit I didn't expect that at the outset. But you have to agree that Laura's done a lot more good than she ever could have when she was working at home. And though the products on sale don't have too much to do with Laura's gift, they're beneficial in a general way and bring in money—'

'But Laura was never interested in money, Dad.'

'All the same, she's got to live. Toby's marketing ability has given the clinic a good financial basis so that she's got something to fall back on. For instance, I think the planning of these tours cost a bit—'

'You mean that Toby's earned the money to plan a project that will turn her into a travelling circus!'

'Oh, now, Cath . . . It's not going to be that bad . . .' But he was shaken by the phrase. It was a formidable judgement. It doubly reinforced his own anxieties.

Laura came home as they were settling in the living-room with the tea tray. Catherine jumped up to greet her with a hug and a kiss. They hadn't seen each other since June.

'How are you?' she cried, standing back to survey her. 'I hear big changes are being planned?'

Laura seemed to her to have changed very little. She was thinner than she used to be, and her soft brown hair was expertly styled now in a long bob which turned up neatly at the ends. She was wearing a gathered skirt of light blue wool with an angora sweater to match, carrying a jacket. There was about her little of the professional woman, nothing to suggest that she could stand on a platform and hold the attention of an audience. She still, in fact, looked schoolgirlish.

'Talk about big changes!' she cried, throwing her jacket on the back of the sofa. 'Look at *you*! That suit must have cost a fortune.'

'Not when you get a discount,' Catherine laughed. 'Come on, sit down, I bet you could do with a cup of tea.'

'I'm dying for one. My last patient had nothing wrong with her, really, she just needed to talk about her troubles and it went on for more than an hour . . . Well, never mind that. What brings you home all of a sudden?'

Catherine was pouring tea. She gave her attention to it and allowed her father to bring up the important subject.

'I rang Cathie because I'm a bit worried about you taking on this tour, love. I thought she ought to know.'

'It's a bit sudden, isn't it?' Catherine took it up. 'You never mentioned it when we spoke last week.'

'No . . . well, it hadn't become a real prospect then . . . Though Toby's been mentioning it to me since . . . oh, I think it was when the second paperback came out. He said then, personal appearances would boost sales. And I said, I couldn't ever sit in a bookshop waiting for people to buy copies. And he said . . .'

'What did he say?' Catherine asked, bringing her tea to her. She sat down beside her sister on the sofa. 'He said he wanted you up on a stage, addressing an audience?'

Laura nodded, looking down to stir her tea although she knew it had no sugar in it.

'And what did you say?'

'I thought he was joking at first. But when I realised he meant it I said I didn't think I could do it. And we talked about it off and on for a day or two, and he made me see . . .'

'What, Laura?'

'Well, you know, stuck here in Hulmesley, people have to make quite an awkward journey to get to me. I mean, if you come to Hulmesley you're not on your way to anywhere else, you fall off into the North Sea if you drive on.' There was a hesitant smile. 'So that must mean that a lot of people never get to me, and perhaps they need me, so Toby made me see that it was rather selfish to stay snug and comfy in my own little nest when there are people out there who are suffering, who need help . . .'

'I see.' The trouble was, the argument made sense. Hulmesley was certainly not the hub of the universe. 'But even allowing for that, there doesn't seem much justification for taking on a big tour—'

'But it's in the Bible, you know. "Whatsoever thy hand findeth to do, do it with thy might" – that means no half measures, no staying in one small corner.'

Catherine glanced helplessly at her father. She'd never expected to deal with quotations from the Bible, nor could she imagine that her sister had read it from cover to cover. Wasn't there a saying that the devil could cite scripture for his purpose? But she'd better not say that because Laura wouldn't like to have Toby compared with the devil.

'Dearie, what we're worried about is whether you're up to a thing like this,' Gerald said gently. 'You've never been one to shine in public, now have you? I can't quite imagine you standing up on your own, holding forth—'

'Oh, but Toby will be there too,' Laura interrupted. 'Of course I could never face it on my own. Toby's going to be by my side.'

'What, on the platform?' Catherine queried. 'He's going to take part?'

'Not exactly. He's going to give an introduction, and then afterwards he'll hand out details of the clinic and the books and things like that. Mr Oliviat says—'

'Who the dickens is Mr Oliviat?'

'He's the man who handles all the details – books the hall, sees to the advance publicity—'

'He goes in for this sort of thing? Organising lecture tours?'

'Oh, not just that! Toby says he's a very big noise in the business world, organises all kind of public events here and in America—'

'An impresario?'

'That's the word,' Laura agreed with relief, for it had been eluding her. Words often eluded her. That was one of the reasons she dreaded making a public appearance.

An impresario? Catherine had some knowledge of show business through her work for Velton's. She knew that an impresario wasn't going to handle someone unless there was the chance of big money.

'Laura, what kind of contract has been drawn up?'

'Oh, Toby deals with all that sort of thing.'

'But he must talk to you about it, dear. After all, you're the basis of any agreement, you must know what's expected, how long it's for—'

'Oh, each tour is going to last two weeks—'

'But how many tours, Laura? Are you expected to go on travelling through the country? Beyond January next year, are there any other tours planned?'

'I don't think so . . . Well, perhaps there's something in the pipeline for next summer . . . But that's so far ahead and it all depends, doesn't it, on whether the first two tours are successful?

I expect I'll be such a bundle of nerves that the whole thing will be a flop.'

'Then why are you doing it?' cried Catherine. 'You don't really want to! It's not the sort of thing you'd ever have thought of yourself! You're letting yourself be manoeuvred—'

'Nothing of the kind. We talked it over and Toby gave me the contract to read overnight before I signed it—'

'You signed it. You mean you're committed.'

'Don't say it in such a doomy sort of voice, Cath, it'll be all right, Toby says that after the first time I'll be fine, he says it's just a matter of reading what's written down and then answering questions from the floor—'

'So who's written the script you'll be reading?' Catherine demanded. 'Don't tell me – Toby!'

Laura's fine skin took on a tinge of indignation. 'There's no need to say it in that tone! After all, he does know more about me and my work than anybody else.'

'And if anybody in the audience gets difficult? I mean, you do remember how hard it was to convince those men on the committee at St Leonard's Hospital – what if you get a troublemaker like that in the hall?'

'Then Toby will step in and deal with him—'

'Oh, will he,' grunted Gerald, who remembered only too well how hard it had been to handle Patterson, the patient who had accused Laura of impropriety. 'It seems to me Toby is going to be all kinds of a miracle man in this affair – he thinks up the idea, gets a management firm to set it up, talks you into it, writes a talk for you to read out, guarantees to see there's no difficulty with members of the audience – what exactly is he, if you don't mind me asking? Your manager? Your representative? Your Svengali? Your handler?'

'Dad,' Catherine said warningly.

Too late. In a sudden flood of tears, Laura jumped up and ran out of the room.

Her father smacked himself on the forehead. 'I handled that well, didn't I?' he groaned.

'Don't blame yourself. It's hard not to get cross at the way things are going—'

'I hate to say this,' Gerald went on as if she hadn't spoken, 'but I think that man is *manipulating* my little girl! The Laura we used to know would never have agreed to get up and try to show off in public.'

'I know, I know, it's Toby's influence – all the changes

towards making money out of her healing ability have come from Toby.'

'Do you really think there's money in this touring idea, then?'

She sighed. 'There could be. I seem to remember reading about huge audiences for faith healers, particularly in the United States. And you know, when you come to think of it . . .'

'What, love?'

'Laura might be ideal for that kind of thing. She's young, and pretty, and easy to control—'

'To *control*? Cathie, what are you saying?'

'Well, we both know Toby's only got to crook his little finger and she comes running. If all she has to do is stand on a platform and read what he's written, she could look very sweet, very appealing. He could set up a sort of show around her that might look good. And if it draws audiences, it will make money.'

'I'm not having that!' raged Gerald. 'No daughter of mine is going to jump through hoops like some tame poodle—'

'Now, Dad, don't get in a state, it won't help. Laura won't hear a word against Toby – I know, I've tried to warn her. So it's no use trying to talk her out of it by being rude about him.'

'That's what you say. But it made her stop and think when I asked what he was up to, now didn't it? I mean, I'm sorry I reduced her to tears, but if it makes her ask him what he thinks he's doing with her life, it might help. Because I don't think he'll have an answer.'

'Oh yes he will. He'll talk her round,' Catherine said. 'In the first place, he won't want to give up the chance of making money. In the second place, he's got the contract to think of – he and Laura are signed up and committed to these appearances. The venues are presumably booked well in advance – I know if Velton's is planning a fashion show in a hotel, we have to sign a contract. To back out now might mean financial penalties, even law suits. Toby will make sure the thing goes ahead as planned.'

Gerald was shaking his head mournfully. For the first time Catherine noticed that he was growing greyer, that there were lines in his face she hadn't seen before. After a moment he said, 'What did you mean, you'd tried to warn Laura? What was that about?'

The last thing Catherine wanted was to recount Toby's sexual exploits. 'That's all in the past, Dad—'

'No, no, if there's something dicey about him, I ought to be told. My daughter's future is bound up with that man. I took him on trust because the Colvilles thought so highly of him, but you seem to think differently.'

'Well, I always thought . . .' She drew in a breath, reluctant to go on. 'My opinion is that Toby took up with Laura to curry favour with the Colvilles in the first place.'

'What?'

'He was trying to build up some boat-making business, if I recall it rightly—'

'Yes, he had a partner, they were remodelling landing-craft or something.' Gerald was nodding.

'Well, Desmond Colville was going to put money into it. So of course Toby wanted to be in their good books, and when they started singing Laura's praises he probably thought it was a good idea to join in. And of course Laura made it terrifically easy for him. She fell for him like a ton of bricks.'

'We-ell . . .'

'She did, Dad. She set out to get chatty with him the very first time she saw him, and of course he played along for, after all, she's a pretty girl – but then up walked Mrs Colville telling him Laura had saved her life more or less, so Toby decided to cultivate her. And then the boat thing fell through—'

'There you are. If you were right, Toby would just have dropped her—'

'But Desmond cooked up this idea of opening a clinic. Now that was a moneymaking proposition in itself, and a way of being in partnership with Desmond Colville, one of the most important men in the county,' said Catherine, speaking the thoughts aloud for the very first time. 'I'd imagine Toby thought he'd been handed an easy way of making a living, at least temporarily. But now, you see, it's opening up into something a lot bigger – the Mertagen Message is going out to the public in a big way. I'd imagine Toby's going to push it for all it's worth.'

'Cathie . . . You seem to be saying he doesn't care about Laura at all, only as a way of making an easy living . . .'

She remained silent. Gerald stared at her. 'Is that what you think?'

'I could be wrong. And see here, Dad, as long as Laura's so involved with him it does no good to drag in my opinions – it would only drive her away, and we don't want *that.*'

'Oh, lord, no. One day she may need us, so we've got to stick by her.' He paced about, sometimes almost wringing his hands in his concern over this elder daughter who had always seemed to need more protection than her sister.

They said no more for a time, each trying to come to terms with the new situation. Gerald was perhaps regretting he'd been so uncritical of Toby's outlook. But then, young men these days seemed so much more pushy than those he'd grown up with – he'd thought the difference in point of view had been just that he himself was out of date.

Catherine was wondering if it had been wise to admit her grave reservations about him. She knew her father had always been more protective towards Laura – but then Laura had always needed it because she'd always been the more vulnerable.

'Go up and ask her to come down,' he suggested. 'She never drank her tea.'

But even as he said it they heard Laura's footsteps on the stairs. They looked up expectantly as she reached the landing outside, but she went on down to the outside door and out to the street.

'She's gone out!' Gerald exclaimed, springing up. 'Cathie, we must stop her—'

'Why should we? Come on, Dad, she's a grown woman. If she wants to go out, why shouldn't she?'

'But she was so upset—'

'I expect she's dried her eyes and powdered her nose by now. Come on, sit down, I'll make fresh tea.'

He was reluctant, but after all, what could he do? Run after her? And if he caught up with her, what could he say? That he was sorry to have spoken harshly about Toby? That wouldn't be true. Now that he was beginning to examine the matter, he felt he should have been even harsher.

They watched the television news and had supper. At last around nine o'clock they heard the downstairs door open. Footsteps and voices could be distinguished. The living-room door opened, and in came Laura with Toby at her elbow.

She was glowing. Every trace of her distress had been banished. 'Well, here we are!' she carolled. 'Back from buying the car—'

'You went to Norwich?' Gerald asked, surprised.

'Yes, went by train, met Toby at the car showroom and he drove me back in the new car – wait till you see it, it's a Bentley Continental in such a smart steely blue with red leather seats—'

'Good evening, everybody,' Toby said, partly drowning out the flow of delight about the car. 'Nice to see you, Cath – I heard you'd come up from London.'

'How are you, Toby,' said Catherine, with a nod of greeting.

'Cathie came because I asked her to,' Gerald announced, getting to his feet to dominate the proceedings. 'I was worried about this new scheme of yours to go touring the country—'

'Yes, yes, Dad, and I told Toby all about that,' his daughter cut in. 'And you know that question you asked at the end?'

'What question?'

'You asked what part Toby would play – was he going with me as my manager or my Svengali – remember?'

'Oh, sweetie, I don't think we want to make too much of things I said in the heat of the—'

'Well, I can answer that now,' Laura said on a note of high triumph. 'He's going with me as my husband.'

'What?'

'We're being married in three weeks' time, Dad. Isn't it wonderful?'

Chapter Thirteen

The ceremony took place quietly in St Mary's, the parish church of Browbourne, Mr Colville's estate. The bride wore a high-waisted late-day dress of oyster silk from the Jacques Heim boutique at Velton's. A stiffened bandeau of the same material and made by Velton's millinery department framed her pale face; she carried a spray of slipper orchids. Catherine as bridesmaid was in a Chanel-style suit of soft grey wool.

Catherine felt she had given all the support she could to the wedding plans by seeing that the two Mertagen sisters looked good. Although she had offered congratulations and good wishes at the news, in her heart she was deeply opposed to the marriage.

She had tried to talk to her sister on the night it was announced. She sat on the end of her sister's bed, as she had on many a night before, and asked her if she was sure she wanted to get married.

'Of course I do,' Laura cried, astounded at the question. 'It's what I've wanted from the very first – to be Toby's wife.'

'Did Toby know how you felt?'

'Oh yes, we talked about it now and then, but he felt that the conventional kind of marriage – finding a house, settling down to start a family – he felt it would interfere with my work, and you know he's always understood how important that is, he's often said it amazes him, it's such a precious thing, so he felt we ought not to endanger it by making a big change . . .'

'But he feels it's right to make a change now?'

'Well yes, you see, everything *is* changing, isn't it? He explained it to me, how it's like a plant growing – the plant's all right for a while in the place where it started but then, you know, it outgrows that spot and it's time to move it, so we're moving out into the big world and he feels it's time to do what we've always wanted to do, become man and wife.'

'He said all this to you this evening, on the way home from Norwich?'

'Oh yes, we stopped the car in a quiet spot and had ever such a long talk. I was upset, you know . . . by what Dad said . . . And I sort of blurted it out to Toby and he was shocked – really shocked, you know, that Dad would speak like that about him, but after he got over it he explained that he intended to propose during the tour and suggest we get married in the spring, because of course it would have been nice to be an Easter bride, but now he saw that it would be right to get married now, at once, without any further delay, because of course married people have this special strength, from being united in this special bond, and that strength would help us in this new idea of going on tour . . .'

'I see. So that did away with any anxieties you had about making public appearances.'

Laura threw up her hands in protest. 'Oh no, I'm still nervous, Cath. But after all, Toby and I together – Mr and Mrs Lindham – nothing on earth can bother us, can it?' In the radiant happiness of her new status of bride-to-be, nothing could really alarm her. Toby loved her, was to be her husband, all would be well.

All indeed would be well, from Toby's point of view. Catherine felt mean-minded in seeing things in this way, but the fact remained that by proposing, Toby had scotched any doubts Laura might have had. Not only Laura, her father too – one glance at him when Laura made her announcement was enough to tell Catherine that he was won over.

Yet in essence nothing was changed. Toby would go his own way as before, manipulating Laura, concealing what he didn't want her to know. Moreover – and this was a cynical but unavoidable thought – it was better from the publicity point of view if he and Laura were married. The partnership between them might have been a little awkward to explain to provincial reporters, might even have caused some harmful gossip.

Moreover, the Colvilles – staunch churchgoers – would approve even more heartily now that the union of the young pair was blessed by clergy. And Laura's father, though less of a churchgoer, was of the same mind.

In fact, only Catherine seemed less than happy. And being in a minority of one made her very uncertain. Nevertheless she felt she had to try to save her sister from what she saw as a mistake.

'Isn't it a bit of a strain for you, going off on a publicity tour just after you get married?' she persisted, her fingers tracing the pattern on Laura's quilt.

'Oh, Cath, you know the only difference will be having a marriage certificate! Toby and I belonged together from the first, you know that.'

'So why rush into it like this? Why not put it off until next year?'

'Don't you want me to get married?' Laura asked, pausing with one shoe off and one shoe on.

'I just don't see why it has to be done in such a rush—'

'Well, if you want to know, you brought all this on, with the things you and Dad were saying earlier this evening!' Unaccustomed anger flushed her sister's cheeks. She threw her shoes into her wardrobe with unnecessary violence and turned, hands on hips. 'I don't understand you, Cath – sometimes you're so *carping* about Toby, I get the feeling you don't like him at all. You were like this that other time, when you tried to get me to believe some silly story about him and Celia Kingsley!'

Catherine had to rack her brains to recall that Celia Kingsley was the woman who, according to gossipmongers, had almost wrecked her marriage over Toby.

'Laura, this is different. You're going to tie yourself for life to a man who—'

'A man who what? Who loves me? Who's devoted himself to helping me with my work, who's always thinking how to do what's best for me? Look here, Cath, if you came in to have a chat so as to say rotten things about Toby, I think we should just say goodnight here and now. Because whatever it is you're trying to say, I don't want to hear it. Understand? I don't want to hear it!' And to emphasise her point Laura put her hands over her ears.

Now as she stood behind her sister in the chancel of the church, with the clergyman's words echoing up to the vaulted ceiling, Catherine knew she must accept the fact. In a moment the marriage would be a fait accompli. She had tried and failed to persuade Laura to wait and she must accept that defeat.

She let her glance wander to the other members of the wedding party. Her father and Toby in dark suits. Fenner – who didn't possess a dark suit and refused to buy one for the occasion – in corduroys and a dark tweed jacket. Mr and Mrs Colville, who had insisted on giving the wedding breakfast at their house. The Colvilles and her father wore that soft smile which seems to go with the marriage service – a smile of hope and optimism for the young couple.

It was a small gathering at the Colvilles' house – a few neighbours from Mitre Lane, Toby's former boat-building partner, the staff from the Mertagen Clinic, and some friends of the Colvilles apparently known to Laura and Toby.

A reporter and a photographer from the county newspaper

arrived. Catherine saw how much it flustered her sister, and wondered how she would fare when the forthcoming tours put her in the public eye. But true enough – Toby was always at her elbow to encourage or soothe.

All through the wedding breakfast, with its obligatory speeches and toasts, the handshakes and congratulations, Catherine smiled and nodded and looked delighted. When the newly-weds drove off to the airport for a honeymoon weekend in Paris, she waved and called out good wishes.

But at home in her Thames-side flat that night, in the darkness of her bedroom, Catherine let the tears overtake her. 'Either she's going to go on fooling herself for ever,' she sobbed, 'or Toby's got to change. And I don't think Toby's going to change.'

'Sh, sh,' soothed Fenn, astonished to find the ever-valiant Catherine Mertagen weeping in his arms. He had never understood how deeply she cared about her sister, didn't understand it now. He himself was an only child from a broken family, learning early to depend on himself and not to expect anything lasting from others.

'Look at it this way,' he murmured. 'She's been happy up to now with Toby, there's no reason she shouldn't go on being happy.'

'But it's all based on an illusion!'

'Cathie, love *is* an illusion. Some are just lucky enough never to see through it. And maybe Laura's one of those.' He kissed her and soothed her with caresses so that the words, which troubled her, seemed just another of his ironic quips. And at last she fell asleep.

Her dreams were full of veiled anxieties and warnings. But in the morning light they melted away; she made a rational decision to hope well for the marriage.

The publicity tour proved a great success. So did its successor. The months rolled by. The newly-weds became an established, busy couple who bought a house on the outskirts of Norwich. Catherine wondered if it might herald a new phase, a settling down and perhaps the starting of a family, but no – the Mertagen Clinic also was moved to Norwich as a more accessible centre, and then was transferred again to Coventry. The Norwich house was sold and a new one was bought near Kenilworth. Money never seemed to be a problem.

It meant that Catherine and her father saw even less of Laura. Gerald went to stay once or twice at Kenilworth and reported to his younger daughter that Laura seemed happy. Yet although he said he had a standing invitation, his visits fell away. He came more often to London, sometimes to attend chess tournaments, sometimes just to be with Catherine. She took him to first nights, she got him tickets for cup finals. But she knew it was a poor compensation for the lonely life he lived now in the flat above the shop in Mitre Lane.

Her own life kept her busy. Her department at Velton's was growing larger with every season – leisure clothes, once thought of as promotable only in spring, were now year-round stock. She still sought out new fabrics, new designs, and besides handling Fenn's work she was beginning to build up an agency of about half a dozen fabric designers whose work she sold on commission. She had a flair for successful design: most of her clients did well.

Fenn had never looked back since she first 'discovered' him but refused to leave the fastness of Somerset. 'What do I need to be in London for?' he said with a shrug every time she suggested it. 'You've dollied-up the cottage so that it's as cosy as a quilt, and now I have a car I can drive up any time I want to.'

'But we could be together more, Fenn.'

'Where? Here?' He glanced about the elegance of her flat. By now she had leased the rest of the floor which contained her studio flat, so that she had a set of capacious rooms overlooking the Thames. 'You wouldn't like it if I took up one of your rooms for a studio, now would you?'

'You could have a place of your own—'

'I've got a place of my own.'

'But it's so far off, Fenn, it means we can only see each other at weekends mostly—'

He made a little gesture that seemed to say, 'That suits me.' Catherine was silent. She often had this feeling with Fenn – an invisible barrier that she knew better than to breach. Fenn was a private person, with a life of his own he wouldn't allow her to share. Well, that was only right. He was an artist whereas she was merely a trader in art. She could make no claim on him even though others might say he owed her a lot.

In the autumn of 1964 Laura and Toby were setting off on a long-planned tour of the United States. This was such a big event that Catherine felt able to suggest a family gathering, a lunch party to see them off, to be held in her flat. It was an opportunity for her father and herself to find out how Laura really felt about this momentous undertaking for sometimes, when she'd spoken about it on the telephone, there had been a quaver in her voice.

With the chestnut trees on the banks of the Thames turning golden, the view from Catherine's sitting-room was stunning.

'We might be moving to London when we get back,' murmured Toby as he stood beside Catherine at the window.

'To live?'

'It's the sensible move, don't you think? This tour of the States will establish her on the international circuit – we can't be stuck in the Midlands after that.'

'Is she happy?' she asked suddenly.

Toby was startled by the question. 'Of course she is. Why not?'

She didn't know why she'd asked him. He was the last person likely to tell the truth. And what could she do about it, anyway?

Yet, strange to say, the imminence of this departure to a foreign land seemed to draw the two sisters closer again. They sat together after lunch with a glass of wine, Laura asking what it was like in New York.

'Well, this time of year it will be absolutely gorgeous – crisp and clear, with a sparkle in the air. The shops will be full of winter fashions and there'll be pumpkins on every door-step.'

'That sounds nice.' It was clear that Laura was extremely nervous. Although by now she had mastered the art of handling her audiences on tour, the thought of facing a large auditorium full of Americans scared her. 'It's not like speaking to people in Manchester or Newcastle,' she murmured. 'I know how those people think, but what do I know about Americans?'

'If they're in trouble or poor health, I expect they think in much the same way as anybody else,' Catherine soothed. 'Don't worry about it, dear.'

'But I do worry about it. It's so much *bigger* than anything I've done before. And we have to fly from place to place.'

'But you'll get used to that, Laura – there's nothing to it. Everybody does it in the States.'

'That's what Toby says.' She sighed. 'I know it's silly to be anxious but I'm not sure if I know enough about the kind of ailments they have over there, I mean, I'm used to having to deal with rheumatism and bronchial conditions and digestive complaints, but what if there are things I don't know?'

'But you always said it had almost nothing to do with knowledge, Laura. You said it was instinct.'

'Well, yes . . . But what if it fails me?'

'It won't,' she assured her, and put her arms around her sister for the first time in many, many months.

'Oh, Cath,' Laura whispered. 'I just feel so . . .' Her voice died away. For a long moment she seemed to hesitate. Then she said, 'Can I ring you?'

'From America?' She felt her sister nod. 'Of course, sweetie – but don't do it when it's the dead of night over here, will you?'

She never expected to get any transatlantic calls but three days later, as she was preparing to leave her office for lunch, her secretary told her her sister was on the line.

'Laura?' she asked in surprise as she picked up the receiver. 'Where are you speaking from?'

'Our hotel room. Toby's gone down to breakfast, he's meeting one of the publicity people. Laura, what do you think! I was on television last night.'

'In New York?'

'No, this is Boston – we got here at noon yesterday. Remember, Toby explained it, people like to try out a thing in other cities first and then bring it into New York. We did the talk and the audience were very friendly, no problems, and then before we knew it we were taken to this TV studio and we were on a chat show!'

'Good heavens! How did it go?'

'It seemed to go well. The man – his name's Randy Veitch, can you imagine anyone in England using "randy" for Randolph?' And Laura gave a nervous giggle.

'That was the chat show man – the host?'

'Yes. He asked a lot of questions about how the healing works and in fact wanted me to give a demonstration there and then . . .'

'Laura!' Catherine breathed, appalled.

'I know. It was just, you see . . . he didn't understand. Toby explained that I could only do it on a one-to-one basis and that I would be receiving patients next day – that's today now – and the minute we got back to the hotel there was this sheaf of messages from people who wanted to see me, and so today is absolutely booked up and more calls are coming in all the time, and honestly, I don't think there's a hope of seeing more than about six or seven and we leave Boston tomorrow morning, so they'll be terribly disappointed, although of course some of them are just sensation-seekers, I suppose, wanting to try out something they've seen on TV, but all the same . . .'

'Laura, don't get upset by it.'

'No.' Her sister drew a faltering breath. Over the transatlantic line Catherine could hear her fighting not to cry. 'It's just all going a lot faster than I expected, Cath. I don't seem to have got my breath back from the flight and here we are going on TV and with mobs of people queuing up to see me and I just don't feel . . .'

'How *do* you feel? Are you all right?'

'Yes, of course, I'm okay, I just feel . . . I don't know, funny, unsettled . . . What should I do, Cath?'

'Just do what you feel you're up to, sweetheart. Don't get bothered or overstrained. You know your gift never works so well when you're tired or overstrained.'

'No, that's right, I keep reminding myself of that and after all, they're people with health problems, people who need me, I don't need to be scared of them . . .'

'Of course not, but if you have the least anxiety about any of them just have them shown out. What are you using for your interview room?'

'It's the ante-room of this suite – there's a sort of sitting-room and a little kitchenette – you should see it, Cath, it's all done out in this sort of avocado colour with a yellow trim, far better than the kitchen back home, in fact, only small of course, and the bedroom's got looped curtains with gold tassels and the most enormous bed and about twenty table lamps which all come on at once if you touch the switch at the door but don't come on if you try to switch them before you do the one at the door—'

Catherine cut in on the nervous babble. 'Laura, Laura, calm down. Have you had breakfast?'

'No, I didn't want to go down and sit there while they talk business. I always feel I'm slow-witted at a time like that.'

'Order breakfast in your room—'

'But the room menu is so peculiar – sweet rolls, d'you know those are iced buns? And biscuits and maple syrup, who wants biscuits for breakfast—'

'Then make yourself some tea or coffee in the kitchenette and just sit down quietly with it. Laura, are you listening?'

'Yes, I'm listening.'

'Once you start the day, just say no to anything you don't feel up to.'

'Yes.'

'Nothing can work unless you agree to it. You're the mainspring, always remember that.'

'Yes.'

'I mean it, Laura. Throw your weight about. Let them see you're someone special.'

'But I'm not.'

'You are, you know you are.'

'But it's not *me*, Cath – it's what I do.'
'Well, nobody else can do it, so stand up for yourself.'
'Yes. All right.'
'Good. Now go and make that coffee.'
'Cath?'
'Yes, love?'
'Can I ring you again?'
'Of course. Any time.'
'Thank you, dear.' And the receiver at the other end was gently replaced.

Her secretary put her head round the door. 'You aren't forgetting your lunch appointment with the sales team from Belucci?'

'Ring the restaurant,' said Catherine, 'and tell them I'll be a little late.'

When she'd gone, Catherine sat at her desk trying to take deep breaths and get the better of herself. The phone call had shaken her deeply. Her sister had sounded on the edge of hysteria.

It kept her worried all day. She wished she'd asked for the phone number at the hotel so that she could call back. She rang her father to ask if he had a list of hotel names and telephone numbers but all he had was the same handout that Toby had given her – a public relations handout extolling the abilities of the healer from the Mertagen Clinic.

'Why d'you want to get in touch with her?' Gerald inquired.
'She rang me this morning. I just thought I'd ring back.'
'But why?' And then, taking alarm, 'She's not ill, is she?'
'She sounded a bit nervy. I thought I'd just have a chat.'
'Well, I haven't got any telephone numbers. Perhaps if you ring the firm that handles the publicity?'

But she shrank from doing that, from sounding like an anxious nanny. She'd wait to hear again from Laura.

When Laura next rang it was Sunday, and she rang Catherine at home in her flat. The phone was in the hall. Fenn was in the sitting-room, feet up on the sofa and the Sunday papers all around him. They had been lazing the morning away before going out for a pub lunch.

'Where are you now?' Catherine asked.
'Atlantic City. That's New Jersey. It's a seaside resort.'
'Seaside? In November?' cried Catherine.
'Oh, it's not a paddling and sandcastles sort of place. It's mostly amusement parks and funfairs. Sort of like Blackpool, I'd imagine.'
'You're giving a talk in a place like that?'

'Actually no, this is our day off. We go to Jersey City tomorrow, I think that's industrial, maybe like Birmingham.'

Catherine bit back what she wanted to say, which was that none of it sounded very delightful. 'How are you?' she asked. 'How did things go in Boston?'

Laura gave a sigh. 'All right, I suppose. But I had to turn two people away, you see. One was so terribly sick I knew I couldn't do anything, it was much too late, but when I told him so he clutched my hands and said he was a good Catholic, so he believed in miracles and knew I could save him, and it was awful, Cath, really awful . . .'

'What happened?'

'I got him calmed down but he wouldn't go, and in the end Toby had to have him practically thrown out. It was so . . . so sad, so awful . . . I . . . just didn't know what to do. And then there was a young woman who wasn't ill at all, she just wanted to ask me if I thought she'd be happy and have a good life if she married this man who's asking her, and I said I wasn't a fortune-teller and couldn't advise her and she went on and on, crying and saying she needed to know because she'd had one bad marriage and couldn't face another, so in the end I said if she didn't feel certain it was better to say no, and she flew at me, really angry, yelling that she could have got that advice for free from her family . . .'

'Oh, Laura, I'm so sorry.' After a second's hesitation she said, 'These people have paid before they see you?'

'Oh yes, the tour managers have insisted on that.'

'But that's not—' She caught herself up from saying it wasn't how things used to be.

'I know,' Laura said, sighing again. There was no over-emotional note to her manner this time. It had been replaced by something that was either melancholy or resignation.

'What's your hotel in Jersey City?'

'The Parador. I hope it's less showy than this one – this one glitters wherever you look, gold and silver and sequins and luminous paint . . .'

'Give me the number of the Parador.' She scribbled it on the notepad. 'What time will you finish giving the talk tomorrow? I'll ring you.'

'Will you? Oh, that would be lovely! Something to look forward to! We should finish in the ballroom about ten-thirty.'

'All right, lovey, we'll talk again tomorrow.'

When she went into the living-room Fenn had gone to put on his shoes and his jacket. She was picking up the discarded newspapers when he returned. 'Ready for lunch?' he inquired.

'Not really. Could we have a walk first?'

'All right by me. Who was that on the phone?'

She hesitated. 'It was Laura.'

'Laura? Calling from America?' He looked vexed as well as surprised.

'Yes.'

'Good God! Has something gone wrong with the tour?'

'I don't think so. She just wanted to talk.'

He gave her a frown of disbelief. 'Conversation at transatlantic rates? A bit odd, isn't it?'

'She needed a bit of comfort and encouragement,' she said.

'Isn't that what her husband's supposed to provide?'

'How true that is. But if you remember, Toby busies himself with the business side of the thing.'

'So she rings you up across the ocean. What is she, a baby chick? A lost waif? When is she going to grow up and handle her own life?' His tone was cross. His Sunday mood of relaxation had been marred.

Catherine tidied the papers into a neat pile on the coffee table. 'You don't understand,' she said. 'I won't bore you with the details but because of the way things went during the war we've always depended on each other.'

'But after all that weepiness about her marriage I got the impression you and she had had a falling out?'

She shook her head. 'Old habits die hard.'

'It's a bit juvenile, isn't it? I mean, she's, how old?'

'She'll be thirty-two early next year.'

'And still crying over the telephone like a schoolgirl?' he inquired with a faint disdain.

She studied him. 'Don't let's talk about it any more,' she said. 'I think we might be on the verge of a quarrel.'

'Oh, it's not worth quarrelling over. It just strikes me you're never going to get over the urge to worry over her. Which is surprising because you're no fool, Cathie, you know in this world it's a case of sink or swim – so if she can't swim, let her sink.'

'Is that meant to be a joke?'

'Not at all. It's good advice.'

'Sometimes,' she said, 'you're so cold, Fenn.'

'So that's me put in my place. Are we going out for this walk?' He was bored by the whole thing, and irritated that he'd wasted time on it.

She fetched her coat and they went out. They walked along the embankment towards Chiswick Eyot, moving briskly, for the day was cold and rather damp. They seemed to have little to say to each other.

She hadn't mentioned that she'd promised to ring her sister. She'd had her warning: Fenn thought her anxiety over Laura was pure self-indulgence. To contact her in Jersey City at about eleven at night Eastern Standard Time it meant that Catherine had to be awake at about four in the morning Greenwich Mean Time. She woke a few minutes after the hour and tiptoed out to the hall so as not to wake Fenn. She got the International Exchange and asked for the number. It rang, and she asked to be put through to the room of Mrs Lindham.

'I'm sorry, madam, but we have instructions to say that Mrs Lindham can take no more patients tomorrow so there's no point in connecting you.'

'I'm not a patient. This is her sister calling from London.'

'Er . . . Who would that be? The name, please?'

'Catherine Mertagen.'

Some delay ensued before the phone was picked up. Toby's voice said, 'Hello? Cath, is that you?'

'Toby? I asked to speak to Laura.'

'Yes, I know you did. Fact is, Laura was so tired she went straight to bed when we came upstairs from the ballroom.'

'She's in bed? Ask her to pick up the bedside phone.'

'She's asleep, Cath. I honestly don't think I ought to wake her.'

'But . . .'

But what was there to say? Her sister was probably exhausted. It would be cruel to wake her. 'All right. Will you tell her I called?'

'Sure thing. Nice to hear you, Cath, but I must get to bed myself, I'm whacked.'

'Goodnight, then.'

'G'night.'

She went quietly into the sitting-room. She switched on the lamp on the coffee table. She sat down in one of the armchairs, pulling her bare feet up under her for warmth. The room outside the lamp's circle was dark and chill. A November wind moaned through the cracks in the old windows, moving the drawn curtains like the skirts of some Victorian lady. The mantel clock ticked like a metronome. It was like a moment suspended in time, cut off from the rest of the world so that she could reach out with her intuition.

Something was wrong with Laura. She knew it, although she couldn't account for the knowledge. Fenn would laugh at her for believing in this feeling but with the wide ocean separating them, she knew that her sister needed her.

And that there was nothing she could do.

Chapter Fourteen

The taxi rushed through the London traffic to the fashion show. Thelma Axworth, resplendent in emerald green tweed with a deep lynx-fur collar, turned her little black eyes upon Catherine.

'You look wan. Got a hangover?'

Catherine smiled. 'I got up too early, that's all.'

'What d'you mean, too early? Six o'clock or what?'

'Four o'clock, actually.'

'Four o'clock? Good lord! Insomnia?'

'I was ringing Laura in America.'

Thelma considered this. Having examined it from every angle she said, 'I take it something's wrong.'

'I don't know. I just feel it's too much for her. From what she says, it's all on a terribly big scale. She's been on television, people have been rushing to consult her – Toby should never have let her in for it, he knows she's not cut out for the fast lane.'

Thelma was to some extent au fait with the news of Laura's American tour. It had been the subject of occasional chat over the office desk.

'So for some reason you rang her in the wee small hours of the morning—'

'Well, of course, it was about eleven o'clock over there—'

'I'd hate to set my alarm for four a.m.—'

'Oh, I didn't do that, it would have wakened Fenn. I just willed myself awake and it worked.'

'He's been with you this weekend? What does he think about Laura and her problems?' Thelma asked with considerable interest. She often put these quiet little questions about Fenn.

Catherine sighed. 'We nearly had a quarrel about Laura yesterday.'

'And is that why you're looking so miserable this morning?'

'Well, it didn't help. I hate it when Fenn and I get at odds.'

'Um,' said Thelma.

'What does that mean?'

Thelma leaned forward to tap on the glass separating them

from the driver. 'Driver, you should have cut through the Gardens.'

The driver shrugged – bossy woman, his back said – and went into Kensington Gardens at the next gate. Thelma ferreted about in her handbag, found their invitations to satisfy herself that they were in time, then looked back at Catherine.

'I suppose you'll tell me it's none of my business, but isn't it time you found yourself a nice, ordinary young man and got married?'

'I beg your pardon?'

'Well, you're not going to marry Fenn. Not ever. Now are you?'

Catherine hesitated. 'No, I suppose not.' She had never told Thelma that somewhere in Fenn's background there was a wife, or had been a wife; whether they were divorced or separated he never said. But certainly marriage was a topic from which Fenn shied away.

'Time's going by, Cathie. You've got yourself involved with a man who isn't interested in domestic bliss. If it's what you want, then well and good. But don't just drift on without considering what you're doing.'

'Are you such an advocate of family life, Thelma?'

'Well, you know I've got a nice, comfortable marriage that fits me like an old shoe. But I don't insist that others follow my example. I just want people – you, in this instance – to think what they're doing. Don't just be content for ever with a makeshift sort of relationship.'

The taxi drew up outside the dress designer's studio in Kensington Church Street. During the business of paying it off, their conversation had to be suspended and, Catherine thought, abandoned. But Thelma had other intentions.

'Come on, let's go and have a cup of coffee – there's twenty minutes before the show's supposed to go on and you know they're always late.'

'But we won't get good seats—'

'That young shrimp wouldn't *dare* give bad seats to the buyers from Velton's!' She took Catherine's elbow, to urge her into a café a few doors up the street. There seemed no point in resisting so she allowed herself to be guided into the café and to a table in a corner. The menu consulted and the coffee ordered, Thelma folded her gloved hands on the table top and looked earnest.

'Now I've started on the subject, I'm going to go on,' she began. 'I've often been on the verge of saying this, Cathie, but you know how it is, one's afraid of being thought a busybody. But what you said just now, about nearly having a quarrel with Fenn about your sister . . . I bet he never wants to hear about her, or anything else to do with your family. Don't you sometimes think Fenn's very self-centred?'

'But that's only natural. He's an artist—'

'Oh, come on, he's a fabric designer! This isn't Vincent van Gogh we're talking about. You give him far too much respect and admiration. And he takes advantage of you.'

'That's not true—'

'Oh yes he does! Who made that cottage of his liveable? You did. Who does all the work of preparing his portfolio? You do. Who negotiates? You do. Who sees that he's briefed in time for the new season? You do. He never has to lift a finger. And what does he give you in return?' Thelma paused for breath, then answered her own question. 'He only comes to London when something is happening that's to his advantage. If you want to see him, you have to drive a hundred miles into Somerset at the weekend. Have you ever asked yourself what keeps him down there in the backwoods?'

Catherine listened to all this with growing astonishment. She took it for granted that she had to take care of the business details for Fenn; that was her role. As to the last question, her answer came easily.

'He likes country life,' she said. 'He likes solitude. That's why he won't come and live in London – he prefers a certain austerity in his life.'

'Huh,' grunted Thelma.

'It's true, Thelma. You remember what that cottage of his was like when we first went there. Only the barest necessities. Now he can afford to live a little better, but he still likes village life.'

'Or he likes one of the villagers?'

'What?' Catherine cried, startled. 'Oh, Thelma, really! You're not trying to suggest there's another woman?'

Thelma drew a deep breath, then gave a faint shrug. 'No, that's not what I'm suggesting.'

'Then what?'

But the waitress came with the coffee at that moment. They fell silent until she'd set it before them with cream and sugar. Thelma took off her gloves, put in too much sugar for the slimming campaign she was always going to follow, and began on a different tack. 'Fenn's a lot more complicated than you know, Cathie. There are layers to his personality—'

'So you know him better than I do?' she interrupted.

'Well, I'm not in love with him. So I look at him without blinkers.'

'And what is it you see?'

'I see a man who doesn't intend to commit himself to any one person. I *suspect* that he wants something from life that perhaps you could never give him, my love.'

'Oh, if you're saying I'm not his equal, not as talented or as coolheaded as Fenn, I know *that*—'

'Stop putting yourself down, Cathie. If you just went back into circulation, men with any sense would grab you.'

'Oh for heaven's sake, I'm very ordinary and we both know it. And that's why I sometimes irritate Fenn . . .'

They sipped their coffee. Catherine resumed: 'In a way I understand what you're trying to say. Fenn isn't an easy man to understand and I don't claim to. But he relies on me, he turns to me for—'

'For business advice, guidance on what to do for the next design conference – he could get all that from an agent.'

'Well, I *am* his agent.'

'That's what I mean, dear. You give him all you have – and he takes just what he needs and gives very little in return. Don't get me wrong, Cathie. I quite like him, I like his work, but I can't help feeling he's wrong for you.'

'That's an awful thing to say!'

Thelma sighed and shrugged. 'I knew I'd regret starting this. I knew you'd think I was a busybody. But I can't help feeling you're – not exactly throwing yourself away on him, because you're good for him in many ways – but it's unequal, and as a businesswoman I don't like to see anybody getting a poor deal.' She paused and made one last plea. 'There are a lot of nice men around, dear. Take a look at them now and again – you might find one you like.'

Catherine was dismayed by Thelma's earnestness. She really seemed to mean all this doom and gloom. But it was time to drink up and go, or the fashion show would start without them.

As the mannequins paraded between the rows of spindly gilt chairs, she had to give her attention to the ideas and outlines of this new young designer. She had to assess whether his clothes would be acceptable to the British public and if so, whether her department could use any of his styles to copy, and in what fabrics. Then back at the office she wrote herself a report about the show. Other business took her attention. It was hours later, as she made herself a bedtime drink, that Thelma's words began to swim to the surface of her consciousness.

She didn't want to admit there was substance to them. Was Fenn Chelburne self-centred?

Well, he was often cool and withdrawn, apt to shrug off Catherine's little displays of affection. He quickly grew impatient if she talked about her family or her office friends.

His view of life was relentlessly disillusioned. He confessed to using his talent to make money so that he could live, but in the life he lived in his country cottage he painted canvases that he wouldn't allow her to see. He said they weren't meant to be gawked at. Once, when he came back from a walk to find her turning one face out from the wall of his studio, he'd led her out and locked the studio door. He had some secret ambition, some serious aim – because otherwise what were the hidden canvases about? What it was, she couldn't discern and didn't dare to ask.

It was an unsatisfactory situation, if she were to be honest with herself. Yet she couldn't give it up. More than four years of her life were invested in this relationship. She felt sure that Fenn needed her even if he didn't love her as much as she loved him.

Thelma had said that he would never commit himself. It was true; as she sat with her hands about her cup of hot chocolate, Catherine admitted the justice of that view. But then she had never asked him to commit himself to her.

Because she knew he never would.

This admission caused her a pang so intense that it was like a physical pain. She drew her hands quickly away from the cup, as if the hot chocolate had burned her. But that wasn't the source of her hurt. She had acknowledged something that had been submerged below her consciousness for a long time.

For the first time in many a long day she allowed herself to look back to her affair with Malcolm. Malcolm . . . Occasionally in Hulmesley she heard news of him, and had schooled herself to receive it with only polite interest. He and his wife had moved on from Manchester, the gossips said. He was doing well. There was a child, a little boy.

When she heard about the child, she had been hard put to it not to give herself away. If she and Malcolm Sanders had married, the child would have been hers. She tried to picture herself with a baby and felt a strange sense of loss for something she had never had.

That long-ago love had been so different. She and Malcolm had shared everything, the joys of the first taste of passion, the hopes of the future, the pain of separation, the determination to endure that and be together at last.

She had thrown it all away. That living, vibrant partnership had ended over a silly quarrel. She should have smoothed things over, she should have been more patient with Malcolm's criticisms – in the end they could have worked it out.

Now what did she have instead? A pale shadow of a love affair, in which there was no real affinity. A union that was somehow bloodless, without real vigour or drive unless she herself supplied it.

Where was it going? What future was there in it?

She got up, threw the remains of the hot chocolate into the sink, washed up the mug and put it in the drying rack. She stood leaning against the edge of the sink, her sleek head bowed in thought.

It can't be, she said, clenching her fists. I won't believe it. I can't have wasted four years of my life on a shadow.

Then she went to bed and slept badly.

The American tour ended without any further telephone conversations with Laura across the Atlantic. Catherine called on two occasions: the first time she was told she was too early, that 'the show' was still going on in the ballroom. She let that night go by because she supposed Laura would be too tired to want to talk. The second time she called the receptionist said that the Lindhams were entertaining a party of guests in the dining-room – did she wish to have Mrs Lindham called out to the phone? She declined, simply leaving a message asking Laura to call if she could. But the tour then reached New York and Laura never had time.

The return was at the end of November on a flight that landed in the early hours of a Sunday morning. Catherine once again roused herself from her bed long before the rest of the world was stirring and went to the airport to greet them. But Toby had arranged for a limousine to whisk them straight from Heathrow to their home in Warwickshire. She had only a few minutes with her sister, who looked pale and fatigued – but who wouldn't, on a cold and dark winter morning after an all-night flight from New York?

'I'll ring you when you've had a night's sleep,' she said, giving her a gentle hug.

Laura nodded. Toby came back from organising the stowing of their luggage. They got into the car and were driven away.

She rang two days later. Toby answered the phone. 'Oh, Cath, nice to hear you. How are you?'

'I'm fine, I'm ringing from the office. Can I speak to Laura?'

'Well, she's having a nap. Better leave it to another time, eh?'

'A nap? In the middle of the day?'

'Well, she's a bit tired after our trip, you know. Just fatigue, she needs a few days to recharge her batteries. No wonder, you know – it was a huge success! And what do you think? We got a contract for a book.'

'A book? What sort of book?' Catherine asked in surprise. 'Another "how to be healthy" thing?'

'No, no, this should be quite a winner. It's about how she does the healing bit. Her special gift, how she first realised she had it, all that sort of thing.'

'You're not serious?'

'Of course I am,' he said, annoyed. 'Let me tell you, there are big bucks in this! The publisher wants her to do a publicity tour when the book comes out, TV stations all across America – you know they've got television on tap there, not like here in Britain where everybody praises Auntie BBC and looks down on the commercial boys.'

'Toby, never mind about commercial TV. Does Laura want to write a book?'

'Of course she does, what a silly question. Spread the word, you see – let everybody know about her message—'

'And what is her message, exactly?' She knew she sounded grim, but she couldn't help it.

'That she's been sent into the world to bring solace and relief to sufferers – the publisher thinks we should have that on the book blurb.'

'You make her sound like some sort of angel from heaven—'

'Well, if seeing her like that is a help to people, why not?'

Catherine couldn't trust herself to speak. She muttered, 'I'll ring again,' and put the phone down.

For the rest of the day his words tormented her. She believed the book would prove to be a distortion of Laura's personality. To paint around her a sort of supernatural aura was wrong. Her sister was a normal, ordinary woman – apart from the gift of healing. She had no guiding spirit, no message from heaven – she made mistakes, suffered disappointments, just like the rest of humanity.

When at last she had a conversation with Laura, she learned that her sister was coming to London in two days' time. 'I'm going to start looking for a house,' she announced. 'Toby thinks it's time we made the move.'

'Well, that will be lovely,' Catherine responded. 'We'll be able to see each other a lot oftener.'

'Yes, that would be nice.' Laura's voice had a listless quality.
'Are you feeling all right?'
'Oh yes, fine, thanks. I'll drop in on you at the flat, shall I? In the evening, say about seven.'
'I'll make us a meal, like the old days,' Catherine promised. 'A great big risotto with lots of mushrooms and almonds – how about that?'
'Yes, lovely.'
Catherine took a lot of trouble over the preparations. She wanted to give her sister a warm, loving, welcome home. When she opened the door to her on that bleak November evening, she saw a silhouette against the porch light, an impression of slightness and chic. When she ushered her up into the warmth and light of the living-room she found a new Laura.
She had lost weight. Her hair had been restyled into a fringe that brushed her forehead and changed the contours of her face. Her make-up was expertly done, with much emphasis on the eyes to make her look serious, almost enigmatic. Her coat was a light green wool by Courrèges, her shoes were lightweight and had heels of the kind now fashionable, thin and spiky. When she took off her coat she was revealed in a white shift dress that looked as if it might have come from some American high-fashion house.
'Good heavens, you look *gorgeous*!' cried Catherine.
'Yes, this is the new me,' her sister said. 'It's what they call a "make-over" in the States.'
'When did this happen?'
'Well, when we arrived the publicity people over there took one look at me and decided I was a mess—'
'Oh, Laura, they didn't say—'
'No, no, nothing was actually said but you could see it in their eyes. So I was taken to a hair stylist and a wardrobe adviser and a beautician, and this is the result, which is a lot more work to put together every morning than the old Laura, but of course as Toby says, it's all for the good of the cause.'
She sat down and accepted a drink – Catherine had provided sherry as a reminder of the old days in Mitre Lane. Something in the way she folded into the corner of the couch made Catherine think she was very tired.
'Are you recovering from that trip?' she inquired. 'I got quite worried about you, love.'
'Oh yes, I'm fine. Still a bit jet-lagged, in a way. But, you know, this book that I'm supposed to write . . . there's a deadline for it, and I haven't the least idea how to go about it, Cath.'

Catherine sipped her drink. After a moment she said, 'What's the deadline?'

'Next June – six months.'

'Good heavens, that's not long!'

'Well, neither will the book be, if you think about it. I mean, I haven't lived all that long so I haven't got a whole lifetime to report. I'm just supposed to tell the readers about my . . . my gift.'

There was a pause. Then Laura burst out with, 'How can I tell them about it? I don't understand it myself!'

'No,' agreed Catherine. 'I don't think it's easy to understand. And perhaps it's not possible to explain it. So wouldn't it be better if you withdrew from the project?'

'We can't do that. We've signed a contract, accepted an advance—'

'You could return the money—'

'No, Toby wants to use that as a deposit on the London house—'

'Oh, for Pete's sake, Laura – do you want a London house? Do you want to write a book? Just say no to it all.'

'No . . . you don't understand . . . Toby's plans—'

'To the devil with Toby's plans! It's you that's important! If you want to know, sweetheart, underneath all this styling and fashion-plate look I don't think you're well – you've lost weight, you look fine-drawn – and half the time when I tried to contact you in the States you were either under the weather or hard at work. It's too much for you.'

Laura was shaking her head at first, negating her sister's challenge. But when Catherine fell silent she looked down, unable to protest any more. She said something in a whisper.

'What?' Catherine said, leaning forward in her chair. 'What did you say?'

'I lost my baby,' Laura whispered.

'Laura!' Catherine was on her knees by the couch, putting hands either side of her sister's face so as to look into her eyes. 'You had a miscarriage?'

'Yes. While we were in Philadelphia. I was in hospital overnight, the doctor said there was no need to worry, there was nothing wrong, things often go amiss with a first baby and I was only *just* three months, you know, but I felt so bad about it, Cath, so sad, I just couldn't seem to get over it, even though I was going through the motions of being all right again, and people seemed not to find me different and I suppose I wasn't, really, but something's changed, I can't explain it, something's been altered in my life . . .'

'Oh, my poor love, poor Laura!' cried Catherine, sitting on the couch beside her and taking her in her arms. 'Poor girl, all alone in a strange country—'

'I wasn't alone, Toby was there, he was wonderful, so kind and understanding, he took on all the publicity side, made two or three television appearances when I felt too tired, spoke longer at the public meetings so that I didn't have to say so much, and so it was all right really, although I couldn't seem to pull myself together properly.' She sighed and leaned against Catherine. 'I'm a mess, aren't I?'

'Nothing of the kind. You've just been pushed into doing too much, that's all. What you need is lots of rest, and time to recover.' She didn't add that she thought Toby ought not to be asking her to look for a house. She'd learned by experience that criticising Toby was a bad move.

Instead she said, 'You're much too thin. Now drink up your sherry and we'll have dinner. You've got to eat up your share of this risotto or I'll be finishing it up for days.'

She reached for her own drink and sat back in the sofa, watching her sister finish hers. Laura put the narrow glass on the coffee table, then sat with her hands empty in her lap. Something in her attitude called forth all Catherine's instinctive concern.

'There can be another baby, dear,' she said gently. 'I know it must be terrible, a loss like that, but there's still plenty of time to try again and—'

'There's something else.'

Their eyes met. The pain and fear in Laura's gaze almost terrified her sister.

'Tell me,' she urged.

'I think I'm losing the gift, Catherine.'

Chapter Fifteen

For almost half an hour Laura tried to tell Catherine what she meant, her voice often choked by the tears that welled up. At last, mascara streaked, lipstick worn away, she sat back exhausted to sip the brandy her sister brought her.

'It's a strange thing,' she said in a firmer tone. 'Often at first I wanted to be rid of it, I didn't understand it so it frightened me, I'd have given anything not to have had to deal with it, yet now . . . now that it's beginning to leave me, I feel . . . scared, lost. Because you see after a while it became second nature to me, like being able to see or to hear, I just knew it was there, waiting to be called on, and it never failed, never. Ever since that first time, on the esplanade, when Desmond had his attack, I've known it was there, a sort of friendly force, unseen, unmeasurable, but dependable. To think it might fail me . . .' She faltered into momentary silence. 'Does this make any sense to you, Cath?'

Catherine nodded, unwilling to halt the flow of confidence. 'Go on.'

'The first time I reached out and found nothing . . . it was just before we left for the States. I had a patient with eczema. A girl, about sixteen, very distressed because she couldn't go swimming, her shoulders and upper arms were covered with sores and scars, she felt she had to wear long-sleeved dresses and blouses. After I'd examined her I put my hands over her shoulders as I always do, close but not touching, and I made smoothing motions. And . . . and . . . nothing happened. It was like a power failure. The light didn't come on, the fan didn't work – do you see what I mean, Cath? Do you? There was no current of healing, no sense of helping or improving, no response in my fingertips, no sensation of warmth in my spine or weighing on my shoulder-blades . . . nothing, just nothing . . .'

'So what did you do?'

'I waited. I was sure it would come. But minutes went by. Then I thought perhaps if I broke off and tried again, so I stopped and had some tea brought in and we chatted a bit and then I asked her to lie down again and I tried. And it was just the same. Nothing.' Laura wiped new tears from her lashes with her knuckle. 'She was with me for almost an hour. Do you remember, Cath, during the war, if there was an air raid, the radio would go down to a whisper just when we wanted to listen to a programme in the evening, because the transmitter had been powered down? It was like that. Almost at the end there was this little whisper like the voices that used to come from the radio – a faint echo of what used to come in full force when I summoned it. I told my patient I thought she'd need further treatment and to come back in a week, and when she came everything was all right, I was able to help her, but then during that same week I had an elderly man with terrible arthritic pains in his feet and when I waited for the flow of power it just didn't come. Worse this time, we waited and chatted and I tried again, but it was a blank, a total blank. I had to tell him I couldn't help and I told him I was going abroad but to come back at the end of November, but I checked and he never made an appointment so I suppose he just lost faith in me and I don't blame him because I failed him, I just totally failed him.'

'Laura, don't blame yourself—'

'Who else should I blame?' Laura flashed back, with startling anger. 'It's my gift, I ought to know how to guard and nourish it . . .'

'But you've never had to "guard" it, love. You were born with it, it just grew stronger and now perhaps it's grown weaker. Perhaps it ebbs and flows, like a tide.'

'In the States,' Laura resumed, urged on by a desperate need to share her troubles, 'the same thing happened on two occasions. There was a third case but the man was so determined I was going to cure him that he convinced himself he was better. That's happened before, people who go in for something like self-hypnosis, and that can help . . . but this time I knew it wouldn't. He went off all smiles and gratitude . . . but I knew . . . I knew, Cath, nothing happened, and in a day or two when he got over his self-delusion the pain would be back and he'd be taking aspirin tablets by the score. I'm expecting to hear from him, I dread it, he'll write and tell me I'm a fraud, and I am, Cath, I am!'

'No, no, dear, you mustn't say it or even think it. You've had – what? – half a dozen failures—'

'The worst one was when I lost the baby.'

'What?' exclaimed Catherine in horror.

'If it means anything, surely I ought to have known that the baby was in trouble? I should have sensed it, the healing power should have protected us, if I couldn't summon it up at a time like that what right have I to say I have the gift of healing? To me that was the proof. Whoever, whatever gave me this gift is taking it away again—'

'No, no, it's just because you've been under stress, over-tired—'

'It's because I used it for gain,' Laura said bleakly. 'It was a *gift*, meant to be passed on to others. I let it become a way of earning money and this is my punishment—'

'Nobody's punishing you, sweetheart, you've done nothing wrong. All that's happened is that you haven't been strong enough to—'

'Now you've put your finger on it. I've been weak, I've allowed things to be done because I love Toby and let him make decisions for me—'

'Have you told Toby about this?'

'Oh no, of course not! I'd never do anything to hurt him, and if I told him how things have turned out he'd feel so guilty! He'd think it was his fault—'

'Well, isn't it?' said Catherine, greatly daring.

'No, it's mine, because of course how could he understand unless I explained to him that this wasn't a thing you could use to earn a living, it's a thing that you have to pass on, in the same way as you give friendship to friends and love to your family. And now of course I've let him get trapped in all these contracts and things, and there's no way to back out without causing him endless worry, and the only thing I have to hope for is that if I put my whole heart into being open to the power it will come back in the way it used to, and as to the money, of course we have to take it because otherwise we can't meet our commitments, but I've been trying to make sure we don't take on anything else that might seem like money-grabbing, and once we move to London I'll get rid of the old system of booking patients at the clinic and start a new one to ensure that as many as possible are treated free of charge—'

Catherine broke in on the spate of self-blame. 'Laura, don't punish yourself. Don't take on a load that will be too much.'

'It's not punishment, it's restitution.' She finished the brandy, found a handkerchief, wiped her eyes, blew her nose, and tried to look determined. 'I'm going to try to get back to how it used to be. I know it's going to be hard for Toby because he goes in for what's called "forward-planning" and he's got things scheduled months and months ahead, but if I explain to him why I'm trying to cut down on anything that seems too commercial I know he'll agree even if he doesn't quite understand.'

Catherine could only hope devoutly that this would be so. While Laura went to wash her face and tidy up, she put the food on the table. The talk returned to Laura's plight, Catherine trying to reassure her without knowing whether she was doing any good – for she'd never understood this strange gift from the outset. But she kept saying that she was sure everything would be all right if Laura would only rest and relax, and that she wasn't to worry if it took a while.

She was reluctant to let her sister leave. 'Why don't you spend the night here?' she said. 'I've a spare room—'

'No, no, all my make-up and stuff is at the hotel and I've got strict instructions to use it every day and be a "new woman" – I mustn't go back to being the old Laura with a flick of powder on my nose—'

'Why not?' Catherine interrupted. 'Everybody seemed to like the old Laura!'

'Do you think so? Well, things change, you know, Toby explained to me that when I give a talk, audiences these days expect to see someone a bit impressive, not a grown-up schoolgirl in a blouse and skirt. And all those American experts must know what they're talking about because you know yourself, Cath, they practically invented PR, so I better do what I'm told and keep up the good work. Besides, I have to go and see an estate agent first thing – I couldn't turn up in a Saks Fifth Avenue dress and no lipstick!'

In this breathless jumble there was something of her old gentle humour, so Catherine let her go with less apprehension. But next morning as she herself sat down before her mirror to prepare for the office day, she thought of Laura recreating herself: 'a new woman'. Perhaps the old Laura would never have lost touch with her special power. Perhaps the new Laura lacked something that the old Laura had.

Christmas was almost upon them. Fenner Chelburne blankly refused to attend the staff party at Velton's. 'Why the devil should I?' he demanded, with that faint curl of discontent on his lips. 'I don't really know anybody there except Thelma and I hate having to hobnob with strangers.'

'Please come, Fenn. We needn't stay long.'

'London's awful at Christmas. All those carols over public address systems and tatty tinsel strung up in Tube stations. No, I think I'll take myself off somewhere.'

'Take yourself off?' said Catherine, startled. 'Where, for heaven's sake?'

He shrugged. 'Might hop across to Paris, look at the paintings in the Louvre.' He was watching her, heavy lids veiling his ice-blue eyes.

She waited for him to add, 'You come too.' It would have been difficult, but she might have managed extra time off.

Instead he said, 'I might have gone by next weekend, so don't drive down. It's not settled yet. It depends.'

Depends on what, she wondered. Later, she mentioned to Thelma that Fenn wouldn't be at the party because he was going to Paris. Thelma said, 'Why don't you take time off and go too?'

'I'm not invited.'

Thelma frowned at the tone. 'What on earth does that mean?'

'I think . . . I rather think Fenn's already got a companion.'

'What makes you think so?' She was all agog.

'He said something about the dates "depending". Since he's absolutely free to do what he pleases, I can only presume the plan depends on someone else's arrangements.'

'Who is it, do you suppose?'

Catherine sighed. 'Your suggestion was one of the villagers, I seem to recall. Though who, I can't imagine, because in the first place he's never seemed on good terms with any of them and in the second place all the women are housewifely types more interested in growing vegetables than having an affair.'

Thelma studied her. 'You're taking it very calmly?'

And that was true. Apart from being surprised at his decision to go abroad, and a sense of hurt at being excluded, Catherine had accepted the situation without a protest. Later, back in London again, she'd told herself that if she loved him deeply she'd have been weeping and wailing at his attitude.

'We're drifting apart,' she said to her friend. 'I suppose it had to happen. He's artistic, I'm practical, we're just too different. And those things you said to me, before the fashion show . . . Well, it made me stand back and look at the relationship. To tell the truth—' But she broke off.

'What, Cathie? What's the truth?'

'I've been thinking that perhaps I made most of the running in the first place. I found him so intriguing, I was so *thrilled* with him because he was so different, so determined to do what he wanted to do . . . Well, perhaps I built more into it than was really there.'

Thelma took her hand. 'Listen, dear, we're all looking for

something to make our life complete. It leads us astray sometimes, that longing not to be alone any more.'

'But we can't afford to make many blunders, Thelma,' she murmured, thinking of how she had lost Malcolm.

'We learn from them, my sweet. We learn.'

Christmas came, the firm's staff party was a great success. Catherine drove home to Hulmesley to cook Christmas dinner for her father, his chess-playing neighbour, Ernest Goode, and his wife. They spent Christmas day following the quiet tradition of listening to the Royal broadcast and opening presents from under the tree. On Boxing Day, Gerald and Catherine were invited to the Colvilles', where they were joined by Laura and Toby and others of the Colville set. It was a pleasant event, a buffet lunch that merged into an afternoon of conversation and music and dancing.

'Laura's found us a house,' Toby announced. 'I dashed down to London to get a glimpse of it last Tuesday and I must say she's done well, haven't you, treasure?'

Gerald Mertagen sighed. Catherine had been settled in London for a long time and now Laura, after moving out from Norfolk in stages, was going to live there as well. He told himself that it happened in every family, the children left the nest and the parent-birds had to make the best of it.

Catherine, on the contrary, was pleased. It meant she would be able to see her sister much more often.

So it proved. The house was in Pimlico, not far from Victoria Station: 'Very convenient for people who have to make a train journey to come to the clinic,' Toby observed. It was in a little cul-de-sac off the main road. Newly decorated, it had a welcoming aspect. The clinic was to be in the rooms on the ground floor: the living accommodation, quite capacious and handsome, was above. True to her intention, Laura had brought in a new system of booking patients. Toby resisted at first: 'Why should we change? It worked well in Coventry.'

'I just think we should put money a long way behind the chance to do some good,' Laura said.

'But what about upkeep? This place won't stay immaculate if we don't have a housekeeper, cleaning services, and then we've got to advertise the new address—'

'When Laura writes the book,' Catherine mused aloud, 'and has to set out a table of charges – makes it sound a bit mercenary, don't you think?'

Toby hesitated. His fresh complexion took on a ruddier hue.

'Being sensible about money isn't being mercenary. *One* of us has got to keep a grip on that sort of thing.'

'The health paperbacks and the herbal remedies bring in a fair amount, don't they?'

'Well, yes, but—'

'Try it my way, dear,' urged Laura.

Toby gave in, but Catherine was sure he was determined to go back to a set fee for a consultation as soon as he could. Once the book was published without mention of money, he would be free to make changes.

The book. Laura was in torment over it. 'I don't know if what I'm saying is right,' she confided to her sister. 'It's so difficult to put into words, when Toby reads it over he says it's all too vague, but I don't know how else to express it, you know I've never been clever with words, Cath.' In her eyes there was an appeal: Help me.

Catherine would have offered, but she wasn't sure how Toby would take it. And perhaps if she was left for a while to struggle, Laura would find a way to put down what she needed to say.

Catherine herself was busy. Apart from her work at Velton's, her design agency was growing important. She had been asked by an Australian manufacturer to find British fabrics for a range of summer dresses. She had obtained approval for the work of the first three designers and was now looking for the fourth and last.

She thought Fenner Chelburne would fit the bill excellently. But the situation between them was a little awkward now. Since Christmas she had been down to Somerset only once, and though the visit had been quite normal – calm, friendly, civilised – they had not been lovers. In a way she'd been glad. She felt she couldn't any longer give herself wholeheartedly to Fenn, was glad he didn't demand it.

But she needed a fourth designer and Fenn seemed just right. Since he'd always refused to have a telephone installed, she sent a postcard saying she'd be there at the weekend and having arranged to have Saturday off, drove down on the Friday evening.

The first thing that struck her was that there was no light in the cottage. She opened the door with her key, stepped into the tiny hall, and called out: 'Fenn? You there?'

Apparently he'd gone out. She switched on the light. She set down her overnight bag, then walked into the living-room.

No light there – not even the glow from the log fire that usually burned in winter. She went on into the kitchen. It felt chilly. She switched on a light, went to the new Swedish stove, laid her hand on it. Only barely warm. It had been allowed to go out, but that must have been a day or so ago.

Alarmed now, she ran upstairs, switching on lights as she went. The studio was always cold, but this evening it was icy, as if not even the lamps had been on.

And it was empty.

There were no canvases stacked against the walls. No cartridge paper on the table, no water-colours laid out for use, no paint-palette with oils mixed, no box of pencils, no brushes in their jar, no T-square, no sketches finished or unfinished. Only the furniture, the table with its swivel chair and the heavy lamps.

Hot and cold by turns, Catherine stared about her. Then she darted from the room and into the bedroom. She opened the wardrobe. A dozen empty hangers swayed. Drawing back in dismay, she stared at them. Then she opened the top drawer of the tallboy. Empty.

She stood there, stunned.

A tapping at the house door roused her. She went downstairs. Through the glass panel of the door she could discern a heavy figure standing on the pavement outside. She opened the door.

'Ah . . . missy . . . Thought it might be you. Could I have a word?'

The last thing she wanted was to have to talk to Mr Hodge, Fenn's next door neighbour. An ex-sergeant-major of the Artillery, he had thoroughly disapproved of them – of Fenn for his stand-offish manner, of Catherine for being no better than she ought to be. In all the visits she'd made to the hamlet she'd scarcely ever had a civil word from him.

'What is it about, Mr Hodge?'

'It's about this smell of burning, missy. I mean to say, it's a bit much, isn't it?'

Now that he mentioned it, she could smell it. A faint, greasy odour, not from within the cottage but from somewhere outside.

'What is it?' she asked.

'What is it? It's your bonfire, that's what it is. And if you're here to finish clearing out, I'd ask you to be so kind as not to burn anything else. Smouldered for two days, that has, and the smell's only just beginning to go. Mrs Losely on my other side, she's complained to me about it and I said to her, I can't do anything, it's *him*! But seeing he's gone and you're here, perhaps you'll be so good as to put some water on it and finish it.'

'Yes,' Catherine said. She was too much at a loss to say anything more.

'Will you be burning anything else?'

'No.'

'Well, see you don't.' With that he turned and trudged to his own door, where he went in without a backward glance.

Catherine went back through the cottage and out to the long back garden. In the dark she made her way gingerly towards the end fence. About three-quarters of the way along she could discern a faint warmth. She stopped. The smell was stronger here. In the starlight she could make out a mound on the surface of the soil.

She drew in a breath. Burned paint.

For a long moment she stood there, perplexed and apprehensive.

She was to pour water on it to put it out completely. She felt her way indoors, filled a pail under the tap, found a torch in the kitchen drawer, and went back outdoors.

The beam from the torch swayed about as she hauled the heavy pail to the site of the bonfire. Once there, she set down her burden and played the light over the remains.

Charred rectangles and squares. A pile of ash. Some pieces of browned fabric blown a few feet away by the wind. She stopped to examine them. Canvas crusted and made stiff by fire.

She stood up. Understanding struck her like a backhanded blow.

Fenn had burned all his paintings.

All those canvases that had stood in the studio, face to the wall. All those paintings she'd never been allowed to see, and now never would, because here they were, a pile of ashes.

The studio upstairs was empty. His clothes had vanished from the bedroom. The fire was out, the range untended.

Fenn had gone.

She turned to hurry indoors again. A note – in such circumstances there was always a note. Propped on the mantelpiece, or leaning against a vase – always a note.

But though she looked everywhere she found nothing. Fenn had gone, without a word, without an explanation. She hadn't even been worth a line of writing to express regret.

For perhaps half an hour she moved about the house, picking things up and putting them down, convinced she must find some message if only she persisted. But there was nothing to find.

Then anger seized her. She became still, breathed deeply, clenched her fists at her side.

All right. So it was over.

She went out to the garden, picked up the pail of water, and emptied it all over the remains of the bonfire. A cloud of ash, a little smoke, a faint spluttering, a rancid smell of wet cinders. Then the sound died, the odour lessened.

She threw down the pail, stalked back indoors, picked up her overnight case and her handbag from the hall, and walked out, not even bothering to switch off the lights or lock the door.

Chapter Sixteen

She spent the night at the inn in Bridgwater, slept badly, woke late, and breakfasted on tea and toast. Before starting out for London she rang Thelma Axworth at her office. Velton's opened till one on Saturdays.

'Will you be at home this afternoon, Thelma?'

'Why, yes, I expect so.'

'Can I come and talk to you?'

'I thought you were in Somerset?'

'I am—'

'But not at the cottage because there's no phone there. What's happened?'

'Fenn's gone.'

'Gone? To Paris?'

'I've no idea.'

'Cathie!' A sharp intake of breath. 'Come as soon as you like.'

From the country she drove straight to Thelma's splendid flat in Regent's Park. Her friend was on watch for her and despite the cold came hurrying downstairs and out into the January drizzle to welcome her. A late lunch was awaiting her on a tray, hot soup and crisp rolls, a toasted sandwich and plenty of fresh coffee.

Thelma's easygoing husband had been sent off to spend an afternoon with nearby friends. The two women settled down by the fire in the drawing-room.

'Now tell me,' Thelma commanded.

Catherine described what she'd found at the cottage. 'He's gone for good,' she ended. 'The burning of his work tells me so.'

'Why on earth did he do that?'

'End of an era. He's going on to something else.'

'Well, it's outrageous.' Thelma's plump features were rosy with indignation. 'Not even a note!'

'I think the message was clear enough without a note.'

'But no goodbye – no words of regret – and after all you've done for him!'

Catherine half-nodded, half-shook her head. 'I don't pretend to understand him. I don't think I ever did. The thing is, Thelma, what ought I to do now?'

'Forget the brute and get on with your life.'

'Yes, but more immediately – I mean about the cottage – I've left some of my things there,' she recalled, able at last to think a little less chaotically. 'Some books, a hairbrush and stuff like that.'

'I'll tell you what we'll do. We'll go down tomorrow and pick up your things. Then we'll put the place up for sale.'

'It doesn't belong to me, Thelma. Fenn rented it.'

'So much the better – it'll be easier to be shot of it.'

'Tomorrow's Sunday. Didn't you have anything planned?'

'Only a visit to some boring people for brunch – I'm glad of the excuse to cancel.' She saw Catherine looking doubtful but surged on: 'I'm a great believer in prompt action so I think we should go tomorrow and be done with it. And dearie, I want you to stay overnight with me—'

'Oh no, I—'

'I don't want you all alone in your flat tonight. You'll stay here, I'll cook us a special dinner, we'll open a bottle of Côte de Beaune, and Bob can roast some chestnuts for us afterwards.'

No use to protest, Thelma had made up her mind. And truth to tell, Catherine was glad not to have to face the solitude of her flat that night.

In the morning they set off in Thelma's big, comfortable and capacious Mercedes. Traffic on a winter Sunday was very light so they made good time, arriving at the cottage before lunch.

As Thelma drew up in the narrow main street, Mr Hodge was out of his door. 'Here!' he bellowed. 'What d'you think you're up to, leaving all them lights blazing and the door wide open all night?'

Catherine didn't even remember the omission. 'I'm sorry, Mr Hodge—'

'I switched everything off and shut the door, but I hadn't got a key, now had I, so I couldn't lock up. Served you right if you'd been robbed of every stick.'

'That was very kind of you, Mr Hodge—'

'And I sent for—'

As he spoke the door of Fenn's cottage opened and a tubby, middle-aged man in a checked tweed jacket and twill trousers came out. 'Miss Er . . . ?' he queried.

'Mertagen.'

'Ah yes, Mertagen, of course. I'm Abel Strood, from Brookheath and Chisholm – the house agents?'

'Oh yes.' They shook hands. She was a little surprised that he thought it important enough to come out on a Sunday. She saw him glance at Thelma. 'A friend of mine, Mrs Axworth.'

He nodded a greeting, then got down to business. 'Your neighbour, Mr Hodge—'

'Yes, he just told me. I'm afraid I don't remember how I left things on Friday evening.'

'All's well, I believe – the place looks neat, undisturbed. Shall we go in?'

He led the way, Thelma bringing up the rear and closing the door firmly in the face of Mr Hodge's curiosity.

'I . . . er . . . gathered from Mr Hodge that Mr Chelburne packed up and left?' remarked Strood, turning to face Catherine in the tiny hall.

'It seems so.'

'Yes.' A pause. Mr Strood clearly expected something from Catherine. She had nothing to offer. 'It gives me reason to think this departure is . . . er . . . final.'

'Yes, I get the same impression.'

Strood seemed to follow his own train of thought for a moment but came back to the point. 'The tenancy . . .'

'I know, the cottage is rented in Mr Chelburne's name. I'll be packed up and gone in a few minutes.'

'No, no, no hurry!' exclaimed Strood. 'Although, in fact, Mr Chelburne's quarterly rent *is* due.'

'It is?'

'Quarterly in advance, you know. He generally comes to the office to pay in the last week of the quarter that's ending. This time, though, he didn't. And though a couple of weeks had gone by he's – he *was* in general so regular that we had no anxiety. But it seems he . . . er . . . knew he was leaving.'

'Not spur of the moment, you mean,' Thelma put in. 'It was planned.'

'I have other reasons to think so . . . Well, perhaps that's not germane. The point is, Miss Mertagen, we feel it's only good manners to make any suitable arrangement with you. In fact, I would have written to you or phoned, if we hadn't met on the doorstep like this. I can't help being aware, you know, that it was your money that paid for the improvements to the cottage—'

'How on earth—?'

'Oh well, the builders you employed were local men, word got around that it was your name on all the cheques. It is so, isn't it

– you put in the new stove and improved the bathroom and so on? And most of the furniture is yours?'

'Yes, that's true.'

'In view of that . . . I mean, you clearly have an interest in the place. If you would like the tenancy transferred to your name, we would have no objection—'

'No!' exclaimed Catherine. 'I never want to see the place again as long as I live.'

'Er . . . I see . . . yes, understandable, perhaps.'

'If you'll excuse me,' she hurried on, 'I just have a few things to collect.'

'Certainly, certainly.'

Catherine swept through the cottage like a winter wind, snatching up her belongings to throw them into a cardboard carton she found in the kitchen cupboard. Within ten minutes all that had been hers was ready to be taken away. She went back downstairs to find that Thelma and Strood had removed themselves to the living-room and were standing in deep conversation.

She thought they looked up rather guiltily as she joined them. But that was probably paranoia on her part – she felt the whole village must be talking about her.

The estate agent took the carton to carry it to the Mercedes. Thelma got in and opened the boot; he stowed the box, then came to shake hands in farewell. 'It's probable that we'll put the cottage up for sale. In that case, some part of the price will be derived from the furniture and fittings you're leaving. We might come to an agreement about how much you should benefit from the sale—'

'No, thank you, keep the stuff, or pull it all out and sell it, I don't care. I'm not connected with this place any more, Mr Strood.'

'Very well, Miss Mertagen. Mrs Axworth.' He raised his hand to wave them goodbye. The Mercedes rolled away, out of the village and in a moment on to an open country road.

They drove for about five minutes in silence, Thelma looking out for signposts to tell her where to turn so as to get back on the London road. 'How do you feel?' she inquired once that was accomplished.

'Angry,' Catherine said. 'Baffled.'

'Would you like an explanation?'

'Of what?' she asked in surprise.

'Of Fenn's behaviour.'

'You think *you* know why he left?'

'I'm sure I know why he left. I think I know why he didn't leave any message.'

'But you can't possibly—'

'That estate agent gave me the explanation.'

'Strood?'

'Yes.'

'But how can *he*—'

'You didn't notice, I suppose, but he said something about having reasons to expect Fenn's vanishing act. He's quite closely involved, strange to say.'

'But that's impossible—'

'Look, we'll be back in Bridgwater in a minute. What say we stop there for a bite to eat and I'll tell you what I've found out.'

'Tell me now.'

'It'll go better with a drink in our hands,' Thelma replied with a sigh, and gave her attention to her driving.

In less than five minutes she had found a decent-looking place on the outskirts of the town, advertising home-cooked food and local ale. They went into a big entrance hall with stags' heads and a log fire. The locals clearly liked the place because they were sitting around in tweedy groups, sipping pre-lunch drinks. The two strangers caused some slight but friendly interest as they were ushered on into a wainscoted restaurant.

Thelma, taking charge, ordered a bottle of Burgundy and the table d'hôte. The wine came almost at once, was opened, tasted and pronounced passable. The waiter filled their glasses.

'Now,' said Catherine as he left.

'Fenn didn't leave without a companion,' Thelma began.

'Well, I'd guessed that. I suppose it was the woman he went to Paris with.'

Thelma took a sustaining draught from her glass. She set it down and reached a hand across the table to Catherine. 'It wasn't a woman,' she said.

'I beg your pardon?' Catherine genuinely thought she had misheard.

'Mr Strood said Fenn went with the son of his employer, Martin Brookheath—'

'No!'

'Catherine, it's true. It all came out last week. The whole town is talking about it, Strood said. Martin Brookheath was supposed to be learning the estate agency business, worked in the office. That's how he met Fenn.'

'Martin Brookheath.' Catherine forced her lips to form the words. 'How old is he?'

'Just turned twenty-one before Christmas, it seems. He had some money coming to him from a legacy from his mother, and inherited on his birthday in November. He used some of the money to take a trip to Paris—'

'Paris?'

'To Paris. The estate agent's office was closed for quite a long holiday, going from Christmas to New Year. Mr Strood said he'd been restless and unsettled ever since then.'

'I can't seem to take this in, Thelma—'

'I know, dear, I know. Shall I stop? There isn't much more, really.'

'Tell me the rest,' Catherine said in an unsteady voice.

'Martin Brookheath told his father last week that he was throwing up the estate agency job and going abroad to live. To be an artist, he said. It seems he's always had ambitions in that direction but his father "talked sense" to him. But once he got his mother's legacy he was independent and of age, so Mr Brookheath couldn't stop him. They had a frightful row in the office, shouting and yelling – our Mr Strood couldn't help but hear, his desk is just outside Mr Brookheath's door.'

'You mean he was eavesdropping.'

'Not intentionally – well, perhaps he was. If you have scruples about that, perhaps I shouldn't say any more.'

'Don't play games, Thelma. Tell me.'

'He heard Mr Brookheath shout that he wasn't going to let his dead wife's money be used to let his son live in sin. He said he would speak to the lawyer and have it stopped. Martin faced him out – quite brave, I gather, for his dad's a bit of a war horse. Anyway, Strood heard him say that nothing anyone could do could prevent him from going to Greece with Fenn. So that's how Strood knows.'

The waiter came with their soup. Both women sat silent until he had gone. Then Catherine said, struggling for the power of speech, 'You're telling me that the man who's been my lover for over four years is . . . is . . .'

'Yes, Cathie.'

'But that can't be true!' she cried, throwing out a hand to ward off the thought. 'Fenn was a married man—'

'Married? You never told me that!'

'There was no reason to. It wasn't an issue between Fenn and me.'

'But you're not the sort who'd break up a marriage—'

'The marriage was broken up long ago. I only got vague hints. I think they married while they were both still students and as far as I could gather it was the girl who walked out.'

'Mm . . .' murmured Thelma. 'Perhaps now we know why.'

'But Thelma—! He and I – you know what I'm trying to say – How could he possibly have—'

'It's not as impossible as you seem to think, dear. You have to realise how hard society is on people of Fenn's persuasion. Look how Mr Brookheath reacted about his son. Other countries aren't so severe in their outlook, I believe, but here in Britain . . . Naturally it's something a man would try not to believe about himself. You know the phrase, "a natural bachelor" – we say that about men who never seem to want to marry and have a family. Who knows, perhaps they've had to make a hard choice, to live entirely alone because society won't let them have the partner they want.'

'I've never . . . I don't really follow . . .'

'Just recently, the social climate seems to have softened a bit. Look at all these boy pop stars jigging about on stage in their flowery shirts and tight trousers – some of them make no secret of their sexual outlook. And though it was a while ago, the Wolfenden Report brought the issue into the open—'

'I never read the Wolfenden Report—'

'Neither did I, only MPs and social workers would, I suppose. But it was discussed in the newspapers and there's been a change – it's beginning to be possible to talk about things like that.'

Catherine shook her head vigorously.

'No, love, I suppose you don't think it's possible to talk about it,' Thelma said with a soft kindness. 'But you're a country girl, really, aren't you? Living in the big city all my life as I have, associating with men of all categories . . . Well, it doesn't come as a shock to me.'

'You suspected, didn't you?' Catherine challenged. 'Why didn't you tell me?'

'Cathie, it's not the kind of thing you rush to say to a friend – "you're sleeping with a man who probably prefers boys"—'

'Oh, don't!'

'I'm sorry.' Thelma went red, and was flustered. 'But he's always been different . . . elusive, guarded. As he had to be, because the big masculine chaps can be awfully cruel about a thing like that.'

'And I was part of his protective armour, is that it? "Look, I'm normal, I've got a girlfriend"—'

'Don't judge too harshly, dear. Perhaps for most of his life he's been trying to be the kind of man that fits in with everyday life. He tried to settle down with a wife but that didn't work. He tried living alone and perhaps that was too arid, too desolate. And then you came along, and – don't take this wrong, my love – but you're the gamine type, slim and boyish; not aggressively female, but kindhearted, and eager to be a friend to him. He was tempted and I don't blame him.'

'I can't be so tolerant, Thelma. I've thrown away more than four years—'

'But you were always telling me – and yourself – that you didn't expect anything from him. Your instincts were hinting to you that it would never work. In the end Fenn found someone he could be happy with and he left. And my dear, he didn't leave you a note because he couldn't bring himself to tell you all this. At least I believe that's the reason.'

'I'll never forgive him,' said Catherine.

Thelma studied her, sighed, and picked up her soup spoon. 'This soup's cold,' she said when she'd tasted it. 'Waiter, take this away, please.'

Catherine began to laugh. 'Oh, right – let's get things into proportion! Here's a real tragedy, the soup's gone cold.'

'Now, sweetheart . . .' There was anxiety in the other woman's voice. 'Drink some wine.'

'I can't!' Catherine got up and hurried from the room.

Thelma Axworth stared after her without getting up. She stayed to finish her wine in an unhurried manner.

'Is your friend unwell?' the waiter inquired, eager to be helpful.

'She's not too grand,' acknowledged Thelma. She rose. 'Don't bring the main course until we get back.'

'Certainly, madam.'

She found Catherine in the ladies' room, on the bench in front of the dressing table, arms on its surface and her face buried in them. Another lunch guest was hovering over her, saying anxiously, 'Would you like a glass of water? Shall I get you an aspirin?'

'It's all right,' said Thelma. 'I'll deal with it.'

'Is she ill?'

'Had a shock.'

'Oh dear. Serious, is it?' said the kindly countrywoman.

'Well, it's serious at the moment,' said Thelma, and leaned over Catherine's bowed figure to signify this was no time for chat.

When Catherine at last looked up, she had to wipe away the tears before she could make out her friend's reflection in the dressing table mirror.

'Oh,' she groaned. 'What a fool . . .'

'Nothing of the sort. A good cry has probably done you the world of good.'

'Not that, Thelma. I've been a naive idiot. I never understood Fenn at all.'

Thelma patted her on the shoulder. She knew this stage had to be endured – the painful acknowledgement of a long, serious blunder. Catherine mopped her eyes with a tissue from the supply on the table. 'I look a wreck,' she remarked.

'Yes you do, but here's your handbag, tidy yourself up.'

'Thelma, he probably despised me all the time.'

'No.'

'But he certainly never loved me.'

'No. But he liked you.'

'What?'

'He liked you.'

'How can you possibly know that?'

'In the same way that I knew your friend Toby was up to no good. I've been bargaining and arguing with people for thirty years. If I hadn't learnt to read them, I wouldn't be so good at it.'

'You really think he . . . had some affection for me?'

'He liked you as much as he was capable of liking anyone. Look here, Catherine, we've just discovered that Fenn's run off with a new lover but that doesn't mean Martin Brookheath is going to find him any easier than you did! Fenner Chelburne is an awkward, selfish cuss and poor Martin had better have a lot of forbearance.'

Catherine began to chuckle, and this time with something like genuine amusement. 'You mean the path of true love isn't going to run smooth?'

'Why should we care? Let them dree their ain weird, as somebody – I think it's the Scots – are supposed to say.'

'What does it mean?'

'It means they have to live out their own destiny, I think. At any rate, we certainly can't live it for them. So how do you feel now, duckie?'

'Exhausted.'

'No doubt. If I remember rightly, you ate very little last night and nothing at all this morning. So let's go back and have some lunch.'

When they had re-settled themselves, the roast beef and vegetables were brought. Their waiter was eager to cosset them. Thelma chose her own helping and Catherine's too, paying no attention when her friend said it was too much. 'Eat!' she commanded, pointing at the plate.

Catherine picked up her knife and fork. She paused. 'Where did you say they were going? Greece?'

Thelma hesitated, perhaps considering whether she should tell any more. But Catherine seemed steady enough now, so she retailed what she knew.

'Mr Strood said Martin had been talking about Greece. I gather Fenn has always wanted to paint the Grecian landscape.'

'He has?' Was that what the canvases had been? Imaginary Greek islands? 'Go on, Thelma.'

'Mr Brookheath was roaring that he'd make sure his late wife's money stayed in a British bank. Martin retaliated by transferring the account out of the Bridgwater branch to some branch abroad – in Greece, presumably. That's all I know. Mr Brookheath hasn't made any move to find out where he is. He's washed his hands of his son, he says.'

'Poor man.'

'Yes, it's tough.'

'Poor boy, too. Life's going to be difficult for him.'

Thelma nodded agreement, her mouth full of roast potato. She was reflecting that if Catherine could find it in her heart to be sorry for the absconding pair, she had made the first step on the road to recovery.

Later, when they were on the road again, Thelma resumed her campaign to find another man for Catherine.

'The right one is waiting out there somewhere,' she insisted. 'All you have to do is go out there and find him.'

Catherine managed a smile but made no response. Inwardly she was saying, I had the right one once. But I let him go.

Chapter Seventeen

Thelma might reflect that Catherine had taken the first steps on the road to recovery but the steps were hesitant and the road was long.

The first phase entailed a great deal of self-blame and anger. How could she have been so stupid? What had happened to her judgement, her perception, her intuition, her intelligence?

She found herself inclined to dissolve into tears for no reason. She felt terribly alone. Since her earliest years she'd had someone to love and care for. First it had been Laura, but Laura had turned in the natural process of womanhood to the man who was to be her partner. Next had come Malcolm Sanders, with whom she'd expected to share the rest of her life. But that had never come about, and now Malcolm was married, a family man, pursuing his career without ever remembering her.

Lastly there was Fenn. Fenn had wanted something totally different from the love she was offering. So now there was no one to yearn over, to do things for, no sweet and dear friend, no soulmate.

And no one to turn to for comfort except Thelma. Laura, her former confidante, was ruled out. She was certain that if she told Laura what had happened, Laura somehow – perhaps inadvertently – would pass it on to Toby, and she couldn't bear the thought of his amusement when he heard how stupid she'd been.

The only other person who cared about her enough to want to listen was her father. But he would be so shocked when he heard about Fenn . . . No, it was better to keep it all to herself. When, in the normal course of events, her father inquired about him, she said simply that he'd gone abroad for a while to paint. She said this with so much studied calmness that he accepted it without question.

Thelma never intruded on her pain but was always there, ready to offer consolation or advice. But Catherine drew back from continually begging for sympathy. She felt she deserved it very little. She'd been a fool, and must learn to live with the fact.

The best antidote to her misery was work. She threw herself into it, extending her activities, putting into action plans she'd scribbled down in odd moments of the past. One of these was to hold high-fashion events at Velton's: she instituted shows in the leisure-wear department of the greatest verve and charm.

Some of the styles from her new stable of clothes designers verged so much on the bizarre that they got exceptional press coverage. This encouraged a new generation of clients to come to Velton's. The store had never been much of an attraction for youngsters but now the place rang with the chatter of teenagers. Catherine encouraged them by playing the Beatles and the Rolling Stones over the public address system in Leisure-wear. It raised some eyebrows among senior management but no one could deny that the young customers kept on rolling in.

Skiing was beginning to be within the financial reach of larger numbers. Ski and après-ski clothes became important. Catherine imported the Afghan look, with its bell-skirted coats of goatskin edged with coloured embroidery, its shaggy hats, its soft, knee-high boots. To wear under this the youngsters bought mohair loosely woven into gathered skirts, which had the look of sacking but cost a fortune.

The group of fabric designers for whom she acted as agent benefited from her addiction to hard work. She travelled the country, talking to manufacturers, showing portfolios of new work, negotiating contracts. She bought new fabrics for Velton's, for her own department and the evening wear salon.

But even all this wasn't enough to keep her from soul-searching. So she volunteered to help her sister with her book. She knew this had been hanging fire, chiefly because Toby took it upon himself to write in comments and alterations among the pages Laura had painstakingly pecked out with two fingers on a portable typewriter.

Laura was in a dilemma. She felt that in this one instance she knew better than Toby, but didn't want to hurt his feelings by telling him he was wrong. So the book remained in a roughed-out state because she couldn't nerve herself to make a ruling on it.

'Let me take it over and see what I can do with it,' Catherine suggested. And even Toby, who seldom liked to let control leave his hands, agreed thankfully.

Catherine read this first draft with interest. She truly wanted to know what her sister had to say about her gift. Not by any means to her surprise, Laura found it very difficult to explain.

'I was always able to heal small creatures. I was drawn to them in some way if they were hurt. Once the farm cat caught a bird and the bird escaped but was injured and I could hear it crying and fluttering so I found it among the raspberry canes where it had got caught and when I gathered it up it went quiet. People might say that that was because it was terrified but it wasn't, I could feel its heart beating quite steadily and it looked up at me with so much trust in its little eyes so I stroked its feathers and told it it was going to get better and not to be afraid. I'd have put it back into its nest if I could have found it but it was a thrush and you know they nest pretty high and the leaves were well out because I think this was May and I couldn't see it among the branches, the nest I mean, so I hung a shopping basket on the washline and put the thrush in that out of reach of the cat, and it just settled down there, the bird I mean, not the cat, and I knew it would get I better and it did.

In the midst of this flood of words Toby had scattered some red ink marks indicating he thought the sentences should be shorter, as well as inserting occasional words or phrases. He had amended 'I knew it would get better' to 'my special powers told me it would get better', and at the end of the paragraph about the bird had added, 'This was just one example of the way I helped with my magical gift.'

Laura, distressed, had circled this sentence and others like it in pencil but hadn't dared to reject them.

There were about a hundred pages of typing, and it didn't get any better. Laura rambled; Toby tried to improve it by giving it a tilt towards self-aggrandisement too obvious to be bearable to anyone as shy as Laura.

Catherine gave up all her spare time to it in the weeks between the end of March and the end of June, which was the deadline. Luckily one of Laura's intentions had been to encourage others to try out their own powers: her message was that the healing gift is more common than people believe. Taking this as the main theme, Catherine gathered the threads together.

She felt empowered to make it easier to understand. She brought to her task of editor the experience gained by writing reports about business matters, an ability to organise and clarify. She included some thoughts of her own, because after all she had been a witness to Laura's powers. She introduced such thoughts with words like 'an onlooker would have seen' or 'watching the result, a witness would realise'. She told Laura that if she didn't like her contributions, she was to strike them out.

She accepted many of Toby's alterations because they made the narrative less schoolgirlish. She even accepted some of the attempts to make it all seem somehow supernatural, a gift divinely given. Because, after all, it *was* strange, it *was* wonderful, and ultimately inexplicable. Laura would never have made any such claims herself but Catherine let Toby make them for her.

When she delivered the finished work, which she had retyped and arranged neatly into chapters with headings, she was half-expecting rejection. Laura would protest that too much was being made of her gift, and Toby would say it wasn't a good enough sales pitch.

But the deadline was upon them, Laura had no idea what else to write if this was no good, and enough had been left of Toby's publicity gambits to make it acceptable to him.

Toby flew with it to New York. A suspenseful wait ensued. Then Laura telephoned in delight. 'Cath, Toby's just been on the line, he says the publisher's delighted with the book.'

'No!'

'Yes! Otto – that's the editor-in-chief – he says he was expecting one of those things about being visited by heavenly spirits and singled out like Bernadette or somebody, but instead he's so pleased because my book encourages people to think they might have some of that ability inside themselves waiting to come out. He says "self-help" books always do well and he's really delighted.'

'Thank heaven,' breathed Catherine.

'He says he's going to put a "rush notice" on it and have it out for Christmas because people like to buy books like this as Christmas presents – wouldn't that be nice, to think that American people were giving each other my book? And he says the paperback version should maybe be out by next June when he'd like us to come over to do a publicity tour – you know, chatting about the book on local TV and radio and signing in bookshops, although I always think that must be awful, sitting about waiting for people to come in and buy. And he wants to sign me up to do another one, but I told Toby to tell him I don't think I've any more to say and besides, it's so hard for me trying to put it into words and I can't expect you to tidy up another one, so I want to thank you, Cath, deeply and endlessly, for sorting it all out and making it work.'

'Glad to do it, love,' Catherine assured her.

With the book safely out of the way, she accepted an invitation to act as temporary consultant to the Australian dress firm for whom she'd found the fabrics. Using her three-week holiday allowance from Velton's, she flew to Sydney in July, midwinter on their side of the globe. The dresses were being made in readiness to show to the buyers in August, to be on offer to the public by the start of the summer season in October.

She herself thought the colourways of the British designs too subdued for the Australian sun. She would have chosen stronger tones had she been asked. She suggested a contrast binding might brighten the dresses and happily the buyers loved the result. She came home in August with thanks ringing in her ears and a substantial fee in the bank.

So she had had what she might think of as two successes one after the other, first the book and now the Australian fashions. Both business achievements – so perhaps that was where she should turn her attention. If she couldn't have love and any version of domestic bliss, she could have attainment.

She said to Thelma, 'I'm thinking of resigning from Velton's to set up a full-time agency.'

'Oh – my dear, is that wise? The top brass think the world of you.'

'Well, isn't that the time to go?'

'But if you wait a year or two they are sure to promote you.'

They were in Thelma's workaday office after closing time. The building was mostly silent, although the occasional whine of the lift told of others lingering to finish a display or check an account. The windows of the office were open to the hazy blue-grey of the summer evening sky. A warm breeze blew in, stirring the swags and samples of cloth that were pinned to Thelma's cork display board.

'I think I'd rather go and do something on my own,' Catherine said. 'As I go round the country I come across dozens of talented youngsters, some of them fresh out of art school. Working part-time on agenting, I can't take them on as clients. But I believe I could do well for them if I were more serious—'

'Nobody's more serious about fabric design than you are,' Thelma said with her incorrigible grin. She raised the front of her dress from her ample bosom and blew into her cleavage for coolness. 'This isn't just a moment's fed-upness? I know you're still suffering the after-effects of the Great Exodus, but you've survived pretty well – don't muck it up now.'

'No, this is not something I'm doing on the rebound, Thelma. It's just that I feel I'd like to have something of my own.'

'I see.' And Thelma did see. Catherine had no husband, no

lover, no children, no companion. Because she had good sense, she wasn't going to dash out and grab the first man that came along, no matter what Thelma said about finding Mr Right. Instead, she was looking for a challenge, to build an agency of her own specialising in fabric design, of which she had great experience.

'Well then, if you're sure you know what you're doing, go ahead. And the first half-dozen young geniuses you find, send them to me.'

'Sure thing, if they're right for Velton's.'

She handed in her notice, and left at the end of September. She had to sign an agreement that she wouldn't poach any designers with whom Velton's had an exclusive arrangement, which irked her because she never had any such intention. But on the other hand she received a handsome little antique cabinet as a leaving present, a permanent staff card entitling her to a discount at the store, and was given a lavish send-off.

She took a second holiday – a working holiday – in Italy where she renewed acquaintance with manufacturers in Milan. All through the winter she was busy visiting art colleges, interviewing young designers, chivvying existing clients, all the while gradually building up the agency.

She had her father to stay with her in London over Christmas, then gave a Boxing Day party in her flat. Partly it was to continue the festive season and partly to celebrate the publication of Laura's book.

Advance copies had arrived a week earlier. The hardback was rather thin, but had a dramatic cover in blue and black and gold, with the title *The Power Within* splashed diagonally across. The title had been altered by the publisher who thought Toby's choice, *My Life of Wonder*, too vague. The books were on display on a table in the entrance hall with a poster produced by Catherine saying, 'Meet the Author!'

It was a big, talkative gathering. Gerald Mertagen was there, smiling proudly at his daughter's achievement, and Laura herself in a shimmering blue silk shift dress. She was hemmed in by other guests demanding that she autograph their copies when Toby joined the party at about nine-thirty.

'Hi there darling!' she called, waving to him to join her.

He waved back, but sought out the drinks table. Many of Catherine's former colleagues from Velton's were there, and Thelma with the ever-attentive Bob. Bob had volunteered to act as bartender.

Thelma drifted up to Catherine soon after Toby's arrival.

'Duckie,' she whispered, 'I don't want to seem an interfering old woman, but should your brother-in-law be sporting a smear of lipstick quite different from the one his wife's wearing?'

'A smear of—?'

'Dear old Bob noticed it. Toby went for a drink when he arrived, then stood chatting, and Bob says the light caught it for a moment. It appears the lady of the Elizabeth Arden Crimson Rose has been nibbling his left ear.'

'Oh *lord*!'

'Quite a picture, isn't it?' Thelma remarked with an ironic smile. 'Wifey's at a family Christmas party, Hubby's sharing cosmetics with another woman.'

I'll strangle him, thought Catherine. With a little nod of thanks to her friend she threaded her way among her guests to reach Toby, who was with a group of men discussing the Boxing Day sporting events.

'Toby,' she murmured.

'Not now, Catherine, Ron here says he can get tickets for the Chelsea match on Saturday.'

'Toby,' she said, speaking almost against his shoulder, 'go in the bathroom, look in the mirror, and wipe the lipstick off your ear.' She felt him start. 'Be quick about it before Laura sees it.'

Without a word he hurried from the room. Ron, a window display artist at Velton's, said in surprise, 'What'd you say to him? Went quite pale!'

'I told him somebody was trying to break into his car,' lied Catherine, and moved off.

All through the rest of the evening Toby avoided Catherine's eye. Thelma drifted up again to say, 'Sorted it out, did you?'

'Yes, and now I wonder why I did. Perhaps it would have been better to let her know.'

'Well, maybe, but not in front of a roomful of people invited to cheer about her book, eh?'

'No, that would have been brutal.'

The guests didn't leave until nearly two in the morning. Laura stayed to help clear up. The sisters had had little chance to talk all evening – Laura had been in demand because of the book.

'Did Toby tell you we're doing another tour?' she inquired.

'The American one for the book?'

'No, that's not till June. No, we're going to lecture on the Continent for the first time – isn't it thrilling?'

'When was this cooked up?' Catherine said, only too aware

that she'd been too busy in the last few months to keep up with the news.

'Oh, Toby's had it more or less planned since early this year. It's for the beginning of March – we're starting in Holland, doing Amsterdam and The Hague, then Cologne, West Berlin, Regensburg, Munich, Zurich and Geneva. Toby's thrilled about it. He's arranged for copies of the book to be sent by air from New York direct to Amsterdam and then we'll take them with us on the rest of the trip – he's been told that lots of Dutch people speak good English and buy books in English and anyway he's hoping to interest publishers in the translation rights, isn't it clever of him to think of it?'

'Are you sure you want to do another tour?' Catherine asked. 'The last one was—'

'Yes, I know what you're going to say, but we've got to do the American tour to publicise the book and I feel pretty sure it'll be gruelling so Toby thought this would be a good rehearsal – a sort of easy run-in, because we won't have enormous audiences like we had in the States, much easier to handle, you see?'

Catherine had to admit there was a sort of logic to it. Her main worry was whether her sister was equal to it. But since the period of poor health that had followed the American tour, Toby was more inclined to listen when Laura said she was tired.

'You will be careful, Laura, won't you?'

'Yes, I will, I promise.'

Laura went to kiss her father goodnight and fetch her coat. Catherine took the opportunity to have a word with Toby. He flinched as she came to him in the hall. 'Don't start,' he said. His expression was full of dislike and resentment.

She paid no attention to his attempt at evasion. 'Who was it?' she inquired. 'Still that smart girl with the sports car we saw you with outside the Bellamy Hotel?'

He was absolutely stunned. His mouth fell open, he looked behind her to see if Laura was coming.

'I haven't said anything to her, if that's what you're wondering.'

'Well, thank God for that. No sense in making trouble—'

'I didn't keep quiet for your sake, Toby, I did it for Laura. And I won't mention tonight's little mishap either, but you've got to give me something in return.'

'Such as what?'

'I want your promise that you'll look after her on this Continental tour.'

'I always do.'

'No you don't. You let her get ill in America because you got so carried away with being in the limelight. *She lost her baby.*'

'Well, she never told me about that until it was too late. Don't preach at me about it, I'd have kept things a lot quieter if I'd known how matters stood—'

'I hope that's true. But you're so sure of your hold over her that you're getting careless, Toby.'

'It won't happen again—'

'Since you can't mean you'll give up chasing women, I take it you're going to remember about lipstick.'

'My, we *are* sharp tonight, aren't we? No wonder the artistic boyfriend fled the country.'

She gritted her teeth so as not to let him know how he had hurt her. 'Look,' she said coldly, 'Laura's your meal ticket, isn't she? Without her special gift, without her open goodheartedness, there's no one to attract the public to these lectures. The whole thing depends on her.'

'All right, so she's an angel and I don't deserve her. Stop being such a nag, Cath,' replied Toby, fretting at having to listen to her and feel that she was right. 'I'll look after her. You don't have to harp on about it.'

'That's what you say now. I wish I thought it could be relied on.' Against her will, she found herself pleading with him. 'She's done everything for you – adopted your view of life, let herself be remodelled and turned into a public personage, made money for you – she *deserves* something in exchange. And she doesn't ask much. Be a bit decent to her, for heaven's sake! If you had any sense you'd see that a bit of love and consideration send her into seventh heaven. Her whole world lights up – and if she's glowing with happiness, surely that's better when she meets the public?'

Laura came into the hall with her coat on and the conversation had to be given up. Catherine and her father stood on the doorstep waving goodnight. Catherine had the satisfaction of seeing that Laura's husband put his arm around her to guide her across the icy pavement to the car. Perhaps her words would have some effect.

'Still as much in love as ever,' Gerald remarked as they went indoors again. 'They make a lovely couple, really, don't they?'

Catherine contented herself with a nod and a smile. No sense in spoiling his holiday by saying what she really thought.

She made an effort to drop in on Laura and Toby at their Pimlico house two or three times between Christmas and their departure for Amsterdam. A honeymoon period had dawned for them; Laura seemed happier and more confident than Catherine had seen her in a long time.

She went to the airport to see them off, and was able to ring her father that evening with the opinion that everything was fine. 'They had quite a little group of reporters there, and the photographers took pix – no wonder, Laura was really looking her best.'

The obligatory postcards arrived from first Holland and then Cologne. It was all the more of a shock to hear Laura's voice on the telephone at noon ten days later, from Munich.

'Cath! Cath, I can't go on! I don't know what to do! Help me, Cath, help me!'

Chapter Eighteen

A Lufthansa flight took Catherine to Munich that evening. Before booking the seat she rang the publicity firm to find out the telephone number of the hotel in which Laura was staying, the Herrentur. By the time she had got through, it was more than an hour after Laura's cry for help. The hotel receptionist told her that no calls were to be put through to Mrs Lindham.

She explained that Laura had just rung her, that she was Laura's sister. 'Yes, madam,' said the receptionist, 'but the doctor said I was not to put through any calls.'

Doctor's orders! She felt her heart thump with fear. She got in touch with the travel agent who handled her business and asked him to arrange the flight, then rang her father.

'I don't know how serious it is,' she explained, 'but I'm flying to Munich.'

'I'll come too,' cried Gerald, immediately in a fret of anxiety.

'No, Dad, that would mean waiting until you could get to Heathrow, we might not get off until tomorrow morning. I'll ring you when I find out what's wrong.'

'But I might be able—'

'I haven't got time to argue, Dad, I've got to leave for the airport.'

All through the flight she'd been trying to work out what might have happened. When the taxi set her down at the Herrentur she saw elegant placards still in place, announcing the visit of 'Laura Lindham, *berühmte Heilerin*'. There was no additional poster announcing cancellation. Did that mean it was nothing serious after all?

Yet there had been desperation in that short phone call.

At the desk the receptionist told her in excellent English that Mrs Lindham was not seeing any visitors.

'I'm her sister, Catherine Mertagen—'

'Ah, Miss Mertagen, so pleased you are here! Dr Brunheim said you were to be shown up at once.' He summoned a pageboy with a flick of his finger. In German he told him the suite number. He turned back to Catherine. 'The doctor asked me to say he will be here again later this evening. In the meantime he has given Mrs Lindham a light sedative. I was instructed to say that you should not disturb her if she is asleep but that it would be good if you would sit by her. In the meantime, madame, can I offer you anything? Coffee—?'

'What happened?' she cut in.

'Really, Miss Mertagen, I am not able to say. I was not on duty when the event occurred. All I know is that Dr Brunheim, our regular doctor when there is need, was called. He says Mrs Lindham is not to be disturbed and that only her sister – that is to say, yourself, madame – was to be allowed into her room. Anything we can do, of course, madame . . .'

From the exceptional eagerness to help, Catherine could tell that the management wanted to be sure it couldn't be blamed. Could there have been an accident?

The door of Suite 301 was opened by an elderly maid. She began by making negative motions of her head but after a few words from the pageboy she stood back, then left with him.

Catherine set down her overnight bag in the vestibule. The next room was a sitting-room, the furniture handsome though heavy. Opening off from that was the bedroom, whose door stood open. She tiptoed across to peep in. Her sister, looking wan and small, was asleep in one of the twin beds.

She took off her coat, threw it over a chair, then went into the bedroom to check that all was well. Laura was sleeping soundly, her breathing even and regular. There was no sign of any bruise or cut or physical damage on her pale cheeks nor on the arm that was flung across the pillow.

Catherine tiptoed back into the sitting-room. She lifted the telephone and quietly asked the receptionist to put her through to her father's number in Hulmesley.

'I'm in the hotel, Dad. Laura's asleep in the bedroom. She looks all right as far as I can tell.'

'Have you found out anything?'

'Not much, the man on the desk says he wasn't on duty when she was taken ill. The doctor's coming back later, he says.'

'Ring me again, Cath, as soon as you know anything.'

'Of course. But try not to worry, love.'

Useless advice. She could picture him sitting by the phone until she called again.

About nine o'clock Laura made a little moaning sound and moved restlessly. Her eyes opened.

'Laura,' Catherine said softly.

'What?' Laura's unfocused gaze travelled across the room to settle on her sister. 'Cath!' she gasped, throwing out a hand.

Catherine hurried to take it. She sat on the side of the bed. She had a pang of recollection – this was how they used to be at home, when they were preparing for bed and sharing their news of the day just gone by.

'How are you, love?'

'I'm . . . not too bad now. The doctor gave me something . . . I was upset . . .'

'Do you want to sit up?' She helped her to do so, bringing pillows from the other bed to support her. 'Shall I order some tea?'

'No, no, just sit there, Cath, just *be* there.' Lying back among her pillows, she let her eyelids slide shut again.

For some minutes there was silence. Then Laura roused herself. 'What time is it?'

'About five past nine.'

'I've been asleep for over seven hours!'

'You feel better for it?'

'Oh yes. I was a mess when that doctor came – what's his name? Brunberg?'

'Brunheim,' said Catherine. 'Why was he called? Do you feel like telling me?'

Her sister put a hand up to her trembling lips. Her eyes brimmed with tears. 'It was too awful, Cath! I was just . . . empty. Nothing happened. At first I felt that it would be there if I just waited, so we sat and tried to talk but you know, I don't speak any German . . .'

'You're talking about the patients—'

'The first appointment was at half-past nine,' Laura said, looking back as if at a great distance. 'Was that just this morning? We sat trying to get acquainted for half an hour and I managed to understand what her ailment was, but then when I tried to help her . . . So she had to leave, because the next patient was waiting, and by this time it was ten-thirty and – oh, Cath, you can't imagine – it was useless, useless—' She broke off, overcome by the memory.

'Don't tell me if you don't want to, Laura,' Catherine murmured, patting her hand. 'Perhaps you'd rather—'

'No, no, let me say it. It's as if . . . I need to tell . . . it's like going to confession, maybe . . . This man came in with Toby – Toby has to be there when it's a male patient, of course, and somehow that made it more difficult, it was even worse this time, so I said to Toby that I couldn't do anything and he said I must try, so I did, I waited again, but I knew it was hopeless. So he left, the man, the patient, very disappointed, he had built up his hopes, you see, I felt dreadful – as if I'd been unkind to him, but truly, Cath, I couldn't *do* anything.'

'Sh, sh, don't be upset about it, dear, it wasn't your fault—'

Laura gave a little gesture of disagreement. 'I shouldn't offer help that I can't provide, that's terribly wrong, and I think I knew this morning from the very outset . . . Well, then the next man too – I couldn't feel anything, and almost at once I said to Toby that it would be better to cancel, so he took me into the bedroom – in here, you know – and he told me not to be silly, that there were three more patients in the afternoon and was I going to go on in this silly way, and I said that I couldn't do anything if the power wasn't there, and he said . . . he said . . .'

'What, Laura?'

'He said, "Fake it!"' There was horror in her tone. 'I was so shocked!'

Catherine could find no soothing word to utter. She knew her expression was grim. It was just the kind of advice she would have expected Toby to give.

After a long hesitation, as if she were looking for the strength to continue, Laura whispered, 'I said . . . I said I couldn't do that, and we had a row, and he grabbed me by the wrist and tried to turn me so as to make me go back into the sitting-room and he told me not to be a fool and ended by shouting it again, "Fake it!" And the patient – Mr Leichtwoller – he heard, and he came rushing in here, and he was so . . . so . . .'

'Bewildered?' prompted Catherine, trying to picture the scene.

'No, he wasn't bewildered at all, he was angry,' Laura replied with an indrawn breath of remembered distress. 'Because you see, Cath, he spoke good English, as quite a lot of them do, and he heard what Toby said and he was outraged – he hit Toby, he cut his lip, and Toby was furious and was going to hit him back but I caught his arm, and Mr Leichtwoller went storming out of the room saying he'd unmask me as a fraud, and Toby turned on me and told me I was an utter idiot and now look what I'd done and I . . . I just . . . I just flew out at him, it all seemed to spill over, I told him that I was never going to forgive him, because you see, Cath, last night . . . last night . . .'

She had been on the verge of tears from the outset but now she began to weep. Catherine put her arm round her and drew her head onto her shoulder. 'That's right, duckie,' she whispered, 'cry it out. Let it all go.'

For a long time they remained like this, until at last Laura's sobs diminished. Catherine brought her some tissues from the dressing table. She mopped her eyes. She lay back again amongst her pillows, almost exhausted.

'Perhaps you should try to sleep again, dear,' Catherine ventured.

'No, I want to tell you, I owe it to you to tell you, because I think you always knew and I wouldn't listen.'

'What?' Catherine said with a sinking heart.

'About Toby. You tried to tell me a long time ago – about that Celia Kingsley story, I wouldn't believe you, but now I think . . . I know . . . it was true, wasn't it?'

Catherine nodded. She had longed for her sister to wake up from her long enchantment but now it was happening she found she couldn't be happy about it.

'And perhaps there were others too. Because last night . . . last night . . .' She paused, took a shuddering breath, and went on: 'Last night . . . was it only last night?' She frowned, making herself concentrate through the haze caused by the sedative. 'We did the lecture in the ballroom and it went quite well, you know the management here are terribly clued-up, they have business conferences often so they have an interpreter who speaks through a mike offstage and anybody that needs a translation can listen through headphones. And the questions were easy enough to handle though it took a lot longer because I had to have the translation but I got on all right and we did the usual thing about the book and sold quite a few, and then Toby said he was glad about the book sales because he could report that to the German publisher.' She hesitated, and a faint colour tinted her wan cheeks. 'He had a date to have drinks with him in the bar but he urged me to go upstairs because he said I looked tired, and I *was* tired, the session in the ballroom had gone on for three hours—'

'But he was supposed to make sure you took things easy!' Catherine protested.

'Oh, you can't take things easy when people need answers, Cath, it was all right, I'd tried to pace myself. But I was tired so I came up here and tidied up a few things before getting ready for bed but somehow I was strung up, you know? So I thought, this is silly, I could be having a drink with Toby and the publisher, so I went down, but Toby wasn't in the bar so I asked the barman and he said no, he hadn't been in. So then it occurred to me he might be having this meeting in Mandy's room—'

'Mandy?'

'Mandy Wellesley, the publicity girl from Oliviat's office, she's been with us from the beginning, very bright, very pretty, and she always has a room in the same hotel, we use it more or less as an office, she does all her telephoning from there and deals with any mail that comes in and has the stock of books and everything so we all have keys. So I went up there and opened the door. And I found them . . . found them . . .' Her voice trailed away.

After waiting a moment Catherine prompted, very gently, 'Go on.'

'So you see what he told me about the publisher was just a lie. Just a lie like others, I suppose, when I think about it. What a fool I've been . . .' She was shaking her head at herself, at that naive wife who, as the story goes, is always the last to know. 'Well, I turned around and walked out. I couldn't speak, I just walked out. I came back here and sat down and turned on the television and there was this man chattering away in German and I sat there for about ten minutes staring at him and then Toby came in.'

'And told you it meant nothing and you mustn't take it to heart, or something like that.'

'Something like that. But I couldn't let him say that, Cath. If it meant nothing, why was he there with her? For quite a while now, things have been so good between us, Toby and me, I mean, if he'd really meant all the sweet things he said to me he couldn't possibly want anyone else. So it must mean something if he was with her, or else nothing he ever says is worth believing, and I couldn't take that in, it was just . . . impossible . . .'

'Poor love,' mourned Catherine.

'Oh, don't be sorry for me! I see now that I brought it all on myself. I let him think he could just tell me any old tale and I'd accept it. You should have heard the way he went on when he was trying to wheedle me into believing him, but the more he talked the more it seemed cheap and horrible, all full of worthless excuses, and I began to think I didn't know him, never had known him, really, and when he saw none of it was working he tried to take me in his arms and kiss me and it was like . . . like being *accosted*, and I think I got hysterical and he stopped and stormed out and I didn't see him again that night. I suppose he went back to Mandy.'

'Oh, Laura!'

'Oh yes,' Laura said with a strange calmness, 'I didn't have to ask him, I knew that's where he'd been, when he turned up in the morning. I told him I didn't want to speak to him but he said we had to talk about business and he'd ordered breakfast in our room, and then he spoke to me very seriously about the patients who were expected, and I said I thought I ought to cancel because I didn't feel well – I hadn't slept, you see – and he said I mustn't let them down. He told me it was my duty. So I put on the Balenciaga dress and the make-up and got ready and the first patient arrived and nothing happened . . . Did I tell you that? Nothing came, I couldn't help her, it was all a big emptiness, Cath.'

'Laura, don't worry. This happened before, remember? Your gift went away, but it came back again after a while—'

Laura was shaking her head wearily. 'Not this time, Cath. I can't explain it to you but it's gone. There's nothing but a blankness. It's over.'

To argue would have been useless, and besides, what grounds did she have? She knew nothing of the experience except what she'd witnessed in the old days in the flat above the shop – and so the knowledge was from the outside, useless in the face of her sister's certainty.

They sat for a time in silence. Then Laura made a move to get up. 'I think that doctor's coming back,' she said. 'The manager called him this morning after that Mr Leichtwoller went storming out, he came up all worried at what he'd been told and I suppose it looked awful because I was screaming and crying and carrying on . . .' She shrank into herself in distaste at the recollection. 'I ought to wash my face, comb my hair. I expect I look a mess. But what does it matter, really?'

'It doesn't matter but you'll feel better. Come on, kitten, tidy yourself up.'

When she pushed back the covers she proved to be half undressed, in slip and stockinged feet. She padded across to the bathroom, closed the door, and in a moment Catherine heard the water running.

There came a knock on the outer door of the suite. Catherine went to open it. A burly man in his thirties stood there, dark suit, sparkling shirt, sombre tie.

'I am Dr Brunheim,' he announced. 'And you are the sister, *ja*?'

'Yes, Catherine Mertagen.' They shook hands. He glanced towards the bedroom. 'She's awake, she's in the bathroom washing her face,' she explained.

'How did she seem when she awoke?'

'Dazed at first, then very pent-up.'

'Pent-up?'

'Anxious to tell me. It came out like a flood.'

'Ah, that is probably good. Perhaps you could explain to me what has occurred. I was summoned, but I found her confused, frightened perhaps – some man had attacked her?'

'No, it was her husband who was attacked – Toby Lindham.'

'Mrs Lindham attacked him—?'

'No, no, another man – it would take too long to explain, doctor. The main thing is her husband had caused her tremendous distress—'

'Ah, the husband.' Dr Brunheim had put his bag on a coffee table and was getting out his stethoscope and thermometer case. 'She was sobbing and crying that he must go, that she couldn't bear to have him in the room with her, so I put him outside. He at first didn't wish to go but I insisted. What exactly does he do?'

'He's the business manager of the Mertagen Clinic.'

Brunheim cleared his throat. 'And . . . um . . . what is this clinic? A medical enterprise of some sort?'

'My sister is a trained nurse,' Catherine said evasively.

He let that lie. 'I was concerned for her. Her forehead was perspired, she was trembling, unable to answer my questions. I commanded the manager to allow no one into the room. When I told her so, she said she had telephoned to you and was longing for you to come, so I altered the command. But the husband – the husband had to be kept out because the mere thought of him makes her' – he made fluttering movements with the fingers of both hands – '*bewegt*?'

'Agitated?' Catherine suggested.

'I think that is the word.'

They heard the bathroom door open. Catherine went into the bedroom. 'Dr Brunheim's here, love.'

Laura sought about for her dressing-gown. Catherine found it in the wardrobe, and noted at the same time that only her sister's belongings hung there – no men's suits or shirts.

She told Dr Brunheim her sister was ready. He went into the bedroom. Catherine glanced about the sitting-room for signs of Toby's occupancy but there were none – no briefcase, no documents, and on the luggage stand no suitcases except her sister's.

So he had moved out. She imagined him hastily throwing his things together on Dr Brunheim's orders. Had he left for the next stop on the intended tour? Or gone back to London? Or merely to another room in the hotel? Mandy's room?

By and by Dr Brunheim came out of the bedroom. He took the stethoscope from around his neck and began stowing it away.

'The hotel manager informed me a tour was intended?'

'Yes, they were supposed to go on tomorrow – perhaps to Switzerland, but—'

He was shaking his head emphatically. 'Out of the question. She does not wish to go, and she is in no state to go. She needs rest, peace and quiet, perhaps some help with sleeping, and who knows what more? I am not a psychiatrist, Miss Mertagen, nor a counsellor of marriage, but it is clear to me there has been some tremendous event, I think you say climactic?'

'That sounds about right.'

'Between Mrs Lindham and her husband. For the present, at any rate, she cannot be with him. It would be better if she were at home, at rest.'

'Yes, I understand. If she's able to travel I'll take her home tomorrow.'

'I think it would improve her condition just to be on her way home, but it will be a help if she takes these light tranquillisers – I leave them here – perhaps she takes two before the flight, *ja*?'

'I understand.'

'And the husband, even if it is just the usual marriage problems, keep him away for the present, until she feels stronger.'

'Yes, thank you, doctor.'

'Her own doctor should see her when she gets home. Try to get her to eat. She may not be ready to sleep for a while but if you can persuade her to eat something and then take the sedative capsule which I also leave with you' – he put one out in the ashtray – 'I think she may settle down in an hour or two.'

She nodded acquiescence and saw him out. He shook hands punctiliously. 'Goodnight, Miss Mertagen, let the manager know if you need me again but I believe your sister is calm now that you are here.'

'Thank you.'

Laura came into the sitting-room as the doctor left. She sat down in one of the heavy armchairs, looking small and pale against its dark brocade. 'I'm sorry to drag you here like this, Cath. Were you in the middle of something?'

'Nothing that can't wait. Dr Brunheim says you can fly home tomorrow if you feel up to it.'

'Oh yes!' cried Laura, clasping her hands together. Then she caught herself up. 'No! Toby will turn up there—'

'You'll come and stay with me, of course.'

'Oh, thank you, Cath, that would be so . . . so nice . . .'

'Dr Brunheim says you should eat. Shall I order something to be brought up?'

'No, I'm not hungry.'

'Please, Laura – try to eat.'

'No . . . well . . . I wouldn't mind some tea.'

'Tea and biscuits?'

'Yes, all right.'

Catherine ordered them from room service. No sooner had she put down the phone than it rang. She picked it up. 'Suite 301,' she said.

'Cath? Is that you?'

'Toby?' she exclaimed, startled.

Laura gave a cry, throwing out her hands as if to ward him off.

'It's all right,' Catherine said, 'I won't let him come in.'

'I heard that,' said Toby's angry voice on the line. 'What the devil does she think she's up to? We've got to talk.'

'No, you haven't.'

'Look here, Cath, don't be stupid. We've got a tour to finish, people expecting us all along the line as far as Geneva. I've got to see her to—'

'No, absolutely not.'

'Don't say "absolutely not"; what on earth am I supposed to do? Decisions have got to be made – I mean, even if she's not well enough to go on to Regensburg we've got to get in touch there, explain the delay—'

'Where are you, Toby?'

'I'm in the hotel lounge.'

'I'll come down in a minute. Wait there.'

Laura dragged herself out of the chair, came and clutched her arm. 'Don't go, Cath. Don't have anything to do with him.'

Catherine made soothing sounds. 'I think someone's got to talk to him. He said decisions have to be made and that's true, dear. But don't worry, I'll make it plain you're not going anywhere except home.'

She waited until the tea had been brought, poured a cup and made sure her sister had started to sip it before she went out. As he had told her, Toby was in the lounge, with a whisky and soda in his hand and papers spread out on the coffee table before him.

It was a satisfaction to her to see his handsome features marred by a swollen lip – from the blow administered by Herr Leichtwoller. He looked tired; his tie had been loosened, the button of his collar was undone. Not quite the immaculate businessman he used to be.

He rose as Catherine came up. It was the first time in years that he had shown her this politeness. She guessed that he was scared, needed her on his side.

'How are you, Cath? It's good of you to come running like this. Can I order anything for you?'

Thirsty, she ordered a fresh orange juice. 'The first thing I have to say to you, Toby, is that you have to cancel the rest of the tour.'

'What?'

'Dr Brunheim says Laura isn't fit to go on with it. I'm taking her home.'

'But—'

'I don't care what problems it causes, the tour is cancelled.'

'Look here, I've been on the phone almost all day with Oliviat and he's *fuming* – he's not going to let us cancel just because Laura got a fit of the jimjams—'

'Oliviat? That's the impresario who arranged the tour?'

'Yes, and he's got a lot of money invested—'

'I couldn't care less about Oliviat and his money—'

'Oh, great, you don't care, but he can sue me for all I've got—'

'I hope he does. I hope you're left without a penny in your pocket. But it's not going to happen, you're too clever to get caught. You have insurance against ill health—'

'Yes, but not to cover everything. There are penalties for breaking the contract—'

'But you insured against that too,' Catherine countered.

'No, I didn't. How the dickens could I ever guess she'd just refuse to go on?'

Catherine gave him a cold smile. 'But you're not going to tell Oliviat that she just refuses to go on. You can get a certificate from Dr Brunheim to say that she's not fit to continue. Stop trying to keep hold of the leash by pretending you're going to be ruined. Even if you are, Laura doesn't care any more.'

'Yes, she does! Just because of one mistake, she's never going to—'

'Just one mistake?' It brought a grim laugh from her lips. 'I told you, Toby, you were getting careless. Laura realises that this isn't by any means the first time.'

'You told her, I suppose!'

'About your charming proposition the day you met me at

the station? No, I've never mentioned it. But there were other occasions, and others tried to tell her, and now she sees it was all true.'

'It's all just silly gossip. I can explain everything. Just get her to talk to me—'

'Not on your life! You've done enough damage.'

'Oh, for heaven's sake, where's the harm in a little variety? You don't know what it's like living with Laura – it's like being married to a bar of milk chocolate, all sweet and cloying. A man's got to have a bit of ginger in his life.'

'Shall I convey that message to her?' Catherine inquired, in a tone that was edged like a guillotine.

'Oh, Cath, come *on*! You know she can't live without me! She may think it's all over but I can soon talk her round—'

'No, Toby, you haven't got the message. This is something you can't talk your way out of. Because you see, it isn't just about your playing around with other women. You've destroyed what gave meaning to her life.'

Toby gaped at her. 'Now what are you talking about?'

'I mean the power of healing. It's gone, and you drove it away.'

'Oh, right, I'm to blame, I'm the bad guy—'

'I couldn't have put it better myself—'

'But you can't claim I have any effect on that healing stuff—'

'If you destroy Laura's world, you undermine her in every way—'

'Oh, all that weird business, she's got no idea how she does it and neither have you! If it's not working for the moment it's got nothing to do with *me*!'

'All that weird business, as you call it – it's certainly not working for the moment and Laura is saying it never will again. Don't you understand? Her belief in herself is gone! And you did it—'

'No I didn't—'

'She found you with this girl, Mandy or whoever, and there was a quarrel, and you marched out and didn't reappear until morning – isn't that right? Do you really think Laura's going to take you back after you blatantly spent the night with Mandy? Or are you saying you slept on a sofa in the lounge?'

'Well, I—'

'And next thing we know, you're persuading her to see patients when she's all broken up over what's happened, and as if that isn't enough when her healing gift won't come you shout at her to fake it. And you think you're not to blame?'

He had gone red and was trying to control his anger. He knew that without Catherine's help he would achieve nothing. He said shortly, 'All right, all right, I handled it badly. I shouldn't have said what I did.'

'And now you're going to have to tidy up the mess.'

'It can all be sorted out if only she'll be *reasonable*,' he burst out. 'Cancelling is out of the question. We can get away with a delay, but—'

'Hasn't it dawned on you yet? She can't go on with the tour. Her healing talent has vanished. And she can't, as you so charmingly put it, "fake it".'

'She could give the talks. We could cancel the private consultations—'

'You really expect Laura to get up on a platform and talk about her special powers when she knows she's lost them? You don't understand her at all, Toby.'

His control finally snapped. 'You're enjoying this,' he snarled. 'You never liked me and let me tell you, it's mutual! I should have known better than to expect any help from you but let me tell you, if that stupid sister of yours lets me down now, it's finished! Do you understand? Finished! I'm not going to stay tied to a nincompoop like her for the rest of my life – the opportunities we've had that she wouldn't grab, because of some daft idea that she didn't feel right about it – I tell you she's been a drag on me for years, scarcely a day's gone by when I haven't wanted to tell her to drop dead, and now she's gone too far! I'm not going to let her pull me down to some fiddly little do-gooding job, *she* can sink to being a nobody if she wants to, but not me, not me!'

Breathless, he came to a halt. He was glaring at Catherine, but almost unconscious of the fact that she was still there. He had been speaking to Laura, venting all his grievances, paying her back for being the kind of woman he could take advantage of.

Catherine got to her feet. 'Is that settled then?' she asked, without disguising her repugnance. 'You despise Laura and want nothing more to do with her? Can I tell her she's free of the threat of ever having you in her life again?'

'Tell her what the devil you like.'

She nodded and walked out. That, she was sure, was the end of Toby's influence in her sister's world.

Chapter Nineteen

Laura had gone to rest on the bed in the spare room. Gerald Mertagen was pacing to and fro in Catherine's sitting-room clasping and unclasping his hands.

'I can't believe it! There must be some mistake!'

'Dad, calm down. Of course there's no mistake. Laura could hardly have got it wrong.'

'But Toby—! I mean, Toby *wouldn't*—!'

'Toby would and Toby did. And not for the first time.'

Gerald stopped short. 'You know that for a fact, Cathie? Or are you just saying that because you're angry?'

'There were stories back home in Hulmesley, and I saw him with a girl here in London—'

'I can't take it in! Toby has been having affairs with other women?'

'Would you call them affairs? He's just the sort that tries it on with any girl who takes his fancy – and a lot do, I think. But he usually had the good sense to keep all that under cover. Then he got careless.' Catherine thought of the party here in her flat when she'd warned him.

'My poor little girl,' Gerald mourned. 'She looked so *ill* when she came in.'

'She's depressed and exhausted. She needs a good, long rest.'

Gerald clutched at his thinning hair. 'To think I was happy when they said they were getting married—'

'Well, that was just to make sure Laura didn't back out of that first tour. I expect he had a long-term plan, heading towards that American venture.' Catherine sighed. 'In a way he's pitiful,' she remarked. 'Anything to hang on to his source of income. But it's not even a huge, lucrative income. Better than nothing, I suppose, but you'd think he'd find himself a really rich woman to sponge on.'

Gerald was shocked at the views she was expressing. He still hadn't got used to the idea that Toby was worthless. 'I thought he was so straight and dependable,' he groaned.

'You weren't the only one. The Colvilles, for instance – they thought a lot of him.'

'What will happen now? Divorce?'

'That's up to Laura. Certainly Toby let me know in no uncertain terms that unless she went on with the European tour, he'd have nothing more to do with her.'

'But the clinic, Cathie? What's going to happen about the clinic and all that?'

'I expect Laura will close it down.'

'And do what?'

'Dad, if I knew that I'd be happy!' Catherine burst out. 'She's got *nothing* left, nothing! He took it all away.'

Her father was silent for a long moment, then said, 'Well, she's got us. We'll help her to sort it all out.'

But it wasn't going to be easy. Laura joined them at suppertime. She was quite self-controlled but quiet all through the meal. When they tried to include her in the conversation she replied briefly, then fell silent again.

Next morning at Catherine's suggestion she unpacked the suitcases she'd brought back from Munich. The bed in the spare room was covered with bright garments in the very latest styles. The cosmetics case yielded lipsticks and lotions from the great salons.

'I'm giving all this to the Salvation Army,' she announced.

'What?'

'I'm never going to wear any of these clothes again.'

'But Laura—'

'They were never right for me. I only bought them because my "fashion adviser" told me to. And all these bottles and jars and things, they never really suited me and I'm glad not to have to bother with them any more.'

'But Laura—'

'At the back of my wardrobe in Pimlico there's boxes of my old clothes, so come with me, Cath, and I'll get them and then I can be my old self again.'

'Well, of course, if that's what you really want.'

They took a taxi. There was no one at the clinic except for the receptionist, who leapt to her feet at the sound of Laura's key in the door.

'The clinic's not—' she began, then sat down again in astonishment. 'Mrs Lindham! I thought you were still abroad!'

'I came back last night. Mrs Gower, I'd like you to contact anyone that you've booked for a consultation and tell them the clinic is closed.'

'Excuse me?' queried Mrs Gower. 'Of course I haven't booked anyone for the period you were supposed to be away—'

'Contact everyone who has an appointment. Tell them the Mertagen Clinic will not reopen.'

Mrs Gower gaped. 'I don't think I understand.'

'As from today, the Mertagen Clinic ceases to exist.'

'Did Mr Lindham send these instructions?'

'Mr Lindham can send instructions until the cows come home but if I give up the practice the clinic has to close. Is that clear? How long will it take you to contact patients?'

'Er . . . a day or two . . . I could do a form letter . . . some I could phone . . . Mrs Lindham, what about my job?' ventured the receptionist.

'If you'll tell me how much is owing to you in salary I'll write you a cheque for that plus a month's money in lieu of notice.'

'But Mrs Lindham—!'

'Please start contacting the patients now,' Laura said, and walked on, through the reception area to the consulting room and through that to the stairs giving access to the flat above.

Here she sank down on the nearest chair as if her legs had suddenly given way. Catherine, who had witnessed this encounter too stunned to speak, leaned over her. 'Are you all right? Shall I get you a glass of water?'

'I'm all right, it's just that . . . I've never dismissed anyone before.'

'You're sure you're giving up the clinic?'

Her sister stared up at her from haunted brown eyes. There was no need for her to put her answer into words.

When she had recovered Laura led the way into the bedroom. There she pulled out cartons of clothes – dresses, skirts and sweaters, sensible shoes, a raincoat. Catherine went out to fetch in the taxi-driver and enlist his help to bring out the boxes. They loaded them aboard. Laura wrote Mrs Gower's cheque, told her to put her key through the letterbox when her task was completed, and said goodbye.

They were carried back to Hammersmith. Here the clothes were unloaded, the high-fashion garments were piled into the boxes thus emptied, and the driver was paid to take them to the nearest Salvation Army Citadel.

'There,' said Laura, faintly but with bitter satisfaction. 'That's an end of that.'

Her father, who had witnessed the beginning and the end of this foray, stood half-protesting and half-approving. He'd never really liked all those hard, smart clothes. It would be good to have the old Laura back.

But the old Laura didn't reappear even though she was wearing a familiar tweed skirt and sweater. After that burst of defiant activity she seemed to shrink back into herself. She would stay indoors until after dark, at which time she would go out for a walk along the Embankment with her father and Catherine. She would sit with a book in her lap but never turned a page. She would find a music programme on the radio but her attention was elsewhere.

After four days, Gerald began to worry about the shop at home in Hulmesley. 'Come home with me, dearie,' he urged Laura. 'You'll be happier if you're home.'

Laura looked at her sister. 'Am I too much under your feet?' she asked.

'Of course not, love.' Laura had the spare bedroom, but her father was sleeping in the little room Catherine had turned into an office. If anyone was under her feet it was he. His shaving tackle and spare shirt took up space in the filing cabinet, his pocket chess set was in her in-tray.

Gerald left for Norfolk and Laura stayed on in Hammersmith. March turned into April. Sticky buds began to unfold on the chestnut trees along the riverside, mallard ducklings scurried about behind their mother on the Thames. But in Laura there was no upsurge of new vitality. She remained quiet, well controlled but without any desire to take hold of her life again.

One evening, Catherine came in after a day of hard bargaining on behalf of one of her clients. She went into her office to put the papers in the files and to open her mail. Laura came in bringing her a reviving drink.

'Oh,' she faltered, her eye caught by the bank statement her sister had just taken out of its envelope. 'I've never thought . . . I ought to offer you some money . . .'

'Nonsense, don't be silly—'

'But after all I ought to pay my way—'

'Not at all, I wouldn't hear of it.'

'I think I ought to, Cath, though I don't think I've got much left in my handbag, but tomorrow I can go to the bank.'

Catherine ceased to argue. Anything that would get Laura out into the world, even just to visit her bank, was welcome.

The next day was a Friday. Catherine had a client coming to the flat to look at a portfolio of work over lunch. He left just after two. Catherine was tidying the designs back into the holders when Laura came in using the spare key.

'Hello, love, did you get on all right at the—' She broke off. Laura's face was white, her eyes were dull with the after-effects of disaster.

'What's happened?' Catherine gasped, springing to her feet so that the drawings scattered around her. Hurrying to her sister, she drew her down on the sofa.

'Cath . . . He's emptied the account.'

'Toby?' But she knew it could be no one else.

'Only a few shillings are left.'

'But how could he do that, Laura?' Even Toby, she felt, couldn't bedazzle a bank.

'It's a joint account, the signature of either of us can be accepted, of course I almost never signed cheques or made deposits or withdrawals, Toby did all that. So when he went there after he got back from Munich and wrote a cheque to cash, they accepted it without question.'

Catherine was too appalled to speak. She sat with one of Laura's hands in hers, trying to come to terms with this last act of cruelty.

At last she said, 'Sweetheart, it doesn't matter. Let him take the money. It was what he cared about in the first place.'

'Yes, I know that now.'

'Have you come straight home from the bank?'

'Yes.'

'Did you get any lunch?'

'Lunch? No, I . . . But I'm not hungry.'

'Come along, love, there's some soup left from the meal I gave Joe Parsons. Come on now, have some hot soup. I'll make you some toast.'

Thus coaxed, Laura let herself be led into the kitchen where Catherine prepared a snack for her. Catherine herself sat down opposite with a cup of coffee. Laura dipped the spoon in the bowl two or three times but after a moment she laid it by.

'Cath,' she said.

'Yes?'

'Do you think it means Toby's gone away?'

'I suppose it must mean that.'

'For good?'

'Yes.'

'I was thinking . . . The Pimlico house . . .'

'What about it, sweetheart?'

'We have to make quarterly payments out of our account to cover the mortgage. If the account's closed . . . ?'

The two sisters sat looking at each other in silence. Alert hazel eyes looked into troubled brown ones.

'Wouldn't you have heard from the finance company?'

'They don't have this address, if there's any correspondence it would be at the clinic.'

'We ought to go there.'

'No!' wailed Laura. 'I can't go there. *He* might be there!'

'I'll go, then,' said Catherine.

Her sister nodded, unspeaking. Catherine set aside her coffee, fetched her coat and bag from her room. Laura came hesitatingly to the door with her to give her the key.

'If he's there . . . If he's there tell him I despise him.'

But the clinic was utterly empty when Catherine let herself in. The heating and the electricity had been turned off but daylight showed the reception desk already gathering dust. The doormat was hidden under a sea of correspondence.

Catherine stepped over it, then walked on through the ground floor to the stairs for the living quarters. Toby had clearly been there, packing up. His wardrobe was empty, a few discarded items were scattered on the floor, the sailing trophies were gone from the living-room mantelpiece, the onyx lighter and cigarette box from the coffee table, and the autographed photos from the wall of his study.

'Goodbye for ever,' muttered Catherine as she surveyed the scene.

As she was leaving she gathered up all the envelopes and packets on the doormat. It made such a big collection that she found a discarded carrier-bag in which to take them back to Hammersmith.

Laura was watching for her at the window. Catherine answered the unspoken question as she came indoors. 'The place was entirely empty, Laura, and all his personal belongings are gone. Here's the mail.' She slung the carrier-bag on the sofa.

They sat down with the bag between them to sort out the contents. All advertising matter was put in the wastepaper basket, all official looking envelopes were opened by Laura, and all personal letters from patients were set aside for further consideration.

'Oh!' gasped Laura.

'What?' Catherine asked with a sinking heart.

'The finance company . . . They're asking why the bank account has insufficient funds. They queried the bank when the regular payment didn't arrive.' She handed the letter to her sister.

It was a formal letter but the tone was stiff. As Catherine was finishing it, Laura passed another to her. It was a reminder about the electricity bill. In due course Laura opened reminders from the water board and the local council inquiring about the rates. There were bills from the printer and from the suppliers of the herbal products.

All in all it came to a very large sum. And there wasn't enough in the Lindham account to settle even the rates.

Laura's assets, when examined, proved to be the contents of her purse, a pearl necklace with matching earrings, her engagement ring with a solitaire diamond, and a gold wrist-watch.

'Never mind, Laura, I've got a bit saved up and Dad probably has a—'

'No, no, I can't take your money!' Laura cried in horror.

'But lovey, we've got to pay or you'll lose—'

'Lose the house in Pimlico – well, let it go, I don't care, I don't want to own it, I never want to see it again, never!'

'But you've paid up quite a lot on the mortgage, you'll lose it all if you don't pay—'

'And what about next time? And the time after that? We haven't got that kind of money, Cath! We could never keep on paying the premiums—'

'But don't you think we ought to try—'

'No, I don't, I don't want to keep it, I never want to see that house again as long as I live, never, never!'

It would have been useless to try to argue with so much emotion. And besides, Catherine wasn't sure what the best course might be. She let it go for the present.

She found the tranquillisers the Munich doctor had supplied. After their evening meal at which Laura ate nothing, she persuaded her to take a capsule and go early to bed. Then she rang their father.

It took him nearly a quarter of an hour to calm down. Unaccustomed to using bad language, Gerald soon ran out of names to call his son-in-law. He ranted and raved against him but ended with anxiety for his daughter. 'How is she?'

'It's set her back, Dad. She was quiet but in control of herself until this happened. Now she's all of a tremble again. I think I'll try to persuade her to go and see a doctor tomorrow.'

'If I ever lay my hands on that man—!'

'What do you think we ought to say to Laura about all these debts?'

'God knows. I've got a little nest-egg put by and of course there's an endowment policy I could cash in—'

'No, no, you mustn't do that, it's only ever worth a fraction if you cash it in early—'

'What does Laura say?'

'She wants to let the house go.'

'Maybe that would be best. The upkeep would be enormous and what use would it be to her if she's serious about giving up the healing?'

'Oh, she's serious about that, Dad,' Catherine sighed. 'The fact is, she can't do it any more.'

'But that's only temporary—'

'She says not. She says a door closed.'

'My poor little dove,' groaned Gerald. 'We've got to look after her, Cathie.'

'Oh yes, and we will.'

When the weekend was over Catherine went to a lawyer for advice. He looked over the demand from the finance company, then glanced up at her. 'As far as I can see, Miss Mertagen, your sister has no need to worry about payments on the property. The house is in the single name of Mr Tobias Lindham, according to these documents, and it is to him that the finance company must turn for payment.'

'Really?' cried Catherine. 'Laura isn't liable?'

'Not in any way. Of course, it means she is without a roof over her head if he is defaulting—'

'It's not a roof she wants, in any case,' Catherine replied, and hurried home to pass on the good news.

The good news was received with only the faintest of smiles from Laura. 'That's a relief,' she acknowledged.

'And if we look more carefully at the other bills, we'll probably find they're all in Toby's name too,' Catherine urged.

'Then they won't get their money?' Laura said.

'Oh, I think they have ways of tracking down people who skive off without paying bills.'

Laura was shaking her head. 'I hope they find him,' she murmured, 'but I hope I never know about it.'

They spent a less unhappy evening. Catherine passed on the good news to their father. She went to bed with her mind much relieved and hoping that in the not too distant future her sister might be strong enough to go out into the world again and find an occupation. Not to be a healer again – that seemed ruled out. But Laura was a trained nurse, she ought to be able to find work that would help rebuild her self-confidence.

Catherine had unavoidable business in the Midlands next day.

The first sample of work by one of her clients was to come off the loom; she was required to be there to hear any criticisms or suggestions.

She got home late, as the dusk of May was turning to the pale blue of evening. Coming in, she called, 'It's me, I'm home!' But there was no answering call from the sitting-room or the kitchen.

She was disappointed. She'd been coaxing her sister this morning to do some cooking for the evening meal, in the way they used to do at home in Hulmesley. No doubt she was sitting in the dark with a book in her lap.

She went into the sitting-room, switching on a light. It was empty. The kitchen, too, had no one at work. Could she have gone to bed so early? Perhaps – she seemed to have very little physical energy these days.

She tapped at the spare room door. No reply. Gently she opened it far enough to put her head round. The room was in darkness but enough light came in from the street to show her that there was no one in bed.

Alarmed, she switched on the light. The room was empty. She went into the little office, but there was no one there. She was alone in the flat.

A stab of anxiety went through her. But then she thought, Don't be silly, she's gone out for a walk.

With great calmness she went into the sitting-room, took off her jacket, poured herself a drink, and sat down. Laura would be back in a minute.

But ten o'clock came, and no Laura. Ten o'clock was too late for Laura to be out alone. Thoroughly scared now, she got to her feet. In the spare room she opened the wardrobe.

Most of Laura's clothes were gone. And tucked under the base of the lamp on the bedside table was a slip of paper.

> I have to be on my own to work things out. Don't worry about me. Sorry to have been such a trouble to you and Dad. Thank you for everything.

Chapter Twenty

Gerald wanted to go to the police.

'We can't do that, Dad,' Catherine objected. 'She's perfectly entitled to go away if she wants to—'

'But she's not herself! She shouldn't be on her own!'

She was inclined to agree with him, but didn't say so. 'She'll be back in a week or two,' she assured him.

But two weeks went by, then three, then a month. Not a word from Laura. Gerald came to London, as if that would be any help. When the fifth week of absence ended, he insisted on consulting the police. They went to Hammersmith Police Station.

The sergeant who listened to their tale looked vaguely sympathetic but shook his head even before they showed him the note Laura had left.

'There really isn't anything we can do,' he told them. 'Mrs Lindham's an adult, and if she wants to make herself scarce she has a right to. All the more so if there's trouble in the marriage, as you seem to be saying.'

'But she's not well,' Gerald insisted.

'In what way?'

'Well . . . upset, unhappy—'

'That's just *when* people walk away from it all,' the sergeant said. 'And generally they walk back when they've sorted themselves out. My advice is to leave it be, sir. Your daughter will come back.'

'But she hasn't any money—'

The sergeant thought about that. He looked as if he'd heard this kind of thing many times before. 'Does she have any skills, any qualifications?'

'Well, she trained as a nurse—'

'There you are then, Mr Mertagen. She's probably found herself a job somewhere, some hospital with living accommodation. I mean, she's not some crazy fourteen-year-old. I shouldn't worry.'

Good advice, but hard to follow. Every time the phone rang in her flat, Catherine leapt to answer it, hoping to hear her sister's voice. Every time she telephoned her father after his return to Hulmesley, she expected to be told Laura had been in touch.

Then came the summer, and she had to travel to Los Angeles on behalf of one of her clients. The autumn was taken up with the succeeding negotiations – special fabrics were needed by a costume designer in one of the big Hollywood studios.

Tired but triumphant, Catherine at last invited her young client to sign the contract one evening in November, drank some celebratory champagne with him, and saw him out. She was promising herself a long, hot bath and an early night when the phone rang.

As always, she hoped it might be Laura and expected it to be her father. Instead she heard quite a different voice.

'Is that the home of Miss Catherine Mertagen?'

'Who wants to know?' she said guardedly.

'Catherine? Is that you? This is Malcolm.'

'Malcolm?'

'Malcolm Sanders – do you remember me?'

'*Malcolm*?'

'Is this a bad time to call? I can easily—'

'No, no, it's not inconvenient—' She broke off. What had made her respond like that?

'I hear you're very busy these days. I'd quite understand if you didn't have time to talk.'

'I'm just completely taken aback.' And that at least was totally honest.

'Of course – it's like a ghost from the past, isn't it.' The rich velvety voice had deepened a little over the years. But it was unmistakable. It still had the power to stir her blood. 'How long is it – eight years? Nine?'

She could have told him exactly how long it was. 'It's a long time,' she rejoined. Then, with more crispness, 'What made you ring me?'

'Well, it's the most extraordinary thing. I was in Cyprus—'

'Cyprus?' She remembered that his wife was a Greek-Cypriot beauty.

'And I was in this bar in Limassol that expatriot Brits like to go to because it has British beer—'

'In a bar?' What on earth was Malcolm doing, taking his wife to a tourist bar?

'I got talking to this fellow, it's always the way. We say it's a small world and groan at the cliché, but the fact is that almost everywhere you go you *do* seem to run into someone who lived in the next street or served in the army with you. And when I mentioned to this chap that I came from Norfolk, he said, I know a girl who was born there, in a town called Hulmesley. And what do you know? He knew you!'

Catherine drew in a breath. 'What was his name?' She'd already guessed.

'Fenner Chelburne, he's some sort of painter. I got the impression he'd just moved to Limassol from some little Greek island – some problem about getting money transferred there from a British bank. But wasn't that strange, that he should know you? He says he did some fabric designs for you.'

She could tell that Malcolm was nervous. He was talking too much, too eagerly. She said, to put distance between them at this moment of renewed contact, 'Fenner was what you might call my first "discovery". So how is he?'

'Hard to tell. I think he and his friend . . .' He hesitated, and she guessed the friend was the boy from Bridgwater. 'Well, anyway, he was having disagreements with someone over money. But never mind that – he told me you were a big success in the design world. How are you, Cath?'

'I'm . . . I'm well, Malcolm. And you?'

'Oh . . . you know . . . good and bad. I've got this big job in London now, in the City, at the HQ of Norfolk Regal, I handle a big section of the investment funds. And I was wondering . . . you know . . . if we could meet up some time? For a meal, or a drink, or something. For old times' sake.'

'Oh, I don't think—'

'Please, Cath – don't just turn it down,' he broke in, quick and intense. 'I'd really like to see you again. I'd like to apologise for some of the things I said all those years ago.'

The last thing she needed was to go out for a drink with a married man. She began, 'I don't really need an apology, Malcolm. We were both to blame—'

'No, it was my fault, I was prejudiced and thick-headed. I've thought of it so often and wished I could tell you . . . and hear how you've got along since then, and catch up with all your news. I'd so much like to see you, Cath . . .'

She said very carefully, 'Your wife would be there too?'

'My wife's in Cyprus,' he said.

Something in the way he said it gave her a message. There was a heaviness in the words, as if it was a weight he had to carry all the time. His wife – her name was Mari, she remembered

– was in Cyprus but not just for a short visit: was that what he meant?

While she was still coping with this unexpected thought, he said again, 'Please let's meet, Cath.'

She knew she was a fool. But she couldn't resist that rich, warm voice. Besides, his wife was in Cyprus . . . whatever that meant. 'Well, all right. Just for a drink, then.'

'Oh, that's great, that's marvellous! Tomorrow evening?'

'Tomorrow. Well, yes, that would be all right.'

'Whereabouts are you? I looked you up in the phone book, it seems you're in Hammersmith – shall I come out your way?'

'This would be after your office day, would it?'

'Yes, up in the City. Things go pretty dead here after the offices close.'

'It would really be better if I came into Town so we could meet halfway – I work from home so I could pack up any time.'

'Well then, shall we say six o'clock? Now where – how about the Savoy bar?'

The Savoy bar. What a contrast to their old days in Hulmesley – a trawlermen's pub by the harbour had been their rendezvous. But those had been different people; young, poor, at the very beginning of life. Now they were experienced, sophisticated. Weren't they?

'All right then. Six o'clock tomorrow.'

'I really look forward to it, Cath. Six o'clock at the Savoy.'

She replaced the receiver, then sat staring at it. She could hardly believe she'd been so silly. She wouldn't go, of course. She'd only agreed so as to get him off the line. She'd telephone the Savoy tomorrow evening and ask them to pass on a message – she couldn't come, unexpected pressure of work.

This was what she told herself all next day. It was difficult to explain to herself, therefore, why she changed into a new white mini-dress and white knee-high boots. All the way in the taxi she was deciding to tell the driver to turn around and take her home. But she was still sitting there when the taxi turned off the Strand for the Savoy Hotel. Even as she was handing in her coat at the cloakroom she was asking herself why she was doing this.

The bar was warm and relatively quiet. Shaded lights sent a muted glow over the fine wood panelling and the dark green leather. From a table against the far wall, Malcolm rose to greet her.

'My word, you're a sight for sore eyes,' he remarked, taking both her hands in his. 'I won't say you haven't changed a bit, but only for the better!' At his nod, a waiter appeared. 'What will you have to drink?'

She asked for a Cinzano. While he was passing on her order she took the chance to study him. He was clad in a dark City suit with a blue shirt that had a white collar and cuffs. His dark hair was well barbered. He was leaner than when she'd last seen him, with lines at the corners of his lips and at his eyes. His mouth had a set that seemed to tell of words often held back – for business reasons, she supposed. Working in the investment department of a big insurance company must call for discretion.

'What I heard from this fellow in Cyprus,' he said, picking conversational ground, 'was that you were something big in Velton's department store. But you said on the phone that you were working from home?'

'Yes, I was with Velton's but I run an art agency now.'

'What – Barbara Hepworth? David Hockney?'

'Hardly! No, my clients are designers.' Their drinks came, and she spent the next few minutes explaining about fabric designers.

'So you're doing well?' His glance at the fine wool of her dress, at her expensive handbag, backed up the question.

'Pretty well. What I like about it is that I enjoy it.'

'Yes, I can see that. You have that sparkle. And so how is everybody – your father? Laura?'

'Dad is pretty well. As for Laura . . . well, Laura's off on her own somewhere.'

'How do you mean? I remember my mother saying once that she was married to some bright lad – or is my memory playing false?'

'No, she was married – still is, I suppose – but they split up.'

'Ah.' He said it with just the faintest lift of the shoulders, not exactly a shrug but as if to say, I know about that sort of thing. 'And you haven't tied the knot, or so this chap in Cyprus said?'

'No, I've never married.'

'Career-girl, eh?'

It was her turn to shrug a little. She sipped her drink. 'How about you? I can see you're doing well. How is your family? I think I heard you had a little boy.'

'Yes.' For a moment he said no more. That in itself was a clue that things had gone wrong. 'I've a son – Leonidas – he's just passed his seventh birthday.' He sighed. 'I don't see as much of him as I'd like.'

She said nothing. She knew there was more to come.

'He's in Cyprus too. I don't quite know how I allowed it to happen but I only see him when I can get time to fly out there.'

'I'm sorry,' she said. 'You speak as if it's a permanent situation?'

'Pretty permanent. You see, you can't argue against it. A child should be with his mother.'

'Of course. But . . . why . . . ?'

'It was never a good marriage,' he said in a sudden burst of confession. He was frowning, listening to himself say it and disapproving, yet unable to prevent it. 'I blame myself – because I married the wrong girl.'

'Malcolm—' It was a protest, a warning.

But he had begun to speak of it, and couldn't be put off. 'If I hadn't been so pigheaded you and I could have made things up, Cath. But no, I was determined to show it didn't matter that we'd split up, and went rushing back to Nicosia to find Mari.' He gave a wry smile. 'You ought to see a wedding in a Greek Orthodox Church, it's quite an experience. Her family went deep into debt to pay for the banquet.'

'Into debt? But I thought . . . I'd heard that she comes from a fine old Cypriot family?'

'Oh yes, their name is mentioned in all the stories about Cyprus and the Crusades. Unfortunately they seem to have backed the wrong side in various later wars so they ended up with lands that are mostly barren mountainside. Mari had very little in the way of dowry—'

'Dowry?' exclaimed Catherine.

'Oh yes, that's still important there, and that's where the trouble lay. Mari's brothers intended to marry her off to some neighbouring landowner who would take her for the few acres of hillside she'd bring him. But then I arrived back on the scene. I'd met them while I was doing my National Service, and now here I came, appearing to Mari like the perfect escape from a marriage with a narrow-minded curmudgeon.'

Catherine gave a sympathetic shake of the head. 'I'm sure it couldn't have been as calculated as that, Malcolm.'

'I certainly didn't see it that way at the time. I thought it was tremendously romantic to fly in from England and save her from being married off against her will.'

A cheerful group came into the bar, demanding rounds of drinks before the performance in the theatre next door. For a moment Catherine and Malcolm watched them. Then she said, 'Go on, Malcolm. Tell me.' Because although she had warned herself against becoming involved again, she found she wanted to hear everything he had to tell.

'Mari came to England with all sorts of wrong ideas. I realise now that she thought of England as synonymous with London. She pictured herself leading a fashionable life in Mayfair, shopping at Harrods, the theatre every evening, nightclubs and parties . . .' He paused, looking back at that sad illusion, a cynical smile touching his lips. 'In fact the branch I was given as the new start to my career after National Service was in Manchester.'

'Oh dear.'

'You can say that again. She never got accustomed to the grey skies and the cold weather. Of course there are fashion shops and nightclubs in Manchester but my salary didn't run that far. We had innumerable quarrels.' She could hear the regret with which he remembered. 'The last straw for her was when I was promoted to a bigger branch in Newcastle. That promotion was forecast for almost six months and she was sure I was going to get a London branch. She was so disappointed it truly made her ill. She endured two days of the cold winds blowing along the Tyne, then packed up and went back to Cyprus. And of course she took our little boy with her.'

Just a simple domestic tragedy. What could she say? She could be direct and honest. 'I'm so sorry, Malcolm.'

'Don't be. It's my own fault.'

'How long is it since she went back?'

'Almost six years now. She never comes to England. I go there as often as I can, to try to keep in touch with the boy.'

'You couldn't—?' She broke off. This was a delicate subject. 'You haven't thought of divorce? I think you have grounds, after such a long separation—'

'But she'd get custody of Leo!' he said, in a voice of so much pain that she winced.

Yet since he had told her his problem, perhaps he wanted advice, or at least suggestions. 'If you had a good lawyer—'

'Her brothers would contest any decision made in London by an English judge. The family has a lot of prestige, their reputation would suffer if they seemed to give in. You must understand, the situation in Cyprus after the breakaway . . . well, it's not favourable to someone like me walking in and taking away Mari's son.'

'And what about the little boy? What does Leo say?'

'Oh, Leo . . .' His gaze softened, his eyes looked at a picture off in some dreamworld. 'He's still at the stage where he's thrilled with a new Dinky Toy and plans on being an airline pilot. He likes "modern" things – planes, tape-recorders, he's the only one on the farm who understands the workings of the electric pump that gets the water out of the well.'

'A perfectly normal little boy, by the sound of it,' she commented, smiling.

Rather to her surprise Malcolm said nothing to that. She'd thought he'd want to run on for a while about his son. In fact, as if he felt he'd spent too long on his troubles, he turned the subject. Catherine was just as glad. She could tell he was in a very stressful situation, and vulnerable too – a man separated from his wife and little boy, lonely, rejected, anxious . . .

So they talked about the business world – about Harry Hyams and the continued emptiness of his tower block Centre Point, about the shops opening all over the country to cope with the demand for up-to-date hi-fi systems, about whether changing the front page of *The Times* from small ads to news would make any difference to circulation. They even tried to decide the meaning of the recently-invented word 'psychedelic'.

At seven-fifteen Catherine rose to leave.

'I couldn't persuade you to stay and have dinner with me?' Malcolm suggested.

'I'm afraid not. I've another engagement.'

'Of course. Perhaps I could ring you?'

'Why not?' she agreed, and shook hands.

She took the Tube home, and as the train rushed through the tunnels she was asking herself why she'd invented another engagement. Why not have dinner with him? Where could be the harm?

The harm, she knew, lay in the fact that they were immediately becoming too close. She had felt an instant rapport with him. The years between seemed done away with – but that was illusion. They weren't the same two people who had been so passionately in love – he was a married man, she was no longer an eager girl. Yet though life had taught them both its bitter lessons, there had been no chasm between them at this meeting. As he spoke she caught, as she always used to, not only the words but the layers of meaning beneath them. They were instinctively close – and that was dangerous.

That night she didn't go to bed until very late. She stayed up dealing with correspondence until midnight, then turned on her record-player to listen to Joan Baez. But after a while she switched it off, for the words of the songs were full of challenges that she hadn't the energy to face. Her own problems were enough for her.

What was she going to do if Malcolm telephoned again?

She resolved to tell him she was too busy to meet him. Then her own sense of justice would prick at her – why should she reject his efforts to resume their friendship? But the answer was plain: what had been between them in the past was never friendship. They had been deeply in love.

So they ought to steer clear of each other now, for fear of falling in love again. But loneliness lay all around them, like a wasteland – why shouldn't they meet, offer each other a little warmth, a little comfort?

Because, her hard commonsense told her, it would be difficult to limit the relationship to mere comradeship.

In his service flat in Highgate Malcolm Sanders was having exactly the same argument with himself. What right had he to be in contact with Catherine Mertagen? He was a married man, with a wife who knew how to make life difficult and a little boy he missed constantly. These were two circumstances that should have caused him to steer clear of further trouble.

Yet the moment the rather drunk man in the Mosaika Bar had mentioned Catherine's name, he knew he was going to look her up in the London telephone book the moment he got back. When he rang her, he'd been prepared for rejection – she had every reason to tell him to get lost. He had been an arrogant fool all those years ago, daring to tell her that she must make her sister give up her work as a healer. He – what right had *he* to make conditions about how Laura lived her life?

When he looked back down the arches of the years, he knew that his parting with Catherine had been the biggest mistake of his life. To pay her out, he'd rushed off to Cyprus where he knew Mari would welcome him. Mari had made it plain that she couldn't continue to see him merely as a friend – her brothers had warned her it was harming her reputation. So when he went back he knew he was going as a suitor.

Pride buoyed him up: the Mirtiados were so delighted to have him as a brother-in-law. They imagined his prospects were glitteringly splendid. He had done his National Service, had university qualifications, was a 'professional man', an executive in a big company.

In the middle of the wedding banquet, Malcolm had a cold and awful moment when he knew it was all a terrible mistake. It was as if he'd woken up from a strange dream – and fallen at once into a nightmare. He was married to Mari. He couldn't get out of it honourably.

He took his beautiful bride home to England. His friends in Hulmesley had given her a warm welcome – so beautiful, almost exotic, dark and flashingly bright, with a delightful foreign accent, how could they not welcome her? If she was surprised by the provincialism of their daily life, she hid it well. She accepted that in fifties Britain servants were not so cheap to hire as in Cyprus. Perhaps she imagined that once they went off to settle on their own, she would be able to establish the kind of household she was used to: a spacious, airy house with someone always at her beck and call for the tedious tasks.

He tried to make a home with her in the cold, grey climate of the Midlands. He knew it was up to him to make the marriage succeed and saw with apprehension that he was failing her. She disliked housework, found household shopping boring, thought having only a part-time cleaning woman was beneath her dignity. A great source of discontent was when she noticed that her bright dresses looked wrong under the cloudy skies of the north. She resented changing to duller though more fashionable tones. It seemed to rankle almost more deeply than anything.

Malcolm hoped the birth of their son would mend the marriage. But some things are not capable of being mended. Mari had a bad time at Leo's birth, never seemed to get back her vitality, became even more contemptuous of their way of life, and at last packed up and left. At first it had been for a holiday in the sun to restore her health. Then it had grown into a separation.

To begin with the Mirtiados brothers had been on Malcolm's side. It was a wife's duty to be with her husband, she brought shame on the family by living apart from him. Mari cried, pleaded, stormed and cajoled. She made herself ill with dislike whenever it seemed she might be forced by family pressure to go back to England.

Recently, however, the brothers had changed their tactics. They supported Mari's claim that the northern winters were bad for her. It was up to her husband to make a home for her in the sun, where she could be well and happy. He must transfer to a branch of his company in the Levant.

He explained that the Norfolk Regal Insurance Company had no branches in the Eastern Mediterranean. Very well, said Georgiou and Nikko, he must get a job with a different firm – in Athens, perhaps.

He explained that to move out of the Norfolk Regal at this point in his career would be suicidal. He had been given a very important role in the investment planning of the company. He knew of no other insurance company who would take him on at the same level. Very well, said Georgiou and Nikko, he must set up in business in Cyprus or in Greece on his own, as an investment counsellor.

He explained that although he spoke Cypriot-Greek fairly well by this stage, he didn't have enough grasp of the Greek language to conduct delicate business negotiations. Moreover, to set up on his own needed capital, and he couldn't raise anything like enough – certainly not for an office out on the fringe of stock exchange activity.

And there the matter rested. Mari's menfolk were adamant that their sister couldn't, shouldn't, return to Britain. It was up to Malcolm to solve this problem.

He had begun to suspect that it was some sort of ploy, a delaying tactic. They knew very well that he couldn't move out to the Eastern Mediterranean and set up in business, yet they kept suggesting it as if it were the solution. He didn't understand it.

And all the while he was anxious about the boy, who was not faring well on the farm on the arid mountain slopes.

Leo had had a collapse the previous summer. He had had headaches and vomiting. The family had written it off as heat-stroke, a common enough occurrence. The elderly housekeeper had applied cold towels and kept the little boy in a shaded room for a couple of days. When he didn't recover quickly she changed her diagnosis to mild food poisoning or perhaps summer fever, of which there were always cases during the hot months. She was so sure the boy would be up and about in a week or so that they didn't even bother to contact his father.

Malcolm arrived for a visit in October, when the heat was waning. He found his son listless and pale. He insisted on taking him to a doctor in Nicosia, who examined him thoroughly, took some tests, and prescribed hexamine.

'He's had some slight infection, I believe,' said Dr Ladas. 'Something that has lingered on perhaps a little too long. If I had seen him earlier I would perhaps have prescribed antibiotics. Well, it will take time before he can pick up strength but with a quiet regime and a light diet I have no doubt he'll be as good as new by spring.'

Spring came, and it was true Leo was better. But he had little nervous spasms, little attacks of weakness in his limbs that seemed to occur when he was under stress. He fell behind in his schooling.

He wasn't the same little boy who used to rush to greet Malcolm when he drove up to the farm.

'He's not picking up as well as Dr Ladas predicted. We should take him to London to see a specialist,' Malcolm urged Mari.

'He's much better than when you came in October. He'll improve even more now spring's here—'

'You see him from day to day and don't realise how he's changed, Mari. He doesn't seem to laugh as much as he used to.'

'Oh, he'll be dashing about next time you come.'

'But don't you think it would be a good idea to take him to a London doctor?'

She shook her head with vehemence. 'If you think you're going to drag me back to that dreary wet climate again, you're wrong! And if Leo needs a doctor, there are plenty of specialists in Nicosia.'

Short of taking Leo away by force, Malcolm could see no way of getting the child the attention he seemed to need. The Mirtiados family shared the view held by many in that part of the world – that if God wished a sufferer to be made better, he would see to it in His own good time. Rushing to doctors was to question the intentions of the Almighty, and rushing to London doctors was an insult to the care and attention he was given here at home.

The dilemma was still unresolved. Malcolm didn't know what to do for the best. Wherever he looked in his private life, there were dark clouds.

Into this sombre scene the name of Catherine Mertagen sent a ray of brilliant light. Merely to see her, to hear her voice, would be balm to his weary spirit. He knew it was wrong, he knew it was dangerous, but nevertheless he couldn't stop himself from getting in touch.

Logic seemed to play no part in this process. Now that they had met, now that the first difficult encounter had taken place, nothing could prevent him from asking to see her again. If she agreed to meet him he would go to the rendezvous with a foolish but stubborn hope.

A hope for a second chance, however unlikely it might seem.

Chapter Twenty-one

For Christmas that year Catherine went home again to Hulmesley. She'd offered to cook Christmas dinner for her father and had invited his chess-playing neighbour Ernest Goode and his wife Nell. It was a sort of thank-you to them for the kindness they'd shown to Gerald over the last few lonely years.

Catherine drove to Norfolk loaded with all kinds of festive goodies from the best London stores. Invited to the feast were not only the Goodes, but Malcolm and his parents. The Sanderses had scarcely seen Catherine since the break-up of the engagement with Malcolm so many years ago. It might prove to be a rather embarrassing encounter, she felt. Since Malcolm had contacted her, they had been in touch only a couple of times. These occasions had been nothing more than an hour or so in each other's company, a rather cool friendship. He was after all a married man.

Whatever they might think of the renewed acquaintance between their son and Catherine Mertagen, Jim and Mary Sanders were determined not to summon up the past by any word or deed. On the contrary, Catherine sensed in them a particular warmth towards her.

As they were setting the table together for Christmas lunch, Mary said to her: 'Jim tells me I'm not to be tactless but I can't help saying, dear, it would have been a lot better if Malcolm had've married *you*.'

'There was no way to foretell it would turn out so sadly,' Catherine countered, half-hoping to end the conversation there.

'Well, I always thought it was a mistake,' Mrs Sanders insisted. 'Of course she was a real beauty, was Mari, still is from what I saw in the last snapshots Malcolm took with the boy. How old is she – thirty-one? Thirty-two? But the fact is, she was always a bit at odds with me while she was here. You know what I mean, thought our house was poky and cold, was astonished to see me doing my own washing-up . . . Well, thought I, you'd better get used to it because Malcolm's salary won't run to a fleet of servants.'

'She was expecting something different.'

'She certainly was!' Pink with remembered vexation, Mrs Sanders banged down table mats with unnecessary vehemence.

'But she's given you a lovely little grandson,' Catherine said. She too had seen snapshots, taken on Malcolm's visits to Cyprus. They showed a skinny little boy in shorts, his medium-brown hair curly and thick, grey-blue eyes, brown legs ending in little bare feet in dusty sandals. He had a serious look as he gazed into the camera.

'Oh, from all accounts he's a dear little thing,' agreed Mary. 'But you know we've only seen him the once since she took him away. We went out for our holiday – what was it, four years ago, Jim?' She called into the living-room for her husband's verification.

A grunted agreement came from him. He was listening to a description of chess from Gerald.

Mary went on, 'We didn't impose on them, we stayed in a holiday hotel in Limassol and drove out to the farm to see them each day. But I don't know, it wasn't very enjoyable, Mari was on her guard all the time in case we tried to persuade her to come home with us and they didn't like it that the little boy enjoyed being taken out for rides in the car. He wanted to drive it – dear little thing . . .' She sighed. 'Goodness knows how it's all going to end. She isn't ever going to come back to England, if you ask me, and Malcolm can't go out there without taking a tremendous step down in his career – and except for Leo, what's to take him there? It's not as if she's pining away for love of him.'

'You think she doesn't love him?' ventured Catherine.

'Oh, never did, dear! Thrilled to bits to get away from the farm, and no wonder. Farming out there isn't like here – goats on a hillside nibbling at scrub, a few vines . . . If Malcolm'd been as rich and important as she imagined, it might have been a happy enough marriage – she was really looking forward to her part as a happy young bride and all that. But I had my doubts from the minute she was unpacking and asked me who would press her things that came out creased!'

Catherine suppressed a smile. She could imagine Mrs Sanders' indignation.

'I mean to say, we know we have to press our own things, now don't we? But out there, though they don't seem to have two pennies to rub together, we found they had a maid who cleans the house and a maid who does the washing and ironing, and a man who looks after the garden and keeps their old car running . . .'

The two women set out cutlery and wine glasses, folded napkins into waterlilies, arranged a centrepiece of ivy and Christmas roses.

For a time conversation was limited to their task. Then Mary inquired, 'Did Malcolm tell you the boy's not too well?'

Catherine looked up, surprised. 'He's never mentioned it.' But then, they'd only really met twice more since that first drink at the Savoy. And they'd each kept to general subjects, 'safe' subjects.

'Malcolm keeps asking Mari to bring him to London to see a doctor. But she won't. She seems to think it's some sort of trick to get her back to England and make her stay. As if he would, against her will!' she ended with indignation.

'What's wrong with Leo?'

'Nobody seems to know. He's just poorly. He had some sort of illness the summer before last and never rightly got over it. The doctor there keeps saying he'll grow out of it but . . . well . . . it's a worry . . .'

One o'clock struck on the mantelpiece clock. It was time to put the vegetables on to cook and get the turkey out to cool for carving. The two women gave up their chat to concentrate on the final preparations for lunch. Malcolm, who had been out visiting old friends in Hulmesley, came in in time to open the wine.

It was a long, enjoyable afternoon, including the Queen's speech and a late tea of traditional mince pies (from Fortnum's) and plum cake. The guests said farewell and made their separate ways home, the Goodes to their house a few doors down and the Sanderses to other friends in Hulmesley.

Catherine was putting away the last of the crockery when the doorbell rang. She went down to answer it. On the doorstep were the Colvilles.

Catherine had only had glimpses of Desmond and Phoebe Colville since the break-up of Laura's marriage. It seemed they were too deeply embarrassed by what had happened to want to be in touch.

They blamed themselves for having brought Toby Lindham into the quiet life of Hulmesely. He had been their protégé, a young man of whom they'd had a high opinion. When news filtered through to them, first that he had vanished from Laura's life without a word, and second that he had taken almost all the profits from the clinic they had helped him start, they were stricken.

'Cathie my dear!' carolled Phoebe. 'Now don't be worried, we're not here to spoil your Christmas party—'

'No, no, not at all,' Catherine said, stepping aside to usher them in. 'We had friends for Christmas dinner but they've gone—'

'We're on our way to an evening affair,' puffed Phoebe as she climbed the stairs. 'My, how this brings it all back . . . I remember so vividly, my first visit here!'

She reached the landing, out of breath. Catherine took the chance to nip in front of her to give her father a little warning before they entered the living-room.

'Dad, it's Phoebe and Desmond—'

'Oh!' He rose from his chair, upsetting his chessboard. Gerald had always felt awkward with the Colvilles, for to him they were landed gentry whereas he was an artisan, a frame-maker. After Toby disappeared, he had been nurturing some rancour against them because he couldn't help blaming them in some way. Months had gone by since they'd done more than nod hello to each other in the streets of Hulmesley.

And now here they were to wreck his plans for a quiet evening with the Christmas programme on the BBC and another stab at the Euwe opening of 1917.

But, after all, it was the festive season, peace and goodwill to all men. 'How are you?' he said with forced cordiality. 'Have you been having a good Christmas?'

'Not bad, not bad,' said Desmond Colville, shaking hands. 'We just felt, Phoebe and I . . . you know, you look back over the year and start thinking about New Year resolutions—'

'Yes, and I take them seriously, you see, I make them in church so I really mean to carry them out,' his wife took it up. 'One of the resolutions I was going to make is to do something about this estrangement that's grown up—'

'Because, of course, we blame ourselves terribly for what happened—'

'No, no, you mustn't—'

'But we *were* at fault, we let ourselves be blinded—'

'Oh, you weren't the only ones—'

'The sad thing is that we had warnings, hints – that partner he had, the one he was involved in a boat-building business with—'

'He let him down horrendously,' Desmond said, his anger causing him to raise his voice and drown out his wife. 'The poor fellow's gone into bankruptcy. And we hear there are debts elsewhere. Not to mention rumours about his love life, if you can call it that.'

'So you see, when I told Desmond the other day about my New Year resolution, he said, "Why don't we do it for Christmas?" So here we are.'

Catherine had been trying to take coats and hats and receiving the off-putting gestures of people who only intend to stay a minute. 'Let me get you a drink,' she offered.

'No thank you, my dear, we're on our way to the Withineys, we can only stay a minute, truly.' Phoebe fumbled in her capacious handbag. 'I brought a couple of little things—'

'Oh, Phoebe, you shouldn't have!'

'No, no, it's nothing. It's just that when I was doing some Christmas shopping in Lincoln, I happened to see this new book about chess in the shop window, and I thought it would be ideal for you, Gerald. But then – almost as if it was *meant* – I found the ideal book for you, Cathie.' She produced two slim packages in Christmas wrapping. She handed them to their recipients.

Rather more embarrassed than they would have liked to admit, Catherine and her father opened the presents. Gerald said, 'Oh, my word, thank you,' when he saw the title by a much admired chess journalist: *Capablanca re-examined*. But Catherine was rendered speechless when she saw hers.

The Power Within, she read on the blue and yellow cover. It was the paperback edition of Laura's book.

'Well, I shall certainly have a go at some of these problems over the holiday,' Gerald was saying in a much more natural tone. 'These classic chess games, they still cause us to put our thinking caps on. Cathie dear, what did you—?' He broke off, astonished, when he saw what she was holding out.

'You didn't know it was out?' Desmond said, glancing from one to the other.

Gerald looked at his daughter. She shook her head. 'We had no idea,' he said.

'You're not in touch with Laura *at all*?'

'I . . . I'm afraid not.'

'But that's . . . that's terribly sad,' Phoebe burst out. 'You were such a close family!'

'Yes . . . well . . . there you are,' Gerald said with a world of regret in his tone.

'But Gerald, hasn't she ever been in touch since . . . when was it?'

'Spring of this year.'

'But where did she go? What's she doing?'

'We've no idea,' Catherine said, and felt her eyes brim with tears at the awfulness of the confession.

Laura's ghost had haunted their Christmas gathering. Even the fact that Malcolm had come to share the meal with them hadn't banished the ache of Laura's absence. Where was she, how was she faring? Father and daughter had hoped for at least a Christmas card, but all through December they had asked each other the same question when they spoke on the telephone: 'Anything from Laura? No, nothing, nothing.'

'When she went away she left a note for Cathie,' Gerald said. 'She wanted to be on her own to "sort things out".'

'But it's such a long time!'

'I know, we went to the police after a few weeks, but they said there's nothing they can do. If she wants to be off by herself, who's to stop her?'

'And you've never tried to find her?' Phoebe asked.

'I wouldn't know how,' Gerald admitted.

'No,' agreed Phoebe. 'It's not the sort of thing anybody's used to—'

'And maybe it would be wrong, anyhow,' her husband put in. 'We think the world of Laura and miss her – but you have to look at it from Laura's point of view. A marriage break-up is a tremendous blow, and the way Toby did it made it worse than most.' He bit his lip at the recollection.

'It wasn't only that,' said Catherine. But then she stopped, for Laura's confidences mustn't be repeated to anyone else. Sighing, she turned over the book in her hands. 'She never really thought she should be writing this,' she said. 'It was just one of the things that Toby talked her into. I don't understand how this comes to be in the bookshops, but I suppose there was some sort of contract with the American publisher that's got to run its course.'

'I hope Toby's not earning any money from it!' Gerald said with a flash of resentment.

'That's not likely,' Desmond Colville remarked. 'That poor boat-building partner has heard on the grapevine that Toby's in the West Indies, trying to get together a consortium to build a yacht marina.'

'Lord help anybody that invests in it,' Gerald said.

A silence fell. They were all thinking that Toby had managed to come well out of the disaster of his marriage, whereas Laura was lost somewhere, still trying to heal her wounds.

'Well, we must be going,' Phoebe said, standing up and buttoning her coat around her buxom figure. 'We just wanted to drop in and give you the books and wish you a Merry Christmas.'

'Yes, thank you, and the same to you,' chorused Catherine and her father.

'And you will let us know if you hear from Laura?' Desmond

asked as Catherine went out with them to their car. 'It seems so wrong that she's off on her own like this, when we owe her so much . . .'

Catherine was in complete agreement but could see no way to alter the situation. Perhaps she had more respect for her sister's wishes than the others: if Laura said she wanted to be alone, she had a right to solitude.

All the same, it was a subject she found herself discussing with Malcolm when they met next day. They had arranged to drive out into the countryside and have a pub lunch. The land lay around them, sleeping under a light blanket of snow. The sky was a clear steely blue against which the winter trees looked like delicate Chinese scissorwork. They sat in the bay window of the inn, looking out at the scene, each a little preoccupied.

'It shook me, Malcolm, seeing her name on that book,' she murmured.

'I don't doubt it. Mrs Colville thought you'd be pleased with it, of course.'

'I suppose so, but she's heard all the gossip about the break-up of the marriage and Laura's vanishing act. Part of the reason for her visit was to find out if we knew where she is.'

'You really have no idea?'

'Not the slightest. Phoebe seemed to think we ought to make some effort to find her, but in the first place I don't know whether we ought to, and in the second place I wouldn't know where to begin.'

'Well, as to whether you ought to . . . that's up to you,' he replied after a moment's thought. 'But as to where to begin – what about the book?'

'*What* about the book?'

'I don't know much about the book world. But it's Laura's book, right? She'd have to give her permission for it to be published over here – it was published in the States first of all, wasn't it?'

'Yes, in a better edition, hardback with a dramatic cover. Then it was supposed to be coming out in paperback there in the summer, if I remember rightly. But I heard nothing about a British publication.'

'There you are, then.'

'Where?'

'Write to the publisher. Ask for her address.'

'Oh, they wouldn't give it out, Malcolm.' But all the same she felt a frisson. Surely the publisher must know where Laura was living?

She left the thought to simmer in her mind. She turned the subject to Malcolm's trip to Cyprus, which was to take place in time for the Greek Orthodox Christmas in two weeks' time. 'You've wrapped all your presents for Leo?' she inquired.

'Oh yes, he loves that, lots of separate parcels to unwrap. I've got him a kit to build a model aeroplane – I hope it isn't beyond him.'

'He's how old – seven? Doesn't it say on the box what age group it's for?'

'Yes, it says eight to ten . . . but you see he has this tremor in his hands.'

'What do you mean?'

'Oh, he had an illness the summer before last – some sort of glandular fever or something. He's never been quite right since then.'

'Your mother said something about it yesterday. But you've never mentioned it?'

He shrugged. 'Why should I load my troubles on to you? You've enough of your own, for heaven's sake.'

'But I want to hear!'

'No.' He was shaking his head with emphasis. He wanted – he longed – to spill it all out to her, because he knew her sympathy would wrap around him like a warm shawl. But they were coming too close too quickly. They were friends again – more than friends – yet he mustn't overload the relationship.

He flew to Cyprus with a crowd of winter sunshine seekers. Catherine went back to work. But one evening alone in her flat she heard again Malcolm's words: 'Write to the publisher. Ask for her address.'

What harm could there be in merely asking? She sat down at her desk. Now that the festive season was over, companies and firms would be back to normal. It was time to write.

She hoped for a swift response but nothing came the following week or the week after that. Malcolm returned from Cyprus on the Sunday of that week. He rang her from the airport.

'Cathie, can I come and see you? I've something very important to tell you.'

She could tell he was struggling under intense emotion. His deep voice almost cracked on the words. Something very important had happened. To the little boy? 'Where are you?' she asked, hearing loud background noises that spoke of a public phone.

'I've just landed, I'm waiting for my bag to come off the carousel. I thought – if you didn't mind – I'd grab a taxi and—'

'Of course. Come right away.'

During the two hours it took him to get out of the airport and be driven to her flat, she worried herself into a fever. She darted about the living-room gathering up Sunday papers, straightening cushions, and then made herself busy setting out a tray of sandwiches in case he was hungry. She flew to the door when she heard the taxi outside. He was paying it off as she got the house door open. 'Is something wrong? You sounded odd,' she asked as he crossed the pavement.

'I don't know how to look at it,' he said. She took his raincoat and newspaper from him while he carried his travel bag. They went upstairs to her flat. All the time she was trying to read his expression. When he came into the warm, cheerful living-room he seemed to sigh with appreciation. 'I'm sorry to burst in on you like this, Cathie, but I've been going over and over it all on the plane and I just don't know what to think.'

'What is it? No, wait – would you like something to eat? A drink?'

'I ate on the plane – at least I tried to. A drink would be good.'

She fetched him a scotch and soda. He sank down in an armchair to drink it. 'Ah, this is good.'

'Now,' she commanded, sitting opposite and watching him with anxiety, 'tell me! Is it about Leo?'

He was shaking his head in perplexity. 'No, not Leo. At least, not directly. Cathie . . . Mari has asked me for a divorce.'

Chapter Twenty-two

Painfully the story unfolded.

'On Christmas Eve we went to the local church, as we always do, and I was introduced to this chap Yannis Artidias, "friend of the family", nothing remarkable. Then I noticed he turned up once or twice during the next few days of festivity . . .' Malcolm frowned. 'I thought nothing of it except that the brothers seemed awfully keen to be on his good side.'

'Mari's brothers?'

'Yes, very much the bosses in anything to do with the family. I could understand their wanting to be on good terms with him, he's clearly got pots of money. Leo mentioned him to me once or twice – "Uncle Yannis" – it seems he's been around for something like a year.'

'And it's because of him . . . ?'

'Yes, but it's not as simple as that. You see, he's from mainland Greece, a property developer, looking for a place to build a tourist hotel in Cyprus. And the Mirtiados family desperately want him to buy their estate. Well, I didn't know any of this until last night. Last night . . .' He stared back at it as if it were in the distant past although it was a bare twenty-four hours ago.

'What happened last night?' Catherine prompted.

'We went out to have dinner in Limassol. I thought it was a family party until I realised as we were getting into the cars that neither of the wives were coming.'

'The wives being—?'

'Elena and Evangelina, married to Georgiou and Nikko – they got left at home. They were standing at the gate looking daggers at us as we drove off.'

The tragi-comic picture this conjured up almost brought a smile to Malcolm's lips. But he shook his head and continued: 'I'd have thought it was a business gathering, men only, except that *Mari* was included in the party – I couldn't understand it. We went to the best hotel in Limassol, there was a table booked, wine flowing like water – not the sort of thing Georgiou and Nikko can afford.

They're perpetually hard up. I know for a fact that the money I send out to support Mari and Leo somehow leaks into their pockets . . .' He sighed.

Catherine couldn't help thinking that to marry into a family like that was a problem in itself. She waited for the rest of the story.

'Well, I discovered that Artidias was the host of the evening. It was the weirdest thing, as if he were trying to butter me up for something. I'm such an idiot, I never cottoned on. And then somewhere around midnight, when we'd eaten and drunk enough for a regiment, out it came: Georgiou and Nikko want to sell out to Artidias, Artidias wants to buy but wants Mari for his wife as part of the bargain, Mari wants to marry him and asks me for a divorce.'

'What did you say?'

'Nothing. I was absolutely stunned. To tell you the truth, I was also a little drunk. I couldn't take it in. Then they all began persuading me it was the right thing to do, and I got angry – don't ask me why, I just felt I was being set up. So I got up and walked out for some fresh air to clear my head. I was stamping up and down the main street of Limassol in the dark, muttering to myself. And then it dawned on me.'

'What?'

'Mari had part of the land as her dowry. And as she's married to me, she can't sign it away without her husband's permission. That's the way things work there.'

'Well,' Catherine said carefully, 'you'd give your permission, wouldn't you?'

'Yes, but why did they have to go through all that rigmarole? Why not just come out and tell me? I couldn't understand their way of thinking. Georgiou came out of the restaurant to find me and I told him I was going back to the farm and drove off in a temper, and they all piled into Artidias's limousine and drove after me. They started the argument again in the farm living-room. It went on nearly all night!'

No wonder he looked exhausted. She said, 'Does Leo know about this?'

'Well, yes, in a way. You see—' He broke off, colouring with anger. 'Artidias doesn't like Leo. Don't ask me why, but it's mutual, as a matter of fact – Leo doesn't like Uncle Yannis. So once Mari and Artidias are married he's going to send Leo to boarding school somewhere outside Athens. That's the plan. And Leo's been told about it and is terribly down in the dumps about it.'

'Oh, Malcolm, how awful!'

'In some ways, it would be better for him,' he replied musingly. 'There are four other children – Georgiou has a son and a daughter, Nikko has two daughters. By the way, that adds to their problems, they need money to get the girls well married in due course. But at the moment they're still kids and I think they pick on Leo – he's different, you see, and even more different since he's been ill. It might be better for him if he didn't have his cousins to deal with.'

'But boarding school, Malcolm? If he's delicate I'd think that's not—'

'I'm certainly not having him packed off out of the way just because Artidias doesn't like him. I just won't allow it!'

'What does Mari say to it?'

'I don't think she was keen on it at first. I look back now and I realise that something's been bothering them all year. Her brothers have been trying to force me to some sort of ultimatum. Now they've come out with the real situation. They're *desperate* to sell to Artidias, and to have Mari married to him as well would be a tremendous advantage.'

'But does she like him? I mean, is it all just a business proposition?'

'Oh, she likes him. She's been to Athens more than once as his guest, and I think she finds him pretty dazzling. And it would give her terrific status in the family, which is very important. Then you know, it's an awful lot of money, enough to let Georgiou and Nikko build separate modern houses for themselves – and I don't blame them for wanting that because really their family home is falling to bits. Big as it is, they're all under each other's feet. Two sets of parents, and Mari, and five children, and the servants – they have to have servants otherwise they'd sink in local esteem. And then there's the education of the children – they're "highborn", you see, they can't just go to the village school, they have to have English lessons and French lessons and heaven knows what else.'

It sounded like a different planet. Catherine said helplessly, 'And they sprang all this on you at a dinner party?'

'And then went on for hours afterwards at home, all talking at once. I gather that the brothers would get a share of the profits when the hotel gets going. It's an ideal spot; great views, water available from underground sources – that's very important in the building of the hotel. In a way it's a perfect business deal – Artidias wants to buy and they want to sell and Mari wants to go and live in

Athens – the difficulty is Leo. Artidias can't disguise the fact that he wants to get rid of Leo and start a family of his own. So Mari in the end has had to accept that he's got to go away.'

Catherine held her tongue. She didn't want to say what she felt – that the little boy was being talked about by the Mirtiados family as if he were a parcel.

'Well, once I'd got my head clear, the solution was obvious. I told Mari that if we got divorced Leo had to come and live with me. And after the first surprise, the menfolk were in unanimous agreement. Mari said no, and we all staggered off to bed about four a.m. with things in that state. In the morning she'd had time to think it over, or perhaps her brothers had got at her – I don't know. But she said over breakfast that she agreed with my plan as long as she could visit Leo when she wanted to. I really think she thought I'd say no to that.'

'Oh, surely she wouldn't think that—'

'You don't know – we've had some terrible rows in the past . . . Well, I had to drive to Nicosia in my rental car to catch my plane. She generally comes to see me off, mainly to bring Leo to see the planes – he loves that. She and I more or less settled it in the car, talking over Leo's head – I'm to file for divorce on grounds of desertion, and we'll get the lawyers to work out an agreement about Leo coming to live with me.'

'And what does Leo feel about it?'

For the first time a gleam of happiness shone in Malcolm's eyes. 'He's thrilled to bits! Of course he doesn't really take it in. All he understands is that he's going to London with Papa and will fly in an aeroplane and see a Tube train. And of course he won't have to see Uncle Yannis, for whom he's got the most almighty dislike.'

'So long as he's not unhappy, that's the main thing,' she murmured.

'Do you think I'm doing the right thing?'

'I don't think you could have made any other decision, Malcolm.'

'Yes, but when he comes, what am I going to do? He can't live with me in a service flat! There's hardly room to hang your hat, and nobody there except cleaning staff during the day when I've got to be in the office. I've got to get somewhere else to live, and find a housekeeper or a nanny or something. How do you go about that, Cathie? Have you any idea?'

'But it's not urgent, is it? I mean, you've got to file the divorce and so on—'

'Oh, no, I made it a condition that he comes almost at once.

He needs medical attention, Cath! He's at the stage where he's growing but he's not putting on flesh as he should. And there's this weakness in his hands and feet – there's something wrong with the muscles or the nerve endings or something. I want him to see a Harley Street man as soon as I can get him there.'

She listened as he went through all the problems that he would have to face. After a while she coaxed him into eating something, and they sat afterwards drinking coffee and talking.

A little after midnight he dragged himself to his feet. 'I'd better go, Cathie. I'm sorry to have loaded you with all this but I didn't know who else to talk to.'

'I'm glad you did. If there's anything I can do . . .' She longed to say, Don't go, stay, you're too tired to go back to an empty service flat. But he was in too much turmoil to be able to deal with anything more. So she rang for a taxi and waved him farewell.

Next day about lunchtime he telephoned. 'I want to apologise for talking my head off last night. Did I give you a headache?'

She laughed. 'No, but I couldn't sleep. And I had a thought, Malcolm.'

'What was that?'

'You know, I work from home. I'm here most of the time. And this is a big flat with a spare room. Why shouldn't Leo come here?'

'What?'

'It seems logical, doesn't it? Better than having to rent a house or a flat at a moment's notice and hire somebody you don't know to look after him.'

'But Cath—!'

'You don't think it's a good idea?'

'I think it's a marvellous idea! But it's too much to ask.'

'I want to do it, Malcolm,' she said with great earnestness. 'Of course I don't know anything about small boys but I'd try to make him happy, until you could sort out something else. What do you think?'

'I . . . I think it's too generous . . . I couldn't accept . . .'

'Malcolm,' she said, 'think about it.'

'Yes. I will. Listen, I've made an appointment with a lawyer for this afternoon after the close of dealing – could we meet later? Or have you something else arranged for this evening?'

'No, that would be fine.'

They arranged to meet once again in the Savoy bar. Catherine had telephone calls to make in the morning and business appointments for the afternoon, but her thoughts were never far from

Malcolm throughout the day. Once again she dressed with care for the engagement, shaking her head at herself for bothering about clothes when more important issues were at stake.

Malcolm still looked drawn and tired but his expression was hopeful. 'Mr Aymes says the divorce should be routine,' he reported. 'He thinks it ought to be before the court in late summer. He's drawing up an agreement about the custody of Leo and he'll send it out to the Mirtiados' lawyers in a week or so. Then I'll go out to get the signed papers and fetch Leo. I rang the farm to tell them I'd started the ball rolling and got them to put Leo on the line. He's still excited at the idea of coming to London.'

'Did you tell them you'd made arrangements for him to stay with me?'

'No – and do you know, they never asked what was going to happen about him . . . They're totally taken up with the money they're going to get when they sell out. Well, I hope they enjoy it,' Malcolm said with a shrug.

'Have you been in touch with your own parents?'

'Yes, just after I rang you at lunchtime. They offered like a shot to have Leo, but I think it would be too much for him. Too much of a separation. I'd only see him at weekends and Mum and Dad are – well, you know, they're getting on, and set in their ways, and Leo is an odd little thing. Poor little lad, coming to a strange country and having to start a new life . . .'

'It'll be all right,' soothed Catherine.

'But everything's so different here.'

Strange to say, Leo Sanders took it in his stride. He proved to be a quiet, thoughtful little boy, keenly interested in everything he saw on his ride back from the airport. London in early March was looking her best – crocuses out under the trees in Hyde Park, the sun glinting off the towers of the Houses of Parliament, red buses queuing up to go round Trafalgar Square. Malcolm had brought him into central London on the Tube and from there to Hammersmith by taxi, so that he could see the sights.

'I've seen pictures of it in books,' he told his father gravely, 'but it's better when it's real.'

He accepted the idea of staying with Catherine Mertagen as just another part of his new life. He was still full of excitement when he dashed out of the taxi, and ran at once to the rail of Hammersmith Embankment to stare at the Thames flowing muddily past.

'It's such a lot of water,' he remarked in wonder. Where he had lived almost all his life, water was never plentiful.

When introduced to Catherine, he shook hands with exquisite politeness. 'How do you do, Miss Mertagen,' he said, in excellent English, 'Papa has told me much about you.'

'And he's told me much about you,' Catherine responded. 'Now, tell me, are you hungry? Would you like something to eat and drink? Or would you like to see your room first?'

'May I see my room?'

There was an audible gasp of pleasure when she showed him in. She had put up new curtains patterned with characters from space comics, and had had a matching bedspread made. There were plenty of shelves for the precious belongings he'd brought with him, Dinky Toys and toy trains and the half-finished model aeroplane from Christmas.

When she showed him the bathroom, he was overawed. He turned on the bath taps to watch the water gushing out, then stood staring. 'You have a very powerful water pump,' he said.

'No, the water comes from a big pipe under the road, and that's linked up with a reservoir.'

'How often can you turn on this tap?'

'Any time I like.'

'But, Miss Mertagen, don't you empty the reservoir?'

Malcolm, bringing up the rear in this tour of inspection, tried to explain that the reservoir was enormous, containing millions of gallons of water. Leo nodded, accepting that if his father said it, it was so. But the fact seemed to overwhelm him. Life in London was going to be much more extraordinary than even his wildest dreams.

Dreams soon claimed him. He began to droop from weariness. Catherine made him a cup of cocoa, but he was only able to drink about half. She had to help him undress because he was too sleepy to undo buttons and sandal buckles.

Malcolm laid him in the bed in the spare room and tucked in the brave bedspread of space voyagers. 'He's been on the go since dawn this morning,' he said fondly. 'No wonder he's tired out.'

They went into the living-room. Catherine had a snack meal ready to serve at any time so they sat down to it. Malcolm brought her up to date with the latest developments – his visit to the family lawyers in Nicosia, the signed documents he was taking next day to his own solicitor, Mari's promise to visit her son within a few weeks. But Malcolm too was weary, and excused himself with a quick handshake at about nine.

'You'll be back in the morning?'

'Yes, of course, I don't want him waking up in a strange new place and all alone.' He added quickly, 'I don't mean that in the way it came out – I know you'll look after him but when he wakes up I'd like to be here.'

He was much too late, however. At about five o'clock next morning Catherine was roused by the sound of the toilet being repeatedly flushed and the bath water running at full tilt. She pulled on a dressing-gown and went to investigate. Leo, thin as a bird in his blue cotton pyjamas, was standing in the middle of the bathroom floor admiring the Niagara he was causing. His light brown hair was on end, his grey-blue eyes alight with curiosity.

'Miss Mertagen! Look, all the taps give water at the same time!'

'Didn't they back home?' Catherine asked, yawning.

'Well, no, the pump is rather old, it can't bring up enough for more than two taps at a time. But you know,' he added, 'even here this container' – he tapped the lavatory cistern – 'has to fill up before water flows when you pull the handle.'

'That's quite true,' she agreed. 'And now, since you're up and about, would you like some breakfast?'

He followed her to the kitchen. While she got out cornflakes and milk and raisins, he pottered about turning on the taps at the sink, then examining the cooker, the refrigerator, and the electric kettle.

'You are very modern, Miss Mertagen,' he observed.

'I try to be,' she agreed, hiding a smile. 'What would you like to drink? What do you have at home?'

'Fruit juice.'

She thought to herself that it was probably pressed straight from oranges grown on the farm. She apologized for having to pour his from a bottle. But he was fascinated. He had never seen orange juice in a bottle before, only wine.

'Papa will be here by and by,' she told him, in case he was worrying.

'Yes, he told me all about that on the plane.' He supped up large mouthfuls of cereal, giving himself a milk moustache. 'Why doesn't he live here too?'

Caught off guard, Catherine almost replied, 'Because we're not married.' But that was far too complex an issue for a little boy. She said instead, 'Because there isn't room.'

'Of course.' And that was that.

She supervised the brushing of teeth and the taking of a shower. He was apparently no stranger to a shower – it seemed to be the accepted form of taking a bath back on the hillside farm. But the temperature of this one could be regulated by turning a knob. He turned the knob up and down, alternately scalding and freezing himself, until she dragged him out.

He told her that of course he could dress himself, rather offended, she thought, and appeared in due course in cotton shorts and a short-sleeved shirt, hardly suitable wear for March weather in London. She made a mental note to take him to the Broadway shops as soon as possible to buy him at least a sweater, and some shoes to replace his sandals.

Even though it was still so early, she began her day. She showered and dressed and washed up the breakfast things. When she came into her office to start work, she found Leo had taken off the casing of her electric typewriter to see how it worked. When she exclaimed in horror, he quickly put the cover back. 'It's all right, it's quite safe, it isn't plugged in, Miss Mertagen,' he explained.

'I understand. But I need to use it in a minute.'

'There you are,' he said, slithering down from her office chair. He surveyed the room and his eye lit on her tape-recorder. 'I've seen pictures of that in a magazine,' he said longingly.

'Would you like to use it?'

'May I?'

She was about to say, I'll show you how, but he was already plugging it in and switching on. He needed no help from her. He talked into the tape-recorder in his faintly accented English for twenty minutes or so, giving an account of his journey from Nicosia to Heathrow. 'Food came in little plastic boxes,' he told the tape-recorder, 'and the name of the airline was printed on the napkin very neatly.' After that he sat for a long time watching the traffic on the river. Occasionally he asked about the craft he could see – was that a police launch, what was that with all the other boats tacked on behind?

By the time his father arrived at eight o'clock he'd shortened Catherine's name to Miss Merta, and later in the day it became Merta alone. She accepted the change without comment. She saw Malcolm smile at the rapport that had developed between them.

They went out to the shops at mid-morning and had an exhilarating time fitting Leo out with long-sleeved shirts, a sweater, a raincoat, and suitable shoes. They ended up in a restaurant where the exhausted adults had a meal and a glass of wine and the equally exhausted child had a salad and a milkshake with a straw – through which he made the expected gurgling noises.

Catherine's first day as surrogate mother drew to its close. By the time it ended the little boy had completely captured her heart. He was so totally without artifice, so alert and alive to the new world around him. For his part Leo accepted Catherine as a friend, someone who would be his guide to the wonders he was meeting in London, although as the next few days went by he realised she was no expert on things mechanical. She let him ride up and down on the escalators in shops but couldn't explain how they worked. She couldn't tell him how many miles of tunnels there were in the Tube system.

Catherine had been worried that he would pine for his mother. By and by she learned that this was by no means the first time he'd been apart from her. Moreover, he was enjoying the sheer delight of not being bossed about by his cousins. She gathered that they had tended to gang up on him, all the more so since he was interested in things they thought peculiar – who cared why the waterpump only brought up so many gallons per hour, who wanted to delve about in the oily innards of their old car? He was odd, their cousin Leonidas – but then for all his name, he wasn't really Greek . . .

After a week to settle in, Malcolm took Leo to see his own doctor in Highgate, to get a recommendation to a Harley Street paediatrician. The specialist, Dr Pryory, examined him thoroughly, tried him out in one or two physical ability tests, let him play with some jigsaws, and asked to have him back in a day or two. At that time he took samples to be sent for laboratory tests.

At the next consultation he advised having Leo admitted to the children's ward at St Mary's, where he had some beds at his disposal for special patients. 'I'd like to have him in overnight for observation, Mr Sanders.'

'But is that really necessary?' Malcolm protested. 'He's only just come to England from abroad – it's a bit much to ask him to go into hospital.'

'Well, there's no immediate hurry. We can put it off for a week or two. But I need to have him in a hospital ward with equipment, to do more tests.'

Malcolm frowned. 'Are you saying it's something serious, doctor?'

'I haven't enough information to make a judgement as yet, Mr Sanders. This isn't a straightforward case – the illness he suffered from took place nearly two years ago, I'm rather late in the field, you know.'

'I know. I'm sorry. Of course if you need to take him into hospital . . .'

'It would only be overnight. You could bring him in about lunch time and take him home the same time next day.'

'Yes. I understand. Let me talk it over with – Let me think about it and come back to you.'

When he reported the news to Catherine she was distressed, but accepted the necessity. 'If we're going to find out how to help Leo, we've got to let the experts take a proper look.'

'I don't want him to feel . . . frightened, or lonely . . .'

She understood only too well. She had the same protective instincts towards the little boy. But she saw how his hands would tremble when he was tired, how he sometimes stumbled as if his feet were getting away from him. Now and again a nervous tic would seize his facial muscles, especially when he was excited.

'We'll explain to him that it's only for twenty-four hours,' she said, 'and that it's to help make his hands steady so he can get on with finishing that model plane.'

Leo went into St Mary's without protest. The visiting hours on the children's ward were very open, so either Catherine or Malcolm was able to be with him almost all the time except when the actual tests were going on. As to those, Leo didn't enjoy being poked and pricked, yet he couldn't help being fascinated by the equipment.

'There's a machine that makes a long buzzing sound,' he reported to Catherine, 'and when it stops the lady comes out from behind it in her big apron and later she comes back with this great big picture of the inside of your body!'

X-ray machines, encephalograms, surgical beds that could be raised and lowered at the touch of a switch, pulleys at the beds of young patients with broken limbs – they entranced him. He was almost sorry when the time came to go home.

Three days later Dr Pryory's receptionist telephoned to ask Malcolm to come to hear the results. Catherine volunteered to keep Leo amused by taking him to the Science Museum.

This proved to be almost too much of a success. He ran about from one exhibit to another till in the end he was exhausted. Catherine had almost to carry him out and was lucky enough to flag down a taxi at once. At home she calmed him down with some hot milk and a chocolate biscuit, then set him down on the sofa to watch children's television.

About five-thirty Malcolm arrived. She studied him anxiously when she opened the door. 'What's the verdict?' she asked, leading the way into her study.

'To put it briefly, there isn't much that can be done to improve things but he isn't likely to get worse.'

He sat down on the chair generally used by clients. She went to fetch him a drink because he looked as if he needed one. When she came back he said, 'He gave me a terrible jolt at first.'

'How was that?'

'He says that what Leo had a couple of years ago was a form of meningitis.'

'Meningitis? But that's terribly serious!' She was shocked. Her hand, holding the drink, trembled so much that she spilled some.

'That's right, and when he said it I nearly hit the roof! It's never been mentioned before, even by the so-called specialist that Mari went to in Nicosia.'

'Didn't that doctor say it was some sort of summer fever?'

'Dr Pryory was careful not to say anything critical of a colleague. All the same I got the impression that he didn't think much of him. He said that luckily the "home nursing" that Leo got was along the right lines for cerebro-spinal fever but if a doctor had been called he'd have given penicillin or maybe even something better – strepto-something. Anyhow, as far as I can gather, the disease has somehow damaged some of the nerve connections in the brain. What did he call them? Synapses, was it?'

'That sounds right.' She handed him his drink, gesturing at him to swallow some. After he'd done so he relaxed a little.

'Well, the long and the short of it is that the disease wore itself out and he's free of it. But the damage to the nerves is still there. Dr Pryory says he runs a remedial clinic on Saturdays. Leo's to attend, to learn exercises for the muscles that aren't responding properly. He's to do these exercises every day and see the clinic nurse every Saturday to learn new ones as he goes along.'

'That's not too bad, Malcolm . . .'

'Oh, damnit, I hoped he'd prescribe some pills or some tonic and it would put everything right!' He set his glass down with a bang on her desk. 'I'd like to fly out there and wring everybody's neck! Why didn't they send for a doctor?'

Catherine had no answer to that. All she could do was to listen while Malcolm went over the doctor's opinion again, and urge that they should follow his advice. When she thought of the exhausted little boy she'd brought home from the Science Museum, she felt it might be a long time before remedial exercises made him anything like the equal of other children.

For her own part, Catherine kept quiet about a disappointment in the post that day. Malcolm had enough to think about without hearing her troubles. She'd at last had a reply to the letter she'd written to the publisher of Laura's book.

The reply was polite but unhelpful.

> Thank you for your interest in *The Power Within* by Laura Lindham published by Brinslow Books. As to contacting Mrs Lindham, we recommend that you look up p. 155 of *The Power Within* where you will see the address and telephone number of the Mertagen Clinic. I enclose a catalogue of other Brinslow Books which might interest you.

That was no use at all.

As she'd followed Leo round his tour of the Science Museum she'd been asking herself if she should telephone or call in person at the publishers. If she explained that she was Mrs Lindham's sister . . . ?

But they hadn't suggested she might write care of their office so that they could forward the letter. That seemed to imply that the only address they had was the one in the book, the Mertagen Clinic in Pimlico.

And who knew better than Catherine that the Mertagen Clinic had been closed for a year?

Chapter Twenty-three

Leo began attending the remedial exercise class at once. Swimming was recommended, so Catherine joined the local swimming club, held at the indoor pool. Here Leo underwent fifteen minutes of panic at the sight of the big rectangle of water, but he was soon jumping in and out at the shallow end. In the succeeding weeks Catherine taught him to swim. He paddled about like a happy tadpole.

Easter came, and a visit to his grandparents in Hulmesley. He had the fun of decorating the shells of hardboiled eggs with various harmless dyes, then rolling them down the slope of the church boundary. The sun came out, the trees were putting forth their leaves.

'It's so *green*,' Leo said in wonder. And then later, as they sat in the garden of Granny and Grandad's house, 'Is this summer?'

'Not yet, laddikins,' said Jim Sanders with a grin, 'though it may not get any warmer in this benighted country.'

Leo lifted his face to the mild blue sky. 'I like it benighted,' he murmured.

It was time to think about his schooling. Inquiry found a small private school for boys not far from Catherine's flat, close to Hogarth House, an easy drive to deliver him there at nine-thirty and bring him home in the afternoon. The headmaster, anxiously consulted about Leo's state of health, asked only, 'Is it infectious?'

'No, no, it's just some damage left over from an illness two years ago.'

'In that case there's no problem. And I'll keep an eye on him to see he doesn't get over-stretched.'

Catherine and Malcolm suffered the same tremors as parents of five-year-olds when they consign them to the care of the infant teacher. In fact, when Catherine went to collect Leo in the afternoon of his first day, she'd made herself almost sick with anxiety.

Leo in his new school uniform ran out to join her at her car. 'Merta! What do you think? This school has a *science lab*!'

He could hardly wait to tell her about his first science period. They had measured a rod of copper, heated it in a bunsen burner flame, then measured it again. 'And do you know what?'

'It was longer?' suggested Catherine.

'You've *done* that experiment?' he gasped, regarding her with awe.

When Malcolm arrived about five o'clock, Leo was waiting on the doorstep. 'Papa! We did science! And Merta had done the experiment already! Did you know Merta could do science?'

'Well, I suppose I did,' Malcolm said, looking back to schooldays in Hulmesley. It made him smile.

All through Leo's supper, which Malcolm and Catherine shared to the extent that they drank tea with him, he talked almost non-stop about his science experiment. Any fears they had had about his liking the school were banished.

Now that Leo was in school and she had some free time again, Catherine had a lunch date with Thelma Axworth. At first Thelma dominated their talk with news of the coming summer season and what Velton's was offering its customers. Then Catherine reported how things were going with Leo.

She came to a stop when she saw that her friend was regarding her with an ironic smile.

'What?' she asked.

'Do you know that you're sounding just like a fond parent?' Thelma asked, wagging a plump finger at her. 'Next thing, you'll be showing me snapshots.'

Catherine in fact had some snapshots in her handbag, taken at Easter. Glad she hadn't produced them, she defended herself. 'I *have* been standing in for his parents – or at least one of them.'

'Cathie dear, are you sure you really want to devote yourself to some other woman's child?'

She thought about it, as she had a dozen times since Malcolm first brought Leo to her. 'It just seems right, Thelma.'

'And the divorce is going through?'

'Yes. It's been scheduled for the Michaelmas term.'

'So are you and Malcolm . . . er . . . ?'

'Oh no, we have to be very discreet. In the first place we wouldn't want to put anything in the way of the divorce going through, and you know the court can be very difficult over "morals". And of course there's Leo to think of.'

'But you and Malcolm are getting married?'

'That's for the future, Thelma. We'll deal with that when we come to it.'

Thelma shrugged and let it go. She dearly wanted to see her protégée happily married but so far it hadn't happened.

'And what about your sister?' she inquired. 'Any news?'

Catherine sighed, pushed away her plate of linguine, and told Thelma about the disappointment over the publisher.

'But Cathie, the book must earn money, and they're duty bound to send the cheque somewhere.'

'Perhaps they send it to Pimlico and it comes back, marked Not Known Here or something.'

'But they must have had an agreement before they could publish, surely? Someone must have signed some sort of contract?'

'I don't know. Perhaps the American publisher bought it all up in the first place and it's with them that Brinslow Books are dealing.'

'Oh, come on. Your wily friend Toby would never have let Laura sign away that book outright. He'd want her to keep hold of it so as to keep re-publishing it for the clinic.'

'Well, yes . . .'

'Have you been to these people – whoever – Brinslow Books?'

'I thought about it.'

'Hm . . . Tell you what, love, let me see what I can do. I've got chums in the publishing game – women who come to Velton's – I'll see if any of them can do anything.'

'Would you, Thelma? I'd be so grateful!'

Two days later Thelma rang to ask Catherine to a fashion show at the store. Catherine was about to refuse on the grounds of being too busy but Thelma went on: 'One of my book-publishing ladies is going to be there, and she's going to stop for a drink in my office afterwards. And my love – I got her to talk to your friends Brinslow Books.'

The publisher was part-owner of a firm that produced travel guides. Over a glass of Pimms she was quite ready to tell Catherine what she'd learned but, she said, 'It's not much. One of the editors at Brinslow Books saw *The Power Within* on sale in New York and chased it up. The American publisher gave them the address they had for Laura Lindham but, I'm sorry to say, the address is the Victoria Street branch of the Eastern Counties Bank.'

'Oh,' Catherine said, high hopes totally dashed.

'I'm afraid it may be a dead end, my dear. You know what banks are like about giving out information.'

'Hopeless,' agreed Thelma.

Not so hopeless as they thought. When at last Catherine told the tale to Malcolm, he thought it over for a minute and then said, 'Well, you know, I've got friends in banking.'

'Malcolm! Do you think you could help?'

'One or two people owe me favours here and there.'

'But – isn't it illegal or unethical or something, to give out information about a bank client?'

'I dare say it is. Let's see if anything can be done. It may take a while.'

Something could be done, and it did take a while. But in late July Malcolm passed on what he had gleaned.

'Your sister's account with Eastern Counties in Victoria Street is the same one she had with Toby. The manager won't divulge much but I explained you were anxious about your sister. When I mentioned Toby's behaviour he knew what I was talking about and got sympathetic. I had the impression that Toby's powers in the account have been nullified.'

'Did he say Toby had agreed to that? I thought he was overseas somewhere.'

'I think the law firm that handled the clinic's affairs negotiated the cancellation. The branch manager apparently feels some guilt over letting Toby make off with all the funds – it was a large sum and he feels he should have asked for the signature of both parties. So he fell in with the lawyers' application to make it a single account. The account is no longer with his branch. He wouldn't say where it had gone specifically but it's somewhere down in the West Country.'

'The West Country?' cried Catherine. 'But surely Eastern Counties Bank doesn't do much business down in the West Country?'

'Exactly. West of Swindon they have facilities in about half a dozen of the branches of the National Bank. Here's the list.'

She opened the folded sheet of paper. 'Bath, Taunton, Salisbury, Dorchester, Plymouth, St Austell . . . That covers a very wide area,' she muttered, hopes fading once again.

'It's about one for every hundred miles,' Malcolm commented, 'and I'd imagine it's for the benefit of commercial travellers and people like that. And if Laura is using an account at one of those branches, it's going to be hard to find out where she's living.'

Catherine's heart sank. She'd been hoping to get an address, or at least the name of a town. But this . . .

The school holidays had begun. She took Leo with her to Norfolk for a visit, he to stay with his grandparents, she with her father. The two families spent a lot of time together. Leo and her father struck up a friendship based on chess lessons, which developed into lengthy and quite serious games. They would sit in the evening, one young light-brown head and one iron-grey, in the little patio garden at the back of the shop, bent over the chessboard.

Catherine felt it right to tell her father she'd been trying to find Laura. Although she had little progress to report, he praised her for her efforts. In his turn he talked about it to Desmond and Phoebe Colville, with whom he was on friendlier terms than ever before.

At a Saturday afternoon cricket match, Desmond and Phoebe sought Catherine out.

'My dear,' began Phoebe, 'your father told us about how you'd learned that Laura is perhaps in the West Country.'

Catherine nodded. 'But it's a big area . . .'

'Well, dear, Desmond and I haven't had our holiday yet this year, and we've been saying to each other, Why don't we do a tour of the West Country?'

'A tour?'

'Which just might take in Taunton and Salisbury and St Austell and so forth.'

'And what would you do?' Catherine said, somewhat at a loss.

'What we thought, dear,' Desmond put in, 'is that we'd go to those offices and ask the manager if Laura does business with that branch, and perhaps get an address.'

'Oh – but would he tell you – I mean, Desmond, it would be against his training and the regulations.'

'That's true, and perhaps we'd have to descend to a bit of subterfuge. But then, you know, Phoebe and I . . . we don't look like rogues and vagabonds, now do we? It might be possible to persuade a bit of information out of a friendly soul.'

'And you'd really do this?' Catherine asked.

'We feel it's the least we can do,' Phoebe burst out. 'It's our fault that she ran away to hide. And it's up to us to find her.'

'But perhaps she doesn't want to be found?' faltered Catherine.

'Cathie dear,' said Phoebe, 'this has gone on long enough. If we have luck and we find Laura, we can ask her if she wants us to let you know. If she says no, we'll back off. But I tell you here and now I'd do my utmost to persuade her to contact you. I don't think she ever intended you to go on breaking your heart for a year and more.'

They were determined to go. And truth to tell she didn't want to dissuade them. Even if they had no luck, it would be something at least to know they had tried. It seemed wrong to let the days slip past and not hear anything about her sister.

Catherine and Leo returned to London in August because his mother was coming to visit him for his eighth birthday. It was to be a great occasion, much talked about and looked forward to. She was staying at the Waldorf so Malcolm was to take Leo there for lunch, after which a trip to the Zoo was promised.

Catherine put out Leo's favourite clothes, a pair of blue jeans and a T-shirt from the Science Museum with the mystic letters $E=mc^2$ on the front. She watched him brush his unruly brown hair and clean his nails.

Malcolm, clad equally casually in jeans and a madras shirt, collected him at noon. 'Do I look all right, Papa?' Leo begged to know. 'Will she think I've grown?'

'You look fine,' Malcolm assured him. 'Now, how shall we go to the Waldorf? Shall we take a taxi or go by Tube?'

'We must go on a red bus,' said Leo. This was his favourite form of transport. His ambition at the moment was to drive a London bus.

Catherine kept busy all afternoon with work of her own. Around six o'clock she began making a salad for the evening meal. The pudding course, a birthday treat, was to be a home-made strawberry tart.

As soon as she heard the voices at the downstairs door she hurried to let them in. One glance was enough to tell her the afternoon hadn't gone well. Leo went obediently to wash his hands then took his seat at table, but even the strawberry tart couldn't tempt him. Listlessly he sat through the meal and then went without protest to bed.

'What happened?' Catherine asked when Malcolm came back from tucking him in and lowering the blind against the summer evening light.

'It was a disaster,' he replied with a grim shake of the head. 'She brought Yannis with her.'

'Oh no!'

'It's clear to me they're staying at the hotel as man and wife. Well, that's their business. But surely she should have known Leo wouldn't want "Uncle Yannis" there when he met his mother again after five months!'

'What happened exactly?'

'We met them in the lounge at the Waldorf. Mari had a load of presents for Leo – a sort of sailor suit, and a tennis outfit – clothes, mostly; Riviera-type clothes. Leo said a nice thank-you but I could see he felt she was saying that his jeans and T-shirt were all wrong. We went into the dining-room and it was the same as that awful night in Limassol – Yannis was trying to make an impression by spending money like water. He'd ordered a big birthday cake with candles and there was a hoo-ha because Leo couldn't blow them all out without help and then, would you believe it, the man insisted we had to take the remains of the cake with us in a box.'

'But you were going to the Zoo?'

'Yes, Leo and I in jeans and plimsolls, Mari in high heels and Yannis in a linen suit and a Panama hat. To tell the truth I thought when we left the hotel that Yannis would drop out but he didn't, and he kept warning Leo not to tilt the cake box because it would wreck the icing, so Leo fed the cake to the elephants and then ran off.'

'Oh dear,' said Catherine, suppressing a chuckle.

'You can laugh! It took me ages to find him, by which time Mari was fed up – her shoes were a big mistake.'

Catherine could only shake her head.

'Well, the next thing was a trip on the Regent Canal in a narrow boat, which was rather restful. But Yannis got bored to death and kept asking when we'd get back. So Leo threw Yannis's Panama hat into the canal and Mari smacked him. And when we stepped ashore I said we'd call it a day and all the way home Leo was trying not to cry.'

'Poor little lad,' mourned Catherine.

'We've planned another outing for tomorrow, but I'm going to put my foot down about Yannis.'

The whole thing was too delicate to discuss. She mustn't put herself in the position of appearing to criticise Mari. Yet she couldn't help feeling that Leo's mother had very little understanding of her son.

That evening, when Catherine and Malcolm were sitting over a cool drink in the gathering dusk, a sudden harsh cry came from Leo's room. They rose as one and hurried to him. He was twitching about on his bed, twisting his head from side to side, clenching and unclenching his fists. Catherine could hear him grinding his teeth.

'What is it?' Malcolm said in alarm. 'Leo, Leo, what's the matter?' He tried to take the little boy in his arms, but he seemed rigid and unyielding. 'What's wrong, Leo? Wake up, wake up!'

Catherine ran to the bathroom for a cold, wet cloth. She pressed it to the child's forehead, wiped his cheeks. After a moment his rigidity relaxed. He went limp in his father's arms.

'Leo, you've been having a nightmare,' Malcolm soothed, rocking him a little. But the child didn't wake up. He breathed more deeply, for a few minutes almost stertorously, then he seemed to fall into normal sleep.

For a time they remained like this, the little boy asleep in his father's arms, Catherine bending over both in concern. But it seemed clear that Leo had gone back to normal rest. Malcolm laid him down, drew up the covers around him, and moved away.

'What was *that*?' he whispered to Catherine in a fearful voice as they went out.

'I don't know. It was like a more serious version of those little nervous spasms he sometimes gets when he's excited.'

They went back into the living-room. The episode had been so brief that the ice in their drinks hadn't had time to melt. They sat down again by the window, watching the light fade from the pewter surface of the Thames.

'I'm going to ring Dr Pryory in the morning and ask for an appointment,' Malcolm decided.

'Yes.'

'Cath, could I . . . could I stay here tonight? Just in case anything . . . you know . . .'

'Of course, Malcolm.'

'I can sleep on the sofa—'

'There's a divan in the office. Dad slept on it when Laura was staying here and he says it's quite comfortable.'

'Thank you.'

They stayed up very late, too anxious and troubled to want to sleep. When Catherine went to make up the bed in her office she heard a distant clock striking two. She longed to cross the gap that still separated her from Malcolm, to open her arms to him, but the time wasn't right. The shadow of the unhappy day, the disappointment and distress of the little boy, the anxiety they both felt for him – this shadow was as deep as the night that spread around them.

To her surprise, she slept late, and so did everyone else. Leo, usually the first to wake, came lethargically out of his room after nine o'clock. Even the unusual sight of Papa drinking coffee at the kitchen table failed to enthuse him.

As soon as it was reasonable to expect Dr Pryory's receptionist to be at work, Malcolm telephoned. He was lucky enough to get an appointment for eleven-thirty, someone else having cancelled. He then rang the Waldorf, to tell his wife. But there was no reply from the room. The receptionist reported that the occupants were expected back for lunch – they had booked a table.

'What should I say?' Malcolm asked, putting a hand over the mouthpiece. 'If I leave a message that I'm taking Leo to the doctor, it might give Mari a fright.'

'When were you to meet?'

'Twelve-thirty.'

'You certainly won't make that. Can't you just say you'll get there as soon as you can?'

'I suppose so. Can I leave this number for them to call and you can explain?'

They looked at each other. So far Catherine had had no contact of any kind with Malcolm's wife. But after all, why not? Mari was fully aware Catherine was looking after Leo. She nodded assent.

Leo showered, dressed, and at their urging ate a little breakfast. Malcolm carried him off with him to Highgate, where he would shave and change. Catherine had a pair of young designers, man and wife, who were coming to show some of their work. She tidied up the flat, changed into a dark summer dress and black sandals, and was ready when they arrived. The interview took longer than she expected and so it was almost noon when they left. Her phone was ringing as she showed them out.

'Miss Mertagen?' said a female voice with a faint accent.

'Speaking.'

'This is Mari Sanders. Malcolm left some strange message that I should ring you.'

'Yes, Mrs Sanders, I'm to tell you that Malcolm and Leo won't be able to make it to the Waldorf by twelve-thirty. In fact, they may not be able to come at all—'

'But what is this? Malcolm *promised* he would never prevent me from seeing Leo—'

'It's nothing like that. Leo's not too well today—'

'Come, if he ate too much birthday cake and icecream it isn't a reason to—'

'No, no, he had a bit of an upset late last evening – it really quite worried us so—'

'Miss Mertagen, if you have persuaded Malcolm not to live up to his agreement that I can see my son—'

'Please, Mrs Sanders – Mari – it's not that at all, Malcolm has taken Leo to see his doctor.'

'His doctor!'

'We were really worried by the attack he had last night and this morning he's not himself at all. I think yesterday was a bit too much for him.'

'I think Malcolm will do no good by – what is your word – mollycoddling? How is he to grow up manly and strong if he is allowed to complain after a day of activity—'

'Mari, it wasn't just the physical activity. I think he was very upset.'

'Upset? What was there to upset him? He had a splendid birthday party, we took him where he asked to go—'

'Never mind that. The point is, he's with the doctor now and I don't think it's possible for them to get from Harley Street to the Waldorf by twelve-thirty.'

'Ah. Well, I don't know the distance but it may be true.'

'I should think Malcolm will ring you from Harley Street.'

'Hm . . .'

'Will you be at the hotel?'

'Of course. We are lunching here.'

'Well, then, would it be a good idea just to go ahead with that and wait to hear?'

'This upsets all our arrangements! We have hired a car at three to be driven to Windsor Castle, we have booked a table for dinner at a famous hotel—'

'I rather think . . . that might be a bit much for Leo. He's usually in bed by nine—'

'Oh, these absurd English hours! At home the evening is just beginning at ten—'

'Mari, let's not get into that. You can discuss it with Malcolm when he gets in touch.'

'Very well,' said Mari in a fretful tone, and hung up.

The rest of the day went by. Catherine kept herself busy. She tried not to think that she would have been a lot more worried than Mari if she heard her son was having to see a doctor. She wondered what the specialist would have to say. She wouldn't let herself envisage the gathering that was probably taking place now at the hotel.

It was after seven when Malcolm and Leo arrived. The little boy looked pale, tired, but not unhappy. Malcolm had an air of grim satisfaction.

'Well, what did you do today?' Catherine asked with perhaps too much brightness.

'We went to the Tower of London,' Leo said. 'But we couldn't stay long because it was almost closing time by the time we got there.'

'But did you like it? What did you see? Suits of armour? The Crown Jewels?'

'Yes, all that,' Leo agreed. He wandered on into the kitchen. 'Is there any of that strawberry tart left from yesterday, Merta?'

'Almost all of it.'

'Could I have a piece and a glass of milk?'

'Help yourself – and then brush your teeth and wash your face and it's early bed for you, young sir.'

When Leo had gone to find his supper, Catherine said, 'What happened?'

'It's a long story. I'll tell you later.'

While Leo ate his strawberry tart and drank his milk, they chatted about the Tower. He went off to bed yawning, but somehow more normal than the previous evening.

'What did Dr Pryory say?' Catherine begged as soon as they were alone.

'More of the same. Nervous disorientation, we must be on our guard against letting him get too excited. He's prescribed some medication for him to take. I left the prescription at the chemist on the Broadway – could you collect it tomorrow? He asked me what had been going on to bring on the attack so I explained the situation. I don't think he'd quite taken in how difficult it's been. The result was, he asked to see Mari. So I rang from his consulting rooms, and she turned up with Artidias at her elbow. Not in a very good mood, I may say, because Dr Pryory could only see them then and there so they had had to interrupt lunch.'

'Oh Malcolm, come on, Mari must have been worried when the doctor asked for her—'

'Yes, of course, I meant Artidias was annoyed.'

'He must be a very difficult man.'

'The funny thing is, where Mari's concerned he's great. He absolutely dotes on her. That's the problem, I believe – he's *jealous* of Leo. Well, anyhow, Dr Pryory wouldn't let Yannis into the room, he spoke to Mari alone. Yannis was furious at being shut out and Mari was upset because he was angry. But she went into the consulting room and was there quite a time. She came out very subdued. I think he must have read her quite a lecture.'

'You've no idea what he was saying?'

'I imagine he was telling her what he told me – that Leo has got to have peace and quiet or he'll have these attacks. You know, before I brought him away, none of the family would acknowledge that he was ill.' Malcolm shook his head in perplexity. 'I don't know why, exactly – perhaps because they didn't want to feel they'd failed him when he had the fever, or because they didn't want it known that the Mirtiados family had a weakling in its ranks.'

'Mari said on the phone that she wanted Leo to be manly.'

'Oh yes. That's very important. Well, we all came out into Harley Street avoiding each other's eyes and drove off in a taxi to the Waldorf. Leo and I had lunch while Yannis had a long talk with Mari in their room – their suite, I should say; you should see it, you could hold a ball in the bathroom . . . I imagine he wanted to question her about Dr Pryory's talk. He was still cross over that incident.'

'And then you went to the Tower?'

'Not immediately. Mari took Leo out to look at the river from Waterloo Bridge while Artidias and I had a heart to heart talk. You should hear him! He says things like, "I have told Mari . . ." and, "The matter is settled . . ." He's decided that the English doctor's orders are to be obeyed and she must not interfere.' Malcolm interrupted himself to make a special point. 'You understand, it suits him perfectly. He thought Pryory was going to say just the opposite.'

'That Leo needs his mother.'

'Yes. I imagine when Mari reported the discussion he was tickled to death. But *I* said the boy ought to see his mother sometimes and out of decency Artidias had to agree. All the same, I could see he won't let her come to London on her own and he himself doesn't like being with the boy so it looks as if she won't be here much.'

'Poor Leo. What does he say to all this?'

Malcolm sighed. 'Poor kid. In a way, Cath, he's been ahead of us in all this. I think he's known for over a year that if it came to a choice between him and Artidias, his mother would choose Artidias. Family pressure, you know. And she does want the kind of life he can give her.'

'It would never have suited Leo,' Catherine said. 'He might have acclimatised to boarding school, but a stepfather who doesn't like him . . . ?'

'A bad situation,' Malcolm agreed. 'And to tell the truth, Mari herself admitted to me that she's never really understood him. So what I have to do now is to try to make it up to him, to give him a happy life.'

'Oh, yes, that's absolutely the first priority—'

'And the way to do that is to get married and settle down to be a family.'

'Yes?' she said, knowing that more was to come.

'This is my way of saying I want you for my wife, Catherine.' He was smiling, knowing it was the understatement of the year.

'You're sure you're not saying you want me for Leo's mother?' countered Catherine, joining in the joke.

'That too.' He grew serious. 'He asked me when he saw my service flat this morning, "Why don't you live with Merta and me? It's much nicer there." It was all I could do not to answer, "I want that more than anything in the world." So what do you say?'

'I see that since I've got all the qualifications for the post – good relationship with your son, a flat ready to move into – it would be foolish to say no.'

'You've forgotten the third qualification, darling.'

'And what might that be?'

'That I love you.'

'Ah yes. And I love you, Malcolm.'

'Well, I know *that*,' he said, taking her in his arms. 'I knew that the minute we met again. I didn't know what to do about it – I'd no idea then that I'd ever be free to ask you to marry me, but I wasn't going to let you go. I knew it was selfish but I didn't care. Do you forgive me?'

For answer, she raised herself on tiptoe to kiss him. Kisses, gentle, exploratory, turned to fierce embraces. They went with arms about each other into her bedroom. Her sad thought of the previous night was forgotten. The time was right, the time was now.

Foolish anger and pride had driven them apart. Their dream had been wrecked, the years had rolled over it so that it had almost been lost. But now with a passion that seemed only stronger for the long absence from each other, they made the dream live again.

The days of Mari's visit passed away. On the last of them Catherine was invited to share the outing, the postponed trip to Windsor. Although it was still officially summer, the day was damp and cold. Equally cold was Mari's manner to Catherine, although it was always polite. They made the tour of the State Apartments, went for a walk in the Great Park, returned to have the cream tea which Mari had substituted for the dinner originally planned.

Nothing could have been more ordinary. No one looking at them could have guessed that Mari was saying goodbye to her son, that her husband-to-be was measuring her every word to the boy, that Malcolm was guarding against too much strain for him, and that Catherine was longing for it all to be over.

As they parted at last Catherine stole a moment to speak to Mari. 'I'll look after him,' she promised.

'Yes.' For an instant the beautiful face was dulled by the shade of some emotion – remorse, regret, Catherine couldn't identify it. 'I suppose I must thank you,' she said. 'Some time, perhaps, you might like to bring him to Athens for a visit.'

'Of course. We'll arrange it.'

Mari glanced at Yannis, who was paying off the driver of the limousine. 'Yes,' she said uncertainly. 'In a while.'

'Yes. Goodbye, Mari.'

'Goodbye, Catherine.'

Catherine turned away to say goodbye to Yannis, to make an opportunity for Mari to hug and kiss the little boy. But the parting was soon over. Catherine, Malcolm and Leo went to board a red London bus for the journey home.

They were turning Hyde Park Corner before Leo spoke of the day gone by. 'Everything in the castle was very historical,' he remarked. 'But I like modern things better – things that work, like the Science Museum.'

'We'll go there again,' Catherine promised.

'Mama really prefers modern things too. I suppose Athens is full of modern things.'

'Yes, I think it is. But it's more famous for the wonderful architecture from its past—'

'Oh,' said Leo in a voice too disillusioned for a boy, 'the past – it's better not to think about the past!'

Catherine dreaded the possible results of the parting. And for a few days Leo was unwell – twitchy, irritable, unable to concentrate. He burst into almost hysterical tears when he dropped the model plane with which he was still tinkering. The medication prescribed by Dr Pryory prevented an attack as serious as that of his birthday but he clearly had a lot of progress still to make.

September came, and the boy returned to school and seemed to settle down well. October came, and Malcolm's divorce case came to court and he was granted a decree nisi.

Then came November, and an event that Catherine had ceased to hope for.

Chapter Twenty-four

Phoebe's voice on the telephone was full of triumphant delight.

'We've found her, Cathie!'

There was no doubt whom she meant. Catherine gave a gasp of surprise. So late in the year, after the Colvilles' 'summer holiday' was long past . . .

'But I thought you'd given up when you came back at the beginning of September?'

'Ha! You don't know me, my girl! Once I put my hand to the plough, I never give up. Of course we had to come back in September – Desmond has to talk to his steward about the sale of the crop, and make final decisions about what variety of winter wheat we're going to sow, and all that palaver. But I never let myself forget our project, so as soon as we had some free time I got my old darling to set out with me again. We travelled by train, you know, I didn't fancy driving on unfamiliar country roads at this time of the year. And so now of course you want to know where she is?'

'Oh, Phoebe, tell me – the suspense is killing me!'

'Well, she's in a little village called Stimmet, not far from Glastonbury.'

'Glastonbury!' The name had echoes for Catherine. It wasn't far from the area of the Somerset Levels in which Fenner Chelburne had lived.

'You've heard of it?'

'Well – yes – in fact, I used to know someone who had a cottage not far from Bridgwater and so of course I heard talk of Glastonbury . . . What's she doing, Phoebe?'

'Your sister is a live-in home-help to an elderly couple in a very handsome house with a great big garden and orchard. *And*' – here Phoebe contrived a suspenseful pause – 'what do you think?'

'What, Phoebe? What?'

'She's got a little daughter, something like a year old. Adele, her name is.'

'A daughter!'

'Desmond and I only got a glimpse of her. She was pushing the little girl in a baby-buggy down the village street. We were so taken aback we just stood there watching her disappear into the car park behind the inn. By the time we got ourselves together she'd driven off in an old estate car. But we had no difficulty finding out about her. We just went into the pub for a drink and a sandwich and asked – and we were told Mrs Lindham had been with the Halcombes "for nigh on two year". So there.'

'Did you contact her? Call at the house?'

'Well, no. No, dear, Desmond and I talked it over and we decided to go slow on that. I mean, Cathie dear, we hadn't expected the baby.'

'No,' breathed Catherine, 'nor had I.'

'What should we do?'

'Where are you, exactly?'

'Well, at the moment we're in a nice little hotel in Somerton, a few miles south of Glastonbury. It's raining outside, and we've just got off the bus after a dreary journey, so we're going to have a reviving glass of something and then eat dinner. I've looked up the Halcombes in the phone book and if you want me to I'll ring the house. What do you think?'

Catherine tried to get her thoughts in order. The idea that her long-lost sister had actually been found was overwhelming. 'No, Phoebe, don't ring. Don't do anything. Let me think about it. It's such a shock!'

'Yes, isn't it? I must admit my heart went pit-a-pat when I saw her.'

'How does she look, Phoebe? Is she well?'

'Hard to say. I told you, it's raining. The rain came on just as we got off the bus in Stimmet. I was fiddling with my brolly, and there she was – hurrying to get to the car, I expect. She was wearing a duffel coat and a tammy, and the baby was in a sort of gnome-suit – you know, with legs – and all I got was a glimpse of light brown curls and a snub nose. Desmond,' she demanded, off-phone, 'did you get a better look?'

'She looked all right to me,' Desmond called from somewhere beyond Phoebe's elbow. 'Easy enough to recognise her.'

'Well, it's marvellous, really marvellous. How did you know she was there?'

'It's a long story, my dear, and I'm dying for that drink. Can we call you back later?'

'I'll call you. Give me the number.' She wrote it down. 'You go and have your drink and something to eat. I'll ring – shall we say nine o'clock?'

'Right you are, my pet.'

The call had come through on Catherine's office phone. Halcolm, who had just come in after a long day in the dealing room, put his head round the door. 'Who're you going to ring at nine?'

'Phoebe Colville. She and Desmond are down in Somerset. And they've found Laura.'

'No!' He was as surprised as Catherine.

'Yes, this afternoon, as far as I can gather.'

'But that's great! Did they speak to her? How is she? How did she react?'

'They didn't speak,' Catherine said, and went on to explain the situation.

'Living-in as a home-help? What does that mean?' Malcolm asked.

'Well, I think it explains how she got a place to live. Because you see, I think she knew she was pregnant when she ran off.'

'What makes you say that?'

'I think it's *why* she ran off. I think it happened while she and Toby were on that Continental tour. You know, I said to him that he ought to be more considerate, kinder . . . to Laura.' Catherine shook her head at the recollection. 'I even said to him that it would be in his own interests to keep her happy! So I think he was romancing her along and she was feeling wonderful – and then she discovered that *at the same time* he was playing around with a girl who handled the publicity.'

Malcolm frowned. 'I never met him, you know. But at first Mother seemed to think a lot of him. Why, one wonders?'

'Oh, we were all taken in . . . Laura most of all, of course. I think she was tremendously upset to discover just after I brought her home with me that a baby was coming. And I see now that it explains how mixed-up she was for a while. I think she might even have been trying to decide whether to go on with the pregnancy.'

'You really think so? That's pretty desperate, Cathie.'

'I sensed something was terribly wrong, but I thought it was just Toby.' She clasped and unclasped her hands as if trying to seize the memories and make them clear. 'I used to know her so well, Malcolm! She and I . . . We used to be able to read each other's thoughts . . . But I missed the signs, I didn't guess what was troubling her.'

'You're not blaming yourself, are you, Cath?' he countered. 'It was her doing, after all – you remember, when you and I had our set-to about Laura, she was already going off on her own track. In her way, Laura could be stubborn.'

'I know, and it's silly to think that the sort of telepathy that ran between us as girls would last for ever. But I see now that she needed to get away – that perhaps I was being too protective, too intrusive, and so she left to think it through without interference. And then decided she wanted the baby. But . . . of course she had to have somewhere to live, somewhere not like nurses' quarters where she couldn't possibly have stayed on once it began to show . . .'

'But how did she end up with the Halcombes?'

'Who knows? I don't even know how Phoebe and Desmond found them.'

Leo appeared at that moment, having finished his homework, to demand supper. Catherine asked what he wanted, knowing he would say baked beans, and went to heat them up and make toast. Malcolm settled down with financial reports until it was time to see his son off to bed. After that came a quiet drink and then their evening meal, a time that had become very precious to them as their chance to share their day. But this evening Catherine was trying to decide what to say when she rang Phoebe and Desmond.

'She wanted to telephone the house, Malcolm. I told her to hold off. What do you think?'

'We-ell . . . It was a shock to you to hear the Colvilles had found her. It could be a shock to Laura to learn she's been found. Especially as she isn't in a place of her own. I mean, if you ring her, do we even know if the phone's in some private spot? Could she be overheard if she gets upset?'

'Yes, she's an employee, after all. We've got to consider the Halcombes – Phoebe said they were elderly, but of course we've no idea what that means. I certainly don't want Phoebe and Desmond descending on them and trying to persuade Laura to come home – Phoebe can be quite bossy in her own way.'

He smiled at the description. Much though he liked the Colvilles, he would never have deputed them to handle any personal problem of his own. He knew, of course, that they had been looking for Laura, but no one had gone any further with the notion – and now Laura had been found and the next step had to be faced. Were the Colvilles the right people to make this first and delicate contact?

At nine o'clock Catherine rang the inn and heard the story of the discovery. Having come home in September from a fruitless pursuit, the Colvilles had decided that perhaps the direct approach was wrong. No matter how responsible and dependable they might look, bank managers weren't going to divulge details of anyone else's business to them.

So Phoebe had suggested that instead of 'swanning around the West Country' by car, they should travel by local transport. In this way they would visit the small villages and hamlets they had missed during the summer. A faint glimmer in the eye of the bank manager in Taunton had led them to think that Laura might perhaps be in Somerset. They had gone to Taunton, then by train and local bus had travelled about the area. They had moved their base camp twice, from Taunton to Milverton and from Milverton to Somerton.

Country dwellers themselves, they understood the importance of local knowledge. They had visited nearby villages and hamlets where they would chat in the local post office or pub. They were on their nineteenth such sortie when they actually saw Laura, twenty days into the month of November which they'd resolved to devote to the search.

'So what would you like us to do now?' Phoebe ended.

'I've been trying to think! I talked it over with Malcolm and he thinks we should go carefully. So, Phoebe . . . if you don't mind . . . I think you should just leave.'

'Leave?'

'Go home.'

'Not get in touch with her at all?' Phoebe asked, and couldn't keep the disappointment out of her voice.

'I think it will be better if I write to her. That way, she can either reply or not, just as she likes. If you go to see her, or ring her, it takes her tremendously by surprise. And she might say or do something that she'd regret. I mean, she might tell you to go away—'

'Do you really think so, dear?'

Catherine actually thought quite the opposite. She felt her sister might give in to the well-meaning advances of the Colvilles but regret it later. And then she might very well pack up and leave her present address and go – who knew where?

Desmond had taken over the telephone. 'We'll do whatever you think best, my dear. We've done what we vowed to do – we've found her for you. Now are you ready to write this down? It's her address and telephone number, and I'm reading it out of the local phone book.'

She copied down the details, feeling her hand tremble as she did so. This was where her sister was living. *Hiding*. It was a strange, unnerving thought.

She rang her father to tell him the news. He was astounded. 'In Somerset? What took her to Somerset?'

'Who knows? Perhaps she remembered hearing me speak of it from the days when I used to visit Fenn.'

'I'll go straight away to fetch her—'

'No, Dad! We mustn't do that!' It took a long argument to convince him that his missing daughter should be left alone. Catherine's plan to write and leave the decision to Laura seemed to him to show a lack of concern.

'Dad, she went away to sort things out. We don't know whether she's achieved that yet. How would you feel if everybody you knew suddenly began tumbling in on you when you were feeling a bit vulnerable?'

'Oh . . . well . . . if you put it like that . . .' She could hear his deep sigh. 'All right then. When you write, tell her I'm longing to see her again – and my *granddaughter*!'

It took her two days of intermittent effort to write the letter. At first she thought she sounded reproachful, and then she felt she seemed too businesslike. At length she read it out to Malcolm.

Dear Laura

You'll be surprised to hear from me, but the Colvilles were so worried about you that they decided to look for you. Now that we know you're safe and sound we're a lot happier. This letter isn't to urge you to do anything you don't want to, but we should so much love to hear how you are, and Dad especially asked me to say he wants to know more about his granddaughter.

Your loving sister,
Catherine.

'What do you think?' she asked Malcolm.

He dropped a kiss on the top of her head. 'No reproaches, no demands. A model of tact and goodwill.'

She reckoned it could take two days to reach a hamlet like Stimmet. Then of course Laura would be surprised, and would take a day or two to get used to the idea that her family knew her whereabouts. Let's say a week, she told herself. Or ten days. In ten days I ought to hear from her.

But November ended without a response. Three days of December crept by, four days.

'What will you do if she doesn't reply?' Malcolm asked quietly.

She thought about it. 'Send her a Christmas card?' she suggested, though her voice broke on the words.

He took her in his arms to comfort her. 'I know how much it means to you, love. Perhaps, if she doesn't reply by Christmas, you could write again and say you're coming to see her in the New Year.'

'She might just up-stakes and go, Malcolm.'

'I don't think so. It's not so easy to do that when you've got a baby.'

'Well, that's true . . .'

'So I think a letter like that would – I was going to say force her, but let's make it prompt her – to reply saying, No, she doesn't want you to come – if that's how she feels.'

'I'd rather not do that. I don't want to give her any ultimatums.' She nestled closer to him. 'I'll wait,' she said. 'It's hard, but I'll wait even if it takes months.'

Christmas this year was to be spent in Hulmesley, to let Leo experience all the old customs that were still carried out there – the visits by the waits, the bringing in of the Yule Log, the blessing of the fishing fleet on Christmas Day after morning service and, on the Colvilles' farm, the giving of presents to the animals in the byres and stables. If there was snow, he would build his first snowman.

Catherine and Malcolm made the necessary preparations – presents were wrapped in secret, Christmas crackers were bought and hidden, food supplies were purchased. Everything non-perishable was locked in the boot of Catherine's car.

They would be leaving for Hulmesley at midday on Christmas Eve. On the day before, as she was folding warm clothes into a suitcase, the phone rang. A small, uncertain voice spoke.

'Hello? Catherine? It's me.'

'Who—? Laura!'

'Cath darling, I've been trying to get up courage to—'

'Laura, how marvellous to hear from you! I'd almost given up hope!'

'I know, it was awful of me, I should have replied—'

'No, no, this is wonderful! If you only knew how much—'

'Oh, Cath, I've been so selfish—'

'Don't say that! It's just so great to hear your voice.'

Laughing and crying, both speaking at once, the two sisters had found each other again.

The best Christmas present either of them could have.

Chapter T[illegible]

They spoke on the telephone [illegible] without waiting for answers, [illegible] tions. The story of Laura['s] departure was much as Catherine had imagined.

I went to a little hotel in Devon [illegible]

Why Devon? [illegible]

Who knows. [illegible] London and [illegible] thought about where to [illegible]

[illegible]

Of course you were [illegible]

I know you feel I should [illegible] about Laura [illegible]

I was always [illegible]

You've [illegible] romance like that [illegible]

Is he not [illegible]

Of course not. [illegible] the very idea now seems [illegible]

What's she like [illegible]

Oh, such a [illegible] know, she holds up [illegible] I wonder how I could [illegible]

Don't blame yourself, [illegible]

You've never heard from him, I suppose?

No, we hear he's off in the West Indies somewhere, planning to build a yacht marina—

Oh yes, that's much more his style, [illegible] are owned by rich people, and [illegible] were seldom rich enough [illegible]

Never mind him. What [illegible]

Catherine sat down on the [illegible] telephone [illegible]

[illegible] trusting, easy [illegible]

Chapter Twenty-five

They spoke on the telephone for over an hour, asking questions without waiting for answers, explaining and demanding explanations. The story of Laura's departure was much as Catherine had imagined.

'I went to a little hotel in Devon—'

'Why Devon?'

'Who knows? Maybe because it was a long way off from both London and Hulmesley. Anyhow, I walked along the cliffs and thought about what to do, because I was terribly mixed up, Cath—'

'Of course you were, but—'

'I know, you feel I should have talked to you about it, I wanted to but I felt—'

'It was about having the baby, wasn't it?'

'You've guessed that? I had this feeling that . . . you know . . . with a father like that . . . perhaps it was better if . . .'

'No, no, no!' protested Catherine.

'Of course not, I soon decided I'd have the baby and of course the very idea now seems—'

'What's she like, love?'

'Oh, such a darling! Just beginning to be a *person* now, you know, she holds up her arms to me to be taken out of her playpen, and I wonder how I could ever have thought—'

'Don't blame yourself, Laura. It was a bad time for you—'

'You've never heard from him, I suppose?'

'No, we hear he's off in the West Indies somewhere, planning to build a yacht marina—'

'Oh yes, that's much more his style, because in the main yachts are owned by rich people, and I see now the patients at the clinic were seldom rich enough to please—'

'Never mind *him*! Who are these people you're working for?' Catherine sat down on the edge of her bed, clutching the extension telephone in anxiety as she waited for the answer – for Laura was always trusting, easy to impose upon.

'The Halcombes? Oh, so nice, so sweet – very elderly, they need a lot of help—'

'How did you come by them?'

'I saw an advertisement for a live-in home-help, in the back of a magazine, it said something like, "Own garage flat, no objection to widow with small child," so I rang the number which was for a place in Somerset and Mrs Halcombe answered. I explained I didn't have a child but was expecting one and she said, "Come and talk to us," so I did—'

'I expect they thought you were an unmarried mother—'

'Yes, and I've never bothered to clear that up, because as far as I'm concerned, I *am* an unmarried mother, at least Adele hasn't got a father I'd want anywhere near her—'

'And the Halcombes accepted you with a baby on the way?'

'I think they were sort of thrilled by the idea, Cath! Like having a grandchild, you see—'

'Have they any grandchildren of their own?'

'No, they've been childless and I think it's been a hurt to them so the thought of having one, sort of by adoption—'

'But did you tell them about the clinic and so forth?'

'No, no, I just said I'd trained as a nurse and of course I got duplicates of all my certificates to show them and sorted out about National Insurance cards and all that and really, it went well and I moved in with them early summer of last year. And they're no trouble to look after, Mr Halcombe has tummy trouble and has to be careful what he eats so meals are fairly simple and Mrs Halcombe has dreadful arthritis and has to be helped to get up in the morning and into bed at night, but really it's just—'

'But when Adele was born? What did you—'

'Oh, we made arrangements at the local hospital and got a temporary fill-in for me, and then two weeks later I was back with Adele and they're absolutely *besotted* with her—'

'What's she like? I mean, dark or fair? Does she take after anyone?'

'Well, she's dark, and has grey eyes with a sort of brown fleck, and a snub nose—'

'All babies have snub noses—'

'But what about you, Cath? We're only talking about *me*—'

'Well, you're the one who's been missing—'

'Oh, Cath, I'm so sorry! I suppose I blotted out the idea that you and Dad would be worried, I concentrated on the baby coming and all that kind of thing, but when I got your letter I felt . . .'

'I know, duckie, I know—'

'Yes, that's the marvellous thing! I *know* you understand. I'm just realising how I've missed that, Cath – how I let it go, gradually, because of Toby at first and then because of being in such a muddle over what I was doing at the clinic – I knew it wasn't right but then—' She caught herself up. 'Here I am talking about myself again! Tell me what's been happening to you, love.'

Catherine explained that her life had changed too, that she had a family to think of now, Malcolm's little boy for whom she was trying to make good the damage done by the marriage break-up. 'I'm going to be a step-mother,' she said with a laugh. 'I never thought I'd be playing that part. Of course it's not easy, but he's such a nice lad—'

'Of course he is! Malcolm's son! Oh, I'm so glad you've got together again, Cath!'

Catherine could hear a faint cry in the distance. Laura said, 'That's Adele waking up, she generally drops off for a while before lunch but I expect she's hungry now—'

'Oh, bring her to the phone, Laura!'

'Shall I? Hold on.' There was a pause, and muffled sounds of baby talk and sleepy responses. Then Laura was saying, 'Listen, darling, here's your Auntie Cath on the telephone wanting to talk to you.'

'Hello?' Catherine said, foolishly. 'Adele, is that you?'

She was rewarded by a wail of alarm and resentment. 'Ooh, she doesn't like the telephone,' Laura commented, raising her voice above the turmoil. 'I better go, Cath, she needs changing and a wash before lunch and—'

'Laura, as soon as you're free to do it, will you ring Dad? I'll get in touch now to let him know to expect you. I've got your number and I'll ring you this evening again. I'm going to Hulmesley tomorrow for Christmas, Malcolm and Leo too – why don't you join us for a lovely family reunion?'

'Oh, Cath, I'd love to, I really would, but I can't leave the Halcombes—'

'No, of course not,' Catherine agreed with remorse. 'No, that was silly of me. Look, let *me* come to *you* – we'll talk about it tonight – Dad would love to see you—'

'I've got to go,' Laura said over the noise of the baby crying. 'Don't ring till after eight, Cath, I have to serve dinner and clear up—'

'Of course, of course, anything you say. I've got the Halcombes' number, have you a phone of your own?' She wrote down the number Laura dictated. 'Goodbye, Laura, bye-bye, Adele – oh, good lord, she's got a good pair of lungs.'

Laughing, they broke the connection. Catherine replaced the receiver. Then, after ten seconds of marvelling at having heard her sister's voice again, she seized a pillow from her bed, clutched it to her chest, and began waltzing around the bedroom in exultation. After which short diversion, she rang Hulmesley to tell Gerald Mertagen he'd be hearing from his missing daughter any moment.

'You've talked to her?' he exclaimed. 'How is she?'

'Happy, Dad. She's found a niche for herself with these people.'

'We'll get her to come for Christmas—'

'No, she can't. She's going to ring you. She'll explain.'

Leo came home early from school, anxious to do his own packing: he had books he felt he couldn't do without, a sweater Catherine had bought him in a misguided moment that he adored for its glaring colours. Finding Merta in a very relaxed mood he cadged two chocolate biscuits then went to collect his belongings. Malcolm returned from the City to find his son trying to pack eight books and a chess set into a holdall clearly too small. Catherine was sitting by watching him absently.

'What's going on?' Malcolm inquired, laughing. 'You're not letting him take that lot, are you, Cath? The car's overloaded as it is.'

'What?'

'I said . . .' He studied her. 'What's happened?'

'Laura phoned.'

'Ah!' He sat down beside her to hear the great news. Leo too paused in his struggles with the holdall. After a bit he came to stand close to Catherine, leaning against her side, as close as he could get.

'Your sister?' he queried. 'Will she be my aunt?'

'Step-aunt, I think, if there is such a thing,' Catherine explained with a laugh that was a little unsteady from the joy of the reunion. Yet she felt a shiver of pleasure – Leo had spoken as if he accepted her in his mother's place.

Leo thought of his aunts in Cyprus. Neither of them had ever really approved of him. And now Merta seemed to be thinking more about this step-aunt than about the Christmas visit to the family by the cool northern sea coast. He gave Catherine an anxious nudge. 'We're still going to Hulmesley?'

'Of course, darling! Nothing's changed, except that we're in touch with Laura and that makes things even better.'

When Catherine contacted her again that evening, Laura had rung her father. She was tremulous with the emotion of that reunion. 'Cath, I never realised how much he'd suffered by my behaviour . . . It was all in his voice.'

'Well, yes.' It was no good trying to gloss it over. They had all suffered from Laura's disappearance, but that was all over now.

'He told me he couldn't come at once because you and Malcolm and Leo are expected any minute, practically, but he's coming on Boxing Day, and he wants you to come too, and so do I, Cath, I'm *longing* to see you.'

'Me too, I can hardly wait.'

The news that Merta would be leaving Hulmesley the day after Christmas caused Leo some anxiety. She was going to this step-aunt who seemed to be so terribly important, and who had a baby called Adele who seemed terribly important too, and of course these two were actually related to Merta. Not like Leo, who was really only someone who was staying in her London flat. It was only natural she should prefer to be with people of her own family.

He went to sleep that night feeling that Christmas had been somehow dimmed.

When they reached Hulmesley next day his fears were confirmed. Uncle Gerald, usually so pleased to see him and with a new chess puzzle waiting for him, hardly gave him a glance. All the talk was of Laura – Laura this and Laura that and Laura's baby and they must rush out and buy presents for them before the shops closed and as for Leo, he could find something to amuse him, couldn't he?

Well, if they were going to be like that, he'd rather spend more of his time with Grandma and Grandpa Sanders in their house, which was much bigger than the flat in Mitre Lane anyway and had a garden. They for their part were pleased he seemed to want to help put up their decorations and trim their tree. Usually he wanted to be with Catherine and her father but of course, those two were busy catching up with that strange sister who'd married that dreadful Toby Lindham. To Mr and Mrs Sanders, Laura was an oddity and always had been. Leo found this view comforting.

'So they're rushing off down to – where is it, Somerset? – on Boxing Day. What on earth is she doing down in Somerset?' Mrs Sanders inquired of her son.

'Looking after an elderly couple, I gather,' said Malcolm.

'You mean she's gone back to nursing.'

'More of a home-help.'

'She always was a weirdo,' grunted his father.

'Dad, we have to be open-minded about—'

'Huh! You used to have quite a different view, as I recall, my lad.'

'Yes, but that was a long time ago and I've learned not to be so sure I'm right. After all, I haven't made a very good job of things myself, now have I?'

'Now, now,' his mother soothed, 'that's all in the past.' She studied him from the corner of her eye. When was the boy going to propose to Catherine? They lived together, they were clearly in love again – that's if they'd ever stopped being in love in the first place. She sighed to herself. Malcolm wasn't one to confide his anxieties but presumably they were hesitating because of the boy. Mrs Sanders had no idea what went on in the head of her odd little grandson. There was no knowing how Leo really felt about the idea of his father marrying a second wife.

To Leo's delight, it actually snowed on Christmas Day in Hulmesley. Only a few icy flakes, blown in on a Siberian wind over the North Sea, but it draped the roofs with a lacy shawl of white and edged the leaves of trees and bushes. Despite assurances that there wasn't enough to build a snowman, he set about it, and was delighted when his father and Merta came out to help.

They succeeded in raising a gnome-like figure in the garden of the Sanders' house. His grandfather provided a cigar to put in its lopsided mouth and, laughing, Merta donated her green woollen hat for his head. It was a happy, happy day. He went to bed full of food and embracing the sweatshirt with the picture of the Beatles given to him by Merta.

But in the morning Merta had gone and the snowman had melted.

Catherine and her father drove south in his trusty estate car, its heater going full blast. The day was fine, bright, and cold. Because they had set off early, they had the roads almost to themselves. They sped west along the A47, through sleeping Peterborough and a drowsy Northampton, then stopped for a meal just beyond. Gerald was too impatient to want to eat. They were on the road again within half an hour, sustained by a pub sandwich and a cup of coffee hastily made for them by a landlord only just opened.

They had set out at six. By eleven they were nosing along country roads in Somerset in a light drizzle. It gave Catherine a strange feeling to see this countryside again, once so familiar to her when she came to Fenner Chelburne's cottage. How strange – she could scarcely remember what he looked like now. But she remembered only too well the pain and distress of his going. Hurt pride – that had been her main problem. And perhaps she was to blame in having tried to manage his life for him. She'd been too pleased with herself, taking him up and making him a success.

Sighing, she put away that train of thought and began looking for the signpost for Laura's village. They might very well have missed it had not the local postwoman, alerted by Laura to look out for an aged estate car, run out of her cottage to direct them.

'Left and then left again – Halcombe House, you can't miss the gateposts, they've got heraldic dragons.'

Gerald scarcely waited to thank her. They drove off, and as they sighted the stone dragons a friendly Labrador came out waving his tail. Close behind him came Laura.

Laura in jeans and a sweater. Laura rounded and fresh-faced. A far cry from the model-girl in the A-style wild silk dress, the anxious, nervy creature who had fled from London almost two years ago.

Catherine and Gerald almost fell out of the car in their eagerness to meet her. They made a tangled group, hugging and kissing, the Labrador barking and leaping around them in excitement.

'Down, Goldie – oh, look, he's splashed mud all over your nylons – stop it, you silly thing – oh, Dad, I'm so *glad* to see you! Cath, you look gorgeous! Are you tired? How was the drive?'

'Where's my granddaughter?' demanded Gerald.

'She's indoors – if you'll get in the car we can drive up – there's parking, the garage is full—' She urged them back into the station wagon, climbed into the back with Goldie, and they trundled up the gravelled roadway with the Labrador pushing his nose between Gerald and Catherine in his eagerness to make friends.

The house came into view. It was a substantial stone building from the Georgian era, two floors with attics and a widow's walk round the roof. A lawn stretched before it, with formal flowerbeds surprisingly well-tended. The garage was round the back in what had been the stables. Gerald drew up on the worn paving stones. Laura jumped out with Goldie in hot pursuit.

'This way.' She ran up a flight of iron stairs leading to a balcony with a green-painted door. She pushed it open. They followed her in.

The door gave immediately on to a fair-sized room, carpeted in serviceable cord and with chintz-covered easy chairs, some solid oak furniture, and lamps lighting up the December gloom. But the main item of interest was the play-pen which took up the centre of the floor.

Inside, a pretty little child was glancing up as the visitors came in. She had a snub nose, as her mother had said, and a thin crop of hair which ended in a curled tuft in the nape of her neck.

'Adele,' said Laura, 'here's Grandad and your Auntie Cath!'

Catherine walked to the play-pen. 'Hello, Adele,' she said.

Adele stared up at her from light grey eyes. A long moment passed. Then she held up her arms to be picked up – and Catherine's heart was lost to her for ever.

Gerald was afraid she wouldn't take to him. But she had learned already to love Mr Halcombe, who wore thick tobacco-smelling jackets and had a creaky old voice. So she accepted this new male without demur.

But soon she was tired by the talk and laughter, by the emergence of new toys, by even Goldie's eagerness to play. She began to droop. Laura took her into the bedroom to have a nap before lunch. 'What will you have? Coffee? Tea? Something stronger? Lunch for us will be about one-thirty, you understand I have to serve the meal for Mr and Mrs Halcombe first.'

'Of course, of course. This seems a nice little flat.'

'Oh yes, and they're always trying to improve it – the plan at the moment is to put in a better carpet but I keep saying, "Why bother?" because Adele will only spill stuff all over it until she's three or so.' She went into the kitchen as she spoke to switch on the kettle for a hot drink. Catherine followed. It was so like old times at the Hulmesley flat that she felt tears well up.

The rest of the day was like that. Moments kept occurring when they did again something that had been commonplace with them before Toby came into their lives to separate them.

'Oh, it's so *good* to be together,' Catherine sighed.

'It's my fault we were ever parted,' mourned Laura.

'Now we're not going to talk about whose fault it was. No blame, no guilt.'

'Quite right,' their father approved. He was beaming with delight. He had to be almost forcibly restrained from stealing into the bedroom to sneak yet another look at his sleeping grandchild.

The Halcombes had invited them for afternoon tea. It appeared this was a daily event in winter to which Adele was brought. In summer she had sat out in her cot in the garden, fondly watched over by Mr and Mrs Halcombe as they weeded and tidied the flowerbeds. It was inevitable that the Halcombes and the Mertagens should be good friends from the start since they were united in thinking Adele perfect.

At length it was time to go to the inn where Laura had booked bed-and-breakfast for them.

'I'll collect you about nine-thirty,' Laura said. 'I've got shoppping to do, and I thought you'd like to see Glastonbury—'

'You'll bring the baby?' interjected her father.

'Of course.' Laura was smiling. She understood just how he felt.

Catherine rang Malcolm in Hulmesley to bring him up to date. 'Yes, she looks well, Malcolm – she's the old Laura we used to know. And the baby's *lovely*. Dad's fallen completely under her spell. We're all going out for the day together tomorrow – to Glastonbury, I think, that's the show-place, of course.'

'I've seen pictures of it, I think. How's the weather? It's cold here!'

'Oh, mild and soft. How's Leo?'

'As a matter of fact, not too well,' Malcolm said with reluctance. 'Too many mince pies and being cooped up indoors playing chess by himself, I should think. I'll take him out for a long walk tomorrow to blow the cobwebs away.'

'Make sure he wears his scarf, Malcolm.'

'I will, I promise. Have a good time with Laura. Ring me again tomorrow.'

'I will, love. Goodnight.'

She didn't expect to sleep. She was too wound up, she thought. But in fact the moment her head touched the pillow she was lost in dreams.

Next day was mild and still somewhat damp, but the countryside glistened under a silvery sun. They were ready when Laura appeared in a serviceable medium-sized Ford. Once again she was clad in casual clothes, trousers with a thick flannel shirt and a loose jacket. Her hair was tied back with a shoe-lace. The baby was wearing a jumpsuit of blue and white checks with a tied-on bonnet which allowed a few strands of chestnut hair to show.

'The main thing is green vegetables,' Laura announced. 'We grow our own carrots and onions up at the house but greens we can't manage.'

'You're a gardener too?'

'Oh, I love it! I love everything about the place.' She drove out of the village towards Glastonbury. 'Have you heard the legend?' she asked. 'About the Glastonbury Thorn? I thought you'd like to see it. They say it really is coming out on time this year.'

'What about the Glastonbury Thorn?' asked Catherine.

'Well, after the death of Christ, Joseph of Arimathæa and his followers landed here after sailing up the river—'

'What were they doing here?'

'Converting us, of course. Well, Joseph planted his staff in the soil, and the thorn tree grew out of the staff. And now every year on the birth of Christ it comes into bud.'

'Really?'

'Well, not last year when I was first here, but this year I hear it's in bud.' She hesitated. 'This is a strange place,' she went on. 'It has its own atmosphere. The Tor and the Abbey . . . there's something about them . . . and it attracts special people.' She nodded out of the car window. 'Look.'

A band of youngsters was walking along the side of the country road. They were clad in a variety of strange garments – Afghan jackets, ex-Army fatigues, scarves, bell-bottomed trousers of vivid hues or long, gathered skirts of Slavonic print. They bore backpacks or carried straw baskets from which peeped musical instruments – flutes, recorders, a small harp.

'They've come to see the thorn come into bloom,' Laura explained. 'They come other times of year too. They say there are ley lines – do you know about ley lines?'

'Never heard of them,' said her father.

'They're supposed to be lines of power that our ancestors knew about and so they built their temples and so on where they crossed. Glastonbury is supposed to be a place like that and you know . . . I often feel there *is* something . . .'

She had to give up conversation to deal with traffic on the outskirts of Glastonbury. To the east the grey ruins of the Abbey gleamed in the muted sunshine. Laura explained it was reputed to be the resting place of King Arthur and Queen Guinevere. A signpost pointed towards the Chalice Well which, Laura said, also had associations with King Arthur and the Holy Grail. The great mound of the Tor drew the eye, with St Michael's Tower on its crest like a finger pointing towards the heavens.

'Do you believe all this stuff about King Arthur and so forth?' Gerald asked.

Laura thought about it. 'I neither believe nor disbelieve. All I can tell you is that this is a special place. Don't you feel it yourself, Dad?'

He shook his head, and turned to Catherine for confirmation. But Catherine was less willing to dismiss what her sister said. There was a gentleness, a welcoming feel, that she couldn't account for.

Laura produced the baby carriage from the boot. They shopped in the town centre, and had lunch in the old Pilgrims' Hotel. Adele was as good as gold all the while, dropping off to sleep after a tablespoon of mashed potato and gravy followed by a little stewed apple. After lunch they went to look at the thorn, and in truth creamy buds were showing on the black twigs.

'Any minute now it'll bloom,' murmured Laura.

Catherine felt impelled to make the steep climb to the top of the Tor, and to her surprise Laura elected to come with her. 'I'll leave Adele with her granddad,' she said with a smile. Gerald, delighted to be entrusted with the sleeping baby, said he would sit in the hotel lobby until they came back.

There was little wind and the climb made them hot and sticky. At the top they took off a top layer to get cool. Catherine wandered towards the ruins of the old church. She laid her hand on the damp stone and wondered if Guinevere had ever leaned here to gaze out at the green countryside that lay like a garland all around.

For a time the sisters said little. Catherine asked to have one or two buildings identified. Laura replied. A silence fell. Then Laura said, 'I've something to tell you.'

'Something good or something bad?'

'I think it's good. I don't know what you'll think.' She paused. 'I think the gift is coming back to me.'

Catherine drew in a startled breath. 'The gift of healing?'

Laura nodded.

'What makes you say so?'

'I felt it coming back two or three months ago. Mrs Halcombe was having a dreadful time with arthritis in her hands and I . . . Well, I spread my hands over hers and I felt as if . . . as if I were helping her . . . you know how it used to be, Cath?'

Catherine could remember it only too well. Her sister's gaze, dreamy yet intense. The capable nurse's hands outspread over the area where treatment was needed. The patient lying quiet, trustful and expectant.

'Did Mrs Halcombe's hands get better?' she asked.

'Well, they improved, but arthritis does improve, it has remissions but they're often temporary, you know. Besides, it would be silly to think I could cure her after all these years, too much damage to the joints, nothing could ever restore them to their proper state.'

'But that's only one instance, Laura.' Catherine felt uncertain. Should she encourage such an idea?

'But you see, there've been others. You know that book you helped me write?'

'Of course.' It was the paperback of the book that had started Catherine on the track of her sister.

'Well, you see, in an area like this there are lots of little specialist shops – selling souvenirs and books about the healing powers of the Chalice Well and the Grail and the occult and all sorts of things. And quite a lot of them stock that paperback and of course it's got my name on it, and this is such a small community, in a way, that everybody knows everybody so people began to ask if I was the same Laura Lindham as in the book. And what could I say? So one or two have come to me for help with ailments and you know, Cath . . . I've helped them. The postmistress's son had a damaged tendon after he was in a bicycle race and I think I cured that, and there was a lady who fell when she was apple-picking and I think I sorted out her damaged wrist . . . Oh, I'm not sure, Cath, and yet . . . and yet . . . I feel it.'

'Do you want it to come back, love?'

'Oh yes!'

'But it caused you so much trouble—'

'That was because I was so careless with it! But I've learned my lesson. I know better now. And you know . . . Cath . . . I feel incomplete without it.'

Catherine made no reply. Laura took her arm and turned her so she could look in her face.

'Do you think I'm wrong to want the gift to come back? Do you think I'm just being vain about it?'

'I don't know enough to make a judgement, dear. You're the only one who knows how to live with a power like that. To me it's such a mystery. If you think you're strong enough . . . ?'

'But I think I must be, otherwise it wouldn't come. Would it, Cath?'

'I don't know,' Catherine said. 'I don't know.'

When they returned to the Pilgrims' Hotel they found Adele had woken up and was being pushed up and down on the pavement so that she could watch what was going on. An elderly man in a caftan was beating softly on a hand-drum and singing in some foreign language while a plump woman circled to the rhythm in a simple dance step. No one seemed to think it unusual. This is a strange place, thought Catherine. Perhaps it's the sort of place that Laura always needed.

The visit passed only too quickly. Gerald had to get back to Hulmesley next day to open his shop, Catherine had clients waiting to see her in London where Malcolm would join her with Leo.

They had tea again with the Halcombes, promising to come

back soon. They watched Laura put her little daughter to bed, then had dinner together. Gerald went into the bedroom to kiss his granddaughter farewell for the present. Next morning they set off northwards. All the way along the now-busy roads, Gerald never stopped talking about Laura and his new little granddaughter. Once or twice Catherine was on the point of telling him what Laura had said on the Tor, but she felt that had been told her in confidence.

Gerald dropped her on the western outskirts of London, where she caught a suburban train to Waterloo and thence went by Tube to Hammersmith. She was full of news to tell Malcolm, of plans for them all to visit Somerset soon. She was sure Leo would love Somerset and its soft greenness.

She could hardly wait to get indoors to tell him all about it. But as soon as she closed the door she knew something was wrong. Malcolm came out of the living-room looked worried.

'What is it? What's happened?' she burst out.

'Nothing – don't be alarmed – Leo's had one of his turns, that's all.'

'Oh, Malcolm!' With only the hastiest of kisses she hurried past him to Leo's room. The little boy was lying in bed, a cold cloth on his forehead, his cheeks flushed, his lips dry.

She sat on the bed and took his hand. 'Well now, Leo, what have you been up to?' she murmured.

He turned fever-bright eyes on her. 'Where have you *been*?' he demanded pettishly. 'I needed you!'

She sat with him until he fell asleep in the early winter dusk. As she held his small hot hand, she was saying to herself that something had to be done to cure Leo of this ailment which dogged his life.

Chapter Twenty-six

The early months of the new year were full of anxiety in the financial markets: the United States had somehow got embroiled in trouble again with North Korea so that Wall Street went wild. And a big investment plan for a third British airport fell through, causing gloom in the City. Malcolm was kept too busy to make the trip to Stimmet to see Laura and her new baby. Catherine once or twice slipped off for an overnight stay, but the long-planned visit with Malcolm and Leo didn't come off until Easter.

Easter that year was at the end of March. London had a few daffodils and crocuses in the parks, but it was nothing compared to the blossoms of the West Country. The willows on the Somerset Levels rose up to greet them like fresh green fountains. Primroses peeped out of the grass on the roadside. The apple orchards were a haze of faint ivory-white as the tiny buds clothed the branches in promise of blossom to come.

The White Hart at Stimmet had only two rooms to let, one of which had already been taken when Catherine rang to book accommodation. The available room was given to Malcolm and Leo. Catherine was to share Laura's room in the flat at Halcombe House.

No one thought to ask Leo what he thought of this arrangement because it seemed self-evidently the best one. But the little boy was very upset that Merta should prefer to stay with her sister and that nuisance of a baby. At Christmas she'd dashed off to see them, and more than one Sunday since then had been made miserable by Merta's absence in Somerset.

He was adept at keeping his feelings to himself, however. Life with his difficult family in Cyprus had taught him that. He shook hands politely with his new Aunt Laura and surveyed the toddler with tolerance. He had nothing against the baby as such, it was merely that she took up Merta's time.

Aunt Laura seemed to want to be on friendlier terms because he sometimes caught her looking at him with velvety brown eyes that seemed to see far into him. Once or twice she seemed on the verge of asking him something important. But he shied away from that. He'd decided before ever he set out for Somerset that he was going to keep his guard up. There was only one member of the household in the garage flat at Halcombe House whom he really approved of, and that was Goldie the Labrador.

They went on outings around the countryside. He had to admit it was very beautiful, in the fashion that he found so enchanting, lushly green and full of birdsong. There was nothing here of the harsh aridity of the hillside farm in Cyprus. Privately he loved it, but he didn't let that appear because, after all, his plan was to show little enthusiasm. That way, perhaps Merta would see she mustn't keep rushing off on visits.

On Easter Sunday there was an open-air service on the Tor at Glastonbury. Everyone had to go. Brought up in the Greek Orthodox tradition, Leo understood how important it was to attend the Easter service. But he found it very boring, completely lacking the drama of that wonderful cry: 'Christ is risen! He is risen indeed!'

It was a chilly day. A fresh west wind was blowing across the Tor. He stood between his father and Merta, shivering and unhappy.

During the night he woke up with the strong impression that a brass band was playing loudly in the bedroom. He knew only too well what it meant. The sound of music coming from nowhere was one of the bizarre signs heralding an attack. He pushed aside the bedclothes so as to breathe some air. Perhaps if he lay quite still the attack would go away. He looked across at his father, sound asleep in the other twin bed. Perhaps if he got himself a glass of water everything would be all right. He got out of bed. The familiar weakness assailed him, he felt his legs give way, and then the loud brass band from nowhere ceased to play, and the frightening blackness engulfed him yet again.

The sound of his fall woke Malcolm. He sat up, glancing about in bewilderment for a moment. Then he heard a sound with which he'd become familiar, the stertorous breathing of his son when he was in the grip of one of his attacks.

The routine was only too familiar. He picked up the boy, put him back in his bed, hurried to the bathroom for a face flannel and a glass of water. He soaked the cloth under the cold tap.

Leo was lying on the bed jerking his head from side to side. His hands twitched as they lay on the covers. When Malcolm felt his forehead he could tell his temperature was up.

He put the damp cloth on his brow and sat down beside the

bed. Experience had taught him that there was little more to be done until the attack chose to relent.

By and by it passed. Leo fell into a normal sleep. His father wiped his brow one last time, tucked the bedclothes around him, and returned to his own bed.

Towards seven o'clock, he woke from a light sleep. Daylight was shining in at the lattice window. He debated whether to disturb his son by ringing for early morning tea. After about ten minutes he sat up and was stretching out his hand to the bedside phone when odd sounds from the other bed made him pause. He swung round to look at Leo.

The boy was lying under the bedclothes, eyes closed as if in sleep. But his body was jerking and tossing. His arms thrashed about on his pillows. He was making grunting noises.

Another attack? Only four or five hours after the last one?

In something approaching panic Malcolm pushed away the jumbled bedclothes to help the boy sit up. Leo made a groaning sound. Then he was sick, helplessly and uncontrollably.

'It's all right, son, it's all right,' soothed Malcolm. 'It'll soon be over. There, there, just relax, I'm here, it's all right.'

Quite soon the little boy became limp and passive. Malcom let him lie back on his pillows but kept his arms around him for a time. At last he felt the well-known resumption of normality, the slipping into a normal sleep.

He got the washcloth again, wiped the boy's face and neck, got his soiled pyjamas off his unresisting body. There were no others available so he put on a T-shirt and a pair of summer shorts.

He could hear sounds of activity in the inn. He rang for service. The landlady herself appeared and at once agreed to sit with Leo while Malcolm washed and shaved. That done, he telephoned Laura's flat at Halcombe House.

It was Catherine who answered. 'Good heavens, this is bright and early to be ringing,' she greeted him. And then, her sixth sense prompting her, 'Something's wrong!'

'Leo's under the weather, Cath. We won't be able to come on the picnic.'

'Oh, Malcolm!'

'I know, it's rotten, but he woke in the night with one of his turns, and he's just had another—'

'What?'

'I know, it's scary – that's two in less than five hours – it's never happened before—'

'He hasn't been missing out on his pills?'

'Of course not, I've made sure of that—'

'Then why—?'

'I don't know, Cath. I think . . . I don't know . . . is he getting *worse*?'

'I'll come over—'

'No, no, there's no reason to spoil the day for you and Laura. The pair of you, you go off as you planned and by the time you get back, Leo will probably be better again. But I'm wondering – should we call a doctor?'

'I suppose so . . . But then, what help would we get from a local GP? And besides, it's Easter Monday. It's probably a locum who's on duty.'

'Maybe I should start for home as soon as Leo wakes. I might be able to get in touch with Dr Pryory . . .'

They had a short discussion. Catherine agreed to have breakfast and then set out with Laura and Adele as planned, calling at the inn to see how things were progressing. Sometimes the attacks ended with a short restoring sleep; it was possible he might be sitting up and looking better.

'What's the matter?' Laura asked as she joined her at the breakfast table.

'Leo's poorly.'

'Oh, that's a shame. I thought yesterday when we were on the Tor that he looked peaky.'

'Perhaps he got a chill. Perhaps that brought it on. Malcolm says he's had one of his attacks. In fact, two of them – I don't understand it – it's since he went to bed last night.'

Laura shook her head in perplexity. 'What sort of attacks?'

'Oh – he sort of loses awareness, jerks and twitches about, sometimes he falls sound asleep and gets better at once.'

'You say he gets these attacks often?'

'Pretty often. But never two, one after the other.'

'What does your doctor say?'

'Oh, keep him quiet, make sure he takes his medication, let him sleep it off, get his temperature down. And we do all that, but it frightens him so. When he comes out of it, he's always scared and upset.'

'It sounds like *grand mal*,' Laura said, frowning.

'Oh, we've seen doctors and specialists! They say it's some sort of after-effect of an illness he had while he was still living in Cyprus. It seems to have been some form of meningitis—'

'Meningitis!' Laura looked appalled. All the knowledge from

her nursing training prompted her response. 'Cath, that's terribly serious! He must have been awfully well nursed—'

'Not a bit of it, the family just thought it was mild heat-stroke. That seems to mean it wasn't one of the serious forms, not the bacterial one—'

'Well, thank heaven for that!'

'But we've been told that the inflammation of the brain has damaged some of the nerve-endings there – what-do-you-call-them—'

'Synapses.'

'Yes, they sort of misfire or something, and when that happens he gets these attacks. And even at the best of times he hasn't got a powerful grip in his hands. It seems there's a fault in the nerve connections. So occasionally he fumbles when he's playing games, which makes him furious with himself.'

'Poor little chap,' murmured Laura. She fed a piece of buttered toast to Adele, who munched contentedly. 'You know, I did think when I first met him that there was something about Leo . . .'

'You mean that he's been super-polite to you – quite stand-offish, in fact. I don't quite know what's got into him.'

'No, I didn't mean that. I felt there was something in him that called out to me . . .'

'How do you mean?' Then, after a pause, 'Laura?'

Memories of times past caused that questioning note. She remembered how Laura had sometimes felt drawn to those who came to her for help.

Laura hunched her shoulders, looking almost guilty. 'You remember how that used to happen, when patients came to see me, there were some who seemed to be reaching out to me and I knew from the first that I could do something for them.'

'Are you saying . . . Are you saying that you think you could cure Leo?'

'I don't know, Cath. But I feel . . . drawn to him.'

'But he's clearly not drawn to *you*.'

'That doesn't matter. Don't you remember? Patients would come, sometimes quite sceptical, almost angry with themselves for giving in to the urge to look for help. Yet often those were the ones I did best with.'

'And you're drawn to Leo?'

'Yes . . . I don't know . . . I told you I thought the gift was coming back to me and since Leo arrived I've felt . . . restless

. . . as if a voice is speaking to me but I don't quite make out the words.'

The two sisters sat at the breakfast table, with the baby in her highchair waving a crust and making sounds of enjoyment. The scene was so ordinary, so domestic. And yet something mysterious was being discussed, something momentous.

After a moment Catherine said, 'Will you treat Leo?'

'Malcolm wouldn't let me. He never believed in me – he thought I was a crank.'

Catherine shook her head. 'He's not so dogmatic about that kind of thing, Laura. He told me when he first got in touch again that he . . . he regretted the things he said when we broke up. And besides, he's so worried about Leo. He's been to specialists, he's taken him for tests – at least tell him what you told me, see what he says.'

A frown of anxiety creased Laura's brow. 'If he gets angry . . . ? I don't think I could bear it, Cath, this feeling I have is so new, I don't want it damaged by other people tramping all over it with hobnailed boots.'

'Let me speak to him. If he thinks it's a silly idea you needn't hear him say so. But please, Laura – *please* – if you think you could help Leo – you don't know what it's like, seeing him in so much misery and not being able to do anything.'

It was a mild spring day, blue sky and fluffy clouds overhead, a soft breeze blowing. They bundled themselves into the capacious old Ford. In five minutes they were drawing up outside the White Hart.

The landlady happened to come into the vestibule as they walked in. 'Ah, there you are, Miss Mertagen, just go right up. I've told Mr Sanders that if there's anything I can do for the little chap . . .'

'Thank you. You're very kind.'

Catherine made her way up the twisting wooden staircase. The door of Malcolm's room was ajar. She could see Malcolm sitting by the bed, one hand adjusting the cold cloth on the little boy's brow.

'How long has he been like this, Malcolm?'

'He had the second attack about seven. It was worse than the first but he seems to be coming out of it just as usual. Mrs Pegram wants to call her own doctor but I think that would be pointless, don't you?' He sighed. His face was drawn, his greenish eyes seemed darkened with anxiety.

'Malcolm . . .'

'Yes?'

'Laura's downstairs . . .'

'Yes, well, I don't think there's much use in the pair of you hanging about. I'll stay with Leo, you two go off on your picnic—'

'Malcolm, Laura says she feels she could help Leo.' There, it was out. She watched in trepidation as Malcolm took it in.

He had to pause for a moment to understand her. Then he said, 'You mean, as she used to? With her gift, her power, whatever it was?'

'I know you were never convinced about it, Malcolm, but she thinks there could be a chance—'

'But you told me you had to bring her home from Germany or wherever it was, in a state of collapse because all that had come to an end.'

'Yes, but she told me – when Dad and I came just after Christmas – told me she felt the gift was coming back.'

'In what way? I mean, how does she know?'

'That book – the paperback, you remember? It's being sold hereabouts, and people recognised the name, and asked her. So she tried, and she's helped one or two of the locals.'

Malcolm rose from the chair. He took hold of Catherine's arm to draw her away from the bed. 'Laura thinks she could cure Leo?'

'She . . . thinks she could help him.'

'Where hospitals and Harley Street specialists can't?'

She felt the weight of the question like a heavy stone against her spirit. 'I know you never believed in her, Malcolm, but there was *something*—'

'Yes, I know, you told me and I was an idiot, I wouldn't even listen! Cath, would Laura really do this, after all the awful things I said about her?'

Tears rushed to Catherine's eyes. She put her arms around him. 'Oh, darling, as if that matters! That's all in the past! It's Leo we have to think of now.'

'Cath, if she would – if she'd just try – I'd be grateful to her until the last day I lived!'

They clung to each other, Catherine half-laughing and half-crying, Malcolm filled with an unexpected hope. Their love for each other, always strong since they had met again, seemed to be reinforced a hundred times by this moment. Some great blessing might come to them which, by helping Leo, would make their life perfect. They felt themselves on the verge of a happiness beyond anything they'd ever known.

They drew apart almost unwillingly. 'I'll go and fetch her, then,'

Malcolm said, moving to the door. 'I owe her an apology and now seems like the time to give it.'

Catherine took his place by the bed. She replaced the cold cloth, which had slipped to the pillow. Leo lay in a scramble of bedclothes, eyelids flickering as if strange dreams were chasing through his mind.

In a few minutes she heard footsteps on the staircase. Malcolm ushered in Laura. She came to the bedside, to stand looking down at the little boy with a slight frown between her brows.

'Tell me what happens when he has these attacks,' she murmured to no one in particular.

'He sometimes feels odd – prickly sensations in his fingers, flickering vision. His hands get feeble, he can't hold on to a cup, for instance. Sometimes he hears music first, he says it's like a band in the park but of course there's nothing there, it's all being done by little flashes of some kind in his brain. Then he seems to get confused, sometimes he falls.'

'He loses consciousness?'

'Yes, but only briefly. He goes to sleep quite normally after a bit. Like now, he's just asleep.'

Laura leaned over the boy. 'Leo? Leo, can you hear me? I'm going to try to help you.'

'Is there anything you need?' Malcolm asked hesitantly. He was totally at a loss, desperate for Laura to help his son yet now that it came to the test, afraid it might all be useless.

'There are too many people in the room,' Laura said, glancing about.

'Oh – yes – I understand.' Malcolm went out and down the stairs. He told himself he deserved this dismissal because of his former scepticism. His dragging step brought the landlady out of the inn parlour where she was keeping an eye on baby Adele in her push-chair.

'That was Mrs Lindham that went up,' she remarked.

'Yes, it was.'

'Oh, then everything'll soon be all right – won't it, lovey?' she added, addressing Adele. Adele chuckled and waved a hand.

Upstairs, Catherine had closed the bedroom door behind Malcolm. She stood now quietly with her back to it, watching her sister. Laura was leaning over her patient, studying him carefully.

'Poor little boy,' she murmured. 'Can you hear me, sweetheart? Wake up, Leo.'

Leo slept on.

Laura touched his shoulder. 'Wake up, Leo, it's time to do something to make you better.'

Leo opened his eyes. They looked straight up into Laura's. At that moment some message passed between them. Catherine saw it, as clearly as if words had been spoken. Then the little boy put out a hand for Laura to take and closed his eyes again.

As she'd done many a time before, Catherine stood watching her sister. A change always came over her at such moments. The round, gentle features would grow firmer, the brown eyes would grow darker, a stillness would spread around her almost as tangible as a canopy of muslin.

She never seemed to put forth any effort. On the contrary, it was as if she were accepting some instruction, waiting for some augmentation. Her hands sometimes touched but sometimes seemed merely to hover over the patient. As she sat now on the edge of Leo's bed, she held one of his hands between her palms.

There was no sound except the shallow breathing of the child. Catherine kept still, waiting for the miracle she had seen many times before – the slow opening of the patient's eyes, the lazy glance of recognition, then the dawning smile that told of relief from pain.

Time passed. Leo seemed utterly tranquil, his breathing deeper now, his tousled hair brown against the white pillows, his hand trustingly in Laura's.

Any minute now, thought Catherine, any minute now and he'll look about and ask what's been happening . . .

But Leo didn't open his eyes. Long moments went by.

Then Laura sat back, her hands letting go their hold as if in surrender.

'I can't do it,' she whispered.

Leo whimpered. His hand made a little searching movement.

'Laura, please—'

'I can't, Cath. I'm not strong enough.'

'But it will come—'

'No, it's too soon, I'm not strong enough yet. I shouldn't have rushed into it like this. I'm sorry, Cath, I *want* to help him, and there's a flicker, but it isn't enough.'

Catherine's heart gave a great throb of disappointment. 'You must, Laura, you must! Don't let me down like this!'

'Do you think I want to?' her sister groaned. 'You don't understand, I feel it like a current of power flowing into me but it's too weak, it seems to fade . . .'

'Rest a minute. Perhaps if you rest a minute and try again?'

Laura drew in a quavering breath. 'All right. In a minute or two. Let's just wait a while.' She stroked Leo's hair back from his forehead. 'I'm trying, Leo, I'm trying,' she whispered.

Catherine took the damp cloth, went to the bathroom to refresh it with cold water. When she returned Laura was sitting with her eyes closed, her hands folded against her breast, almost as if she were praying. She roused herself at Catherine's entrance, took the cloth and gently wiped Leo's face.

'Are you going to try again?' Catherine asked with a pleading glance.

'All right.' For a moment or two her sister didn't move. Then she leaned over the little boy, putting her hands either side of his head. The special stillness of the healer returned to the room.

Catherine held her breath.

'I can't,' whispered Laura. 'You've got to help me, Cath.'

'Me?' It was a gasp of disbelief.

'Yes, yes, help me, Cath. Take his hands.'

'But—'

'I can't do this alone. Take his hands!'

Scared, unwilling, Catherine went to the other side of the bed. She took the small boy's hands in hers – hot, perspiring, febrile. She grasped them firmly, feeling the fragile bones against her palms. She looked at her sister for guidance but Laura was staring past her, that dark gaze fixed on some inward vision.

A strange thing happened. A warmth began to steal through Catherine's wrists and fingers. It wasn't the warmth from Leo's sticky hands, it was as if sunlight had been infused into her blood. Confidence flowed through her. She felt buoyed up by a strength she had never known before.

How much time went by, she never afterwards was sure. A great peace seemed to surround the three of them. The little boy began to breathe very deeply, as if he were hauling each breath from the depths of his being. He lay quiet, the agitation behind his eyelids died away.

It was Laura who spoke. She said the boy's name softly.

He opened his eyes. It took a moment for his gaze to focus. Then he smiled – a smile Catherine had witnessed many times before from Laura's patients.

'How do you feel?' Laura asked.

'All right,' he whispered, staring up at her.

'Do you feel giddy? Drowsy?'

'No, not a bit. I feel . . . different.' He became aware of Catherine's presence. 'Why are you holding my hands, Merta?'

'To pull you out of bed and make you get dressed,' she said, hiding behind a joke. 'Come on, lazybones, are you going to get up? The rest of us have been up for ages.' She gave a tug at his hands, so that he sat up.

'I had one of my funny turns, didn't I?' He sounded anxious, regretful; he hated to be a nuisance.

'That's over,' Laura said. 'I mean, for always.'

'Yes.' He frowned, half-shaking his head as if to see if he could understand this news.

He wriggled his hands free. He flexed his fingers in and out, making fists and relaxing them. 'My hands feel different,' he mused. 'You know, I think I could hold a cricket bat properly!'

Both Catherine and Laura burst out laughing. 'Well, that's good,' Laura remarked. 'Perhaps you'll be another Jack Hobbs!'

'Are you going to get up, or lie there all day?' Catherine demanded.

'I'm getting up, I'm getting up,' he said, and with a return of his usual vigour scrambled up out of the bedclothes.

Both sisters watched anxiously as he set his foot to the floor. But he stood up quite steadily, fetched his spongebag from the dressing table, and headed for the bathroom.

When he had gone, Catherine touched her sister on the arm. She felt bewildered, almost scared. 'What happened then?' she asked in a troubled voice.

'You helped me cure him.'

'But *I* don't have any healing power!'

'Yes you do, Cath. I suddenly knew it, when I was losing hope.'

'But how could you know that, Laura? I mean, it's never been so—'

'I wasn't strong enough, you see, but all at once I knew I could turn to you for help.'

'But it can't really be so, Laura. I've never had the least ability—'

'Perhaps it's there in a lot of people,' her sister said gravely. 'Only we never listen to the voice that tries to tell us about it. Perhaps that's been true of you, dear – you wanted to be a success in the world, to have a career. And perhaps I put you off, making such a big thing of it, getting into trouble over it . . .'

'It's scary,' Catherine said. She shivered.

'No it's not. But it takes a bit of getting used to, I suppose.'

'I don't want to get used to it! It's not right for me! I'm absolutely ordinary, I don't want to have a special gift!'

'Don't get in such a state about it,' Laura said, putting an arm about her shoulders. 'There's no law says you've got to use the gift if you don't want to.'

'Don't tell Malcolm!' Catherine cried. 'He'd think I'd gone off my head!'

Laura was laughing now. 'Calm down, calm down. You'll tell Malcolm yourself if you want to. But think of this, Cathie, love – you can help Leo any time he needs it.'

Catherine was shaking her head. 'I'll never be able to do it again.'

'Perhaps not.' Laura shrugged. 'Time will tell. All I know is that today you helped me, and it gives me confidence that my own powers will grow again to what they used to be, and that's wonderful because you see, for me, it was the most important thing in my life. Thank you, Cath, thank you a million times.'

Catherine hugged her sister. 'No, on the contrary, thank *you*, Laura.'

She went slowly downstairs to speak to Malcolm. He was sitting on a bench outside the inn, the baby asleep on the push-chair at his side and Goldie lying at his feet. He leapt up as Catherine appeared.

'Well?' he demanded.

'Leo's in the bathroom getting washed. He seems fit and well.'

'But he usually wakes up sort of woozy—'

'No, he's quite all right.'

'Laura cured him?'

'Well, it seems so. This time. Perhaps he might need another treatment some time. But he was saying he felt his hands were stronger. It really does seem as if he's better.'

Malcolm sat down again on the bench, almost as if his legs had collapsed under him.

'It's a miracle . . .'

Catherine said nothing. She sat down beside him, took his arm, leaned close to him.

'I'll never be able to thank her,' Malcolm said.

'That's all right. She understands.'

'I just . . . just . . . feel as if the world's been changed from grey to gold!'

'Yes, darling, I know.'

They sat in silence, each deep in thought, until at last the door of the White Hart opened to reveal Leo washed and dressed for outdoors, hand in hand with Laura and blinking a little in the spring sunlight.

'Aunt Laura says she baked an egg and tomato pie for the picnic,' he said tentatively. 'Is it too late to go now?'

'Not a bit of it,' cried his father, jumping up. 'So, how are you, Mr Sanders Junior?'

'I'm quite all right, thank you, Mr Sanders Senior.'

Goldie rose to his feet, stretched, and came up to put his nose in Leo's hand. He wagged his tail in greeting.

'Dad, could we have a dog?' Leo asked, patting the Labrador.

'Well, we have to ask Merta, because it's Merta's flat.'

'Of course we can have a dog,' Catherine said. 'But you have to promise to take it for walks.'

Adele awoke as they began to load themselves into the Ford. Leo seemed determined to stay with Goldie, so got into the back with the dog. Catherine followed with the baby. Malcolm stood on the pavement with Laura for a moment, in deep conversation. Catherine guessed that he was trying to say thank you.

'Come *on*, I didn't have any breakfast and I want some picnic pie,' urged Leo. 'Aunt Laura, you'd better drive because you know the way and we'll get there faster.'

'I hear and obey,' said Laura. Malcolm, smiling, took the front passenger seat. They went bowling out of the village. Their aim was a spot on the banks of the river where Laura promised a view of ducklings and cygnets.

'Merta,' Leo asked in an undertone after a while, 'is it true that the flat in Hammersmith belongs to you?'

'Well, yes.'

'In Cyprus houses and things belong to the men.'

'So I've heard.'

'If we get a dog, it would be better to have a house and a garden. Papa could have a house, couldn't he?'

'Yes, of course.'

'And you would live there too? You would leave the flat.'

'Well . . .'

'What's the matter? You'd rather live in a house, wouldn't you?'

'That was always my dream, Leo – to have a house and a garden . . .' She thought about that girlish dream, the one on which she'd turned her back all those years ago.

'Well, we'll get a house for us to live in. I'll tell Papa.'

'But it's not as easy as that. Buying a house is a big thing. Perhaps Papa won't want to.'

'Of course he'll want to. A man should have a house and a wife to look after him – that's what Uncle Nikko used to say.'

'But that's in Cyprus—'

'Oh, I bet it's good in England too. Why don't you and Papa get married soon? Then he would have a wife as well as a house.'

Catherine rubbed her cheek against the silky hair of the baby's head. 'Would you like it if Papa and I got married?' she asked gently.

'Well of course,' Leo replied, as if it were self-evident, then fell silent.

After a while he patted the Labrador on the head, then leaned forward to address his father. 'Papa, we must get a house with a garden and then we can have a dog just like Goldie, only young at first,' he instructed, 'and we'll call him Tawny.'

'Oh, must we indeed, Mr Sanders Junior?' Malcolm said, turning in his seat to view his son.

'Well, don't you think it's a good idea to have a house? Merta thinks it is.'

'Does Merta want to get rid of us, then?'

'That's not it at all. We're all going to live there together.'

Malcolm laughed.

'Perhaps if the house was big enough, Aunt Laura could come to visit us,' Leo went on, pursing his lips as he thought the matter through, 'and we could take the baby for a ride on a red bus.'

'Thank you,' Laura said. 'I think Adele would like that.'

'This is all very unusual,' Malcolm said. 'I got the impression you weren't too keen on the baby.'

'Oh, she's all right,' Leo said with lordly tolerance. 'I'm getting used to her. In fact . . .' He paused. 'I feel different, you know? As if things are better, I don't know why.'

He put his arms around the neck of the Labrador so as to whisper some confidences about his plans for the future, mainly concerned with getting into the school cricket team.

Catherine watched him. He was right. Things were better. Things had changed, and with them her view of herself. Perhaps it was true that she had the same power to heal that had been so strong in Laura. Perhaps in time she would feel the urge to use that power. Perhaps she would tell Malcolm about it and ask how he felt.

But for the moment she was content to accept things as they were, and the future that Leo had sketched. A home with Malcolm and his son, a place to build a family. Her girlhood dream, changed by the vicissitudes of life yet still a golden dream, full of optimism and the possibility of happiness.

Laura too was content. She was thinking of the mistakes she

had made and had paid for in disillusion and self-reproach. Now she had a second chance. This time she would be strong, this time she would not let herself be misled by the misconceptions of others. She would listen to her inner voice, knowing that it would always speak truth to her.

She glanced back at her sister. Catherine caught her eye. They smiled at each other, a deep and understanding smile.

Each had her own happiness, the joy of finding and holding safe something almost lost. Laura had regained the talent that seemed to have withered. Catherine had been sought out again by the man she had always loved. They knew they were lucky; they had insight enough to know the value of what fate had sent them.

The car rounded a bend. The river lay before them, flashing bright in the sun, flowing between green banks spangled with the brilliance of marsh marigolds.

'Isn't that a marvellous view?' exclaimed Malcolm.

'Yes,' said Catherine, 'the view ahead is lovely.'

She leaned forward to lay a hand on his shoulder. His hand came up to cover hers. Their fingers interlinked.

She knew he understood what she meant about the view. And that he agreed.